BENEATH

The

CHIMES

N. P. ARROWSMITH

DEACONSHIRE
TALES

Joy,
the light of home

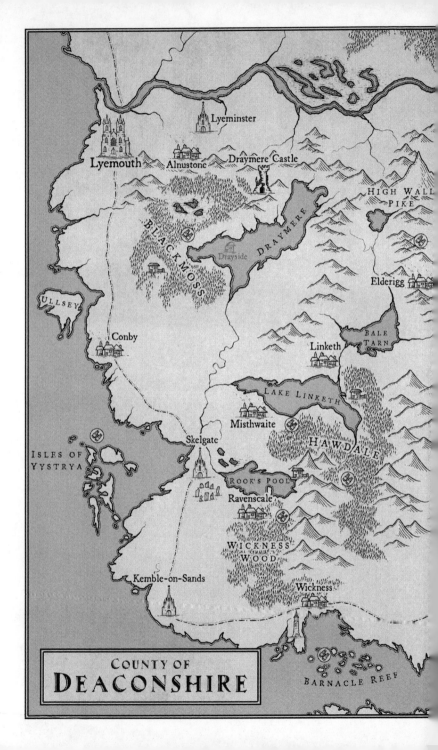

Lyeminster

Lyemouth   Alnustone   Draymere Castle

HIGH WALL
PIKE

BLACKMOSS   Drayside   DRAYMERE

Elderigg

ULLSEY

BALE
TARN

Conby   Linketh

LAKE LINKETH

Misthwaite   HAWDALE

Skelgate

ISLES OF
YYSTRYA   ROOK'S POOL

Ravenscale

WICKNESS
WOOD

Kemble-on-Sands   Wickness

COUNTY OF
DEACONSHIRE

BARNACLE REEF

CHAPTER ONE

THE THIRTEENTH TOLL

Friday 28th November 1879

I now know I will not make it home on this icy evening, and my attempts to seek shelter have failed. The frosting cobbled streets of this unfamiliar village glisten in the warm glow of the gas lamps and the pale radiance of a full moon. A sharp pang of terror overcomes me as I wrestle with the fact that I must survive this bitterly frigid night outside and alone.

I set out this morning with the hope of finding new employment. For late November, it was quite temperate, so I dressed smartly not warmly. However, nearly two hours ago, I stood shivering on the platform at Copsefield Junction while I watched my last train home chugging away into the night. I'd just missed it! The scream of the steam echoed my inner turmoil. My connecting train had arrived too late, and I was stranded. I hadn't enough coins to afford lodgings, and the station porter offered me little sympathy as he took me for a scrounger.

I rushed to the Railway Inn, but the innkeeper scolded me, saying, 'Get out o' here, you lousy beggar. This ain't no dosshouse.'

Indeed, I discovered that the village of Copsefield, which serves almost solely as a railway interchange, has no dosshouse or penny sit-up, and the last omnibus departed before my train.

I was told there was no room at The Causeway House, so my final hope was The Waggon & Horses. I pleaded with the owner, but he said, 'If you're so desperate, you'll trade me that pocket watch to share with the 'orses.'

The gold pocket watch, which hangs on a chain on my waistcoat, came to me after my brother, Charlie, passed away when he was just nine years old. I would rather die than give up such a sentimental treasure.

After that, I returned to the train station. Judging that I would likely freeze if I slept on one of the benches outside, I attempted to gain entry to the station house. I was unsuccessful, so I then tried the entrance to the church, but as I discovered that it was firmly locked, too, I heard shouts.

'Oi, that vagrant's trying to break in,' a man cried.

'He's just stole that timepiece,' said another.

'Get 'im!' said a third.

Those men chased me down several streets. Their false accusation and taunts made me sure that they were the thieves, and they intended to steal my precious heirloom. I finally evaded them when I turned a corner and hid inside

The Causeway House. My salvation was short-lived, however, as I have just been roughly turned out after brazenly refusing to leave. But what else could I do? I have nowhere else to go, and those men could still be searching for me.

So, now I stand, trembling, frozen and fearful, as the church bell tolls eleven times to mark the hour. My residence is sixteen miles north, and I don't know what to do. My coat is smart but thin, I didn't bring gloves, and I have no means to start a fire. If only I could find a policeman or kind-hearted soul, they might spare me my perilous predicament.

Staring at empty avenues shimmering in the spectral shine of the moon, I recall friends who are members of the Lunar Society. I know little of the society except that they meet on nights such as this, when the sky is clear and a full moon illuminates otherwise unlit streets. It begs the question: could I traverse this night on foot and make it home by dawn?

I am expected back in Horton at sunrise, and my absence will cause chaos. I am a lamplighter and a knocker-upper. Failing to extinguish the gas lamps is bad, but if I don't wake my clients by knocking on their window or door, they will be late for their work, and my name will be mud. The whole purpose of my journey today was to gain employment doing much the same work but in a larger place, the city of Lancaster—it was not to anger my current employers. I believe I must walk home to save my job, and if I linger any longer, those thieves may find me.

I walk a few streets looking for signposts to locate a northbound road, but the houses tease me as I search due to how their curtained windows glow with warmth.

Soon, I discover a stone plaque bearing the village names of Thanham and Mosskene, and I find the route I must follow.

There comes a clip-clop of hooves behind me. A hansom cab approaches, and its two bright lanterns illuminate a vacant cabin. The smart driver is seated high up behind the booth and holds the reigns to a huffing, grey horse. 'One shilling to go north?' I call out.

'Not a chance!' he replies with a laugh. His sinister chortle still permeates the air as the glowing lanterns disappear from sight, and it stokes my ire at the dark heart of humanity that has been on display this evening. It may be too meagre a sum, but why would he forgo payment when he could drop me at the next village? He will get no other trade between here and Thanham. Is it worth a shilling to ridicule a pitiful fool?

Seething with resentment, I begin my homebound journey, and it is not long until the candlelit houses and lamp-lit streets behind are lost from sight. As I follow this deserted country lane, I gaze out over a frostbitten landscape. Pallid rays graze the pastures, and silhouettes climb up the horizon as distant hills blot out a night sky speckled with starlight. Fields stretch far and wide, crisscrossed with hedgerows and dotted with the shadows of dense thickets. Soft, shady undulations carve the scene, outlining my trail ahead. My breath sparkles like glacial mist, and the road stretching in front of me twinkles with frost. Skeletal bushes guide my route, and occasionally I pass a gnarly oak tree whose branches, in the light breeze, claw at the stars.

As I look down, the dark, taller vision of myself upon the loose paving acts as a compass pointing north. As the night goes on, the bearing of this peak-capped phantom will drift and creeping moonlight will wash out the stars to the west, so I shall use Polaris to judge north instead. The Plough, which forms part of the Great Bear, dominates in the sky, and its handle points down over my current waypoint.

Wafts of manure come and go, and the only sounds are from my footsteps. I feel the emptiness of the open fields around me. Then, distant screams cut the night air. Whatever it is—animals or otherwise—my route is heading towards the cries, and I cannot deviate or delay. The shrieks continue intermittently, but they grow louder as I approach, and they seem to emanate from a copse of trees.

All is eerily quiet as I enter the wood—except for my footsteps, which announce my arrival to any listening ears. I try to walk more softly, but I cannot silence my steps on this rutted road. It's as though I'm a mouse ringing a dinner bell as I stroll through a cat's lair. And while the fields embrace the moonlight, this copse dwells in darkness. I cannot even see my feet, and I could walk right into a predator's mouth. My only guiding light is a narrow corridor of night sky shining through the trees above, and I judge that the road must follow this gap in the treetops.

I press deeper into the dark thicket, feeling eyes upon me. But whose eyes are they? A screech gives me a terrible start. Bushes rustle, twigs snap, and the cries repeat. The sounds shatter what little composure I have left this evening. A shaft of moonlight ahead reveals the edge of the woodland. I pick up the pace, but my footsteps grow louder. Snapping twigs approach, but I'm nearly out of the copse. Moonlight begins to seep through the thinning trees, and I see one of the bushes nearby shake, then another, then a third. My feet and my breath race. An invisible beast rushes towards me—its shriek deafens. Shadows dash in the evergreen growth, and I spy flashes of red and white. Foxes.

I escape the copse feeling foolish. How can I hope to complete this journey if simple woodland creatures are going to frighten me so? But then, I discover that I have arrived at the unlit village of Thanham, and I rejoice at the progress I've made.

Entering the village, I walk by the few pebble-dashed houses that line the one road through this quiet place, and it is not long before I find a marker informing me that I am six miles from Mosskene. I have walked three miles already! While my progress may be heartening, the path so far has been flat. I am expecting that to change because the hills are close now.

As I leave Thanham, church bells repeatedly clang in a discordant harmony; it is midnight. Soon, I pass a manor that stands proud in broad moonlight. Shadows move through the candlelit windows, and a snorting black horse stands with a hansom cab at the entrance. If they pass me on the road, I will ask for a ride, but it will only antagonise them if I approach them now. Besides, tonight has already shown me that I cannot rely on others—if I must, I shall do this alone. As I continue past the manor, the lane begins to meander and climb.

Before long, the ascent becomes a struggle, and my thighs burn. Sweating, I unbutton my coat. I progress, leaning forwards, staring at my feet and puffing breathlessly as a biting wind picks up behind me. The thought that this is likely to be the hardest segment of tonight's journey provides encouragement to overcome it. It takes all my focus to hold a strong pace, and I frequently gasp out noisily, both in frustration and exhaustion. I regularly retrieve my watch to keep an eye on the time, though it takes some effort to angle the dial into the moon's rays to discern where its hands are pointing. Mosskene is approximately the halfway point, and I strive to arrive by three o'clock.

There is some relief when the lane finally flattens, but this is only a momentary respite. Presently, the road snakes through another dense thicket. There are no screeching foxes here, but there is a light through the trees. As I wind through the lane, I hear huffing and metallic clinking. I must be brave—this could be someone who could save me. I hurry towards the light.

A hansom cab blocks the road at a tight chicane, and a grey horse at the helm is tied to a tree. Has the cab suffered a mechanical failure? There is no sign of any damage or the driver, but he could be keeping warm in the cabin. If I aid the cabman in making repairs, then he would surely offer me a ride.

'Are you in trouble?' I call out, but there is no answer. 'Do you need help?'

A figure emerges from behind a tree. Lunar rays caress a wide-brimmed leather hat tilted down such that it hides the man's eyes. His breath forms crystals of moonlight as he sniggers, and he pulls something out from within his dark overcoat. It glints as I stare down two barrels of a shotgun. 'Run along, pauper,' he says.

I start, and in my haste, I cut myself and my coat on the cab as I scramble past, then I run as fast as I can. Behind me, I hear a familiar but sinister chortle. That man was the same cabman who refused me a ride in Copsefield.

When I reach a safe distance, I pause to catch my breath. Who is that man? To be blockading the road with his cab and hiding with a shotgun, he must be a robber not unlike the highwaymen of decades past. I suppose it is fortunate that he recognised me because he already knows I have only a shilling.

My side burns, but the cut is not bleeding too badly. My injury won't impede my journey, but I cannot stop shaking. Perhaps it is the shock of seeing a shotgun, but the icy conditions are beginning to bite, too.

The plummeting sub-zero temperatures have caused the soft ground to shrivel into its hard cocoon. I now have to stamp to break the small frozen puddles in the mud rather than tap them as I did when I set out. The wind pricks what must be a bright red face with its hidden needles. I cannot stand here shivering, so I continue onwards. The lane ascends once more, and the climb is a struggle.

A shotgun blast shatters the still night. The gunshot startles me, even though the robber could be half a mile back by now. A distant whinny of a horse replaces the blast; I dread to think about what might be happening. I stop and listen; a new silence sits uncomfortably. I am too far away to help, but I pray I do not hear another blast. If the first shot was a warning, the second might not be. I breathe more easily as the minutes pass without another sound, and I recommence my journey.

However, it is not long until I hear the rattle of a cab, but the robber is upon me sooner than I anticipate. His grey horse charges down the lane, and I hurry to get out of its way. The robber snaps the reigns then, seeing me, he tilts his hat to conceal his face and laughs heartily. He reaches into his overcoat, but what he pulls out is not a shotgun. Coins glint as he throws a handful up in the air as the cab rumbles past. 'Call me Robin Hood!' he shouts. As the robber races off, his laughter becomes raucous.

I scramble, collecting the coins off the frozen mud. Shillings are scattered amongst dozens of pennies. Small change for the robber but potentially life-saving for me. There is enough here to afford a cab or lodgings. An ill-gotten gain, perhaps, but the bounty is a boon for me.

It is only as I begin to climb once more that I consider that no inn will accept new lodgers at such a late hour. My only hope resides with another cab passing, which would likely be the robber's victim. If their cab passes me, I can return some of their money and offer to be a witness. But as I trudge up the incline, no more cabs come. I repeatedly check my pocket watch, hoping that time and distance will pass quickly and that this climb might soon end.

Close to an hour after collecting the stolen coins, I hear a clink and clank behind me. Excitedly, I turn and see two lanterns blinking as they glide through the lanes below. A cab speeds along the route I have walked. This is my chance! I will stop the cab and pay for a ride home.

It may be a rickety black cab, but to me, it is a heavenly chariot delivering salvation. My guardian angel races towards me. It hurtles along the lanes so fast that the four horsemen of the apocalypse could not stop it. It jinks left and right, closer and closer. A horse snorts, whips crack and shouts boom from the driver. The cab thumps the ruts in the road, and it creaks and rattles so loudly that it could shake itself apart. There cannot be a passenger as the ride would be much too uncomfortable. I stand in the middle of the road, ready to get their attention.

The hansom cab races around the corner ahead. A black horse stampedes towards me, its nostrils puffing ice like a dragon breathes fire. 'Bella. Hurry!' the cabman shouts. His voice is deep with a distinctive American accent.

'Sir! I need a ride,' I shout as I wave. 'I can pay.'

'Bella. Go!' he instructs his horse.

'Stop! I'll pay double.'

'I have a passenger,' the cabman shouts back. Indeed, a grey-haired man sits slumped in the cabin. His eyes stare vacantly, and his body bounces like a rag doll as the cab jolts.

'It's freezing out here!'

'Out of the way!' the cabman bellows as he cracks the reigns. Clumps of mud fly and stones chip up as the horse rampages towards me. The thought of being trampled and crushed paralyses me. The moustachioed cabman waves his top hat as he gesticulates for me to move aside, but I remain rooted to the spot.

'Out of the way, goddammit!' he shouts again. The snap of his whip jolts me from my paralysis, and I leap out of the cab's path as it thunders past.

I land hard and in a heap. Ice-cold water stings my skin, and there is a dull pain in my side. I lie in a muddy puddle, having broken the ice, and a rock sticks in my ribs. I roll over and out of the icy water in time to see the cab disappear around a bend. 'Damn you!' I shout. 'Damn you all!' I thump the ground, then just sit there, aghast. Why must everyone dismiss me?

I grumble as I get to my feet and straighten my wet clothes. 'No!' I cry out as I glimpse Charlie's pocket watch. Its face is cracked! 'No, I can't have broken it. Damn it! I'm so sorry, Charlie.' My hands tremble as I lift it to my ear. It still ticks. Thank goodness! It's just the crystal that is damaged, and I can replace that. It is often said that a clock stops when someone dies, so as long as Charlie's pocket watch ticks, some aspect of him remains alive and with me.

I walk down the lane. The pain in my side is nothing compared to how angry I am at those who could have come to my aid but refused. I will get home all by myself if I must, but now that my clothes are wet, the cold really cuts into me. My progress has slowed too, so I must pick up the pace.

Eventually, the blurred horizon is interrupted by a definite outline pointing skyward. It is the unmistakable shape of a distant spire, presumably signalling the direction to Mosskene. But just as my long struggle achieves some success, I reach a fork in the road. I cannot afford to lose my way now. With no sign, I have a decision to make: bear right and follow the natural course of the road or turn left up a narrower, steeper lane.

As I stand debating, I begin to shiver and start shuffling on the spot. Initially, I think to follow the road right, but as my new waypoint hangs above the left path, my instinct is to take this darker trail. Remembering a map on the train, I cannot recall any other towns or villages in this vicinity to account for the distant church. I choose to follow my instinct and turn left, reasoning that it is better to quickly discover the wrong route than to shiver any longer.

It does not take long for me to doubt my decision. Large coniferous trees and tall bushes block the moonlight, so I cannot see where I am placing my feet. Once more, I use the skyward hue to guide my earthbound route. I climb blindly to a chorus of hooting owls. The track narrows, and I put my hands out in front to feel for any gates or other obstacles that I may walk into. This tenebrous trail is disorientating, and the church spire that led me this way is out of sight. I promise myself that if this path leads to Mosskene, then I shall allow myself a moment's rest. I continue my trudge uphill. I tread in darkness, one daring step after another.

Exhausted and muddy and cold, I emerge from the track as it opens out onto a small village. Cool lunar light glints off the knobbly stone facades of distinguished houses.

'Yes!' I cry as a sign confirms that I am indeed in Mosskene. The village is unlit, so I open the crystal on my timepiece and use the moon to see horizontal hands—it is seventeen minutes to three. I bask in sheer delight as I behold the holy spire that guided me. The steeple looms high over the settlement as the church sits atop a rise. That I have completed the more difficult half of the journey and kept the pace emboldens me into thinking that this foolish errand may see success.

I walk carefully into the centre of the village as the streets are dangerously slippery due to the hard frost. A few metal benches lie hidden in the moonshadow cast by The Cross Keys tavern. Approaching, I step up onto the pavement, but my foot slips, and I fall. The solid road surface smacks my head, and I cry out in pain.

One hand pressed on my head, I struggle up and shuffle towards a bench. The pain surges as I briefly release the pressure, but I am relieved to see no blood. Hoisting myself onto the icy seat, my ankle spasms—I've twisted it.

I believe a short moment's rest will allow my foot to heal somewhat. I remember experiencing a similar crippling pain playing sports in my youth, and that after a few minutes sat down, I would be back running again. Presently, I must do the same.

I am undoubtedly fatigued. My muscles hurt, my side is sore, my ankle twinges, and my head throbs. The astral canvas arcs as I stare. I switch my position, so I am lying down. I gaze at God's magnificent creation though it swirls traumatically. I'm dazed. I close my eyes but reopen them in a panic—they've grown heavy. I must stay awake, but I still need a moment to recover. I fight for consciousness. As my blinks last steadily longer, I can resist no more.

BONG!

A deep lingering chime rouses my consciousness.

BONG!

The echoing metallic vibrations tremble through my mind.

BONG!

I recognise the tone of a church bell, though an octave or two deeper.

BONG!

I stir at its metronomic resonance.

BONG!

My heart sinks at the realisation of my slumber.

BONG!

Six tolls? I've slept till six!

BONG!

Panic swells within me.

BONG!

My eyes bolt open expecting to see a bright morning sky.

BONG!

I stare into a bejewelled black void.

BONG!

I turn my head and gaze out over the icy, iridescent settlement.

BONG!

I spy the sounding spire looming above the trees behind the emporiums across the street.

BONG!
Towards me, a conspiracy of ravens swoop overhead.
BONG!
Thirteen chimes? Can that be right?

The thirteenth toll lingers like the portentous echo of a scream. Its prolonged shuddering resonates, the tremors building and building as they course through me. It swells into a thunderous quaking that rips and wrenches my whole being. I cry out, a tormented beast's wail. When the vibrations eventually begin to subside, my body keens with aches as though all my bones lie broken. A pervasive coldness creeps into my limbs. And as the trembling chime finally ceases, I am left utterly numb.

CHAPTER TWO

THE BLASPHEMOUS REQUIEM

I sit up with a jolt, glance at my hands, and then frantically check I have movement throughout my body. I breathe a heavy sigh of relief. Other than feeling frozen, I seem to be fine—but what was that excruciating sensation? It couldn't have been a nightmare, could it?

Ravens disturb my quiet moment of recovery with their harsh cries. I turn to see them hopping excitedly on rooftops before a silver-lit sky. I reach for my pocket watch, but the face is unreadable in the dark. How long have I slept? I haul myself up and stagger forwards, but without feeling in my legs, I fall onto moonlit cobbles.

A warmth floods through me, its welcome presence chases away the numbness. Slowly, I climb back to my feet and angle my timepiece to catch the moonlight. Through the crystal, I see the hands in a straight line. My mind strains trying to comprehend. Seventeen minutes to three? That was the time when I last checked. My heart skips. Has my watch... stopped?

A high-pitched singing ahead contrasts the carrion cackling behind. I walk beside the stores lining the east road seeking the sanctuary of a human voice. It is a lady singing. She may take pity on a man left outside on such a cold night and offer me shelter. Now that I am walking again, I don't feel so frozen. Perhaps I can still get home before sunrise.

As I pass the emporiums, her angelic melody hushes the laughing ravens. A muted babbling suggests she may not be alone. The hum of the others bubbles louder; a burst of laughter, a wail of gaiety. Following the sounds, I turn down a side road leading to the church.

The sky is black, yet there is much commotion. Does the singer have an audience? Chatter grows louder and louder as I approach, but still, the soprano eclipses them. I become more and more apprehensive. Who are they? Yew trees lining the sacred ground possess an almost ethereal shimmer as their frosty needles catch the lunar rays. These trees block much of the scene, but there are people in the cemetery—lots of people.

The entrance to the church grounds lies at the corner of a high wall that is more moss than stone. The lych-gate is open, and the high wall casts a shadow over the path that ascends towards the chapel. As I enter, my body numbs at the spectacle I behold.

A divine chorus fills the air. The grandeur of the gothic church is on full display as it towers above the steep bank. Giant gravestones, Catholic and Celtic crosses, tall tablets, stone altars, obelisks and sculptures of angels cover the slope. These monoliths cast long shadows amongst which revellers rejoice.

I hide in the shade created by the wall before I am seen. This is outrageous! Hundreds fill the cemetery. They cluster towards the top of the hill where the soprano stands over them. They dress like figures from portraits hung in houses of the aristocracy, and their dancing creates an ugly, incoherent opera.

The orchestrator of this symphony of the night is a tall and beautiful woman. Her black hair passes her shoulders and sits on her brow with a neat fringe. Her face is distinctive, pale in complexion with a sharp nose, rose-red lips and a foreboding smile. Most striking though are her eyes, dark but wide, she seemingly conducts her audience's trance with her many gestures and leering glare. I struggle to tear my eyes from her witching whites. I am at risk of falling under her charm, and I find part of myself willing it. Her long dress drapes on the ground, and as she sways, it catches the moonlight, revealing a purple sheen. With a mighty soprano voice, she sings without warbling but with only strong tones meant to convey no words. It summons within a warning from tales of devious sirens whose calls lure good men on whom they wreak death and destruction.

This enigma's indoctrinated followers cluster in packs on the slope. Mostly they wear suits and white dresses, and they are seemingly oblivious to this numbing chill. The lady's talent lies in inciting her congregation to rejoice. Some sedately sway; others are wild. Some move precisely;

others whirl around haphazardly with their arms aloft. It strikes me that these hideous flailing limbs, conjured by this enchantress, form part of a daemonic rite. No God-fearing group would dance blasphemously on sacred ground during the dead of night. No, it seems to me their limbs are extending the tentacles of Satan and the immobile tombstones that honour his nemesis are loath to watch. The couples who dance precisely enhance this ridicule as they waltz through the cemetery as if it were a magnificent ballroom. Their expressions are as serious as their motion is smooth, disclosing an element of preparation.

What is this devilish sect? It could never be that of the Lunar Society. While I do not know the group's activities, my friends who are members are decent people. I read in the newspaper on the train about a Manchester clergyman named Sidney Faithorn Green. He had been admonished for performing illegitimate liturgical practices, but the charges against him—mixing water with wine and wearing unlawful vestments at Church of England ceremonies—are mere misdemeanours in comparison to this.

I am left further aghast as several untended children run past. Not only are their perverse parents too consumed by the ritual to care for their offspring, but how they expose innocent children to such vile devil worship is despicable. This vulgar ceremony is a horror the like of which I have never witnessed. I must remain unseen.

I start as the loud church bell chimes. Unlike before, the peals have a typical tone—not deep, menacing or bone-shattering. The bell tolls seven times. It is seven o'clock! And my watch *has* stopped. At this very moment, I should be waking up the men and women of Horton. Will I be relieved of my duties? Will they believe my tale of woe and hold faith in my past record? It is the only employment I have ever enjoyed. Some may think it is beneath my academic talents, and I have held positions in companies where the pay was much better, but they were too disagreeable to my sensibilities. I do not want to go back to that. I want to keep my sedate life as a lamplighter, but I would like to move to Lancaster where my pay will increase. If news of this transgression reaches those who interviewed me, they will not employ me. I shall plead my case, but there is nothing more I can do now.

Huge trees loom over the graveyard, but they are unable to hide the dazzling starlight, and as their long, spiny branches creep towards the chapel, they form a frame around the spire and the heavens beyond. The church gleams under the lunar spell and its steadfast authority and righteousness remain a calming influence counteracting the dreadful charnel wallowing below. I believe God will see that I am safe, but I must stay hidden.

I surmise that the revellers are the residents of this settlement because no one wakes to investigate the singing or the cries. The sect seems extraordinarily large for a village so small, however, and its members dance among tombstones that tower over them. The shadows on the ground lie still and are intangibly long. I watch but there is something about the scene—something beyond the outrage—something which is not right.

Four men adorned with canonical robes join the conducting soprano. These are either imitation priests or corrupted clerics. Their hymn is unmistakeably in Latin as though they are the choir for this mass, but the soprano can overcome their dreary drone at will. These sacrilegious clergymen transform the absurdly profane panorama into the most blasphemous requiem. I seethe at the scale of the scandal. Their emergence is a final insult before the lucid lunar traces subside. The woman's song does now contain words, and I decipher a few phrases from the chorus:

Life and Death... fooled by welcoming fallacy... Hail the Moon, the Sun's gentle twin.

As the choir builds to the chorus, the soprano this time does not sing but shouts aloud, her eyes wide, addressing the gathering: 'The sinister bell resonates for another who has fallen to the curse of the Sun's realm. Soon they will discover the grace of a new majesty. But the forlorn Lunatic for whom the bell tolled has not sought our asylum. So let our invite be heard before fires' ascension.' A crescendo of noise follows, and she bellows the delayed chorus. She is joined by much of the congregation and the macabre mass roars.

A waking village would hear this, yet still no one investigates. The moon drops behind the houses, and the entire graveyard is cast into eerie darkness. Towards the horizon, twilight beckons. With the new light, a haunting thought occurs to me: during the liveliest moments of this ghastly ceremony, the crowd danced and swayed but the shadows on the ground remained still. Can that be true? Where were their shadows? They should have been dancing too. I must be misremembering it—I must be.

The ritual creatures disperse, most heading towards the chapel. A few folks enter the grounds from outside with no qualms about there being a gathering at such an hour. The soprano, however, remains for one final lonely encore.

I stand, still in shock, wholly consumed by her sombre ballad, the words now clear:

Death my friend, where is thy Scythe?
My patience cannot forever abide.
Good hunter, please free his mortal curse,
Swing it swift near our civic hearse.

Eternally, are your words in stone.
Expectantly, I lie alone.
Once upon, this nightmare ends,
Endlessly, our story transcends.

Darling forgive, I urge you no pain,
Dreaming demise brings unholy gain.
Dearly beloved, delirium clouds thee,
No offerings of hope, hast thou forsaken me?

Eternally, are your words in stone.
Expectantly, I lie alone.
Once upon, this nightmare ends,
Endlessly, our story transcends.

Young kin, when shall we meet?
I rue I could not dispel deceit.
O child, did I ever cradle thee?
Do I brood for no written entity?

Eternally, are your words in stone.
Expectantly, I lie alone.
Are the words ill-fated lore,
To stay unembraced forevermore?

With the raucous frights faded and the parade now a small clutch, I stare, pitying the lonely lady. Her mournful elegy soothes my alarm, and her stoic stroll towards the church stands in stark contrast to her fiery exultations. I am captivated to know who she is. I follow the perimeter wall further to keep her in view.

The whole cemetery and its chapel lie in darkness. The church stands atop the mound before a brightening sky which steadily blends greenish-yellow into a pastel blue overhead.

Near the far side of the church, the soprano kneels in front of a comparatively small headstone. Lowering her head beneath the dawn horizon and into the dusky fore-ground, she disappears from view. I am compelled to wait a moment with a newly forming thought. Perhaps, if I ap-proach cautiously, praise her singing and behave as a mem-ber of the sect, she may reveal the mysteries of tonight's events and alleviate my fearful premonitions. As I linger, the dawn tapestry becomes overexposed, and the graveyard begins to absorb the natural light of day.

My eyes have not moved from where she knelt, but she is gone. A glance around finds no one. How has she vanished? Surely, I would have seen her as she stood up to leave. I begin walking towards where she was and appreciate how peaceful the cemetery is in the dawn light. At the base of many of the sturdy plaques are colourful and heartfelt sym-bols of love and remembrance. The more weathered and often larger tablets are typically less likely to own flowers or wreaths. The carvings tell of whole families who are at rest together with inscriptions dating back over a century. I observe no sign of the young woman as I approach the monument where she mourned. She left no memorial gift as the ground is bare. The engraving reads:

IN LOVING MEMORY OF
MARIA CHESTER
WHO FELL ASLEEP ON MAY 17 1836
AGED 37 YEARS

The only other words are at the base; the epitaph reads:

My Love
My Angel Above

I gaze at the tablet, deep in thought. Why had she paused at the burial site of someone who evidently died before she was born?

I move to the front of the church where a large, wooden door bars entry. I crane my neck to view the church's domineering entrance, then I poke my head around the other side of the chapel, but I see no one.

I stand beside the door of the church, unsure what to do. Out of habit, I glance at my timepiece. The hands are still fixed in a straight line. Wait... The crystal... It's no longer cracked. And my coat... It's no longer torn. I check and double-check. How can this be?

A bright crimson sky draws my attention, and I look out over the frosty countryside landscape. As the sun peeks over the horizon, a scorching infernal force throws me off my feet. The pain is intense but rapidly subsides.

Bells chime eight as I lie staring up at the grand interior of the church's sacred hall. What just happened? The door is closed. How did I get inside?

CHAPTER THREE

DWELLERS IN THE CRYPT

I gaze upon a gleaming altar. Figures depicted in stained glass windows cast their colourful rays upon it. High up, behind the altar, organ pipes rise like silver fingers. Can this be real? The door is shut and seems to glow ever so slightly with the morning light behind it, and I can see it is locked as the bolt blocks the sunlight that billows through the crack between the doors. A large keyhole shines brightly too, but I do not see a key.

I saw the sunrise, and I felt scorching pain. Now it is gone, and I am inside the church. Did the soprano open the door and pull me in? Where is she?

I pick myself up, but I don't see anyone. The holy shrine entices me towards it, so I walk down the aisle.

'Hallo,' I call out. The soprano must have the key; I need to find her. 'Is anybody here?'

'This way, quick!' a woman answers.

'Where are you?' I ask.

'Down the steps,' she says. Her muffled voice comes from a far corner, but I don't see anyone. I cut through the pews and pass beneath one of the giant stone archways framing the nave. A hatch lies open in the floor where steps disappear down into blackness. I hesitate before the void. 'Come now, you don't want to get caught again.'

'Do you have the k—'

'Hurry!'

I descend, losing my feet to the abyss. Once I am consumed by it, my eyes readjust. Waiting to greet me at the bottom of the steps is a young woman. It is not the soprano. This lady is younger with cropped hair.

'Long night?' she says chirpily. She wears a white blouse with a brass brooch. The blasphemous revellers dressed formally too, could she be one of them?

I do not answer. I don't know if I can trust her. Instead, I assess the room. Cobwebs huddle in the corners and dust mites breathe the stale air. Short pillars line the basement, connected by arches. It gives the impression that multiple spiders support the low roof. This undercroft is mostly empty with only a few tables and shelves adorned with bibles and crucifixes. Why is this woman in such a dusty crypt?

'My name is Amy, and this is Mr. Isaac Dewhurst.' She points to a man I had not seen. He is slumped against the wall created by the stone steps. 'You'll have to excuse Isaac;

he doesn't talk much. Perhaps you'll be better company,' she chuckles. 'Tell me, don't you think he's the oldest man you've seen here?'

He is smartly dressed and probably in his late fifties. Confused, I merely reply, 'He's not that old.'

'Fascinating. Isaac, maybe you are not such a rare specimen after all.' Isaac grunts. Amy ushers me down the stairs, and I oblige. 'I'm thrilled you've come to end our eternal silence, and I will enjoy gazing into your bright blue eyes—Isaac's are like coal,' she laughs. 'What brought you to these parts?'

'I'm trying to get home.'

'Aren't we all.'

'Do you have the key?'

'The key, the key... what key?'

'The door is locked. I don't know how I got in, but I need to leave. I'm sure my employers are already furious. Do you know how I can get out?'

A croak erupts from Isaac. He lifts his head and addresses the dumbfounded woman before me, 'O Amy, O Amy—be gentle with this poor bastard! Today might not be so bleak after all.' His rasping laughter evolves to become unnerving and shrill.

'Ignore Isaac; he has no decorum. I believe we can help you. Would you kindly take a seat, please?'

'I must get back,' I say. Amy offers a helpless look. 'May I ask what you are doing down here? How did you get in? Are you hiding?'

'In a way, yes,' Amy replies.

'From whom?'

'Please sit down and I will explain.' Amy gestures for me to sit against the pillar opposite her and Isaac. What other option do I have?

'How long have you been here?' I ask as I sit.

'We arrived shortly before you.'

'Who let you in?'

'In good time. Isaac and I are on a journey, but before I divulge all of our secrets, do you mind if I ask you a few questions first?' Amy's response stirs me with intrigue.

'Go ahead,' I say. 'I'm not getting out of here just yet—I've got time.'

'Ha, us too,' says Isaac.

Amy gives Isaac a curt look and adds, 'You didn't tell me your name.' Amy's demeanour, while still friendly, has become formal.

'My name is Edward Webster.'

'Excellent, where were you born?'

'Lyemouth.'

'Is that near?'

'You don't know where Lyemouth is? Are you lost? It's about fifty miles north-west.' I see Isaac shoot a quick glance at Amy.

'Does your family still live there?'

'Yes...' I narrow my eyes, uncertain about the questioning.

'He has a chance,' Isaac slyly whispers to Amy.

'Excuse me? What chance do I have? Huh?' Why does he refuse to talk to me directly? Isaac sits knees up and arms folded, staring at his boots with his firm, emotionless face.

'I apologise for Isaac,' Amy says. 'Let me ask you one final question: what happened last night?'

I explain the predicament I was in and how I'd seen to resolve it. It is when I mention the trembling thirteen tolls that they give each other a fleeting look.

'The Eldritch Chime,' Amy says. 'We heard it too. The thirteen tolls signify that someone nearby has crossed the Ethereal Veil. It is the boundary between the realms of the Sun and Moon. As you cross the Ethereal Veil, the soul and spirit part.'

'I don't understand. The Eldritch Chime? The Ethereal Veil?'

'I mean... that bell rings when someone dies,' Amy answers with a knowing stare.

'Excuse me?'

Isaac hesitates for the briefest moment before saying, 'If you fall asleep during an arctic blast without shelter or warm clothing, you don't expect to survive. That bell rang for you!'

'What do you mean?'

'YOU'RE DEAD, SON!'

CHAPTER FOUR

JOURNEY TO THE GRAVE

Amy berates Isaac, but as she does, something dawns on me. I can be so foolish! This is all an act—two heretics teasing the outsider. Who are these wretches who loiter in a crypt and converse in an equally cryptic manner? All this about Eldritch Chimes and Ethereal Veils—what nonsense! Do they think I'll believe anything? There is no way I can walk and talk so ordinarily for Isaac's heinous assertion to be true. Once again, no one is willing to help me. I won't listen to their twisted dogmas any longer.

Enraged, I stand up and walk to the steps. 'I'm leaving,' I say. 'If you won't help me, I'll find my own way out.'

'No! Don't go up there,' Amy shouts.

'Let him go, Amy,' Isaac says, before adding with a snigger, 'He'll be back.'

I stride up the steps and towards the bright white aperture at the top. The grand ceiling and the tops of stained glass windows come into view. As I enter through the opening, a divine figure stands before me in the coloured glass. A green beam of light blinds me. Searing sensation courses through my body as I am thrown back down the steps. The pain dissipates once more to numbness. I open my eyes; I am under a table. I roll out from underneath and tremble to my feet. I reach out to the table for support, but my hand passes right through it! I grasp only the air. I try again and again until I am frantically punching through the mirage of the table. Petrified, I look at my captors. Amy is distraught, her hands covering her nose and mouth. Isaac looks back at his boots and calmly says, 'And the penny drops.'

'No!' I scream. 'No, it cannot be! What have you done? What occult sorcery have you performed?'

Amy shakes her head and whimpers, 'No one has done anything to you.' I pace around under the arches, my mind spiralling into oblivion. I rush over to a crucifix on the far wall and fall to my knees. It may not be a Protestant cross, but I have no other recourse.

Terrified, I pray to my saviour, reciting the Lord's Prayer. After, I pause for a moment then commence a fresh appeal, 'Pray tell Father, for I know not where I am or what is happening. I yearn for your heavenly guidance. If I did perish, why am I not rising to greet you?' Isaac chuckles. 'I have always been your loyal servant and followed your teachings. How long must I—'

I hear footsteps, and I pause my prayer. The clopping gets louder. I run to the stairs and shout up, 'Please let me out.' Amy turns her head away and sobs quietly. A woman appears through the bright aperture. 'Yes, I am down here,' I cry. She begins to descend the stairs as I stand at the base. 'Will you let me out?' I ask as she approaches. She gets very close and does not react. Before I can get out of her way, she walks right through me. 'No! Can you hear me? Excuse me!'

The woman turns and looks directly over my head and asks, 'Is someone up there?' After a short pause, she turns back, grabs a folder from the shelves and returns, passing straight through me once more. She shivers as she climbs the steps.

I rush up after her but am thrown back again when I reach the light.

I pick myself up, and with my mind spinning, I pace around. My feet sweep across the floor, but the dust doesn't move, then I kick a stone pillar. I feel no sensation—nothing! A puppet feels more than I do. But it's not just that—there is no sound or recoil. The world refuses to react to my presence. I beat the pillar harder and harder in an attempt to feel something, anything! It's hopeless. I'm not fit to even disturb dust.

I stride back and forth, overcome with grief and anguish. Above, I hear the unmistakable chords from church organ pipes. The deep and metallic tones conduct my descent into lunacy and despair.

Multiple climatic songs play as I continue to wallow and flounder in desolation. My poor mother will be so distraught. Mama, I'm so sorry! How could I be such a dunce? Why didn't I opt for an earlier train? Why did I have to be so proud and refuse to sell my watch? What will my family do now? What will I do? I cannot bear the thought.

My mind continues to spin and swirl until after some time, the music abruptly ceases. I move to a distant corner of the crypt and watch as the woman returns the folder of hymns. As she climbs back up the stairs, she seems to fade into the glare of the sunlit church.

Desolate, I sit in a foetal position, burying my head into my arms. Amy tries to talk to me and encourages me to sit with her. 'Show some respect!' I snap. 'You should not disturb the dead.'

Silence protracts for hours. So many depressing thoughts flutter through my brain; it is like a charm of humming-birds in a feeding frenzy, sapping away all that I am—all that I *was*. And what was I? I have no legacy, no meaningful contribution and no offspring, though it is probably for the best that there is no fatherless child. My heart sinks thinking about the ones I love. My mother, Catriona, stands fore-most in my thoughts. My brothers and I would often call her 'Cat' as she saw herself as a lioness protecting her three cubs. But now two are dead! Mama, how could I do this to you?

My childhood was fun, but it all went wrong when Charlie died. I struggled as an adult, either with employ-ment I despised or that paid poorly. Through a lack of confidence, I shied away from potential romances, a bitter regret now. No! I can't be thinking about my life in the past tense. Those bloody trains! They claimed Charlie too. Why am I not reuniting with my little brother? Why couldn't I have just kept some extra change?

I wallow, chastising myself, until Amy puts a hand on my shoulder, and says, 'I'm sorry Mr. Webster, but Isaac and

I need to speak with you before nightfall. We can help—a little.'

I nod, and as I lift my head, I wipe my eyes, only to realise that there are no tears. 'I can't even cry!' I moan. I haul myself up and return to where I had previously sat, opposite Amy. 'So, what is this place?' I ask.

Isaac chuckles to himself, then says, 'Welcome to a gothic nightmare! Here you shall make your bed in crypts and coffins. And no matter how much you invite it, sleep will not come.'

Amy scolds Isaac who merely laughs some more. She then apologises on his behalf.

'I'm dead and not in heaven,' I say, desolate. 'I can hardly expect a good answer to that question.'

'But what Isaac fails to mention is that there is hope for you.'

'I'd die again to find hope in this situation, but I've fallen a long way from my happy, sedate life as a lamplighter. And I don't even understand what it is that I've become.'

Amy's response is not what I expect, 'You're a Lunatic.'

I don't know whether to laugh or cry, but only one of those options is possible now. I thought Amy was the kind one. 'What did you say, a Lunatic?'

'It is a term which many of us use to describe ourselves. We've lost our minds, and we as much as worship our lunar deity.'

'Why do you love the moon so much?'

'This is the Moon's dominion, and our spirit has no feeling—I'm sure you've noticed. Yet, three things remove the numbness. As the moon's soft glow passes through us, it warms and thaws our senses as if we are alive again. This effect is noticeably strongest when the moon is full, hence the festivities last night to celebrate feeling reborn. The moon also acts as our only guiding light because of the second reason: the sun's rays are incredibly strong, it delivers an intense burning and paralysing force, as you've seen. Hence, we are restricted to move only at night.'

'Seriously, son, don't get caught by sunlight or even in a bright room,' Isaac adds. 'Some time ago I got caught outside. I was locked in a terrifying inferno for much of a day until the sun passed behind the rock wall I was pinned against. There may be no lasting damage per se, but the unending agony burns the whole episode into your memory and pushes out something of who you are. In my case, it may have been what I did or where I'm from; I remember neither anyhow.'

'You don't remember?' I ask.

'Memory fades when you... pass over,' Amy says, searching for a kind way to express death.

'It fades bloody fast from what I can tell,' Isaac adds. 'And the sun will purge it almost instantly like touching a flame to dry tinder.'

'I can remember things fine,' I say.

'Not for long,' Isaac says.

'What do you remember?'

'Not much, language for one, so thankfully I don't gargle like a bloody infant—yet. Otherwise, just my name and that searing episode, that's about it for me. Each day can be terrifying and tortuous, and I may be doomed to roam forevermore.' What he describes is terrifying, and I begin to feel sympathy for this loathsome creature.

I ask Amy too. She says, 'I don't recall much more. Most of us remember our name, language and have a general concept of things. I don't remember the name of where I'm from, but I believe it is coastal. My mind clings to an image of a long, sandy beach at sunset, so I'm travelling to the west coast, that's all I have to go on. I will say this though, while it is a curse, it is also a blessing in my opinion. Would you want to remember how you died, what it was like to taste good food and wine, and the thought of your grieving loved ones? I think our blissful ignorance spares us.'

'That is a harrowing prospect,' I say. 'How long do I have? What can I do?'

'This is why we are so keen to speak with you. We don't think you have long. You need to get home.'

'Why?'

'So you may rest in peace!' Amy's tone is deadly serious. 'The dead don't rest until both spirit and soul reunite. They ripped apart when you heard the chimes. You are a spirit now, but a person's soul is seated within their skull. If you find your grave and reunite with your soul, you will be able to slumber deeply and peacefully. I believe it is a most wondrous euphoria, one which evaporates all numbness—that is the third method. But until then, you will never sleep—as Isaac so delicately put it.'

'You never sleep? That's awful,' I say.

'It's much worse than that!' Isaac cuts in.

'We wanderers are always tired,' Amy says, 'so tired in fact that we can become somewhat delirious, but no matter how weary we may be, we never fall asleep. So, you must journey to your grave; otherwise, you will never rest or be at peace.'

'And you must go before you forget where home is,' Isaac adds. 'Each night, Amy and I wander from graveyard to graveyard in the serendipitous hope that one day we'll stumble upon our souls. If you don't hurry, you'll end up just like us, wandering restlessly and aimlessly for all eternity.'

'Oh!' I say, dumbfounded.

'And it gets worse!'

'Give the poor man a minute, will you?' Amy complains to Isaac.

'He needs to know,' Isaac says.

'Know what?' I ask.

'Last night, Amy and I were in some other godforsaken crypt with another Lunatic, and that man was the true definition of the word. His mind was totally gone. He was shrieking at shadows all day; he was so delirious that he barely acknowledged that we were there at all. We tried to calm him—well, Amy did—I knew it was useless. But I fear that will be our fate if we don't find our graves sooner or later.'

'That's horrific!' I say.

'The longer we go without sleep, the more our minds deteriorate,' Isaac adds. 'That's when the nightmares manifest. You might be able to brush them off to start with, but as we saw last night, there comes a point when they take over completely. And we have no idea when that day will come.'

I sit silent and stupefied. Will that be my fate?

'Don't let Isaac frighten you,' Amy says. 'The important thing is that you know where your body will be buried. Lyemouth, I presume.'

With that distressing image of my burial, the hummingbirds of despair leap into flight again to suckle the nectar from fresh flowers of melancholy. 'Yes,' I simply say.

'Then there is hope, Mr. Webster.'

The thought of my funeral brings a passage from the burial rites in the Book of Common Prayer to mind: *ashes to ashes, dust to dust; in sure and certain hope of the Resurrection to eternal life*. 'But what good is hope?' I say to Amy. 'I was full to the brim with hope that, upon my death, I would resurrect to eternal life, yet... I am here.'

'Mr. Webster, I can't claim to understand what this place is, but I presume you're familiar with the concept of purgatory or limbo—an in-between space.'

'Are you saying that this is my final trial? That if I prove my faith in the face of such adversity that I may still enter heaven?' I ask, my spirit buoyed.

'All I'm saying is that you should not lose hope; it will drive you on when there is no other good reason. I don't know if we reach heaven through our graves—but the sensation one gets is heavenly! Or so I'm told.'

'So all may not be lost?'

'Nothing is lost, Mr. Webster—you know where your home is. The moon may not be full tonight, but these nights are long. Each evening the moon will get dimmer and rise later and later. By the half moon, it will be very difficult to travel; you have about five nights to get home.'

'And what about both of you?' I ask.

'We will carry on together for now, until we have a reason to part. I don't remember when Isaac joined me, but the company helps us stave off manic thoughts and to focus on something other than our monotonous journey.'

'Your incessant chirpiness is bloody grating,' Isaac says to Amy, 'but I must admit, purgatory is easier to traverse following you.'

'You really know how to compliment a woman, Isaac.' Then Amy addresses me, 'He's just looking at my buttocks.' Isaac reacts with a creepy chuckle.

'If this is purgatory, am I here because I committed a terrible sin?' I ask.

'I believe saints and sinners alike come here, but I couldn't say with any certainty,' Amy replies. 'I cling to the hope that I was a good person, but I simply do not recall.'

As the brightness above the steps fades, I hasten my questioning. 'I still don't understand what I am. Why can I not touch the table, yet I can lean against this stone pillar?'

'You are a spirit now. Spirits can pass through materials such as wood but not heavier things such as stone. Also, mortals pass right through us, as you saw, but our spirit projections can touch each other.'

'Spirit projection?'

'I believe that when you cross the Ethereal Veil, you retain a mental image of yourself which is normally young and beautiful. This image is perhaps the actual form of your spirit or the form which your spirit projects. I fancy that it depends on what the nature of the spirit truly is. Many Lunatics are young and beautiful because they reminisce their former glory. That's why it's so amusing to see a man as old as Isaac.'

'Clearly, I just kept refining,' Isaac says dryly.

'How rough was the starting point?' Amy jokes, triggering a croaky laugh from Isaac.

'Is that why my watch has the wrong time?' I ask. 'It's the last time I saw. And the crystal cracked last night, but now it appears mended.'

'I expect so. After all, it is only the image of a watch, as you'd want to remember it,' Amy says. 'Also, I introduced myself as Amy—not Miss or Mrs. Rawlins—simply be-cause I don't recall if I married. My spirit projects no wed-ding ring, but that's not to say I never married. I might have lived to the ripe old age of eighty, too. Do you understand?'

'I think so.'

'I know there's a lot to get your head around, but once you embark on your journey, it'll all become clear.'

We continue with sparse conversation until five o'clock when darkness envelops the crypt. Amy asks if I know the way and she is impressed by my skill for navigation. They both stress the importance of only travelling on clear nights and that we can only hope tonight is like the last.

It is time. We stagger to our feet and trace the walls of this black crypt. Climbing the stairs is a struggle. At the top, it is easier to see where we are walking; the stained-glass windows glow with soft moonlight, and the door at the entrance seems to shimmer as if it too catches a trace of the lunar rays. The door is not bright like the windows, but there is a perceptible contrast with the black stone walls. It is enough to suggest that the door is not real, and indeed, we pass through as if it were not.

CHAPTER FIVE

THE GHOSTLY GUISE

The low zenith distorts the moon so that it looks unnaturally large and phosphorescent against a black sky. Its heat is welcome, yet it is like sitting a little too far from a campfire as it is not enough to stave off the numbing chill. In retrospect, in its pallor last night I was fooled into feeling human. In truth, those few moments in its heat were too warm for a night so cold.

Amy leads with Isaac and me in tow. The headstones cast shadows in the moonlight but none of us do. The sight of Maria Chester's gravestone brings a flood of memories. 'Where did the wanderers go that were celebrating the full moon?' I ask Amy.

'They are residents, not wanderers,' Amy replies.

'From here?'

'They lie beneath us now in rapture.'

'Oh, so they are spirits that have reunited with their soul? Why do they surface?'

'Those Lunatics may have found their asylum, but like us, they are still social beings.'

'Speak for yourself,' Isaac interrupts.

Amy continues, 'On clear full moon nights, you will discover that cemetery residents will rise to bathe in the warm rays and socialise with their family and fellow Lunatics. Many will have forgotten the friends they made from previous lunar cycles as well as from life, but I wonder if the residents repeatedly bond with the same people—I think that would show true friendship.'

I pause as we reach Maria's gravestone. Amy stops and asks, 'What's wrong?'

'Is this the grave of the woman who sang last night?'

'It may well be.'

'Was her name Maria?'

'I don't know.'

'If it were not for her singing, I would have continued my walk to Horton. When the sun rose, I would have been caught in its inferno. I may have lost my memory, and I'd have no idea that I need to return to Lyemouth. I was terrified when I saw everyone dancing to her songs, but now, I am truly grateful.' Amy puts a hand on my shoulder as I stare at her grave. 'Who wrote: *My love, My angel above?*'

'Her husband, I suppose,' Amy says.

'His name is not engraved here. If she had a husband her own age, he would be eighty years old now. I don't know many people who lived to be eighty.'

'Perhaps he remarried?'

I remember the last two words of her sombre ballad, *unembraced forevermore*. 'No wonder her final song was so sad. She is lonely. The promise of her love returning is fading, and she may be alone for eternity. She cannot know if she has any children, but even if she does, they may not be buried here.'

'Better than wandering restlessly like us,' Isaac adds.

'Yes, but she will be reminded endlessly that she was once loved and then forgotten. No one is leaving flowers at her grave.'

In a solemn mood, we move from Maria's headstone and towards the entrance. 'How do they rise and return to their resting place?' I ask Amy.

'I cannot be sure. I have never done it.'

'If you cannot pass through stone, how do they get into the stone tombs?'

'Oh Goodness! Imagine if you were locked out.'

'That'll be just my bloody luck,' Isaac says. 'I finally find my home, only then, I cannot enter. Alas, I am doomed to rot in this eternal damnation.' He sighs.

'The soul must open the door somehow. I believe I witnessed Lunatics entering their stone tombs this morning,' Amy says.

We depart the church grounds and approach the main street. I have a terrifying thought: what will I find on that bench where I died?

We turn onto the street. The metal bench glints in the moonlight. There is something on the seat blocking its sheen. I cannot yet see what it is. I inform the others what this place is, but they don't respond. I think they sense my nervousness.

Soon, I see what lies there: a colourful bouquet in the spot where I slept. I approach purposefully. Isaac and Amy wait further back.

I pause in front of the bench, distraught. This is all too real. My family will have left notes with an epitaph. I have to read them, but the apprehension is incredible. The devastating act of crystallising their mourning and grief is unbearable. I fall to my knees in dismay. Not being able to console them or ease their depression is shattering. Even if I could communicate, how could I tell them that while I was able to read their loving messages, I am not experiencing heavenly exultation but instead wandering in wretched desolation afflicted with looming lunacy?

Inspecting the bouquet triggers a desperate frenzy. Where are their messages? I frantically glance all around and closely interrogate the shadows for any note dislodged by the rustling wind. I must know their last words to me! They would have left a note, of course they would. Sour though their words may be, I need this comfort.

I calm myself and stare wide-eyed at the modest arrangement. The single bunch of handpicked flowers is small. These surely were left by a kind villager who, upon discovering such a pathetic human specimen, made this pitying gesture. My foolish mind raced ahead to see only what it wished.

What I would give to read the final note from my mother, but how could she have received the news and visited this spot and returned all in one day? It is unlikely, and would my family even feel the need to visit the site of my last stand for stupidity? If they do come, it might be tomorrow. What if I stay another night? I could still read their epitaphs.

No, I cannot do that. I have seen Maria's heartache, and I know that I am lucky; I *do* have family, and I still have hope of reuniting with them one day—I want nothing more. I must make it home without delay.

I sit on the bench. My patient companions are talking amongst themselves, affording me some privacy. I call over, 'Thanks for waiting. I know we need to press on.'

'How are you feeling?' Amy asks, caringly.

'Sad, but it has strengthened my resolve to return home.' I stand, and, at once, we walk out of the village along to the northbound country lane.

'Your hometown, Lyemouth, does it have a long beach? Or do you know any places that fit the description?' Amy asks.

'My home is a port town, no beaches. There are numerous beaches north and south from there, unhelpfully. If you travel due west, there is a lovely town called Kemble-on-Sands, where the sand stretches out so far it is almost impossible to reach the sea. I have been there with my family and witnessed a beautiful sunset just like the one you described. From there, you should follow the coast north as you will find many other places like it.'

'Excellent, thank you. Is that town near Lyemouth?'

'No, it's perhaps twenty miles south.'

'Very well, but I'm afraid we must leave you then. We will travel west as you suggest. Neither of us can afford to take any diversions. Will you be all right, Mr Webster?'

'Oh!' I pause. I don't want to say goodbye, nor do I wish to travel through this nightmare realm on my own. 'I should be,' I say, bravely. 'I still have my navigation skills. Thank you for setting me on the right path, Amy. I don't know what I'd have done without your guidance—truly.'

'Well, it's not every day you have to tell someone *the news*,' Amy says.

'Seriously, son, find somewhere dark and quiet well before sunrise,' Isaac says. 'The moon will drop faster than you expect. You need to keep your memory intact and the nightmares at bay.'

'I will, thank you.'

'Church crypts are a good place to bed down for the daytime,' Amy says. 'And you may find more wanderers like us. After all, we wanderers are searching for our place of rest, so many will visit churchyards and then stay in the undercroft if the hour is late. It can be helpful to trade knowledge, much like how you've informed us about the towns on the coastline.'

'I don't plan to bed down for many days if I can help it,' I say.

'It is time we set off,' Isaac cuts in. 'Good luck, son.'

'May Luna guide you!' Amy proclaims.

'Farewell,' I say.

Amy smiles as she and Isaac turn and set off on their journey. They walk through the tall bushes that line the road as if they weren't there. Their disappearance not only impinges a sharp sense of loneliness, but it also makes me appreciate how foreign all this is to me. I would likely have walked miles and miles before realising that I no longer need to be confined to roads. This is good though, because travelling as the crow flies will be quicker, and the chance of getting lost is much slimmer if I am careful to follow the celestial compass.

Presently, I follow the lane as it turns slightly westward and towards the direction that I am heading. I gaze over the frosty landscape and then down at the wet, muddy track. I feel uneasy. I am alone now, having to fend for myself. That unease bubbles quickly to a deep-seated anxiety. The world around me is peaceful, the sky is clear and the moon shines brightly. I can make good progress tonight, so why am I so worried?

I sense that it is not simply that I am on my own. After all, last night on my fateful walk, the loneliness did not perturb me. No, there is another source of discomfort—this place is not familiar to me. Amy referred to it as the Moon's Dominion. If ghosts can exist here, then what else might inhabit this place? What I am seeing doesn't look right, either. It appears somehow altered, as though the world around me is a mere illusion.

It is only as I pass beneath a giant oak tree that the discomfort becomes too great. I stop and look upwards. Bright stars pierce through grasping tree branches—through what should be solid wood—and they shine dimly like embers through cinder goggles. The transparency is only slight, but why is it like this at all? As I move, I notice an odd distortion somewhat akin to how objects refract when seen through a glass of water. The combined effect affords the oak tree with an ethereal shimmer.

I look down at the wet and muddy track; there is no frost so far tonight, yet the fields and hedgerows shimmer too, as if there is a thin covering. The trees that loomed over the graveyard last night did not hide the stars either, the woman returning the hymns in the basement faded a little as she climbed into the sunlit nave, and the door at the entrance to the church seemed to catch the moonlight on the opposite side. In this ethereal domain, it is the corporeal world which adopts a ghostly guise.

Not all corporeal objects possess this strange quality, though. Stone walls and buildings don't, neither did the metal benches. I reach out to touch the tree trunk, and my hand passes through. Am I right to surmise that the things that possess this ghostly guise are only the corporeal objects that I can move through? I miss Amy already; there is still so much I do not understand. I feel like an orphan out in the cold. This world may be strange and unnerving, but I must adapt quickly if I am to find rest and reunite with my family one day.

As the lane bends away, I withdraw from the road and pass through a spiny hedge. Moving through almost-solid objects just doesn't feel right, but I emerge from the hedgerow onto a grassy knoll and climb. Beside the knoll is a bog and a forest. A stone circle rises as I continue my ascent, and the ground soon flattens into a plateau. Deaconshire has several of these ancient stone monuments. This one is merely a ring of jagged boulders; nothing as spectacular as Stonehenge. While the boulders are not extraordinary, I do marvel at the length of their shadows. I look at the grass beneath me. The moonlight at my feet is unspoilt. I miss my shadow.

Cresting the hill, warm but distant lights twinkle. They signpost farmhouses and villages, but my route north-west is dark and barren.

I hear quiet voices. Beside one of the boulders are two young women gazing out at the view; both have long hair, one is a short, heavyset redhead, while the other is thin and blonde. Their appearance is quite grubby, and I surmise them to be farmers' daughters. These two women have shadows, but curiously, they have no shimmer. It is odd for two women to be out here in the dark, though they seem at ease.

I have a mischievous thought; what if I attempt to spook them? Nothing sinister, but what will happen if I walk through them? Will they sense my presence? The woman in the church basement shivered after she passed through me. Don't they say that ghosts give people chills? Despite being dead, I can still see and think and move. I am still *here*, so I hope to have some impact on the world, even if it is only slight.

Both women are facing away from me, and I decide to target the blonde lady. Their soft laughter whistles through the air as I approach. I don't want to cause them harm, but I really do want something to happen. Complete non-existence is a horrible prospect. I creep closer and closer. Then, as I go to pass through, the blonde woman squeals with fright.

'Who art thou?' the blonde woman yells.

'I—I—' I stumble for words. I have not walked through her but bumped into her.

'How dare thee!' the redhead shouts. The pallor of each woman bears a striking resemblance to their hair colour.

'I'm ever so sorry ma'am—I—'

'Ma'am—hah—do not *ma'am* us,' the redhead chastises. She turns to the pale blonde woman, and says, 'Art thou well?'

'I am well, Meg,' the blonde woman chuckles. 'It hath been such a long time since a man cometh upon me in this manner. I had forgotten the excitement.' She twists her body and smiles at me seductively.

'Jane and I art covenant sisters, and we do not respect being shunted from behind in the dark,' Meg barks.

Jane steps in, 'He is just being playful, Me—'

'Who art thou?' Meg scolds again. She looks ready to fight me.

'My name is Edward, I'm ever so sorry, Miss.'

''Tis quite unnecessary for thee to apologise, Edward,' Jane says giddily. She is swaying with nervous excitement.

''Tis absolutely necessary, Jane,' Meg says.

'I do apologise,' I say. 'I was confused. I saw that you both have a shadow, and I do not. Are you—'

'Dead?' Meg jumps in. 'Yes, we are both dead.'

Jane coos like a doting mother, and says, 'Meg, he wanteth a shadow.'

'He shalt go wanting.'

'How can you be a ghost and have a shadow?' I ask.

Meg answers, ''Tis a riddle those of thine ilk wilt ne'er resolve.'

'Never?'

'Ne'er. Please do not lose sleep o'er it.' Jane stifles a giggle, but Meg's laugh is like a sharp blast through a French horn. Is it a joke because I cannot sleep?

Jane settles herself and asks, 'Where is thy place of belonging?'

'Lyemouth.'

'We know it well,' Meg says.

'You do?' I ask.

'Beside Lyeminster, is it not? Passed Draymere,' Jane shudders at Meg's utterance of the name, 'is it not?'

'Yes—' I ponder how it is these sisters remember such details and why they speak so strangely. 'May I ask a delicate question?'

'What is it, my darling?' Jane replies.

'When was it that you died? I am told I will lose my memory dreadfully soon, but yours is good.'

'Thou shalt lose much of thy memory before the next moon,' Meg answers. 'We art friends of the moon. We entered this promised land in the year 1613, and we do not forget it. We do not forget anything.'

'How can I be like you? How can I keep my memory?'

'O darling, do not be sad,' Jane says. 'Thou wilt ne'er be like us, but the night is long and clear. There is hope for thee.'

'Thou should'st leave now,' Meg says, 'Time is—'

'Not yet,' Jane interrupts. She shuffles excitedly, 'I have something I wish to do for this man before he leaveth.'

'What is it?' Meg snaps.

Jane clasps her hands together and shakes. 'I wish to make him a prophecy.'

I panic. A prophecy? Covenant sisters? Memory? Shadows? These are witches and not just any witches. 'You are the Havelock Harpies!'

Jane delights in her reply: 'Oh, thou art as clever as thou art handsome.' Meg snorts with laughter. I fear she is the honest one. 'If thou art set for Lyemouth, thou wilt meet our shadowless sister. Let me devise a prophecy for thy journey through the valley of death.'

'No, I don't want anything from you. Please forgive my transgression.' I do not want to meddle with the occult, and nor do I want the occult to meddle with me. I move to withdraw.

Meg steps in my way and grasps my arm. She says, 'Thou assaulted my sister. Thou shalt hear her prophecy.'

I turn back to Jane; she deliberates. 'What shall it be? Hmm. Oh, yes—yes. I think I have one for thee,' she giggles. '*When thou meet'st a nag and a hag—*'

'HAG?' Meg shrieks. Jane sniggers. 'Thou can't call Alice a hag.'

'She is a hag,' Jane titters.

'What say thee to Alice if this peddler speaketh thy prophecy to her?'

'What then—if I say—two mares?' Jane howls, laughing. 'Absolutely not!'

'Prithee Edward, do not repeat thy prophecy to our shadowless sister. It will place her in a foul mood, and worst of all, thy prophecy shalt not rhyme. Dost thou not wish for thy prophecy to rhyme?' I pause, unsure how to respond. 'But, of course, it must rhyme.'

'I take no part in it,' Meg says. 'Let her wrath be upon thee.'

'Edward, darling, please heed my warning: *When thou meet'st a nag and a hag, there shalt be a trick and a trap.*' Jane giggles and claps. 'Yes, that is it. 'Tis a fine prophecy for thee.'

Meg releases me.

'Goodbye, Edward,' Jane calls as I walk away. 'Won't thee remember me?'

The witches cackle.

CHAPTER SIX

THE GHOST IN THE BEDROOM

Many hours pass and progress is good. Interestingly, I find that I have not the energy to run, but walking bears no burden. I also discover that well-tended farms are akin to illusory swamps; not only do they shimmer like frost—although I believe frost is now forming—but my feet sink below the soil, so it appears as though I am wading through lush blades of grass. Fond memories of camping expeditions return to me, including the frustration of splintering countless wooden pegs as the force of the mallet would often fail to breach the impenetrable layer of rock hiding just underneath the soil. It is perhaps logical that in such well-maintained plantations this layer is banished much deeper. My ethereal being is not free from the clutches of gravity, and I suspect that it is this layer of hidden rocks that prevents me falling.

Much of the route crosses undulating moorland filled with thick scrub; the only barriers in my way are drystone walls. My spirit cannot pass through these moss-ridden walls of stone and slate. Instead, I either clamber over or find a wooden gate or a gap.

The cosmos gleams, and thoughts of home swirl through my mind. It was my father, Bernard, who taught me how to navigate using the night sky. It was an imperative skill for him on the merchant ships, and it will be useful to me now.

The day my father gifted his pocket watch is one that stays with me. He was returning on a steamship from North America. That day at the dockyards, my mother hoisted me above the crowd, so I could watch his three-masted steamer come in. I sat on the saddle of her shoulders, holding the red reigns of her hair. That was twenty-one years ago, but I can still remember the smell of the sea air and the blaring cries from the foghorns. My ten-year-old self tingled with pride. That ship was a propelled vessel, made from wrought iron, but now they are being built from steel—modern times, indeed. Papa had a gift for each of my two brothers and me. My little brother, Charlie, was gifted the pocket watch; my older brother, George, got a maritime spyglass; and I received a nautical compass. But following Charlie's death four years later, the timepiece came to me, and I vowed to protect it better than I had Charlie.

Of course, there is another reason why I remember that day so well—it was the day that I saw a ghost! I had woken up early that morning, not just because I was excited to be reunited with my father but because I had glimpsed something as I turned in my sleep. Daylight was beginning to pierce the drapes in my bedroom, but in those drapes, I saw two eyes leering at me. They came closer, and slowly the faint figure of a man in a top hat manifested before me. I cowered in my bed. He peered over me, and I called out for *Mama*, but she did not hear. The phantom simply put a finger to his lips and grinned. After I fell silent, he retreated towards my wardrobe. Still with his finger to his grinning teeth, he disappeared inside. I ran out screaming.

Dearie! There's no such thing as ghosts, was all my mother said. Her voice has a beautiful Irish purr, and when she sings the melodic songs from her hometown of Cork, it soothes all my anxieties. I wish I could hear her voice now. I must make it to my grave, so that one day, I may hear her sing again. But there should already be somebody waiting—Charlie! If I make it home, will we reunite?

The thought makes me both nervous and excited. There was a time in my life when I grovelled at Charlie's gravestone every day, so I may finally be able to tell him how sorry I am. And I will not just reunite with Charlie, but my grandparents too. I never met Grandma Diana, but Papa always spoke of how she would have spoilt me and my brothers rotten had she had the chance.

While I think of my family, more perturbing thoughts, of life and religion, cross my mind. Why is it that those witches had memory and shadows? Should I believe their prophecy? They were happy; they seem to thrive here. Why does this place reward the wicked? Was I sent here to be punished for my sins? Do cowards not enter heaven? Perhaps every person comes here when they die, but the idea of limbo is only merely hinted at in biblical text. Is my faith just a wishful deception, or is this journey truly the last trial before exultation? Am I stupidly naïve, or will my doubt ensure that the pearly gates are locked when I arrive?

Hours pass, and the moon now rests at its highest point. The dim bleached scene remains still, the only exception being the swaying branches of sporadic trees. When the moor collides with pastures, I entertain myself by walking through the sleeping cattle and sheep. I do it for the same reason I attempted to walk through Jane, to see if they feel my presence. None of the animals wake, but does my ethereal being disturb their dreams?

Ahead, the calm scene is disturbed by the distinctive shape of a man in a top hat walking towards me. The middle-aged man is dressed in a suave suit complete with a cravat. Like me, he also appears to be wading through the grass. His pace does not slow, and as he passes by, he touches the brim of his hat and offers the jolly greeting, 'Good evening, sir!'

I reply, 'Evenin',' and we both carry on. It is amusing how nonchalant and mundane it is to meet such an elegantly robed gentleman roaming the fields in the dead of night. A thought occurs to me, causing me to stop and shout after him, 'Sir—wait!'

'Yes!' he responds definitely, 'How may I help?' I believe I can, in fact, help him.

'Do you know where you are travelling to?' I ask.

He replies in a deep and emphatic voice, indicating upper-class status. 'Not exactly, sir, you know what it's like. This cycle I have been arcing my way south. Blindly, I follow the magnificence of our stellar goddess. Most beautiful she has been this cycle, one of the best I'd imagine. In truth, I am infatuated by her, her presence has cast aside the loneliness and dark apparitions on my solitary stroll. I do believe that my destination is south, and the east-to-west arc that the moon traces across the southern sky allows me to scour a wider area as I search for signposts, in the vain hope that I may recognise a name.'

'Do you remember any names?'

My question brings another long doddery ramble from the chatty gent. 'Oh, I say, now let me think—names you see, much like everything else, they run off sometimes, and each time they run farther and farther away. Oh now, crumbs, what was it, argh... A *T* was it? I think the name begins with a *T*, hmm... No maybe it was a *P*. There was a map. Lots of names, one of the ones at the bottom, I don't remember which.' He gets lost going through the alphabet. He may appear middle-aged, but his confused monologue to himself is much more akin to an older chap, presumably due to the curse of fading memory. Then he gives up and says, 'Sorry, you must excuse me. Why do you ask? Where have you just come from?'

'I was just in Mosskene, and before that, I was in Copsefield, d—'

'Ah, yes!' he interrupts with great enthusiasm. 'Of course, that was it—Copsefield!'

'That's where you need to go? That's your home?'

'Oh, no. That was the name on the map! No, no, there was another name, one that really stood out. Now, what was it? Hmm, it's coming to me—Erm—Ke—Kettle. No—Kemple! Yes, that sounds right, yes, Kemple. Do you know it?'

'Do you mean Kemble? Kemble-on-Sands?' I press, not wanting to disappoint the man who was so proud to have remembered the wrong name.

'Oh I say, old chum, I think you might have it. Do you know if I am close?'

'You need to travel west about thirty-five miles.'

'By Jove! Do you really think so? How do you know?'

'I have not been long in this nightmare realm,' I answer.

'Oh, that's a rotten bit of luck. How did you snuff it, if you don't mind my asking?'

'I fell asleep outside and froze to death.'

'Oh crumbs, what a pity, most devastating, it really is. Well, we cannot dawdle all night, you have done me the utmost courtesy, young man. I thank you, and I apologise that I will likely forget the name of the man who led me to salvation—' He pauses awkwardly, so I offer my name. 'Ah, excellent. You have my eternal gratitude, Mr. Webster. You may have just saved the soul of Mr. Reginald Carrington.' We shake hands; it is a weirdly normal gesture, but due to the reduced sense of touch, it is more of a bump. 'Well, off we must. May her gracious beauty grant you fine passage.' Mr. Carrington caresses the brim of his hat once more and strides off in a direction that is more southbound than westbound.

As I walk away, I smirk. The idea that he is blindly tracing a crescent each night, by walking east then south then west in order to keep the moon—that he's hopelessly obsessed with—directly ahead, somewhat amuses me. I'm not sure if I pity him or envy his ability for such optimism in a bleak and endless ramble. Had I not steered his course, I expect he would have continued his southerly arc until Land's End ceased his infatuation with his Goddess. I do worry about his ability to navigate, though, as he did not set off in the correct direction. It's almost as though he wants to keep gazing at the moon despite my directions.

A darker thought comes to mind. If Mr. Carrington does not divert further west soon, he will become lost. He'll end up south of Faunton and on the wrong side of the estuary. Mr. Carrington is out of sight now, so I cannot help him further. He may be doomed, but gazing at the moon, he will be very happily doomed. It is a prophecy all my own.

I have my own troubles presently because the window to the heavens has cracked. Clouds obscure the stars that I use for my compass, and they are drifting towards the moon. It makes me wonder how it is that clouds can blot out starlight, but trees do not. Then I spy a tall tree up ahead, at the corner of this field. It appears solid at first, but it is only as I approach that its ghostly shimmer becomes noticeable. It seems not unlike how a patch of fog becomes easier to see through the closer you get.

As the clouds streak across the moon, it acts as a prism, gifting the lunar deity a hazy rainbow halo that appears as a porthole in the sky. I remember that my father was often mystified by these rare moonbows during the long nights on the merchant ships, and he once woke up me and my brothers when he saw one above our house one evening. Then, I was excited at the strange phenomenon, but now the spectral ring hangs like an ominous portal, ushering in darkness. With the cloud growing thicker and the light fading fast, I approach a coniferous forest. It is very wide but a hill rises about half a mile on the far side, so it won't take long to traverse.

Soon the portal is firmly shut, sealing away all light. Only the faint outline of the evergreen trees contrasts with the cloudy sky. There is no way around the forest, so I press ahead. Inside, the forest becomes dense, and a thick canopy obscures even the slightest contrast. I walk with no visual cues and no solid boundary to follow.

I traipse on and on and on. The forest continues. Is it really so vast, or am I walking in circles with no way to stop it? A drystone wall would be a blessed saviour; it would give me a straight path to follow. Sadly, none emerge. I traipse for aeons, lost in space.

An earthly bunker still eludes me as daybreak threatens. The dawn light helps me to find my way out of the forest. I enter an open hollow and climb a nearby crest. At the summit, a distant source of light interrupts the twilight scene. In hopeful relief, I divert towards my potential shelter. To reach it, I must cross a valley and pass through a wood. As I descend, the light of the solitary sanctuary hides behind the hillside, but I can now use the small thicket of trees as a landmark to fix my bearing.

I traverse to the other side of the valley buoyantly and enter the thicket. Through the trees and the morning mist, the warm beacon gleams. A small cluster of majestic deer, some with huge antlers, stroll through the deep-brown vegetation. I'd love to monitor their undisturbed nature, but I must continue. I emerge into the open and witness the welcoming beams emanating from a single-story farmhouse upon the hill.

Approaching the secluded bungalow, I hear the cries of a cockerel alerting me to the brightening eastern horizon. With Isaac's warning still ringing in my ears, I am desperately relieved to find this farmhouse. I turn to face the front door within a narrow porch. The window to the right is the beacon I saw in the distance. Shadows dance in its warm hue; the inhabitants are awake.

I step through the door into the grubby porch, which is home to heavy coats and muddy Wellington boots. I press on through into a rustic living room that bathes in the glow of a roaring fire and numerous stubby candles that have been unable to contain their white mass, losing themselves down their silvery pedestals. On the floor beside the open fire, an outstretched grey cat rests snuggly; curiously, it appears as solid as stone. Numerous scenic landscape paintings, and one which includes the farmhouse, hang listlessly on the walls and resemble the craft of a skilled amateur. A beige armchair and sofa are arranged to face the fire, and a wooden door stands behind the seats, opposite the fireplace. To my right is an archway leading to a kitchen. A woman is cooking at the stove as an unkempt man sits bent over a dining table reading a newspaper. He lifts the pages, so they receive the glow of the wax-borne flames. Unlike the cat, the couple exhibit the ghostly guise though it is only subtle. I watch them a moment, and as the woman's glances sweep past me, she does not panic at my presence. Despite my morbid reasoning, it is unnerving to be unnoticed.

I stumble upon an invisible barrier as I walk towards the door behind the sofa; the heat of the fire forces me back. I take a wide berth around the fireplace to reach the door. Beyond it is a narrow corridor. I search numerous rooms on either side for a dark place to hide. If it's not dark enough the sun will scorch me and purge my memory. I finally find somewhere that might be suitable, a child's bedroom.

The curtains are closed, but the brightening sky illuminates them. A little dark-haired girl stirs in a small bed in the corner. It is hard to see her face with a pink blanket pulled up close, but she lies awake. This room is suitable because it faces away from the sun and has a wardrobe in which to hide. As I walk over between the girl and the window, the girl lets out a piercing shriek.

The girl, who is perhaps seven years old, sits bolt upright in her bed. She stares at me as she clutches a rag doll. I stop and look around. What startled her? Surely she can't see me, but her eyes are frightfully fixed upon mine. I step towards her urging her to calm down. She screams again. Afraid of alarming her parents, I put my finger to my lips to encourage her to keep quiet. Still holding the rag doll, she jumps out of bed, runs towards the door and darts out the room. She cries for her papa; she has seen me.

Mama, there's a man in my bedroom! I cried when I saw that ghost as a child.

That was when my mother told me that *there's no such thing as ghosts.* I always believed Mama, but I felt so sure that I had seen him that I refused to return to my bedroom until she had checked it was safe. That man was not threatening me, he was searching for a dark place to hide. It all makes sense now—now that I am the ghost.

I hide in the little girl's wardrobe, praying that her father shows less interest than my mother did. She is pleading with her father as vehemently as I did. Will he investigate? It is not long before I have my answer...

Heavy footsteps approach.

The father swings open the wardrobe. I rush to a dark corner where the girl keeps her dolls. The man is holding a wax-covered candlestick, the flame atop irradiates his gaunt face. He scans the wardrobe and the room then pulls open the curtains. The father turns back to face the room and says softly to his daughter, 'There be nothing 'ere, Beth.'

Beth has not ventured very far into the room but says firmly, 'Papa, there *was* a ghost. He came at me!'

'Where is 'e?'

'Could he be under the bed?'

'Ghosts ain't real, darling. And if they did, there ain't no reason for them to be in your room.'

Beth shrugs despondently as the pale all-grey cat enters between her feet. 'Oh, how are you, Gracie,' she says. The little girl squats down to pet the cat, but before she can, the cat rushes away from her and directly towards me. Grace halts a few feet from me and hisses at me angrily. The cat is leering at me with striking lime-green eyes and threatens with long fangs. 'Gracie? Papa, I think Gracie has found it.'

Grace unleashes a shrill, distressed wail, and the warning calls the father over. As he approaches, I swiftly shuffle along the wall and hide under the bed. Grace tracks my movement. She pokes her head under the bed, alerting them to my new position.

'Gracie has never behaved like this, Papa.'

'Go 'elp your mother with breakfast,' her father commands. The girl's feet do not move until her father irritably shouts, 'NOW!' As soon as she's gone, the bed under which I am hiding tips up against the wall with a loud crash.

The anxious father kneels and pets Grace, but her fierce hiss continues. He squints at me and leans forwards; we are almost nose to nose. He thrusts the candle inside my spirit. I scream. It scorches like hot coals. The flame flickers. The man reacts with a throaty cry and takes a step back, retracting the candlestick. His petrified face mirrors my own. I cannot stay here.

The father attacks, jabbing me multiple times with the candle, while shouting, 'Away! Away!' Each blazing stab causes me to be overwhelmed and paralysed.

During a brief respite, I regain motion and, as fast as I can, I pace out of the room and down the corridor. Grace races after me. I rush through the door at the end and into the scalding region surrounding the fireplace. The heat of the log fire hurls me back into the corridor. I pick myself up. Where can I go?

Grace screeches at me. Beth screams because of Grace's distress. Beth's mother shrieks as she runs to her protection. The father shouts as he stomps down the corridor, protecting the flame with his hand. I need to get outside.

I charge through the living room to the porch. I then step through the doors and out into the morning light.

Sunrise is imminent. I dash to a cattle shed. It is too exposed. I continue through and out the other side. Roosters in an open pen frantically bellow the warning of my impending disaster. Close to the cattle shed is a massive mound of manure. Swallowing my earthly reservations, I dive into the dark faecal sanctuary.

CHAPTER SEVEN

THE PIT OF PERDITION

Mercifully, the abhorrent foetor from this mound of manure distresses only my imagination because I do not possess a sense of smell. I worry that at any moment a shovel will expose my hideout to the sun. The only way to tell the passage of time is to reach outside the mound of manure; when my spirit doesn't inflame, it will be night. So keen am I for the accursed sun to abate that I repeatedly engulf myself in a searing inferno.

While the day passes by, I ponder the events of last night, but my mind fixates upon the episodes when I was engulfed in flame. I struggle to focus on anything else; it is like those moments are shouting for my attention.

One question bothers me: how is it that they saw me when the woman in the church cellar did not? Beth's father only caught a glimpse of me when he put the candle through me, and Beth saw me as I passed in front of the gloomy window. Does a spirit distort the passage of light? It would explain the moment in the church because the crypt was dark with no light behind me, but if that is true, how did Grace track me moving between the dark corners? What extra perception do cats possess?

Grace had a shadow and no corporeal shimmer, much like the witches, yet the family were petting her. Do witches and cats exist both in the corporeal and ethereal realms? Is that why cats are thought to serve as their familiars?

I reach out and feel no sensation—finally the sun has fallen. Gratefully, I exit into the clutches of the night. The quiet farm is lit solely by the fiery radiance emitting from the farmhouse windows. The moon's circumference cannot be distinguished, but lambent clouds reveal its location. With each step shrouded by night, I am conscious that tonight is a bad night to advance. Nonetheless, I have to get away from here. I leave the farm and continue north-west.

The terrain becomes rocky as I spend several hours struggling almost blind with no sign of civilisation. All around is the soothing patter of rain. Despite this, the moon breaks through thinner clouds in the south to make an appearance. Its reflections dance hypnotically as rain splashes onto wet rocks. I marvel at the beauty of the gleaming mountainside and at how I cannot feel the droplets as they pass through my outstretched hand.

I traverse the steep sides of this craggy hill, which I believe is Deacon Fell. It is one of the most well-known peaks in Deaconshire as it heralds the start of the mountainous and picturesque terrain for which the county is known. From the top on a clear day, you can see a spectacular expanse of hills, valleys and lakes. I remember a family day out when we climbed to the top then sat to eat while looking out over our home county. Despite the squabbles I had with George and Charlie, we were a loving family.

I have enjoyed visiting as an adult too, finding a quiet place under the summer sun to read poetry by Wordsley and then looking up to try and spy his old house hidden in the panorama. I've loved writing poetry and reading stories since my youth. Back then, Charlie always wanted me to play and all I wanted to do was immerse myself in words. I wished that Charlie would leave me be. He would say, *why do you like books so much?* and I would tell him that he should try it. He thought it was boring, but one day, Mama read the adventures of Robinson Crusoe to us both. Suddenly he was interested in reading, and I was excited to play. We pretended to be Robinson Crusoe and Friday; of course, I was always Robinson Crusoe and I would never relent to Charlie's request to be him *just once*. We played other games too and Charlie helped me to become more gregarious. Then, because of me, my wish came true.

My older brother, on the other hand, had a penchant for a different type of story; George relished teasing me with the grisly details from his ever-growing collection of penny dreadfuls. He still loves a gruesome tale; a few months ago when the newspapers and penny dreadfuls revelled in the horrific murder of Julia Thomas by her maid, Kate Webster, he scared a few street urchins that were pestering him by claiming Kate was Catriona, our mother, and if they didn't let him pass, he might boil their flesh and toss their dismembered bodies into the river Lye. Childhood with George was a trial.

There are lights from distant villages in the valley now, but I must not rush. Despite my visits to Deacon Fell, this is not a route that I am familiar with. In fact, this route is particularly treacherous; big gaps gape in the rocky path, so I must tread carefully. The vegetation rustles, but I cannot determine if it is just from the rain.

A shrill call startles me. I jolt in panic, and then I stumble. Falling towards one of these yawning chasms, I jump in a last-ditch attempt to avoid falling in.

I land on a rock below and stop myself in front of a much bigger crevasse. A flap of wings rushes towards me. A pheasant flies overhead and lands nearby. Whatever spooked it so nearly caused me disaster.

'Help! Help!' a man cries out. The sound rises from below. 'My name is Lord Mason, and I need help.'

'Where are you?' I shout.

'Please, help me. I am down here. I'm stuck in this pit.'

'Down here?' I ask, peering over the edge of the crevasse.

'Yes, I see you. I need your help to get out of this hole. My life was taken from me but a few nights ago, and upon my walk to my grave, I fell down here. I cannot get out. I was set ablaze by the sun; I cannot endure that again. Please, sir, I need your help.'

'What can I do to help?'

'If you were to reach down, I might be able to grab your hand.'

'I shall try, but I cannot see you.'

'Thank you, sir, thank you so much.'

I assess the ground, trying to find a rock to wedge myself against so I do not fall in. 'You said your life was taken from you?' I ask.

'Some scoundrel strangled me!'

'Strangled you—who would do such a thing?'

'Some rotten half-breed from America—that's who. I remember he had a great big moustache and the devil's grin.'

'Why would he strangle you?'

'Money, I suppose. It was only two nights ago, and I can barely recall a bloody thing. The ricochet of a shotgun blast still wails in my ears. I believe my cabman staged a robbery, and when I accused him, the penny-pinching pig throttled me.'

'Two nights ago, you say?'

'That's right.'

'Late at night, on the road from Thanham?'

'Yes.'

'That was the night I died,' I say. 'I was walking along that road, and I encountered an American cabman. He refused to stop for me; he could've saved my life.'

'He was more for taking life than saving it.'

'He tried to run me down.'

'That'll be him. Did you see a passenger perchance?'

'Yes, I saw someone lolloping about like a rag doll,' I say.

'Then you saw my corpse.'

'My goodness!' No wonder he didn't stop for me if he'd murdered his passenger. 'Who was the driver?'

'I don't recall his name. The sun—that's all I bloody remember! Now would you help me out of here?'

'Certainly.' I lie on the floor beside the crevasse, wedge myself amongst the rocks and reach down. 'Can you grab my hand?'

He groans and strains, then he whimpers, 'You're too far away.'

'Can you jump?' I ask.

Lord Mason panics, 'You're out of reach! O God, please. There really is no way out, is there? I shall never rest; this is perdition—perdition! Please God, get me out of here. I don't deserve this fate.'

'Keep trying!'

He huffs and puffs, and his exasperation grows.

'Reach further. Lean over the ledge.' He grows more agitated until he shouts, 'Lean over, boy!'

'Lord Mason, I will not fall in myself. Let me try another position.'

'Don't leave me down here like a rat, boy. Don't condemn me worse than that—that degenerate Yank—that rabid dog!'

'Lord Mason, I am trying to help you.'

'Humbug! Children try. Men do—men act.' Lord Mason's disrespectful tone angers me, but I appreciate he is desperate.

I reach down. 'Try again,' I say.

'Further,' he shouts.

'Jump,' I bite back.

'Boy, are you a squire or a sodomite? Reach further in.'

'Jump higher!' I shout, holding my tongue.

'Nearly,' he shouts. 'Nearly.' He roars with each jump. 'Yes. Yes,' he cries. 'Pull me out.'

I pull. I cannot feel my own hand, let alone his, but I pull my arm up without noticeable effort. Lord Mason clambers up. He is free.

'Thank you, sir.'

'Am I sir or boy, Lord Mason?' I chastise.

'Sir. Thank you, sir. Please forgive my intemperate language. I was so worried that I was set to be in that pit for eternity.'

'Do you know where you are going?'

'Where I am going? Where I am going? O Lord. Where am I going?'

'Was that your manor in Thanham?'

'Yes! Thanham. Oh, bless you, boy—sir,' he corrects himself. 'Bless you, sir. Thank you. And which way is that?'

I point.

'Oh, may God be with you, young man.' And with that, Lord Mason walks away. His rude nature peeves me, but I am pleased to have freed him from the pit.

The rain grows heavy, and the weeping clouds threaten to shroud the moon momentarily. If I do not hurry, I may soon end up in a deeper pit.

I continue, but I do not go far. The ground is precarious. I drop down a series of ledges. The drops are far, but the moon's light reveals that it is safe. Presently, I stare into a black void. It is a shadow cast by a nearby rock formation. It is no longer safe to descend, but there is no way back. I have no idea as to whether the blackness hides a solid surface or a ravine.

I cannot wait for the light of dawn to reveal a safe path because I am so far from civilisation that I will not find a sanctuary in time. An old tree protrudes from the shadow below, but only its warped branches are visible. It is too far in front to jump to, but it tells that there is firm ground somewhere down there. The only option I have available is to jump. The fall won't hurt, but nevertheless, it will be a leap of faith

I stare down. The hideous emptiness below beckons like a gaping mouth. I continue in dilemma as the rain continues to thunder down, and the cloud begins to consume the waning moon. I listen to the sound of the rainfall to try and gauge whether there is solid ground below, but the noise is too universal to make any distinction. The closer to the tree that I land, the better my chances to avoid falling into a pit of perdition. I must make a leap; there is no time for delay.

After a quick prayer, I find the courage. I move to jump, but my foot slips off the ledge. Screaming, I tumble into the abyss.

I land suspended in a dark void. I do not know if I am looking up or down. I search desperately. I turn and see the twisted branches of the lifeless tree. It is close. Thank heavens! I have not fallen into a great ravine.

Behind are small cracks through which I see reflections of moonlight. Could this be a cave where I can hide out? Cautiously, I shuffle towards these narrow slits. Deeper darkness passes overhead as I enter the cave. I cannot stand, but it is deep, and the ground is solid.

Yes! This will be a good place to stay. I can wait here for a clearer moonlit night to safely navigate the perilous pitfalls.

Drowsiness creeps upon me but sleep does not come. One of the branches of the malformed tree hangs in a gloomy scene outside the cave, contorted to unfathomable and distressing angles. A tired mind will hallucinate if starved of sleep, and I cannot shake the idea that the branch is in fact the dangling claw of a preying beast. It sways as the creature breathes, and its bony, daemonic fingers linger possessed, ready to grab anything that attempts to escape. Even the cave's jagged entrance appears to snarl.

As daybreak rises, its appearance remains near-solid as it glistens in the sunlight. I try to shake the silly notion and plan my route in the hope that tonight will be clear, but again, my weary mind fixates on the thought that there is a beast lurking outside.

'Stop it!' I tell myself. What's the name of the village just north of here? Oh, what is it? How can I have forgotten? I've been there. I went there on the way to—. O God! What's the name? I don't remember any of the names. Lyemouth—that's where I'm going—I cannot forget that. Mosskene... I remember Maria from Mosskene. And Lord Mason was from Thanham. Where was I trying to get to the night I died? Har—, Thor—. I cannot have forgotten those names. How can I? No. I cannot be turning. Not yet. I have too far to go. I frantically search for the names, but the corridors of my mind are just too narrow.

CHAPTER EIGHT

THE BEAST THAT WAITS OUTSIDE

I have become entranced by the fiendish, lingering talon of the nameless beast that waits outside. As my sleepless mind grows wearier, my thoughts drift to manifestly wilder ideas. I may sit awake, but I am increasingly unable to tame these strange notions such that I have nearly lost all clarity and concentration. There remains a part of me that knows what I stare at is nothing more than the spiny winter branch of a mildly peculiar tree. And I also understand that my tired mind naturally dwells upon it because it is the only distinctive feature in an otherwise vacant and enduring scene. In my state of conscious limbo, however, it is not possible to shake the perception that what I see is the extension of a malevolent but patient creature that preys on wandering spirits. Rational thoughts exist but typically do not possess the strength to clear the delirious mist. So, I stare at the claw as pastel colours of day and night slide by behind it.

I do not leave this cave for two reasons. Firstly, thick clouds block all moonlight, making it impossible to determine if I am about to fall into a pit of perdition. Secondly, I fear the creature will strike. Thus, it would be wise to wait for a moonlit night.

When the sun rises, it pulls open the curtains of this abode. While the dark and dingy atmosphere persists, the thin cracks in the rock above expose the boundaries of my new home. Outside the narrow entrance, the path towards the old tree is flat, without pits, but what is beyond remains a mystery. I rise to my feet, albeit crouching, and walk as far towards the exit as I can before the burning sunlight becomes too much to bear, but I see little further. All I can do is return to the dark depths of the cave and dwell in a deep depression as the names and faces of my beloved family slip from my memory.

Night-time brings the hope of escape, but I wait longer still for the moon to rise. And when it finally does appear, its light is meek and masked by cloud. The terrible realisation is just how much the moon has waned, and with each coming night, its luminosity will fade further. All hope of travelling this lunar cycle will soon be gone, and it will be weeks until the next bright full moon night. Either I chance my escape from this cave now—running blindly amongst perilous pits while I evade the beast—or I wait. But such a delay would likely lead to a disastrous loss of memory. The thought of being scorched by the sun's inferno while trapped in a pit, even for one day, is too much to bear. Therefore, I resolve to wait for a clear night with full moonlight to safely traverse this mountain.

In my attempts to combat encroaching memory loss, I loudly and repeatedly utter 'Lyemouth' and 'north-west' to keep my destination and route at the forefront of what memory I still retain. This is easier during my more sober moments, but as I stare out at the pastel grey clouds of another new day, I sense the emergence of my drunk and maniacal self.

The scratching of a scurrying rat draws my attention away from the inclement vista. From a rock, the rat emerges, and as it rushes by, I instinctively pull my outstretched legs close to my chest. It hurriedly traces the most inane path, continuously looping round in bizarre patterns, never reaching me or leaving this vault. Growing tired of its unintelligible scuttling, I shout at it to *shoo*. At once, it darts away, runs up the wall, along the ceiling and out through the impossibly narrow crack in the rock overhead. I can be sure that the rat is not real, but it keeps coming back.

Like anyone fighting off the insistent advance of uninvited sleep, physical motion offers the best cure. Though I do invite sleep, only paranoia and delirium are forthcoming. Unless my feverish imaginations are particularly disturbing, I do not apply the antidote. Instead, I encourage my mercurial neural wanderings as a way to entertain my piteous slumber. I regret this choice now, though, because I can no longer stem the hallucinations. And while I continue to utter aloud my destination and route, as the delirious visions grow more lucid and terrifying, my vocal repetition descends into a shrill and frenzied mantra.

———◆———

Days and nights pass, though I do not know how many. I keep fighting for sanity, pushing away the delirious hallucinations of my fatigued psyche, but they come relentlessly. Not only does the beast wait for me to leave my hollow, now I hear its windy breath. Every night since I can remember, I approach the cave entrance in the hope of seeing a full moon, and every night I run back inside, fearing the beast will strike me. When will a full moon come?

———◆———

Briefly, a full moon emerges through the clouds. I stand at the entrance of the cave and bask in its glory. Its warmth burns away the delirious mist, and I see that the beast's claw is just a branch of a malformed tree—somehow, I believe I already knew that. Oh, how wonderful the moon is! But just as soon I step outside, the clouds cover the moon once more. They grow thicker and thicker, then I hear the beast growl, and I scamper back into my burrow. When will the full moon come back again?

———◆———

A pitch black night falls—no stars, no moon—but shadows stand against the darkness. It makes little sense because there is no discernible contrast, yet I acknowledge nebulous eddies of black mist that judder and churn absurdly. The awkward motion is befitting of shadow puppetry, but this display of phantasmagoria is not constrained to the contours of the walls or the floor. In this theatre, the performers leave the stage to tease and taunt. Like any thespian, the puppets feed off the ghoulish gasps and shrieks of a captive audience. They dangle and dance unconventionally beneath the swaying claw outside, and I know it is the beast that controls them. This master of puppets has found the end of my yarn and is effortlessly unravelling terror. The shifting form of the actors often starts plain but, with only a slight change, they are able to create the most nightmarish concepts. Their unrecognisable shapes seem to perfectly fit gaps in my mind so that they create new connections. Once fixed, the actors take harrowing forms which causes these threads to vibrate ever increasingly until the thread snaps, and the puppet puffs into non-existence. Each time one of these threads snap, it rips out the healthy parts of my consciousness to which it was attached.

The puppetry finally dispels due to overexposed flashes from an incredible lightning storm that rages outside. The rain brings a loud scurrying, and the flashes confirm that the number of rats in this cave has increased. I have come to gauge their quantity to indicate the depth of my mania. Tonight, there are many.

The lightning may provide some brightness to guide my exit, but fear of being stuck in the darkness, should the waves of light break, restrains me. Gazing in the direction of the black entrance, the sky frequently illuminates with dramatic pulses of purple, and the streaking bolts echo the gnarly form of the beast's claw. The creature has grown impatient. Its stomps crash overhead in tandem with the display. I transfix my eyes on the entrance and listen intently to the roaring rain. Another bolt irradiates the backdrop, and I glimpse the outline of something that was not there before. The next flash shows nothing, but the following one exposes the unmistakable shape of a person's head and up-per torso. The time between lightning bursts reduces, and the stationary body shifts closer with each staggered image. A faint hope of regaining sanity occurs as the shape dis-appears, but it returns, once again, beneath the creature's grasp. The figure's long hair and shapely form suggest this is a woman. Her face is hidden, but she wears a flowing dress, and the next eruption from the tempestuous storm implies that, much like the blazing bolts, it too has a purple gleam. Surely, she is not real. I cannot think of any explanation why this woman, alive or dead, would be outside this cave on such a night. I wonder, are these visions mustered by my subconscious or mirages conjured by the frustrated beast?

In a slow and well-spoken voice, she says, 'Oh, bless you child, please do not cry.' Her sweet, harmonic voice draws the memory of a bewitching lady; it is Maria Chester. Why is she here? Who is she talking to? She continues, 'Hush now darling, we are nearly inside, please stop crying. Your father may not return, but I shall grant all that you covet.' Another lightning flash reveals that she has found the en-trance. Her arms form a cradle, and her feet remain mo-tionless. But her arms are empty. She is cradling nothing, and there is no crying.

'How are you?' I ask. 'Please take shelter.' I didn't want to give away my presence, but she would've stumbled upon me regardless.

'Please stop crying; this kindly gentleman will protect us,' Maria says. Then, with another electrifying discharge and more thunderous stomping above, I observe that she has advanced inside. The stationary figure looms imposingly a few yards ahead.

'Won't you take a seat and dry off?' I say.

'Oh, he is humorous,' Maria giggles, 'polite and smart too.' I realise that I made an accidental joke—spirits don't get wet. 'Hush now, child. I will sit close so he may guard us.' The darkness shifts as Maria approaches. She chuckles, and I feel a warm sensation against the left side of my numb being. I slide over to be proper and allow her space, but she laughs, and the feeling re-emerges.

All the disquieting aspects of this encounter—the non-existent child, the way she doesn't directly address me, how she can see my smart clothes in such darkness, not to mention why she is even here in this cave—all disappear with the warmth of her touch. In her softly spoken manner, Maria says, 'No longer do I want to be alone, child. Do you think he will accept a kiss?'

A flutter of surprise and excitement tantalises me. Though I sit on solid ground, I quiver, worrying that I may fall. There is a slight change in contrast, and I decipher her silhouette. I lean towards her, but as I do so, bright purple flashes penetrate through the cracks in the rocks, illuminating the beauty whom I'm about to kiss. A grinning white skull beams back.

The jaw opens. A diseased rat scurries out, scampers up to Maria's fringe and hides in her flowing black hair. Her vacant eyes gape, and then her jaw grins wickedly. Loud cries of an infant erupt from her cradled arms—the cries are oddly familiar. I recoil with a start, shriek, and then hurry out of the cave.

I reach the claw, but the beast lets me pass. I follow the natural course from the old dishevelled tree to the rock structure beside it. Fearing that I'm being pursued, I look back without altering stride as the sky is torn asunder by lightning. Maria is not there. In the flickering light, the hideous shapes in the rock form two sunken voids, like vacant eyes, along with that same victorious grin. My horrified gaze averts as I plunge off a cliff edge.

The drop would have killed me was I not already dead. Instead, I climb to my feet and find myself at the base of a sheer rock face. I have foolishly succumbed to the vindictive visage cast by the stone-chiselled daemon, its hex ousting me from its domain. The storm quells its wrath, and I loiter, lost in darkness. My only opportunity to seek shelter will be at dawn. I sense the cruel beast peering down in expectant amusement. It waits to watch the desperate scurrying of an inferior creature that seeks a squalid hollow to which to escape. I am vermin to toy with and torment. The beast will not devour its prey until its primal sadism has been satiated.

With the brightening dawn sky, I distinguish that the sloping ground ahead soon levels out with the typical brush that scatters the moors. This terrain with slight peaks and troughs is a safe path to walk without the risk of falling into some hidden pit. However, with such limited time, I hastily scour the edges of this craggy hillside for a safe hole in which to crawl. Rushing back and forth, I try numerous crevices but abandon each one. I pause momentarily to survey my options. Panicking, I repeat the loop, retrying locations, only to dismiss them once more. Then, gazing up from the ground, I spy a tall crack a few feet above that is wide enough to squeeze into. I dart for the wall, clamber up and burrow into the gap. It extends around a tight corner and provides stable footing. I let out a sigh of relief as this tall, narrow chamber prevents daylight or the predator from invading.

Slumped in the crevice, I stay in protracted silence so as not to alert the beast to my concealed location. My thoughts focus on survival. I cannot shake the idea that I am forgetting something, but that feeling has grown so familiar that I ignore it.

My strategy prospers, and eventually, my glances outside hint at a glistening night sky. But, as I plot my final escape from this haunting hillside, I am horror-stricken by my incompetence to answer a simple question: *where am I going?*

CHAPTER NINE

REUNITED

Tuesday 27th January 1880

A wintery scene welcomes me. Smooth snow softens the sharp rocks. The brilliant white blanket covers the entire landscape, mimicking the waves of an ocean frozen in time. The sky is dark, but the ground up ahead is as bright as day. The moon, hidden from view behind the hillside, shines brightly. The velvety vista subdues my apprehension about the preying beast and clarity rescinds confusion. The true horror of my interment on this mountain of madness returns to mind and extinguishes the fire of hope that this night brings. It is the sobering understanding that my memory lies in tatters, and I do not know which way to go. It does not matter whether the beast is real, though I suspect it is not. All I can do is walk away from this hillside.

I drop from my rocky hollow, and with a sense of urgency, I stride away from the rock face to where the path flattens. A pleasing warmth reaches me as I turn around to see the moon rising behind the imposing fell. The hill has its rocky scars but appears peaceful in its new guise. The cliff face and the surrounding terrain usher me in a westbound direction, and I decide to hold this course until I gain information that will orient me home. I resolve to seek guidance from Lunatics. Recognising that the gibbous moon has not quite reached its peak this lunar cycle, there is hope that rapturous spirits will rise from their graves in a night or two. While it is logical to end my isolation, I cannot suppress the worry within me because I cannot expect a Lunatic to offer useful assistance. After all, what can I ask of them?

I continue to wander silently without the distinctive crunch of snow which rises above my ankles and leaves no footprint. The open moors dwindle to farmland, and there is frequent need to surmount or divert around drystone walls. As I walk through the heavenly carpet, I am captivated by the prancing glistening from the beads of ice which twinkle in every colour but hide as I focus my gaze. I find a new appreciation for walking through pristine snow and not disturbing it. I have no right to feel so peaceful, but as I stroll through the diamond dunes, each foot swallowed with an opalescent glimmer, I feel at ease. This new calm also brings an expectation that the nightmares will not resurface tonight.

One thing does disturb my tranquillity, however. A pocket watch hangs on a chain on my waistcoat. The object sparks an unpleasant sensation within me. It is one of guilt, as though the timepiece is a symbol of some wrongdoing, which I feel equally guilty to have forgotten. I avert my gaze and focus instead on the placid scene.

Chimes from a distant church bell interrupt the still night. I divert towards the source of the sound. The moon hangs a little past its highest point, and its power creates the brightest night. I approach a wooden gate with an inch of snow atop. Beyond are pine trees wearing a heavy white coat, framing an ash-grey bell tower with nine pinnacles. Eight of the spiky protrusions line the square edge of the tower with a larger ninth crocketed pinnacle in the centre. Beneath this hoary diadem are tall, arched windows with stone struts on each side. Snow manages to cling onto each impossibly steep strut as their bulk strengthens towards the ground. Passing through the boundary of pines at the perimeter of this rural shrine, I observe a serene graveyard scene.

Soft sobbing emanates from the snow-crowned tombs and tombstones. A hunched figure, whose face is hidden, kneels by one of the headstones. Her blonde hair and white dress mean she is nigh invisible in the winter shroud. I approach slowly and understand that it is not crying, but a quiet, quivering elegy. From her shaky voice, I hear her utter:

> *Return to me to allay this mocking lie,*
> *So you can sleep to my lullaby.*
> *I will wait till you find your way,*
> *Let us reuni–*

The woman starts, sensing my presence. 'William?' she says with optimism. She turns while raising her posture. As her eyes meet mine, all hope drains from her face, and she slumps. 'Oh,' she sighs, 'I hoped you were my son. I'm not sure I would recognise him, but I can be sure you are not him.'

'Sorry, I didn't mean to disturb you,' I say.

I introduce myself, and she says, 'Nice to meet you. I am Mrs. Joan Wells, but please call me Joan. Formality is rather redundant here.'

'Do you not know where your son is?' I enquire, recognising her heart-breaking sadness.

She gestures towards the gravestone and sorrowfully laments, 'He is here, yet his spirit is lost.' I kneel beside her to show reverence and read the inscription on the tablet:

IN LOVING MEMORY OF
WILLIAM
THE DEARLY LOVED SON OF
JACK AND JOAN WELLS
BORN 16th AUGUST 1860 AND DIED 8th OCTOBER
1869
ALSO
JOAN WELLS
A BELOVED WIFE AND MOTHER
DIED 17th MARCH 1877 AGED 53

At the bottom, it simply states:

REUNITED

I stare at the words as a tingling shiver spreads through me. It is a profoundly sombre shock, and while I could never grasp her grief, I can at least appreciate Joan's burden.

For a spirit suffering from a lack of rest, this ghost land becomes a nightmare realm. And Joan's little boy wanders this realm hopelessly lost. I am a grown adult and have already succumbed to hideous nightmarish delusions, and a child's mind is more active and impressionable.

The unspoken understanding that genuinely stuns me is that I know, in all likelihood, his return is long away. My misplaced case at the tranquil scene is starkly exposed. This could be a haunting foreshadowing of my own destiny. I cannot—must not—be lost for decades like William. It would render my family (if I have a family) in endless turmoil. The young, pale-faced woman looks at my stony reaction. I want to console her with kind words, but my jaw is locked. She acts first, saying softly, 'Where are you going, Edward?'

Swelling sorrow threatens to overwhelm me; I must hold it back. My jaw remains firmly shut, and I am concentrating with more and more effort to keep it that way. My mind flits from imagining the lost and scared nine-year-old boy—venturing in futility amongst the daemons of his night terrors—to an apparition of myself as the hero in my own tragic tale. She asks again, and I need to respond. Releasing the pressure locking my jaw, I cry out, 'I don't know! I've lost my mind! I let slip the only name I had to hold onto.'

I bawl, and she puts her arm around me and places my head on her shoulder. The gesture is reassuring, and it displays the strength of her character. After all, it is I who should be comforting her. 'I cannot tell you where you should go; it may come to you, but it may not,' she says earnestly. 'Our memories fade when the moon dips each cycle. It is hard to retain memory from the last one, so you cannot hope to avoid walking in circles. You can, however, control your direction throughout each cycle. The advice I would give my son if I could is to hold firm in the direction you walk each cycle. That way you will cast a farther net, offering a greater chance of finding your home sooner.' I absorb the information, silently acknowledging the logic amongst the underlying bleakness.

After I compose myself, Joan informs me of a hideout in the church's basement. I believe it wise to stay here tonight.

As the night closes, I ask, 'Have you experienced nightmares or strange visions? I fancy that I have witnessed things that are not real.'

'Not that I can remember,' Joan replies.

'Do you not feel drowsy? I think it is drowsiness and tedium that elicits my apparitions.'

'I don't feel drowsy. The warmth of my soul seems to purge my tiredness.'

'I don't understand. The warmth of your soul?'

'Yes, the ground is lovely and warm here. I can feel the heat from my soul below. It is another reason why I like to sit here.'

'I don't feel it,' I say.

'I believe it is only possible to feel the heat from one's own soul. It might also be that I don't experience these nightmares, of which you speak, because I like to compose and recite poetry to my son below. It concentrates my thoughts. You know, I have probably composed over a thousand poems. I have seen gravestones recently dated,

January 1880. I suspect that I have created at least one poem each night since my death three years ago.'

'You must have a talent for it.'

Joan chuckles. 'I don't know about that. I probably create the same few poems over and over. This is a tedious existence, and if I do keep recreating the same terrible poems, I at least find some enjoyment in it.'

'I need to find something on which I can focus my mind.'

'For me, it is a natural way of coping with such galling torment. *Reunited*—I stare at that word every damn night! How else can I react?'

'I cannot imagine how painful it must be to stare at that word,' I say.

'Do not worry about me, Edward. I do not. I fear for what you and my son must endure. I do not know how I could travel so hopelessly lost while experiencing delirious nightmares. Edward, I urge you to find someone to travel with. It is much easier to concentrate on a conversation than on your own thoughts, and someone else can tell you if what you are seeing is real or not.'

'Yes, I'd like to travel with someone. I thi—'

'Oh, joy! She's back,' Joan interrupts, looking towards the entrance. A scowling middle-aged woman approaches. A blue bonnet contains her curly, brown hair, and she wears a blue gown with a bustle petticoat. Gleaming rows of pearls around her neck encourage you to understand her affluence.

'Who is she?' I enquire, curious at Joan's sarcasm.

'She is the Honourable Elizabeth Walthew,' Joan says, mocking an upper-class accent. Then she adds, returning to her normal voice, 'Mrs. Walthew still cares very much about her social standing. And you should ask her about her story; she will tell you regardless.' Mrs. Walthew walks through the entrance and directly to the chapel without any greeting.

'I will go inside too,' I say as there is a tinge of daylight in the sky. 'Thank you for settling me. The advice will be helpful. I truly hope William returns to you soon; I will keep a lookout for a small boy.'

'I'm coming in with you, Edward.'

'You are? Why? You can rest here, can you not?'

'I will not succumb and abandon William. I will endure as he has done for much longer so that I can guide his arrival. If I rest, I fear I will sleep too long, and if I do not resurrect on the night when he is near, we may never be reunited.' The epiphany of her noble self-sacrifice moves me. For nearly three years, this saintly mother has foregone what promises to be euphoria in favour of the most heart-wrenching and tortuous wait for an event of the slenderest likelihood.

'It is pure devotion to enact such self-immolation,' I say.

'It is nothing,' she says as we walk through the icicled entrance archway. 'Shall we go and hear what Mrs. Walthew has to tell us?'

I enter a dusty, featureless basement. As my eyes adjust to the darkness, the woman's pearls hold my gaze.

'I have had the most frustrating evening, one could not imagine,' Mrs. Walthew says before we sit down. 'It is completely pointless. I'm absolutely positive of that. Once again, I am to spend the day in this filthy, repugnant place.' I sit close to Mrs. Walthew while Joan sits much further away. The stone-faced woman does not attempt introduction as she continues, 'Went to three churches and found nothing, not that I could see half of the stones, but there was indeed no sensation—nothing.' The way she over-emphasises her words is simultaneously amusing and grating.

I introduce myself and say, 'I'm sorry, I don't understand. Do you not know where your body is buried?'

Mrs. Walthew gestures to Joan. 'No, did she not tell you about my plight? I cannot think what else you had to talk about.' She lets out a loud sigh and continues, 'I am stuck in this fusty basement until I find my body. This rural village is my ancestral home. There is surely no question that I would be buried here; the Avingtons are pride of place.'

'Avington?'

'That is my maiden name.'

'How long have you been here? What is the name of this village?'

'This is Lordale, and I have been here long enough that one does not remember. I have patiently waited, but my grave has not yet risen. The past few nights, I have visited other local churches but sensed no soul.'

'I feel my soul's warmth much stronger when I sit down,' Joan states. 'It is like sitting on the ashen remnants of a fire as opposed to the little heat one attains standing over it.'

'Well, this one will not be lowered to dragging her buttocks like a parasite-infected hound!' Mrs. Walthew proudly replies.

A laugh bursts out of me at the absurd image, and Joan says, 'Then I expect that you are stuck here, Mrs. Walthew.' I suspect that Joan would like nothing more than to witness such a spectacle.

A silence lingers until Joan says, 'The full moon is tomorrow. I expect you will get to see your ancestors—perhaps for the first time.'

'Good heavens!' Mrs. Walthew reacts. 'I cannot be doing with that. I abhor idle chatter.'

'Even with your parents?'

'Especially with my parents, I was never overly fond of them. I think I will make haste before they arise.'

'May I ask again that if you see a small boy, that you discern whether his name is William Wells, and if so, escort him back here? I plan to have a search parade for William with my small family and any volunteers.'

'You're wasting your effort,' Mrs. Walthew replies. 'Honestly, he's clearly hopelessly lost.'

Joan visibly composes herself before responding. 'He may be, but please can you ask? Repeating the name should hopefully help him remember if he has forgotten. Can you promise me? I will be attentive to any missing person signs that I see for you and ask the others to look as well.' It is evident that Joan does not like Mrs. Walthew, but her desperation to reunite with her son means she chooses her words carefully.

'Yes, of course, I am a mother too, don't you know. I just see the futility.'

'Thank you.'

'Where will you search tonight, Mrs. Walthew?' I ask.

'I shall re-acquaint myself with Birchwood Manor once more. That is where I am most likely to discover information regarding my passing, and I love returning. The glorious grounds still bring memories back. I meticulously reinvigorated the place after my father bequeathed it to me in the most appalling state. Everything there has been calm and orderly; nothing to suggest when I died or why my burial might be delayed. Of course, my funeral will be a momentous ceremony requiring meticulous preparation, but

I have witnessed none of that. Perhaps that is because my husband, Cuthbert, is too frail to organise such an event, but my son, Nicholas, would not allow it to take so long. It is wonderful to watch my husband reading peacefully by the fire, but he could show a little devastation at my passing. Although, the poor man did get quite a fright when he saw me.'

'He saw you?'

'I believe so. My husband enjoys reading in the tomb room. A few nights ago, I leant in close trying to read his newspaper, and he convulsed with a frightful start. He was troubled for some time, and there was nothing I could do to calm him. Thankfully, he settled himself and has not seen me since. The sconces in the room only create a dim glow, and I believe he saw their light distort as it passed through me.'

'Did you say he reads in a tomb room?'

'Yes, my husband and I collected Ancient Egyptian artefacts. My husband is very scholarly and spends a lot of time in the chamber. Our collection is most magnificent, and we are the envy of all those we dare show.'

'And is there a tomb?'

'But of course. One could hardly refer to it as the tomb room if there were no tomb. The Egyptian reis, whom I employed, requisitioned a sarcophagus of an ancient Pharaoh.'

'And you can vouch for its authenticity, can you?' Joan asks.

Mrs. Walthew does not answer. Instead, she scowls at Joan for her insinuation.

'What does his mummy look like?' I ask.

'I do not know. No one has ever opened it.'

'Never?'

'No centrepiece can impress quite like an *unopened* tomb of an Egyptian Pharaoh. It is important to preserve the mystery. The friends we showed pleaded for us to open it; it is very powerful to say no.'

'How did the reis procure such an item?'

'Via the same means to which he acquired the curios: from secret tombs to which he, and he alone, had knowledge. I expressed quite clearly that it was my intention to have an unopened tomb as the centrepiece of my collection. It was of utmost importance.'

'The reis knew it would never be opened?' Joan asks. She raises a hand to cover her mouth but cannot hide her smirk.

'Mrs. Wells, my dear. One should not entertain conspiracies.' Mrs. Walthew's words, however polite, are delivered with a frosty stare. It is met with silence.

'Fascinating,' I say to break the tension. 'I must say too that your memory is much stronger than mine, Mrs. Walthew.'

'There is something about seeing a familiar face or place that regurgitates memory.'

'I hope I sense that soon,' I say. 'Despite the memories it brings back, you still don't know how you died?

'I do not recall how I perished, but I do not believe it was old age. I am troubled by the vestigial memory of a moustachioed gent with a sardonic American accent and an insidious grin. It incites suspicion of a most egregious demise. Why such a scoundrel might want to murder me is beyond good sense and reason.' At this, Joan smirks again.

'An American?' I ask.

'Yes,' Mrs. Walthew replies. 'I do not keep company with degenerate yanks, so for the boy's impression to linger in my memory, it must serve as some testimony to his dastardly nature.'

I find myself irritable all of a sudden, angry even. 'An American accent...' I ponder. 'I don't know why but that strikes a chord with me.'

'Perhaps he murdered you, too.'

'I don't know,' I say. 'I don't get an impression of his face as you do.'

'Nevertheless, Edward, this is good,' Joan cuts in. 'If something is familiar to you, you should explore what it could be. As Mrs. Walthew attests, seeing or hearing something familiar can reawaken closely-attached memories. If you were able to find this man, you might recall a detail that helps you discover where your grave is.'

The thought excites me. 'What else do you remember of this American, Mrs. Walthew? What did he say to you?'

'I don't recall his words, only his nasal butchery of our fair language,' she replies. 'My fear is that this rodent may have buried my body in a forest, like how flea-ridden squirrels bury their acorns. If that is true, then I shall experience this damnable, restive angst until such time as I chance upon my body or Her Majesty's inept constabulary achieves an unlikely breakthrough. You understand now why I sought to read my husband's newspaper.'

'You were searching for clues?' I say.

'Precisely, so I shall return to my manor at nightfall to see if there may be some new article that sheds light on this vexatious yank.'

'May I come with you?' I ask. Mrs. Walthew shifts a little uncomfortably. 'And I would dearly love to see the fine artefacts that you have acquired.'

'I do not allow just anybody to view my collection of curios,' Mrs. Walthew replies. 'I show only the most esteemed in our society who can also be trusted not to disclose knowledge of such things.'

'I am a ghost, Mrs. Walthew. I cannot tell a living soul even if I wished to, but I can help you search for this man as well as your grave.' Mrs. Walthew grumbles, but I continue, 'And I promise not to disturb your dear husband.'

'Oh, very well,' Mrs. Walthew says. 'My collection astounds the wealthiest of men; it will be amusing to witness the reaction of someone from the peasantry.'

The day expires with Mrs. Walthew becoming increasingly restless and carefully inspecting whether the sun has set. She is manifestly keen to avoid her deceased relatives, which I find baffling. When night finally comes, I exit the chapel with a companion and a small measure of hope for discovering the secrets of my life and death.

CHAPTER TEN

THE MISSING PORTRAIT

A fresh layer of snow and a crisp sky, fading from orange to violet, greets us. The moon has not yet arisen, but it promises to be a good night to forge ahead. The clock on the bell tower tells the time is just shy of five o'clock.

Mrs. Walthew strides off with purpose. I shout ahead, 'One moment.' It has no effect. I turn to Joan and say, 'Thank you for your advice and for calming me. I will seek things that are familiar. Perhaps, Mrs. Walthew and I can aid each other in that endeavour. And any young boy I see, I will ask their name.'

'Thank you, Edward. I wish you good fortune on your quest. But you must go at once, and don't dawdle gazing at her ill-gotten goods. Oh—' she smirks, 'just so you know, you can feel the presence of your soul just fine standing up. I decided to have a little fun with our friend.'

A laugh lurches from my throat. 'Excellent! I won't tell.'

'And I can be quite sure that there is no mummy in that tomb. Good luck, Edward.'

'Farewell.' We smile, and I set off to join Mrs. Walthew.

I walk briskly through the silhouette of a small village. I pass an elderly gentleman who, judging by his frail shuffle, will soon succumb to the mortal curse. I muse morbidly on how he will soon be in for quite a revelation. He will at least regain some dignity in his youthful form, and living so close to this resting place, he should not suffer in purgatory. I catch up with Mrs. Walthew behind the man's stone cottage. We cross a small stream and head into the gloomy countryside hidden in the backdrop of the dark hillside.

'Hours and hours in a room by oneself is bad, but with her, it is most unpleasant,' Mrs. Walthew says. 'Have you ever tried to pass the time with someone whom you cannot abide? Mrs. Wells has the nerve to ask *me* to help *her*, yet she will not help me. I wish she would rest during the day.'

'She is waiting for her son.'

Mrs. Walthew laughs, 'She is deluding herself. Her boy has been lost for a decade; he is not coming back. She must think she is a saint for enduring, yet if she were truly virtuous, she would help me find my grave.'

Mrs. Walthew's rant continues. Attempting to defuse the tension, I ask, 'How long have you been interested in Ancient Egypt?'

'I am not,' she responds bluntly. It baffles me. 'I am interested in what it has done for my family. We are bitterly envied, and as such, it has elevated our social standing to new heights and allowed Nicholas to marry well.' I am aghast. How can she have such a collection and have no interest in it? 'It is my husband who has the fascination. He was not born into nobility and does not truly appreciate the importance of our stature. His interest was merely the seed which became a business venture with an unscrupulous local to unearth lost treasures and transport them to England. It was ever so cunning, and the secrecy added a pleasant spice.'

'So, you did all this to flaunt it and make rich friends?'

'Absolutely. One does not allow former greatness to wither. I would spit on my father's grave for all that he did to my family and me. He led us to ruin and depravity; it has been my life's ambition to undo his misdeeds.'

'Is that why you did not want to meet your father tonight?'

'I do not wish to discuss him,' Mrs. Walthew replies.

I wonder, what did her father do?

The moon sits just above a farm behind us and burns off our numbing cloak. A manor hoves into view, and it's frontage bathes in the lunar light. The gated entrance yields to a broad plain of fresh snow before the imposing stately home. Creeping vines portentously crawl across the ruinous stone façade. The vines are so thick that it is like a lattice of roots sprouting smaller feelers to spread their affliction across every corner. A few heavy vines even hang across the windows, which themselves are positioned unevenly and vary in style. Seven gargoyles standing watch, atop the gables, unnerve me. This rough and asymmetric geometry is consistent across the entire estate.

On the far side of the building is a forest of silver birch. It encroaches so close to the manor that the rear appears to extend into the mass of spiny trees. I imagine that some black magic has permitted the barren forest to grow these vines in an attempt to slowly pull the manor in. I thought Mrs. Walthew had redeemed the building from the derisory state in which she inherited it.

'This place is not what I expected,' I say.

Mrs. Walthew chuckles, 'It's a bit spooky, don't you agree? The Boston Ivy is striking.'

'Is that what those vines are?'

Mrs. Walthew elaborates. 'Yes, oh I adore it, in all seasons. Though it looks like it, it is not actually ivy, hence why it is not evergreen. In the summer the manor is a carpet of green, a vertical wall of life that chirps excitedly with concealed birds. In the autumn the deep shades of red and brown are magnificently striking. Then when it dies away in the winter, the eerie aspect adds a foreboding charm. Some people love it while others loathe it. It is like nothing else, a truly unique place inside and out, though a lot of what is special inside is hidden. You'll see.' She smirks before continuing, 'The idea to grow the Boston Ivy was my grandfather's, Archibald, the 3rd Baron Avington. He was a great man; a gentle giant.'

'So, your grandfather was a Baron?'

'Yes, Walter Avington, the 1st baron, was in Parliament. One only recollects his name from the portraits inside. The title passed to my father, but his terrible attempts at producing a male heir failed, and he lost our family's title. I keep only the courtesy title of the Honourable Elizabeth Walthew.'

Approaching the manor, I feel like a dwarf. I still use my hand to test that I can pass through the shimmery door. I enter.

'Welcome to my residence,' Mrs. Walthew proclaims.

'It is a goodly home,' I comment politely. It is very grand, but a little too ostentatious for my liking. The entrance is a large room with the main feature, straight ahead, a wide set of white marble stairs leading up to a landing where a series of portrait paintings hang in a horizontal line. I glance around the rest of the entrance room appreciating the further artistic décor of landscape paintings.

Mrs. Walthew walks to a room on the left. I go to follow her, but I hesitate. 'Huh,' I say, 'one of the portraits is missing.' All the paintings are of people, six in a line from the left, then a gap where it is clear a portrait once stood, then another three.

'That's intentional.'

My inquisitive mind scours the paintings for a clue. The image furthest right has a likeness to Mrs. Walthew though I am too far away to read the inscription. I deduce that the portraits relate to each Baron and his wife as well as Mrs. Walthew and her husband. Therefore, the missing picture can only belong to one man. 'That's your father, isn't it?' Mrs. Walthew does not reply. 'Why did you dislike him so much? Because he lost your family's title? Is it not a little unfair to remove his portrait?'

'Oh really, what would you know?' I do not answer. 'You assume that because I have wealth that one is immune to hardship? Why do you think that I vacated the church at once this evening? Why would I not wish to reunite with my dear mother and loving grandparents? Why have I never uttered his name?'

'I'm sorry, I shouldn't have pried,' I say, sheepishly.

Surprisingly, Mrs. Walthew shows some understanding. 'You were not to know. He was not a nice man. He was outwardly quite pleasant, but he tried too hard to provide a male heir. He violated the most sacred bond; he should have protected his little girl, not be the one to spoil her!'

I startle at the insinuation, 'Please, you don't need to exp—'

'We'll both forget soon enough. I cannot wait for that day. This place exhumes memories, the treasured and the depraved. I'm sure they will fade sooner if I stop returning. It will be good for my dear Bertie too as I won't accidentally spook him, but I adore that I can still be close to him. It is wonderful to watch him happily exist in ignorant bliss. The caveat is that my memory is still clear on certain events.

'My mother died when I was young. Recollection of her is nigh gone, sadly. She was not well for a long period after I was born and passed away when I was approximately eight-years-old. Then my father and I moved in here after my grandfather died a few years later. He was an unsightly sod, my father, he had bulging eyes and his hair was receding and scruffy—a palpably queer look. He was desperate for a son because he had no brother to pass the title to. Despite his wealth, his appearance and peculiar mannerisms dispelled all potential romances. It was when he was drunk one evening that he woke me up with an unspeakably foul intention.'

I wish she wouldn't tell me this story. I attempt to interrupt, 'Please, you d—'

'As I discovered that night, he was as dumb as he was a disgusting rantallion! I was not even old enough for his heinously incestuous plot to succeed.' Mrs. Walthew glimpses my face, which is pursed like a prune. 'The insufferable man went through with the deed but was racked with guilt the next morning. I did not speak. When the opportunity arose, I ran to my friend's house and refused to leave; it became established that I would live with the Walthews. Rumour spread; it ruined my father as he had ruined me!'

I feel uneasy, 'Pleas—'

'A deep-seated depression lingered, but it was alleviated by my friend's older brother, Cuthbert. In time we courted, became married, and had a happy life with our boy. Upon my father's death, I vowed to restore the pride and nobility that he took from me and our family.'

'I am truly sorry to hear that. I understand why you would remove his portrait; I should not have inquired.'

'Your intentions are earnest. That is why I will show you my collection and not Mrs. Wells. Besides, all families have their dirty secrets. I hope that I forget mine soon and that the sight of him does not bring them back. Now,' she pauses, 'would you like to see the artefacts?'

'Yes.'

'Very well.' Mrs. Walthew leads the way across the drawing-room and through an inconspicuous brown door. Oil lamps light the narrow stairwell to the basement. 'Splendid!' Mrs. Walthew exclaims. 'Bertie must be reading in there as usual. Refrain from getting too close to him; I do not wish for your presence to induce a paroxysm of fright.'

At the bottom of the stairs is a plain black door. I push through.

CHAPTER ELEVEN

THE TOMB ROOM

E ntering the room, I gasp in wonderment. A warm glow lights the chamber with sharp contrasts from the flickering firelight and wall-mounted sconces. The divine brilliance of the golden glints and myriad colours within the glorious and intimidating ancient arcana mystify. The disparity at the far end of the room amalgamates rough chiselled masonry with smooth, sumptuous gold. The heavenly gleam from the lustful metal steals my glare with a corrupting transfixion.

A hacking cough startles me, shattering the covetous spell. An elderly chap sits in a wing-backed armchair beside an open fire. The wizened man, who must be close to eighty, is reading a newspaper. On the table next to him is a tumbler of amber liquid beside a half-empty bottle of whisky.

With the man's head buried in the newspaper, I am able to inspect the front page of the *Deaconshire Chronicle* without him seeing me. The headline on the front page reads: *Mythological Creature Blamed For Man's Disappearance.* Curious, I read the opening paragraph:

The Legend of the Silver Horse is being blamed for the disappearance of Mr. Walter Henderson, a 42-year-old man from Alnustone. Mr. Henderson was last seen arguing with a friend as they vacated The Pickle and Pike Inn near his home. Our reporter spoke to the barman, who stated that Mr. Henderson's friend had enquired about the legend shortly before they left at approximately seven o'clock. The tale supposes that a shining silver horse roams the Forest of Blackmoss near the flooded village of Drayside.

I scan the rest of the front page. Sadly, there is nothing that strikes me as familiar. I recognise none of the few places named, and there is no mention of Mrs. Walthew's demise or an American.

Cuthbert Walthew opens the front page. 'There's a map here!' I say excitedly.

'Keep your voice down!' Mrs. Walthew scolds me.

She takes no interest in the map, but I investigate it keenly. I furiously scan the page and pause on a few names: Mosskene, Horton and Lyeminster. They strike a chord in a vague sense, like hearing the name of someone you went to school with but not necessarily a friend. And, unfortunately, Lyeminster is in the opposite direction to Mosskene and Horton, so it doesn't help me decide which way to go.

I continue to search. West of Lyeminster is a symbol denoting a city, but Mr. Walthew's thumb covers the name.

I will for him to move it, but he's pinching it firmly. I scour the rest of the map but nothing else jumps out at me. In yet another direction is Kemble-on-Sands, but the attachment is weaker than the others. If none of the names were even vaguely familiar, I'd surmise that I'm not from this county, but there is enough to make me think I know this county yet none of the placenames strike me as *home*. There must be a clue here for me.

I read the article associated with the map as quickly as I can:

Deaconshire is a county steeped in folklore. In light of The Legend of the Silver Horse resurfacing, our expert has charted some of these fables and myths onto a map accompanied by a brief description outlining the reported encounters.

The Bog Beings of Mosskene

First on our list is a peculiar sighting near the village of Mosskene. Beside a stone circle just outside the antiquated settlement is a peat bog. Our expert is aware of two independent sightings. Both witnesses reported observing two beings rise from the bog. It was at night on each occasion, and the first witness fled there and then. The second person initially mistook them for a couple who may have accidentally fallen into the bog, but their behaviour was not that of panic. The man described seeing the two beings traipse from the bog to the stone circle. It was when the man caught a glimpse of their hideous and disfigured faces in the moonlight that he fled too. By the time—

'No,' I cry out as Mr. Walthew turns the page. The stone circle sounds familiar, but I need to know more.

'Mr. Webster! Get away from my husband. I cannot have you shouting like that. You'll give my dear husband the fright of his life.'

I apologise, but as I step away, I have a final glance over the new pages to no avail. Disappointment pulls my mood down like a ship's anchor. I'm no closer to understanding which direction I should travel.

I observe the artefacts around the room, but my initial interest has waned. Behind Mr. Walthew is a bookcase filled with dusty tomes from floor to ceiling. A large proportion of these books are devoted to Ancient Egyptian history, mythology and curses. Beside the bookshelf are a series of stone tablets with bizarre inscriptions which Mrs. Walthew explains are hieroglyphs. Some of the tablets are incredibly worn while others retain vibrant colour such as one which depicts a vivid red disc (likely the sun or moon) in a crescent boat-like structure. On the same wall is another set of shelves which contains colourful figurines, amulets and miscellaneous trinkets.

I stroll into the centre of the room to examine the magnificent centrepiece. Mrs. Walthew explains that this is the pride of her collection—the sarcophagus. A worn painting on wood resembles a person with long strands of black hair and big, black eyes. The decorative coffin rests on top of a stone altar with many inscriptions. 'My goodness! Who is this?' I ask. Mrs. Walthew savours my reaction.

'The reis informed us that it is Amenhotep I, one of the great Pharaohs of Egypt.'

'Did you ever invite in a professor of Egyptology, so that he may study it and determine if it has ever been opened?'

'It has never been opened!' Mrs. Walthew snaps. 'And no, an academic would only seek to involve the authorities in a bid to claim these relics for himself. Besides, they have pieces from similar sites; they do not need mine. It was at great expense that I brought these items here, and I would never relinquish them. Despite all the difficulties, to stand amongst such enticing, buried secrets, within a hidden vault in such a characterful manor, is so satisfying. It affords me the ability to bask in my cunning and ingenuity and to bequeath a legacy to my son that will stand him higher than any Baron Avington.' With these words, Mrs. Walthew's eyes inflame with insatiable rapacity. Her zealously egotistical sense of supremacy has become frightful. Not wanting to engage or offend the gluttonous matriarch, I nod and inspect the other items.

Mrs. Walthew points to the far corner of the vault. Carved from a towering masonry block is a figure of a man who is painted in a dull red. His arms are crossed, and he has a comically long beard and an elaborate headdress. I walk over gazing up at the face, which is remarkably distinctive and only a little worn. 'That is Amenhotep,' Mrs. Walthew says. In the other corner is another stone statue. This one is rougher with no painted colour and a simpler headdress. I struggle to resist the obvious distraction of the spectacular gold artefacts that these statues guard. Mrs. Walthew grins voraciously as I inspect the pristine pieces. A sizeable carving of a cat sits amongst many smaller treasures, and above them all is a tremendous golden hanging of feathered wings lifting a shimmery disc that spreads across much of the wall.

'Looking upon familiar objects reawakens the memories associated with them,' Mrs. Walthew says, 'but the familiarity fades over time.'

'It does?' I ask.

'I am sure of it. I greet the pieces in my collection as if they are old friends because gazing upon them rekindles the thrill of acquiring them. When I regard many of the other antiques around my house, however, there is no such sensation. I do not remember their origin or purpose; they have become inanimate. One day, these will all be inanimate too.'

'Do you think you w—'

Mrs. Walthew jolts. 'Do you hear that?' she says. Her expression is full of alarm as she cranes her neck upwards. She looks at my blank expression. 'You do not hear it?'

'Hear what, may I ask?'

'That howling!'

I strain my ears. 'Actually, I do perceive a faint, protracted howl.'

Mrs. Walthew is wincing. 'One is not serious! It is quite deafening.' She looks curiously over my head. 'I fancy that it originates from the wood outside. We should investigate.'

Without a second thought, Mrs. Walthew withdraws from the room. She walks with a determined stride, and I follow her up the narrow stairway and out the front door.

The night embraces me with exotic warmth. I close my eyes to savour the heat that reignites my nullified senses fully, and I sniff the freshness of the air. With my eyes still shut, I bathe in the balmy summer heat of this snowy night. I hear the howling; it is oddly pleasant. A sense of abnormality and alarm does not enter my thoughts until I open my eyes. My ecstasy escapes at the sight of blood-tinged snow. The portent pigment is not a quality of the snow, but instead, it reflects the fiery glare in the heavens. A blood-red moon looms.

CHAPTER TWELVE

THE HOAXING HOWL

The moon's glow is powerful enough to inflame my core, yet it is incapable of thawing the rose-twinkling ice. Does the hellish sky and the continuous wail of a glorious trumpet signal the Apocalypse? If so, will I ascend to heaven or be devoured by the Beast? I panic that I cannot recite or recount biblical text. Am I not worthy? Fearful, I approach Mrs. Walthew to find comfort in shared angst.

'What is happening?' she asks.

'I don't know, ma'am.'

'That howling is so close, and it's—well—it's wonderful. And yes, it is coming from the forest behind my manor,' she says pointing, but she is not pointing to the origin of the howling and it sounds much further away than she claims. 'What could it be? We must go in search.'

Once again, I walk in her wake. We traipse the perimeter of the manor until we approach the edge of the wood. Inside, the pristine coverage of snow is spoilt by the uneven ground, and the foliage is poking through. Excited sounds accompany shadowy shapes as they dance amongst the gaunt trees in the sanguine spotlight.

'The wood has never been so alive!' Mrs. Walthew exclaims.

As we enter the wood, a silent rampage of racing stags startle us as they charge past. We watch as they dart amidst the forest without deviating for the birch trees, but instead, plough on through.

'I'm astounded—the animals have risen too. Look at those antlers,' Mrs. Walthew swoons. 'They're as majestic as my great, great grandfather's trophy in the reception room. We have never known deer here since.' I stroll through the devilish gloom in awe as I behold the resplendent and ghoulish critters that nudge us as they pass.

Moles surface, squirrels dash, rabbits run, hedgehogs waddle, foxes frolic, deer prance and birds sing and soar without flapping. The hoots from nocturnal owls perform in melody with morning birdsongs. I drop to cover from onrushing bats, then, averting my marvelling eyes down, I discover a swirling chase of courting stoats pirouetting between our feet.

I stumble for words as I excitedly switch my glance from one animalistic drama to the next. 'This is magical! There—there is so much life here.'

'Ha! The tree rats can't even pursue their favourite climbs,' Mrs. Walthew adds with unexpected malice.

'You don't like squirrels?'

She squeals as one runs into her in serendipitous retaliation. 'Gormless vermin! They have such stupid bushy tails.' I snigger without her noticing as she picks up the pace. Another deer stampede clatters into Mrs. Walthew, knocking her to the floor. 'Argh! My ancestors ate you for supper!' She cannot be hurt, but it is her pride that took the battering. This forest of the dead is wilder than any living.

Accepting my helping hand, Mrs. Walthew gets to her feet and shouts, 'The howling is still ahead.'

'Are you sure? I can't hear it.' The lively chorus of the day and night creatures is too loud.

'Yes. Are you deaf? It is louder than all these bloodthirsty beasts.' I chuckle as a badger shunts me. It causes me to stumble through a tree. I still reach out in an attempt to steady myself. Mrs. Walthew frowns thinking my laugh is aimed at her. Her temper is frayed, she is not enjoying this enchanting spectacle of nature, whereas I find it enthralling. These woodland creatures, like any playful puppy, have excited me and quelled my underlying fears.

Deep in the forest, the ethereal fauna is so dense and agitated that the ground ahead swirls as rapidly as a white river albeit with no discernible current. Standing still is not so perilous, but any movement will likely intersect the path of some scurrying woodland specimen. I develop a slow-moving technique which allows the hurrying animals time to divert around me while Mrs. Walthew persists with her more belligerent approach. Blindly, she tries to race through, without dodging, and her progress is no quicker due to constant sideswipes and trips. I titter to myself at her latest squeal, and I begin to believe that my more cautious approach is superior, but then I stumble as a rogue fox runs into the back of one of my legs. I begin to recover when its chasing companion hits my other leg causing me to fall onto my back. Dull, painless thumps batter my body as a blur of woodland mice, squirrels, stoats and rabbits trample over my face. I put my hand down so I may roll over, only for a hopping hare to disagree. On the second try, I make it up and immediately dodge another herd of bolting deer.

Mrs. Walthew and I continue to run this gauntlet. My focus is firmly on each step, so much so that I only know Mrs. Walthew's position from her piercing cries of frustration or the peripheral flash of her blue dress when she is upended. I am knocked down only once more, but Mrs. Walthew remains ahead despite countless wails and tumbles. By the time we see a clearing and the frenetic flurry of wildlife calms, I am giddy with laughter and Mrs. Walthew is enraged. She runs as she leaves the woodland. I can run too! This was not possible before, and I feel no exhaustion.

Emerging from the boisterous woods, I am alive with a childish buzz and Mrs. Walthew's sour distaste is bizarrely unstated but evident nonetheless. 'Still ahead?' I ask jovially.

'Yes, it must be over this rise.' As we walk up the grassy knoll, the lively nocturnal symphony subsides to that euphonious but distant howl or whine. It is not close nor straight ahead, more like halfway to the right, but not wanting to antagonise my companion, I keep quiet expecting the summit to provide clarity.

Reaching the peak, I see the lambent light of a small town in a shallow valley ahead. A broad, beaming constellation of dazzling white lights emanates from the base of a soaring church tower on the southern side of the town. Amongst the illuminations, a compact cluster of tangled shapes jostle.

'That mass of light. That's where the howl originates,' Mrs. Walthew says.

I look to the darkness on the right. I point and say, 'Honestly, I hear the sound over there.'

'Whatever it is, that radiant churchyard has something to do with it.' The unnatural bundle of lights is too bold and white to be borne of flame. The shining mass's luminosity remains steady but is not entirely motionless. It is too bizarre not to investigate.

'Do you know the town?' I ask.

'Yes, this is the town of Ghyll. I was searching amongst St. Paul's cemetery down there the night before last. It is a beautiful old town, and many of the avenues felt familiar.'

We both pause for a moment to absorb the breath-taking scene of the settlement nestled within the snowy hills. The sharp, hoary edifices mesmerise as the ice gems that infuse the sprawling town glisten. The stark halo surrounding the church stands in defiance against the blood-red moon that leers down upon it.

'Don't dally, come now,' Mrs. Walthew says as she marches onward. I regard her as she descends the hillside; the assuredness in her gait is something I can only wish to possess. I face towards the darkness from whence the blissful hum of an angel calls. I sense that ignoring it is akin to declining an invite to heaven, but being rational, it is a fanciful notion to follow a strange noise blindly, and it will only result in me becoming lost. I shouldn't lose my way if I stay with Mrs. Walthew, and she is as eager as I to understand the mysteries of this night. And the bright lights down in the valley promise answers.

'This warmth is wondrous,' I say as I catch up with Mrs. Walthew. 'I had forgotten what it was like to feel.'

'It is marvellous,' she replies. 'The concept of heat is most baffling when one becomes accustomed to its absence.'

'Indeed.'

A quiet calm takes hold as we approach the foot of the fell. Once more, I marvel at the appearance of the country-side cast in this strange new glow. A hill rises high across the valley, but a series of dark patches scattered across the ridgeline break the uniformity of the snowy vista.

Something in me stirs. A strange sensation. Familiarity.

I hear laughter, not aloud but in my head. Those patches are dark because it is a rock formation on which the snow does not cling. I know it is a rock formation, but how can I be so sure? I have been here before. I have climbed those rocks. This sense of *déjà vu*, can it be real?

The laughter breaks to a cheerful shout, *Dearie, don't you mount those ladies!*

'The Ladies!' I blurt out loud.

'Good heavens!' Mrs. Walthew cries. 'Why are you shouting? You gave me a start.'

'The Ladies. That's the name of the rock formation. I remember!'

'Yes. That's all very well, but don't yell so suddenly like that.'

'Forgive me, Mrs. Walthew, but I believe I have been here before. I recall too why the rock formation got its name. The shape of the rocks from the town makes them appear like beetles crawling across the ridgeline, except there are holes in the rocks, which affords them with dark spots—like Ladybirds.'

'Yes, I know all that.'

'But so do I!'

'Well hopefully you shall soon recall something a little more useful than the name of a rock formation.'

'I do! I recall a woman telling me not to climb the rocks. Her voice is soft and kind, and she calls me, "Dearie". Could it be my mother? Could this be my hometown?'

'I disclosed that the town was called Ghyll, and you did not react. I would expect you to recognise the name of your hometown.'

'Yes, but perhaps home is not so far away.'

'Perhaps, my dear. Perhaps.' Her words are cold, intended to suppress my excitement. Perhaps that is wise.

We reach the base of the hill and enter the town. Smoke puffs from every chimney; everyone is keeping warm inside. The hour is just past nine and the slippery conditions ensure the streets are empty. Snow covers the roads, though black parallel lines indicate that some bold cabmen do venture out. The occasional gas lamp, in its frustum guard, illuminate the narrow streets. Black slate is invariably the material used to build the rustic houses and cottages in this town, and many of the tiles protrude and serve as a ledge, upon which snowflakes gather to rest. I harbour a great sense of hope with each corner we turn, but Mrs. Walthew was right to caution my optimism—this town is unfamiliar to me.

We walk towards a stone bridge, and we cross. The water cascading beneath turns a downstream waterwheel. I watch the stream bursting with fish that leap as high as salmon and as aggressively as piranha. It seems even ghost fish surface for leisure tonight.

The bridge leads us towards a crossroad and the centre of the town with a variety of shops and taverns. We continue to the main square, which contains a handful of people, but only one moving object casts a shadow—a trotting black horse pulling a hansom. The cab's tall, spindly wheels sink in about an inch and score a new pair of grooves in fresh snow.

A young lady with wispy red hair and a silky green dress rushes out of one of the buildings. She is slim, attractive, and full of the youthful energy that is typical of those who straddle the boundary of womanhood.

She meets the cab and shouts, 'Excuse me, can you take me to Deaconbury? I know the roads are treacherous, but I need to collect something. Please. I will pay extra.'

'Yes, ma'am.' The cabman's response instantly captures my attention. He pronounces the last word as 'mairm', revealing an American accent.

'Oh, thank you so much. No one else would take me.'

'I will always help a damsel in distress, ma'am. Where do you wish to visit in Deaconbury?'

'Deaconbury Manor.'

'Oh! Are you a friend of The Duke of Deaconshire?' the cabman asks.

'Oh, yes,' she giggles, 'he is my betrothed.'

'Congratulations, ma'am.'

'Thank you. It is wonderful to meet an American.' The girl in the green dress steps into the cab and they ride off towards the gleaming churchyard. The cabman's voice coupled with the sight of his cab and black horse stirs a sensation as though I am glimpsing something from a repressed nightmare. I feel bitterness and anger, both towards the cabman but also for my current predicament. If this was the man who could unlock my memories, then it has failed.

I turn back to Mrs. Walthew, but she is accosting two men without shadows or the ghostly guise, 'Excuse me, gentlemen, what is happening tonight? What is that serene howling?'

'A marvellous evening it is indeed, ma'am,' a gentleman wearing a top hat says. 'I am ignorantly cherishing it, however. I wanted to get away from the excitably freakish fellows at St. Paul's church down the way, so I'm afraid I'm not sure why tonight is so peculiar. I do beg your pardon though ma'am, but I am not sure what you are referring to with this—serene howl?'

'Yes, it is quite loud.'

'I am awfully sorry. I did not mean to offend ma'am. It is a wonderfully strange evening, but I do not understand it. I wish I could be of greater assistance.'

The man's friend who wears a peaked cap adds, 'Me neither ma'am but them folk at the church, they'll know. They're a strange sort, but it's an odd night, ain't it, ma'am?'

'Yes, it is,' Mrs. Walthew replies. 'I thank you both kindly. You've been most helpful.'

We bid each other farewell, and Mrs. Walthew and I set off in the tracks of the cart that is now out of sight.

'We are getting close,' Mrs. Walthew says loudly. I do not respond because I would argue that the howling is unmistakably behind us now. I was hoping the two men could help her realise. I don't know how they couldn't hear it, but it is not as loud as Mrs. Walthew claims.

The street leading to the church is devoid of the living. Many of the crooked houses fail to hide their orange glow. At St. Paul's, the hellish moon soars above the heavenly aura. Are the townsfolk sheltering from the snow or cowering from the tormenting sky? Can they see the moon's bloody tinge or the absurdly dazzling lights from the cemetery? The lady in the green dress and the American driver made no mention of it.

At the gates to the cemetery, sharp talons of distress grip me. I halt as I resolve the source of the graveyard illuminations. It is something dreadful.

Chapter Thirteen

THE NIGHT OF THE SOULS

I stand spine-chillingly still, gawping through the cemetery's fiendish, gothic gateway onto a macabre festival.
The omen promised by the crimson moon has been kept.
The leering furnace in the sky breathes its fire over the
boneyard, and the snow-dusted spire appears blood-stained
in its light. The devil's trace extends below as the tainted
tint imbues the soft snow lying on the ground and the tops
of tombs and tombstones. Soaking in the bloodbath is a
ghostly orgy of incubus worshippers. Yet more unsettling
are the torches that these possessed spirits carry. The intense
white light that they emit vividly illumes the wielders, but

no natural or living surface receives any trace of its lustre. It is the torches themselves that unlock a dementing fear that paralyses me. The spectral light from these lanterns beams out from empty eye sockets. The exposed crypt is cramped with ghouls clutching skulls, wailing and hailing.

The sight of these cadaverous tokens excites an unkindness of ravens. A cacophony of caws resounds from their perches within the gangly limbs of gnarly trees. Too enticed to simply watch, many of these envoys of evil swoop low over the churchyard and cackle in their delight.

I try to regain my composure by reasoning that the haunting phantasms in the cemetery are just folks like Mrs. Walthew and me. However, I cannot stem this sense of dread. From the hoaxing howl to the beaming skull lanterns, there are so many aspects that I can pretend are the source, but these are mere manifestations of a deeper lurking fear. The upwelling of amorphous terror is, in truth, the underlying unknown. This uncertainty is what triggers anguish to stampede voraciously through my ethereal being. Tonight is not without its magical quirks, but something is maddeningly awry, and it is not something to celebrate. This eerie culture with its loathsome and grotesque melodrama is frightfully foreign. My instinct is to cower furtively until I assemble some reason or theory to explain the utterly unfamiliar frenzy.

Mrs. Walthew breaks the silence with a terrifying and foolhardy suggestion, 'Are you ready to enter? This is all so mystifying.'

'You are not serious!'

'I must find the origin of that wondrous howl.'

'The howling is not coming from in there.'

'Why do I only hear it? I need to understand,' Mrs. Walthew says, and, at once, she walks towards the entrance.

I have a decision to make. Either I follow her into the frightful parade or face being left alone on this unhallowed night. I try to craft a resolution: 'The gate is closed; you won't be able to get in.'

'Oh, come now. One knows as well as I that the wall is easy to surmount.' She is right, we cannot breach the spiked metal gate, but the stone perimeter wall is little more than waist height. She tilts her head back and starts breathing heavily. 'Oh, the howl, the heat, the singing, it is all so sweet.' She lingers in ecstasy. 'It is calling me!' She writhes in pleasure.

With a groan, her euphoria fades. She glances back at me with a tantalising smirk and says, 'Are you not enticed?' It is the first time that I've seen her smile, and in that moment, I find her strangely attractive. I follow.

She hops the wall with much more grace and enthusiasm than my own reluctant struggle. If Mrs. Walthew were to suggest retreating, however, I know that I could hop back as swiftly and as positively as she entered. We reach the main pathway and walk past a quiet family sitting on the floor by newer gravestones. Like this family, many of the spirits do not wield skulls but those that do certainly catch the eye. Further along the walkway, numerous shining skulls nestle in the snow at the base of a variety of tall head-stones. The spirits are mostly young and well-dressed. A significant proportion of the women wear beautiful flowing wedding gowns and veils. From outside, the teeming mass was intimidating. Inside, however, the small family clusters offer no threat. Many of these groups have several young children and adults, though their actions are wholly distinct from each other. Nearby, a young couple sits in the shadow of their gravestone, though the stray light from someone's skull highlights them. Their heads rest both on the tombstone and the other's temple, so they can gaze at one another and watch events. There are also several cliques who stand or wander in idle conversation. The calmness of these characters acts to ease my nerves further, but they are just peripheral to the wilder, more boisterous activities.

The skull dancers, in particular, perturb me with their profane gyrating. Numerous Lunatics flail their arms high above their heads with one hand holding their skull aloft. As their arms rhythmically swirl, they rotate their wrists causing their lantern's beams to flash across the congregation in a hap-hazard and mesmerising display. A few people dance rigidly as if in a ballroom but at the end of their outstretched arm is not a partner but a skull cradled by their hand. One debonair chap appears to kiss his skull as he leans in at brief intervals. Even more disturbing are those who insert their skull within their own head! Bright light streams out of their eyes while the rest of their face adopts a gaunt and ghastly expression. This spectral appearance differs from the ghostly guise because the soul-light makes something ethereal partially transparent, not a corporeal person or object. Close by is a couple who adopt this same style; a veiled woman and a distinguished gentleman relive the first dance of their wedding, and while one arm links them together, the other supports the emissary of death behind their eyes. Many sing to themselves but their songs are lost to the general chaotic chorus of the crazed crowd.

One group stands out, not because they are nearby and audible, but because the lyrics stir a sense of *déjà vu*. I recognise it as an Irish folk song, and their softly accentuated words pervade a homely satisfaction. All four singers are young men who possess dark, curly hair and pale skin. As I watch and listen, I am struck by the apt lyrics and the repetition of the phrase: *by the rising of the moon*. In front of them a couple sway, four attractive ladies dance merrily, and a group of children and young adults play. I savour the melodic ballad as I gaze upon a new family drama.

A young mother is shouting in an attempt to control four lively children. All the children are amusing themselves with miniature craniums as if they were toys, except the baby who is crying in the arms of a more passive father. I am confident that the skulls they hold are their own and no other spirit seems able to interact with them. The differing sizes befitting their age suggests this inextricably. The youngest is a blonde-haired girl of about four and the two boys are approximately six and nine years old. The dainty but menacing form of the tiny skulls, in the hands of their innocent owners, throws my mind through dark loops of trauma. I watch on in alarm at how the girl laughs as she throws her cranium upwards before it arcs back to the ground. She giggles as it is nearly lost in the snow. Her mother is trying to stop her, but the little girl throws her skull so that it passes through her frustrated parent. Meanwhile, the younger boy is making faceless imprints in the snow while the older boy runs off to scare girls from another family. The mother races after him while the father shouts in vain for the other two to stop.

All the time the murderous ravens mutter overhead and occasionally swoop to harass the mother some more. As the Irish folk singers switch to a more sombre ballad, I reflect on how such a vision can appear before me. How are adults and children alike able to remove their skulls from their graves? How do these skulls act to leave their mark on the living world and be caressed by the dead?

Mrs. Walthew's mood has calmed as she too has been marvelling at the disquieting antics of our deceased compatriots. She turns her stare from the same family, smiles at me, and returns to watch. She is enjoying the bewilderment, and she sways with the rhythm of the melody. She turns back to me, points, and loudly says, 'It is over there.' She lingers, waiting for a response as if she's asked a question. I usher her to lead the way, and we set off. As we weave between the looming memorials and various parties, the sights and sounds vary wildly from rough but good-natured brawls to playful Morris dancing mimicry.

We reach the far wall where the atmosphere is calmer, but Mrs. Walthew's countenance is one of concern. 'It is still further,' she says. A nearby couple remonstrates with each other, but Mrs. Walthew interrupts. 'Excuse me, I am a wanderer. What is happening tonight? Do you know why I hear a sweet howling beyond this wall?'

'Huh,' says the brunette woman in an orange and white gown. 'You are not the first person to suggest there is such a noise past this wall, but neither of us hears it nor knows what it could be.'

'Who was asking? Where are they now?' Mrs. Walthew presses.

'It was a lady, she was about to set off to investigate, but I see her talking to someone. Just wait here a moment, she'll be interested to learn that you hear it too.'

She walks off and when she is out of earshot her husband, dressed in a navy-blue suit and wide-brimmed hat, finds an opportunity to express himself. 'Till death do us part we said. O Lord! Why couldn't that be true? I'm sure in life I realised that I'd made a foolish error. The thought of death was likely a sweet relief to me then,' he chuckles. 'She is turning me insane. I'm glad you interjected. All Mary does is pester and gossip. My frustration must repeat every full moon. I cannot leave her; we are together for eternity. Damn my pubescent hormones!' He pauses as he recognises our discomfort. 'I'm sorry to burden you with my woes. My plight must be nothing to yours. You're both wanderers, right?'

'Indeed,' Mrs. Walthew replies.

'Please forgive me,' he says and then introduces himself as John.

Mrs. Walthew asks, 'Do you have any idea what is going on or how I can find my grave?'

'I do not have much knowledge, but folk are calling tonight the Night of the Souls.'

'The Night of the Souls?' I query.

'Yes, whatever that means, but it's the cause of tonight's strange phenomena.'

'But what is causing this? Why is it so hot? What does it have to do with souls and these skulls?'

John explains, 'My understanding is that the soul resides behind the eyes, which may explain the white beams emitting from the skulls.'

'Does one know what the howl is?' Mrs. Walthew asks. 'I must be so close, what does it mean?'

'I'm not—' John starts but is distracted by his wife, who returns with a young woman wearing a long, pink cuirass bodice, and a short gentleman in a suit and bowler hat.

The trailing pair of Lunatics are deep in animated conversation. 'She's found another one, dear John,' Mary says.

'Oh, it's awful! This chap believes he was accosted by the American too—'

'American?' Mrs. Walthew baulks. The unfamiliar pair abruptly halt their conversation.

'Not you as well?' the woman says.

'Perhaps, my dear,' Mrs. Walthew says. 'There is a conjuring in my mind of a moustachioed man with a big grin. I vaguely recall his degenerate accent but not what he said or did, but I believe it to be something most terrible.'

'That's him!' the man shouts as outrage spreads through everyone. 'The evil bastard! He murdered all three of us. Who is he?'

We all express that we do not know who the mystery murderer is. As we simmer in quiet outrage, Mary introduces us. Lady Priscilla Axham is the sharp-featured young woman and Mr. Henry Carmichael is the gentleman.

'Do you remember how?' I ask.

'It was just a few nights ago, before the snow,' Lady Priscilla says, her hands shaking. 'It was late, and I was a passenger in his cab on my way home. I was drunk. He pulled over on the approach to Ghyll and—oh, it's so horrible. His grin—beneath that—that mop of a moustache. That dastardly miscreant—he—he kissed me softly on my forehead as he did it—oh it was horrible—such a despicable grin.'

'Did what?' I ask. Mrs. Walthew's horrified glance cautions me to my insensitive line of questioning.

Her well-spoken frenzy continues: 'I could not breathe! He—he had his hands tight—around my neck. Before his fatal kiss, I—I remember he whispered something. That he—he would savour watching the light in my eyes fade. That vile Yank! His gratifying grin was the last thing I saw—till—till I was here—welcomed by ominous bells. I watched him jubilantly ride off.'

A stunned silence spreads as Mrs. Walthew and I finally understand the brutal reality of her death. Counter to her current appearance, Mrs. Walthew was a frail old lady, when the dreadful foreigner took her life. Why would anyone do that? To use his cold grip and to smile so wickedly, he must have some abhorrent perversion.

'Why all three of us?' Mrs. Walthew asks. I keep quiet regarding my personal reaction towards the American. Could he have murdered me, too? If so, why don't I recall his evil grin?

'I could not tell you, madam. I thought it was only me a quarter of an hour ago,' Lady Priscilla says. 'Wait a moment. Are you the Honourable Elizabeth Walthew of Birchwood Manor?' Mrs. Walthew affirms. 'My father mentioned that you'd disappeared following an event in Ghyll on New Year's Eve.'

'Oh my!' Mrs. Walthew reacts. 'That means I've been in this spirit realm for approximately one month.'

'I'm sorry I didn't recognise you. My father, the Earl of Ghyll, has spoken of you, but I don't believe we ever actually met,' Lady Priscilla says.

'The Earl must have been distraught to learn of my disappearance.'

'You were known for taking long trips away unannounced, so I believe many presumed that you'd taken another.'

Mrs. Walthew grumbles, and then she asks Mr. Carmichael how long he's been here in this spirit realm.

'A few days before Lady Priscilla. He's fast at work. I remember him standing over me with that ghastly grin, and it was in a cab too. That bastard! I had just concluded a trip that marked the start of a new business venture, and I was heading home. I took his cab to get a train south. I don't remember much else other than his face.'

'I don't believe this!' Mary cries. She turns away and expresses her outrage to others.

Mr. Carmichael sombrely adds, 'The last few days I was going mad in someone's basement. I don't know what to do.'

'We must find our bodies,' Mrs. Walthew declares. 'Did the cabman leave your corpse?'

'No, he took it!' Lady Priscilla wails. Many onlookers are now eavesdropping on our conversation, and Mary is remonstrating with another group.

'If this despicable scoundrel has taken our bodies, he most likely has a place to dispose of them. We need to find that place,' Mrs. Walthew says. She ponders a moment. 'Do you both hear that howl? In that direction?' she points out towards the hillside away from the centre of town. They both nod. 'Mr. Webster, you say that you also hear a howl but a distant one in a very different direction?'

'Yes,' I answer and, in that moment, I understand the point she is making.

'Tonight is the Night of the Souls, yes?' Mrs. Walthew says.

'That's how they try to explain this madness!' Mr. Carmichael reacts.

'Yes, the souls emit light, but perhaps they cast sound too...' Mrs. Walthew hypothesises. Mr. Carmichael's look is one of confusion while Lady Priscilla's is surprise. 'No one else I've asked has heard it, but I understand that they're all residents, not wanderers like us. I surmise that a soul calls out to its spirit but only if it has not been reunited. So, it is logical to argue that this deviant Yank has buried our bodies together, and if we follow the howl, we shall find them and finally be able to rest.'

'We must try,' Lady Priscilla says.

'Agreed,' Mr. Carmichael adds.

If Mrs. Walthew's assertion is correct, then I couldn't have been murdered by the despicable man as he would surely have buried my corpse beside theirs. In part, such knowledge would be a relief, but it wouldn't explain why the man's voice is familiar to me.

Lady Priscilla attempts to move through the crowd, which has grown as a result of Mary's gossiping. 'Excuse me, sir,' Lady Priscilla says.

A bald spectator leers and shuffles to one side. He crudely asks, 'Did 'e do anythin' else to ya miss? Were you as rosy as you are tonight, miss? Ay miss?'

'It is "*Lady*" you odorous peasant!' Lady Priscilla snaps. 'How ever did such a fopdoodle come to be buried here?' The others show the utmost respect to the victims and offer their sympathy as we pass through. I must confirm if the theory is correct. If it is, it is fantastic news. It will set me back on my path towards home.

We cut past the crowd and approach the wall with many eyes upon us. The air has grown quiet with tension, and the dizzying swirls of the soul-streams have quelled considerably.

The hush exposes the bellows of a man and the frantic shrieks of a woman. The shouts emanate from close to where we left the path through the cemetery, but I am unable to discern what they are saying. Our audience turns to attend this new theatre; the latest sordid flame draws these slavering gawkers like entranced moths. They skulk forwards and steadily spread, slowly finding the ideal vantage point from which to pry. Lady Priscilla rushes to watch the unfolding drama too and not wanting to leave without her, we follow suit. Fresh screeches and diving ravens thrill the gasping crowd.

CHAPTER FOURTEEN

THE RAVENS' CONSPIRACY

L oud menacing squawks cut the muted tension, further feeding the sense of unease. The unkindness of ravens has taken dominance of this amphitheatre as their guttural croaks surround us. Birds swoop low over the audience, arousing frightened yelps. The chilling chirps produce a reply from a larger bird that takes flight from its perch on the church and soars towards us.

With its wings spread wide, it passes into the face of the blood moon. The raven's shadow stretches across the spectators, averting their leers. It succeeds in hypnotising them to its gloomy and doom-laden arrival. The ruffled silhouette lingers in the sanguine disc. It seems to savour its perception as an omen of death by opening its cadaver-ripping beak and releasing a reverberating set of foreboding squawks. My eyes remain upon this feathered fiend as it leaves the limelight to land high on a thin branch, which bends and strains under its weight. It stares down upon its prey. Its feathers are silky black, but it does not possess the ghostly guise; it is as though ravens are as much at home in the land of the dead as they are in the world of the living.

I follow the gaze of its evil eye to the tiny blonde girl I saw earlier. 'Go pick it up, Charlotte!' her mother yells. Charlotte waddles over and does as she is told. She turns to her mother and holds it up high. Another raven dives from a tree and connects with the skull. It is a solid contact, and the skull flies out of her hand and embeds itself in the snow. The little girl titters playfully while her mother bellows, 'Sod off pests!' Charlotte collects her toy only to repeat the charade, dispatching another raven.

'Stop encouraging them, Charlotte!' her father shouts, still cradling the crying baby.

'Malicious black rats, the lot o' ya. Go and bother someone else!' the mother screams. Charlotte continues to laugh and plays for another round.

There is discontent in the audience:

'This is bad. She shouldn't be doing that.'

'Pick it up, girl!'

'She doesn't know what she's doing. What parent allows their child to play with such a thing? They're asking for trouble.'

The father stands and shouts, 'What have I told you? Huh? Stop playing with them. They are not your friends. Go and pick it up and sit quietly.' The little girl's expression turns grumpy. She walks away from her father and her disquieting toy, and she sits in the snow, arms folded.

The whole theatre takes a sharp intake of breath when the portentous raven plunges and lands beside her skull. The raven hops forwards and sideways to check if this peculiar, and presumably pungent, prey reacts. It remains motionless with Charlotte sitting several yards away. The father is next to the raven, and the bird ignores his attempts to scare it away. The raven hops within touching distance and investigates this unfamiliar carcass with a nudge of its beak and immediately hops back a few steps. With a calmer but definite tone, the father instructs, 'Charlotte darling, pick it up. This raven wants your skull. It is yours, not his, go and claim it back.' Charlotte does not react. The raven has a nibble at the skull, lifts it, drops it, and has another nibble. It taps the skull firmly. The girl turns.

Tapping!

The sound of beak on bone shudders through the crowd, wrenching them into silence. It's as if the raven has found the nerve on their heartstrings. The unspoken will is for the girl to act and cease the relentless tapping. I yearn for it too. The girl is in mortal danger, I know it, I feel it, but I do not understand it. What can they do to her? She is already dead.

Tapping!

'CHARLOTTE!' her father roars. The raven clamps onto her skull. The girl rises. A grating alarm call resounds from the other birds. The little girl reaches out as she runs, desperate not to lose her toy. The raven takes a hop away then lifts its head to pompously display its trophy. The girl rushes to grab it. The skull escapes her grasp as it rises into the sky. The mother shrieks. A chorus of flapping feathers fills the auditorium as a dozen birds clamour to join the lead raven. The girl starts screaming as she follows the raven with her arms reaching up to the sky. The excited ravens laugh in mockery.

Like a lighthouse during a storm, the light streaming from the girl's soul flashes over terrified faces as we await the ship to wreck. The raven taunts the desperate throng as it weaves in a figure-of-eight pattern overhead. Turbulent cries rise from the company united in despair and anger in a vain attempt to avert disaster.

The girl sobs wildly and rushes into her mother's arms. Her mother consoles her with reassuring words and loving sentiments while her father shouts at the ravens. A few of the onlookers try to tempt the raven down with their shining lanterns.

I foresee no reason why the ravens would relinquish their reward. Not only would it make a magnificent nest ornament, but its ghastly odour will likely entice maggots and other juicy treats for them to snack upon gluttonously.

The raven ascends, going high, and the flock trails. Their frenzied croaks amplify with fevered expectation and growing impatience. The avian thief circles once more. The ensuing conspiracy of ravens divert and circle in the devilish gloom above the church's gothic spire. The spectators are agitated and aggressive to the point that the father's bellows can scarcely be heard. The raven glides close to the church from a great height. The skull plummets! As it tumbles and spirals, it ejects rapid flashes of brilliant white and encourages a flurry of fervour in the fluttering gaggle. The crowd holds their breath.

The impact is hard, and the skull rebounds off the snow-dusted church roof with an audible crack. The ravens clamour over the spot and a streak of the brightest, holiest aura billows upwards with incredible dexterity. It shoots into the black and chaotic cloud of ruffled feathers where it is consumed.

An intensely shrill shriek accompanies the reverberating crack and shrivels agonisingly before being abruptly silenced. The soul-devouring daemons triumph wretchedly above the stunned bystanders as they perform breath-taking aerobatics and cruelly cackle. I tear my eyes from the display of the raucous fiends and see darkness behind the eyes of the fallen skull. It rests wearily in the snow with a visible cavity gouged from one of its eye sockets.

The mother's keening hysteria overshadows the murmurs of discontent. I watch the family and witness her pleading prayers and the dumbstruck father clutching the baby and his boys. Empathy sits within my heart and seems to weigh upon the crowd too. The little girl is not in her mother's arms. She is gone.

Has she run off? Where would she go and why is no one else looking for her? A mournful silence spreads and the insinuation is grave. How can it be? She has vanished into oblivion. My instinct throughout the whole drama was correct, she *was* in danger. The dead can die!

But where has she gone, and why? Did she enter oblivion because her soul escaped her skull or because she was gobbled by the winged scavengers? If the soul is the secret to there being an afterlife, why would their parents allow the girl to treat it like a toy? But how could they stop her, if only she could hold it? Why do the other children not play with their skulls?

Whispers and mutters are the only sounds from the sheepish assembly as no one dares to break the sacred stillness. Solemn faces and bowed heads unite the gathering from its previously insular but outlandish festivities. This sombre funereal atmosphere finally befits the graveyard setting.

Equally pertinent to this sobering sacrament are the uncertain and frightening thoughts that flood my mind. We Lunatics are not indestructible. Where do we go when our soul is lost? Is it blank emptiness, wild rapture, or the inception of another cursed existence with its own novel laws of death?

Amongst the sedate shuffles, Mrs. Walthew looks over her shoulder towards the perimeter wall. She is anxious to exit but understands the disrespect it would show. Lady Priscilla and Mr. Carmichael are preoccupied interrogating the scene, and Mrs. Walthew returns to looking on in fake reverence.

'Isn't it such a pity, a girl so young,' a soft male voice to my left whispers. I glance and see that this unfamiliar man is indeed addressing me as he leans in close. 'It is most enviable to be blessed with such playfulness and ignorance for all eternity. She'd never turn into cynical charlatans like you and me.'

Despite being a little affronted by the casual accusation, I ignore the comment and continue to stare out at the grief-stricken commotion.

The man continues, 'I'll be honest with you. I'd have slain my own daughter in the first life when she was a mere child if I knew she could exist for perpetuity with such honest carelessness.' Disturbed, I give the man a curious glance. 'I mean that. I'm no barbarian, I promise. That girl had the gift of eternal joy. Before this event unfolded, I witnessed my daughter screeching at her husband. No father wants to see his daughter distraught and sentenced to linger in misery, repeating petty squabbles forever. She was a lucky lass that little girl, bless her soul. Those ne'er-do-well ravens will cavort long into the night with their new ephemeral elixir. It was smartly seized; I grant them that. I wo—'

BONG!

The man is suddenly cut off by a deep and rasping clang from the belltower. It penetrates through the earnest atmosphere. Lady Priscilla darts a look of outrage at Mrs. Walthew. Open mouths gape as the dumbstruck crowd intently listens to the macabre tolls. It is the Eldritch Chime!

CHAPTER FIFTEEN

THE PHANTASMIC PARADE

'He has killed again! It is surely that—that dastardly miscreant,' Lady Priscilla cries out in the stunned silence. 'Those cold crushing hands have strangled another. O God, who is this monstrous brute?'

'Where is he? Where is that vile American?' Mr. Carmichael shouts in anger. Mrs. Walthew gazes out over the wall nearby in search of a clue.

Questions abound from the mystified onlookers. Seizing the opportunity, Mary jumps onto a snowy tomb to address the congregation. 'This poor lady, Lady Priscilla Axham, daughter of the Earl of Ghyll, was murdered in cold blood just two nights ago as she rode in the back of a cab. This was after that same driver struck down Mr. Henry Carmichael as he was on his way to the train station. Yet, he is not the first victim amongst us tonight. The despicable American slayed the Honourable Elizabeth Walthew a month ago. And tonight, there is no doubt, he has claimed another!' Her speech stirs discontent amongst the crowd, which bubbles to palpable anger. Frustration at the group's perceived helplessness vents with wild vengeful bawls.

'That Yankee bastard!' one man yells.

'Who let this foreigner in?' bemoans another male voice.

'Where did he do it, ma'am?' a woman shouts. Mary looks at Lady Priscilla who points towards the edge of town, the same direction in which they claim to hear the howling. 'Perhaps he is still there,' the woman adds.

'We should all go and commandeer the scoundrel!' Mr. Carmichael bellows. 'If we find him, we'll give him the fright of his life!' His rallying cry is received with a tumultuous roar. It ignites a tinderbox, and the whole place rumbles with riotous protest. Many raise their skull torches aloft, and some shine their soul's aura high into the sky, so the collective soul-streams create a near-unbroken ring of silvery spotlights that penetrate deep into the void. The dissenting rabble has amassed into a mob set on lynching the villain, and as Lady Priscilla and Mr. Carmichael walk towards the wall, a great horde follows with silent footsteps and vicious barks.

The barks are villainous and xenophobic, and I feel intense unease, but the tales about the man remind me of the beautiful girl in the green dress in the town square. Her voluptuous beauty held a captivation over me, and she spoke both sweetly and with kindness. The man with the

American accent promised to aid the damsel in distress. The thought of his betrayal and the chance to learn more about my own fate causes me to bite my own bitter seed and join the hunt.

Lady Priscilla vaults the wall with much of the congregation in tow. Most surmount the stone barrier with grace as if it were routine, but a few stumble, and one man drops his skull but breathes an audible sigh of relief as it finds a soft landing in the powdery snow. Mrs. Walthew, John and I march at the right-hand edge of the throng, about ten rows back from Lady Priscilla, Mr. Carmichael and Mary, who lead the hunt.

We walk through the narrow streets, leaving the church behind us. There are numerous vocal taunts and shouts around us, but due to the uncertainty of what we may encounter, the three of us remain in tense silence. It is only when I look behind that I shudder at the sight of the immense and haunting rally.

The mob is young and glamorous with their ball gowns, wedding dresses, suits and tuxedos. They billow out from the church and fill the quiet streets. Their appearance is the epitome of elegance, but the sea of skulls, with their jawless gapes and dazzling eyes, induces terror. The houses and cobbles do not accept the light from the deathly totems. Instead, the ghostly aura from the skull lanterns only serves to illuminate the vitriolic gestures of the zealous, macabre pageant. This skirmish of skulls surpasses all the phantasmic sights that this night has held, and it is no dream or hallucination.

In the grounds of the unlit graveyard, the festivities garner no attention from the living. There appears to be an unspoken acknowledgement that the barrier between the two worlds is not breached. The living do not walk the graveyards at night, in respect for the dead, and the dead do not leave the cemetery with their skulls, so they do not frighten the living. We have broken the balance! The dead walk the streets and the sight of a thousand floating skulls would greet any mortal's glance that fell upon the scene. When I left Birchwood Manor, I feared the blood moon would bring the Apocalypse upon us and the Beast would rise. Presently I fear *we* are the Beast and it is us who are delivering the Apocalypse.

Thinking about the likely fate of the girl in the green dress, I want justice—I want retribution. But at what cost? What happens when we terrify the living? If we deliver hell on earth, earthlings will seek revelation and revolt. The omen of the blood moon hangs like a noose around our necks; the splinters of the noose salivate, ready to accept all.

The Beast is within us, and I sense it grinning as its claws sink deeper. I harbour terrible discomfort that the nature of our vast procession of undead ghouls is malevolent, yet I do not withdraw. The parade's genteel attire may reflect the prosperous past lives of these townsfolk, but their behaviour and language in no way portrays the sophistication of high society. I observe no nobility as I inspect this barbarous pack slavering in uncouth and vengeful mania.

My fears of disrupting the balance are eased as we exit the town via an empty rural road with parallel cart tracks in the snow. The procession follows the country lane around a gentle bend until the silhouettes of the treeline show the road straightening. I catch a glint of bright white up ahead. Before long, it steadies to a constant glow, and the shimmering orb dangles beneath an overhanging tree.

Without any audible instruction, the horde halts. Whispers start flooding back from the front. I cannot make out what they are saying, but from this position at the side, I see Lady Priscilla and Mr. Carmichael approaching the orb. The closer I look at the distant brightness, I begin to make out the shape of a crouching person who faces away from us. Mrs. Walthew has understood this and she makes her way forward, as do I. At the front, Mary is facing the crowd, and after an initial reaction upon seeing us breaking the line, she quickly withdraws her protest when she recognises us.

A quiet sobbing grows louder as we approach. Despite having red hair, the crying lady wears a white dress. I breathe a sigh of relief, but guilt is quick to follow; she may not be the girl in the green dress, but she has just died.

The young woman sits slumped at a pull-in at the side of the road just before where the lane veers left and towards the hillside. Her whole body shakes as she sobs with her head down in her hands. As we squat down beside Lady Priscilla and Mr. Carmichael, she lifts her head and says, 'Lady Priscilla? Is that you?'

I recognise her kind voice and beauty, and I recoil in horror. It is indeed the girl in the green dress.

CHAPTER SIXTEEN

THE GIRL IN THE GREEN DRESS

The imprint of hooves and thin narrow bands cross the road, indicating the cab likely turned around here. Beside the weeping victim, there is a significant disturbance in the snow and a small blood-red colouring. My sleuthing suggests the girl put up some fight and may have injured the assailant, albeit it was likely only a minor wound.

I glimpse the horrifying lynch mob looming, and I understand the need to keep the newcomer to this nightmare realm facing away from them to help restore her calm and not subject her to another traumatic ordeal. I understand too that this young lady's spirit projects a white dress, despite her wearing a green dress at the time of her death.

'Lady Priscilla, you look well,' the young lady says.

'Miss Jeanette Davies, you are always so kind,' Lady Priscilla replies.

'I'm so glad you're safe. The Earl was so worried—we all were,' Miss Jeanette adds. 'I took a cab to Albert's, and on the way back—the driver—he—' Lady Priscilla embraces her as she bursts into a fit of sobs. A torrent of empathy floods through me.

Miss Jeanette breaks the embrace asking in a shaky flurry, 'What happened to you, Lady Priscilla? Where were you? How did you find me?'

'My darling, I went through the same ordeal as you. That wicked cabman brought me here too.'

'No! We thought it was a businessman turned outlaw. A police report stated that a married businessman had gone missing nearby after withdrawing his family's savings. With stories of two people missing within days of each other, we thought they were connected. The rumours were that he had swindled his wife and then kidnapped you, while others thought that it was a secret affair and that you had run off together.'

'That's outlandish!' Mr. Carmichael protests. 'Why would they think that of me?'

'Please, Mr. Carmichael,' Lady Priscilla somewhat manages to quell his rage though he is enthusiastically shaking his head. Lady Priscilla explains, 'I'm afraid these are just devilish rumours, people do love to speculate on fantastical notions. Mr. Carmichael here is that businessman, but we are not eloping or any such nonsense. Unfortunately, he too was a victim like us.'

Miss Jeanette adds solemnly, 'Not quite like us, I suspect.' She looks over at the disturbed snow and small patch of blood. 'I don't understand, Lady Priscilla. I am having this strange out-of-body experience as if this is all a nightmare. I remember him smiling as he clasped my neck, and then, not long after, I saw myself lying over there in the snow. I was barely clothed, and he—he was on top of me!' She releases a tremendous wail and cries, 'What's happening? What's wrong with me? Why am I in a white dress? Why is it so warm?' Lady Priscilla holds her once more.

Mrs. Walthew, Mr. Carmichael and I stare at each other in a stunned and awkward manner. In these quiet few moments, we each complete the puzzle and realise the unthinkable events that transpired to this ill-fated maiden. This revelation exposes a new sickening characteristic of the killer as he did not seem to target young women for carnal thrills until this night.

We watch with painful sympathy as Lady Priscilla enlightens Miss Jeanette to the true nature of where she is. Her initial reaction is surprisingly minimal as she appears numbed by the disclosure. She sits quietly listening to her friend's explanation, until she asks desolately, 'So, I will not become Duchess of Deaconshire then?'

'No, I'm sorry,' Lady Priscilla says. Miss Jeanette sits in sombre reflection.

'Miss Jeanette, please forgive me as I know it is hard to come to terms with this, but I am eager to see my money returned to my family,' Mr. Carmichael says. 'I gave your fiancé, the Duke of Deaconshire, a large payment to start our business arrangement. You said the rumours stated that I withdrew our savings, which is correct, has his grace returned it to the police or my family yet?'

'He did not mention it, but I am sure that he will,' she replies.

Mr. Carmichael grumbles nervously, then says, 'With your help, we can get the bastard that put us here and destroyed our dreams. Where did he go?'

Miss Jeanette lifts her head, and with a nod down the road, she softly states, 'He went back that way. He could be long gone, I'm afraid.'

'Perhaps, but we suspect he may stop to—well—dispose of your corpse.' Miss Jeanette whimpers at this thought, and Mr. Carmichael receives a stern stare from Lady Priscilla. 'I'm sorry, Miss, but it could be an opportunity to put the fear of God into the bastard so that he may not strike again. The whole cemetery has joined our hunt.'

'What do you mean?' Miss Jeanette asks, and Lady Priscilla ushers her to look over her shoulder. As she obliges, she lets out a scream and jolts backwards into Lady Priscilla's arms.

'We could get him Miss, but we have to go now,' Mr. Carmichael insists.

'I don't understand. But whatever you can do to him—do it.'

'Come on,' Lady Priscilla instructs. 'We do need to go, but Miss Jeanette, you've been through enough trauma tonight. I'm not sure what we'll find if we accost that dastardly miscreant. I'd like you to go to St. Paul's with one of the kind ladies. We must all go to try and find our burial place, and I will come back for you.' Miss Jeanette shrugs her shoulders, and as Lady Priscilla helps the quivering girl to her feet, Mr. Carmichael gestures for the hunters to rally once more.

As they approach, Lady Priscilla ushers over one of the ladies, who comforts Miss Jeanette and shields her from glimpsing the monstrous procession up close. The four of us join up with Mary at the front, and with renewed conviction, we lead the charge.

CHAPTER SEVENTEEN

THE DASTARDLY MISCREANT

Our phantasmic parade proceeds along the slow left turn until the road straightens. The hunters' ghastly cursing and shouting return following a short pause to gawp at the poor girl. Amongst the angry shouts are vulgar insinuations relating to her beauty, her ginger hair, and the events that may have occurred.

Mrs. Walthew thankfully distracts me from my outrage at their impolite manners. 'We're getting close, the howling is this way.' Her words are loud, and Lady Priscilla nods as she overhears.

A slight right turn brings us upon a narrow, rustic stone bridge. The sound of trickling water wholly disagrees with the sight of feverish and ghostly fish.

The stream marks the boundary between cultivation and the untamed wild. On the right is a small thicket of silver birch trees that bustle with creatures of the day and of the night. On the left, the tall hedgerow gives way to a low stone wall, behind which is the steep, tufty hillside. The lane rises with the moorland and turns away to the right.

Mr. Carmichael shouts excitedly alerting me to a yellowish hue through the trees. There is a crescendo of unruly cheering as word spreads to the back of the brigade. Mrs. Walthew points into the thicket. 'In there—that alluring howl—it is in there.'

As we turn the corner, our suspicions are confirmed. A hansom cab is pulled over on the left with the black horse that steers it facing away from us. Footprints lead further along the lane and across to the other side where the snow atop the stone wall has been disturbed. A dark figure lurks in the woods with the enthralled animals that gleam in the ethereal light of the hunters' torches.

Mr. Carmichael reaches the cab first. I am close behind. 'Miss Jeanette's body is not here,' he tells the mob.

'There is someone in the wood,' I say. 'He would not have left her corpse on display lest another cab came by.'

I walk past the snorting black horse whose breath steams the air. I am followed by two smartly dressed young men who carry their skulls. From their conversation, I deduce their names to be Myles and Douglas. Both men shine their skulls ahead but only illuminate the lively woodland creatures. I track the footsteps in the snow. Gruff groans emanate from beyond the wall where the shadowy figure toils.

The horse lets out a distressed and jittering neigh. I turn around to see its front hooves flailing high in the air. Myles and Douglas stand in front of it. Their levitating skulls must have spooked the poor mare. With another frightened neigh, the horse bolts!

The black mount charges and knocks both men's torches to the floor. The horse narrowly avoids trampling on their lanterns. As the charger rampages, it pulls the cab along with it. The wheel of the runaway chariot rides up one of the skulls. It fractures. The chariot tips to the side as a narrow burst of blinding white light darts into the heavens. A brief cry, permeated with intense pain, echoes as I witness Douglas rapidly dissipate into non-existence. Before anyone can react, the cart crashes down on top of the rocky wall with terrific momentum. The connection with the wall pulls against the horse, but its stampede is unstoppable. The carriage violently swings back into the road, and the wagon topples as it hurtles into me. The iron chassis knocks me aside.

'BELLA!' I recognise both the voice and the name. The shout comes from the trees behind the wall against which I have been flung. I witness the relentless steed flee, dragging the cart as it scrapes away the road's snowy embellishment. In the middle of the road lies a cracked skull and an up-side-down top hat.

'DOUG!' a woman from the crowd shrieks.

Black boots land beside me. 'BELLA! BELLA! Skittish filly—goddamn!' the deep voice holds an unmistakable American twang. His leather boots hold still below a heavy overcoat. The man lets out a deep sigh knowing a chase is futile. He walks calmly into the lane.

Moonlight caresses the profile of his stern, square-jawed face. Beneath a large pointed nose, his thick moustache is a grandiose marvel of masculinity, the sharp tips of which almost connect with prominent sideburns. Surveying the wreckage, the tall, imposing man squints as he furrows his hand through his short, dark hair. He casually reaches down to retrieve his hat as a war cry surges from the teeming mass: the rabid hunters' thirst for blood!

The fevered hunters charge, wielding their cranium clubs high in the air with spiteful snarls and hate bleeding from their eyes. As the onslaught of undead warriors advances, the chiselled American expels a throaty growl which rapidly transforms into a bone-chilling scream. Staring down the ambush of enchanted skulls, he hurriedly steps backwards. He slips on the icy surface, topples rearwards and is unable to stop his fall. His head rebounds on the hard surface exposed by the dragged cab. The raging horde engulfs the predator-turned-prey. The vicious pack gnashes and barks, and though it is hard to discern through the crowded melee, I surmise that the Lunatics are clubbing him.

The Beast spreads its wings and the pack becomes a savage swarm. The vitriol of the hunters portrays the Beast laughing. One of the baying mob cries that their prey lies motionless, and she erupts in hellish laughter. While some appear to ease off their barrage and heckling, the wrath of others persists. As more of the hunters revert to hysteria, it is clear they are unable to quench their bloodlust. More cries suggest that the man had been convulsing with a heart attack brought on by the fright while others proudly profess to delivering the decisive blow.

BONG!

The menacing reverberation from St. Paul's confirms that their prey has been slaughtered. Drunk with venomous ire, the mob jubilantly howls with exhilaration at the success of their hunt. Witnessing the animalistic decay of once forthright and civilised townsfolk is horrifying. It sours what, in truth, is a great justice as their action prevents their target from claiming another victim.

The crowd disperses. The perpetrator lies still, his carved face bloodied.

After the thirteenth toll echoes through the frenzied atmosphere, a figure rises from the fresh cadaver.

CHAPTER EIGHTEEN

THE LANTERN'S LIGHT

Dazed and confused, the brutal malefactor stares, eyes wide, down at his corpse and then out at the goading celebrations of the crowd that, from his perspective, have suddenly appeared. 'Who are you? What is happening?' he shouts. Initially, no one answers, but a few young girls giggle as they skip past him. 'What is going on?'

No one directly answers the man's question but cries of 'Good Riddance,' and, 'You can't hurt anyone here,' rise from women in the gathering.

'You evil swine!' an enraged woman then shouts. 'My dearest Doug is gone forever.' She kneels at the cracked skull in the road, its light extinguished.

'Don't give him the satisfaction, ma'am,' Myles says, touching her shoulder.

He then approaches the baffled figure, who eyes his skull before forthrightly addressing him. 'Sir, I demand that you tell me what is happening.'

'Welcome, my new friend,' Myles says with a smug smile. 'Welcome to a place where your deeds can be returned in kind. For some—including those you were so eager to send here—this is a place for rest. For others—particularly those far from home—this dwelling is a dank charnel house where the only person who'll come find you is Madness.'

'What are you talking about?' growls the American.

'There is much to discuss, so let me introduce myself, I am Myles Greene.' He offers a handshake with a sly grin but, perceiving his subtle derision, the American scowls at it.

Of the two men, the self-satisfied Englishman stands slightly shorter than the American, wearing a brightly-coloured blue suit with white stripes and a billycock hat. Now appearing with his top hat reaffixed, the American's spirit projection is no different from his living self, and he looks to be approximately fifteen years older than his boyish counterpart, whose attempt at facial hair doesn't pass muster.

'May I inquire as to your name, squire?' Myles asks.

The American ignores him initially to survey the assortment of leering freaks. I cannot imagine what he must be thinking. Calmly, he obliges with an answer. 'My name is Vincent Bartholomew Lawrence of Cambridge, Massachusetts.'

'I think you mean your name *was* Vincent Bartholomew Lawrence.' Myles chuckles and Mr. Lawrence squints. 'Will there be anyone to mourn your death?' Myles succeeds in suppressing a laugh this time but still fails to continue the façade as he is unable to resist extending a wide grin.

Presently, the gaggle surrounds Mr. Lawrence jibing him with more taunts and mocking cackles until someone a little further down the road announces with urgency, 'Time is running out! We must hurry back.' Many in the freak-ish parade gaze up at the red moon, and in response, they hasten their triumphant traipse back towards the church. They shove Mr. Lawrence along with them, and he is lost amongst the gloating ghouls.

I stand up but do not pursue them. Instead, I hop over the drystone wall and enter the thicket. A glimmer of green catches a ray of the red moon. Again, I am struck with sadness because the girl in the green dress lies in death and indignity. Her semi-naked body is sprawled in the snow, and her eyes gawp vacuously at the moon. Her life promised so much, but her death, at least, has been avenged.

Mr. Carmichael and Lady Priscilla look on from the lane. 'It's her,' I tell them, with a heavy tone. Lady Priscilla ex-hales; it is the despondent sigh of someone who was expect-ing bad news but is aggrieved to hear it nevertheless.

Mrs. Walthew remains, too. She is several yards further into the thicket, amongst the feverish creatures that she detests and beside a distinctive disturbance in the snow. A spade protrudes from a half-dug grave, and the earth has been deposited in a pile to the right.

Mrs. Walthew, in her blue dress, kneels several feet fur-ther right in an oddly pristine patch of snow where no grass pokes through. 'I am here! I can feel it,' she shouts excitedly.

I am desperately happy that she will be able to rest. Mrs. Walthew may be a difficult, obnoxious person but no one deserves the torture of purgatory. I have gained respect for her strength and will, and if it were not for her encouragement, I would not have achieved the most wondrous discovery. The howl is my soul beckoning me home. There is hope.

I wait a moment to respect her privacy, but I want to offer my farewell. In a moment of calm, I perceive a slight cooling of the atmosphere and a reduction in the pace and quantity of the rushing critters. The howling has quietened too, and I note its north-western origin in anticipation that it will soon fade altogether. The sky is still clear, but a darkness creeps over the blood moon. I know this to be the reason for the change.

'This will be us too,' Lady Priscilla tells Mr. Carmichael.

As I step forward to offer my appreciative send-off, the blue outline of Mrs. Walthew sinks softly and uneventfully down through the velvety snow until she is no longer there. She has gone; she didn't even say goodbye.

'Huh, so that's how that happens,' Mr. Carmichael says. I continue to gaze dejectedly at the smooth patch where Mrs. Walthew descended. She did not care to wish me well. 'I will rest too,' Mr. Carmichael adds, finally breaking my melancholy stare. 'What about you, Lady Priscilla?'

'I shall console Miss Jeanette and stay with her till the morning. Farewell, Mr. Carmichael.'

'Yes, farewell ma'am.' Mr. Carmichael vaults the wall and he walks to his burial site giving me a little nod and touch of his bowler hat. I return the gesture and hop back into the now quiet lane, which is a scene of carnage. I join Lady Priscilla, and we walk back to the church a reasonable distance behind the marching brigade whose pace has grown.

'Do you know how it is that they carry their skulls?' I ask.

'I don't understand it,' she says, 'but they somehow plucked them from their graves when the lunar eclipse started.'

'Oh, I was worrying that the Apocalypse was coming.'

'No, it's an eclipse, but I can't explain why the souls react the way they do to the red moon. I believe they need to return their skulls before the eclipse terminates; it is not long away.'

By the time we pass the murder scene, much of the ghoulish mob is out of sight as they rally through Ghyll. Only those at the rear of the procession, not yet lost amongst the narrow streets, are visible; the bold brightness of their lanterns starkly contrasts with the dimly lit houses.

Shrill shrieks erupt. Jets of brilliant white dash into the heavens. They streak like fireworks from behind smoking chimneys. It is the same as when the raven dropped the girl's skull. Her spirit was lost as the light in her lantern went out.

The origin of the screams and streaks cascades towards us. Those at the back of the parade race out of the town. Skulls fly into the air as they ride a bulging wave. Many crash and break against the houses, sending their souls streaming into the beyond and condemning their spirits to oblivion. Lady Priscilla and I share a nervous glance as the wave rumbles towards us and those fleeing the procession.

A runaway chariot bursts through the rear of the column. Skulls fly towards us, and one achieves great distance, exploding at our feet. A charging grey steed races at us, unleashing a frightful neigh. It pulls a driverless hansom as it stampedes upon us. A terrified elderly woman sits in the cabin. Lady Priscilla and I dart out of its way. We watch it hurtle down the lane until the glow from its lamps disappears behind the thicket.

Keening screams and angry shouts replace the last cries of obliterated spirits. Events have not gone unnoticed by the townsfolk.

Lady Priscilla and I rush to the edge of town. A sense of grisly fascination permeates my dread regarding the unspeakably foul and inevitable nature of what I know is to come. The sacred divide between the living and the dead has been destroyed.

CHAPTER NINETEEN

EXODUS AND REVELATIONS

W hat greets us is pandemonium. Skulls scatter the street and fill the gutters. Ghouls scramble on the floor in a frantic search for their gleaming, jawless totems. They are lucky; their skulls have not broken else they would be acquainting themselves with oblivion. However, relief is not what is imprinted on their faces as they hastily glance at the darkening moon. Their wide-eyed countenance perfectly encapsulates fear and desperation.

'You must leave now—you will be locked out. The moon is turning,' a man without a skull shouts to a wailing woman. I recognise the woman to be the mother of the little girl who fell prey to the ravens.

'Hurry, hurry, hurry,' she shouts. She has her skull, but her two young boys are scrabbling in the gutter. She cries as she takes another look at the moon and whimpers, 'I'm sorry.' Sobbing, she runs towards St. Paul's, leaving her boys to search on their own.

A stern-faced villager opens his door and steps into the street. He holds the skull that broke his window. A Lunatic swiftly plucks the skull from his hand and rushes off. The man hits the ground hard as he faints.

Another mortified villager has stood dumbstruck in the street since we arrived. He is a bald-headed brute of a man in shabby worker's attire. He attacks one of the skulls as it flies by. It falls to the ground. With a heavy boot, he stamps right through it. The man recoils backwards glaring at both the skull and his boot as the ghoul makes a screeching departure.

The exodus of Lunatics who have retrieved their skulls is replaced by townsfolk leaving their warm houses and gawping in disbelief.

I watch terrified at what the ramifications might be. The townsfolk have no means to learn the truth, only wild hysteria can flourish. The remaining Lunatics scurry with such maniacal frenzy that I believe their fate is already sealed. I think they know it but refuse to accept it. Judging by the number of souls that billowed into the heavens, I estimate approximately fifty Lunatics are already lost. There is no hope for them, and their remaining family will reel for eternity.

A man shouts to the two boys as he discovers two small skulls beneath his own. He races ahead, towards the church, as the boys fall behind collecting theirs. Another man leaps out of a broken window nearby, skull in hand. The bemused occupant looks out from inside. The man who leapt out joins the young boys. At once, they move towards St. Paul's, but then they halt.

The skull lanterns visibly dim. The howling ceases. The world becomes numb. The moon is blood-stained no longer; it is a sliver of silver.

The man with the two boys yells out in despair. My heart aches at their plight. They are locked out of rapture. When Judgement Day came, they were left behind. With the townsfolks amassing, they face hell on earth.

The more curious villagers cautiously surround the three skulls they hold in mid-air. The man encourages the two boys to run while he keeps the crowd's attention—a protective act from a stranger. The boys escape the mortal mob, and the man attempts to flee too, but the bald-headed brute grabs his skull, slams it on the ground and smashes it with his boot for good measure. He roars with delight.

'Good heavens!' Lady Priscilla recoils.

'This is terrible. We should never have left the cemetery,' I say.

'This is a nightmare.'

I stare at the few searching Lunatics that remain. A thought crosses my mind about how they may still find rapture. If they cannot enter their grave, they will still be able to rest if they take their soul someplace dark and quiet. I think to the cave where I was losing my mind. It is not close, but there may be others nearby.

More of the townsfolk come outside. They gasp in horror when they observe mostly cracked skulls strewn across the narrow street. Outrage simmers under hushed breaths until the bald man crushes another skull, annihilating a young lady.

'What are you doing, Mr. Talbot? Who is responsible for this?' a woman asks from her doorway. She wears a man's coat over her nightgown, and she speaks with affluence.

'CRUSH THEM!' The bald man commands. 'All of you. CRUSH THEM!'

'They'll do no such thing,' she says.

'The crushed ones don't flutter off and leave, my lady,' he adds with sarcasm.

'What on earth are you talking about?'

Another of the men in the street disobeys the lady and stamps on a skull. A shriek cries up from around the corner. Lady Priscilla and I wince.

'Mr. Peterson!' the woman scolds. The man does not respond.

'They're killing them all. How do we stop them?' I ask.

'Mrs. Bagshaw needs to assert some authority,' Lady Priscilla replies. 'I do not hold out much hope for that.' I forget that Lady Priscilla still remembers things so well.

One of the Lunatics close to Mr. Talbot finds his skull and tries to creep past the brute. Mr. Talbot points to the cranium levitating just above the ground. Mrs. Bagshaw gasps and cries, 'What sorcery is this?'

'Be more careful,' I plead, wincing in the apprehension of the Lunatic's imminent demise.

'Could be them Havelock Harpies, my lady. If you crush them—' Mr. Talbot stamps; the Lunatic obliterates, '—they stop.' Mr. Talbot smiles at Mrs. Bagshaw and opens his arms to make his point that the skull lies still. 'It is rather satisfying, my lady, they squeal like plague-ridden rats. You should try it; you may prefer skull-squashing to fox-hunting.'

'Don't be ridiculous. Has anyone consulted with the vicar?' Mrs. Bagshaw asks.

'No,' Mr. Talbot replies.

'Well, don't you think someone ought to?'

A tense silence cuts through the street. Mr. Talbot concedes the standoff with a mocking bow. 'Yes, my lady.'

The mortal horde shuffle towards the church, steadily growing in size and voice. Mr. Talbot assumes leadership at the front and searches for more skulls to squash while instructing others to do the same.

Another Lunatic, a young man, moves one of the skulls in the street. 'Be careful,' I say approaching, 'wait for the rest of them to leave. The church is not safe. Run for the hills; find a cave or somewhere dark where you will not be disturbed.'

'Yes, thank you,' he replies.

'We need to go,' Lady Priscilla says, and I agree.

We walk the gloomy streets towards St. Paul's. Shouts rattle windows, and the flames of hysteria are thoroughly fanned by those that spill into the streets. Evidently, the cart ploughed through many avenues, and Mr. Talbot's command is being heeded. It is a massacre.

I offer the same advice to the few Lunatics remaining while the townsfolk amass on the church and the vicarage.

The arguments in the streets and the yells from windows are frightfully fierce. Those who saw events encourage the crushing of skulls and shriek about witchcraft and the devil, while those who did not are aghast at the delusion and brutality of their fellow residents. They all speak the name of one man though—the Reverend Matthew Thornton—for he will have answers.

The commotion in the street is calm in comparison with the cemetery. Those prevented from returning their skulls to their graves panic, terrified. The crying of their families only enhances their exasperation. Lady Priscilla and I do not enter the cemetery. Instead, we follow the mob as they round on the graveyard's gothic gateway, where Mr. Talbot starts rattling the gates in noisy protest. The other streets are quiet, but several people emerge with perplexed expressions. One man wearing a clerical dog collar rushes from behind us to meet Mr. Talbot's clanging alarm call. The hatless middle-aged man, presumably the Reverend, is tall with unkempt blond hair, and Mr. Talbot desists upon his arrival.

The gates remain shut, but several unruly boys jump the wall of the cemetery. 'Get out of there! It is sacred ground,' the Reverend shouts.

'We have to crush the skulls. You did not see it,' one of the older boys in the cemetery shouts back.

'I did witness it, young man,' the Reverend responds to the crowd's muttered surprise.

'Well? What is it?' the boy asks. 'Witchcraft? Necromancy? They went in here. They must be destroyed.'

'Your dear Grandpa and Grandma rest in there, young man. Would you crush their skulls?'

'What if they are vessels for them Havelock Harpies?' Mr. Talbot asks. 'Would you want your body to be exploited for the devil's work?'

'Most certainly I would not,' the Reverend replies, 'but the Havelock Harpies died over two hundred years ago when a spate of paranoia and misunderstanding gripped good men and women like yourselves. This is no time for rash action, we shall discuss this in a civilised manner in the church hall.'

'This *is* witchcraft!' one man shouts at the Reverend. 'Dig them up and burn them. Cleanse the cemetery!'

'If you dig up my wife from the grave. I will see that you enter yours!' another man bites back.

'Please, ladies and gentlemen, be civil,' the Reverend urges. 'Let us discuss in the church hall.' He walks away from the cemetery gates ushering Mr. Talbot and the crowd to follow. They obey the Reverend, which encourages the boys to cease their assault and jump back into the street.

'This is escalating to civil unrest,' I say, worried.

'The vicar is a good and well-respected man, he can calm them,' Lady Priscilla replies.

'Calm them? How do you calm someone when a skull comes hurtling through their window and then floats out again? It's preposterous!'

'Come now, I need to find Miss Jeanette.' I follow Lady Priscilla, and we vault the wall to re-enter the churchyard. We follow the path towards a large gathering where a dozen or so people still clutch their skulls. Two of them are the boys who escaped the mob.

'YOU!' their mother shrieks when she sees Lady Priscilla. 'You're the reason that I'm about to lose my two boys.'

'I did not ask for any of you to follow me,' Lady Priscilla replies.

'What are my boys to do now?'

'They cannot stay here,' I say, then I shout so the others hear my instruction. 'That mob is intent on crushing every skull they find. If you still have yours, you need to get away from here else face oblivion.'

'And where should they go?' the mother asks.

'There are caves in these hills; I have spent a long time in one. They need to vacate soon via the quieter streets.'

'So, I should send my boys off into hills and never see them again?'

'Do you want them to rest in peace?' Lady Priscilla snaps. 'How dare you?'

'Please, both of you,' I interrupt. 'Everyone who still has their skull should go as one group. I am afraid that if you replaced your skull in the grave, you won't be able to rest if you join them. But those who leave won't be alone, they will have each other.'

The mother looks to her boys and hugs them both. The father, still cradling the baby, joins their embrace. The mutterings amongst the others who are locked out imply that they are acquiescent to my suggestion. I hate the idea of separating families, but I don't see another recourse for them.

'When do we go?' one man shouts to me. I hesitate. Am I now the organiser too? If it fails, I will be to blame, and I don't have a detailed plan. The only place I can think to suggest is the caves to the east. Is it a good plan? The man repeats the question.

I look at the clock tower, 'Twenty minutes,' I reply, 'we'll go when the church bell tolls for eleven. From the wall on the opposite side of the church so that we are as far away from the crowd as possible.' Did I say, *we'll* go? Why did I say that? I have my own troubles. I need to return to my own journey while the night is still young.

'I'll 'elp you, pal,' says a man with short, black hair in tight curls. His eyes bulge, and his appearance is counter to anyone else in the cemetery. He has a dark complexion and a vibrant suit, which must have cost a pretty penny at some point in time. It consists of a light-blue shirt with purple waistcoat and trousers, and I must say, I think it is rather stylish.

'Thank you,' I reply.

'Good to meet you, I'm Mr. Frank Grant. You're one of the few talking sense around 'ere.' I thank him again, and within minutes we are on first-name terms. He offers to assist me, and concludes, 'I'll go spread the word, meet you there at eleven.'

'Mr. Webster,' Lady Priscilla then says, 'I will find Miss Jeanette and make sure she is all right. They do not want my help, I feel.'

'It is for the best that you ease Miss Jeanette's arrival. I cannot imagine what she must be going through.'

'Be careful, Mr. Webster. I wish you good fortune in your own search for rest.'

'Farewell, and thank you, ma'am,' I say, and Lady Priscilla leaves for the church.

As I walk to the far wall, I see the moon is close to half full. The sooner we vacate the graveyard, the better. With less light, it will be harder for the villagers to spot the skulls, though gathering clouds in the west threatens to spoil what good light there might be for my own subsequent journey once the moon has returned full. I feel a sense of duty to help these men, women and children rest in peace. I will escort them to the edge of town, but then they will be on their own.

I observe that the west road remains empty. This will be a good way to start because it is away from both the gathering in the church hall and the avenues with scattered skulls. It will then be wise to move south because it is the shortest distance out of town.

'Bloody 'ell, Eddie,' Frank says as he returns. 'Seems you lot 'ad a right ball when chasing that murderer.'

I feign a laugh. 'I never expected so many would follow. Did you?'

'No, I bloody didn't. Leaving the cemetery was asking for trouble.'

'Are there many joining us?'

'About twenty 'ave been locked out, I reckon, they're all coming. Saying goodbye to their families. If only they 'ad a bit more common sense, ay?'

'I still don't understand it. How did they pluck their skulls from their graves?'

'Ah, you're not a long-term resident I take it.'

'No, I'm a wanderer.'

'There's no use to being a vagabond in this world, you know.'

'Yes, once we have assisted their escape, I shall make my own way.'

'You're a good man, Eddie, to devote yourself to 'elp others.'

'I'm not so sure. I have a terrible feeling that I am a sinner. You see this pocket watch,' I say, pointing to my timepiece, 'it conjures a terrible sense of guilt whenever I look at it. How can that be so if I am a good man? Perhaps being a perennial wanderer is the justice I deserve.'

'I only see a kind and 'elpful chap in front of me, and I'd wager that my first impression is not all that wide of the mark.'

'I don't know.' I can get lost in conversation with Frank, so I bring it back to my question. 'So, how did they pluck their skulls from the grave?'

'Well, when the moon turns red like that, the souls get extra energy somehow. I can't explain that part. I wasn't a scientist—well, I don't think I was. It's like the invigorated soul swells, it grows brighter, and the entire skull becomes encased within its engorged ectoplasm. A spirit can interact with their soul, so if you can grab the soul, you can grab the skull that 'olds it. Tonight though, because the skulls were encapsulated inside the ectoplasm or what 'ave you, I could retrieve it from my grave.'

'So, you had yours out too?'

'Yes, I mean I didn't do anything daft with it, they get fragile over time, but I and the others 'ad a little dance and a jig.' Frank mimics and has a chuckle. 'It was merry. There's a bit of a technique to retrieve it, Joshua nearly cracked 'is going too fast.'

'Joshua? How so?'

''E's my son. Don't worry 'e's an adult, not like that poor girl. Joshua wasn't slow enough. It's hard to explain. It's like the ethereal ectoplasm shrouding the skull turns solid objects into a viscous fluid as it passes. Go too quick, and it is still solid, you 'ave to ease it through like.'

'And you have to return it while the moon is still red?'

'Aye. It must be returned before the shroud recedes back inside the cranium which is when the red moon fades. They were so foolish it amazes me. They were behaving like a pack of wolves. They got the chap though I saw. That was impressive.'

'I just hope it was worth it. He won't kill again, but a lot of Lunatics have passed on tonight.'

A crowd of those left behind gathers around us, snivelling after their farewells. The two boys are joined by two older boys with pubescent spots, several young men and women, and a balding older man with a black suit and greying beard. Their appearances range from wedding dresses to labourers' clothing, and tuxedos with dickie bows to silk nightgowns.

'You got a plan?' Frank whispers.

'A loose one,' I reply.

'Splendid, I'll try and boost the morale of these sorry sods.'

Frank addresses the gathering, 'God, look at you!' A silence grows. 'I've never seen such a motley crew.' To my amazement, Frank gets a smattering of laughter. 'Tonight 'asn't gone very well so far, so it's time to make amends. If you succeed, you'll be able to rest in peace once more. Some of these people in this cemetery were your friends in life, but because you don't share a stone with 'em, you don't remember 'em and, more to the point, you don't care. Now, you 'ave each other. Don't all cry at once,' he chuckles to himself. 'Mr. Webster and I are going to 'elp you start your new family. We will 'elp you reach the countryside then you're on your own.'

I tell them my plan, explaining that I want them to travel in a line of pairs through the streets while keeping their skulls low and in the shadows. I add that I want them to cross roads one pair at a time so they are not so easily spotted. 'Understand?' I call out. There is a murmur of nervous acknowledgement. 'Then we are ready.'

We walk to the corner of the graveyard, and then I vault the wall and cross the road. The westbound road remains clear, so I usher pair after pair to come.

Once half have joined me, a commotion rises from the church hall. The townsfolk are spilling out in a raucous voice.

'Quick!' I shout. The remaining Lunatics frantically rush towards me and Frank. 'Keep your skulls low,' I remind them.

I glance at the crowd of mortals, they're breaking off into small groups, seemingly heading home. A group move towards us, but the only safe place is to get out of the town.

I ask Frank to stay at the back, then I lead the group along the westbound road. All is fairly quiet but shouts from the small crowd of townsfolk grow in volume. At each junction, I go ahead to check all is clear then call for the Lunatics to join me a pair at a time as planned. We make it through several streets, switching between southbound and westbound roads. We listen intently to the shouts of the townsfolk as they filter out amongst the avenues. On a few occasions, Frank shouts ahead to inform of their movements.

Escape comes into sight. A forest lies beyond the junction at the end of a narrow road. If they reach the tree cover, they'll be safe. Up ahead, there is a side street, and I tell the couple at the front to wait while I check to see if it is clear.

'See anyone, Frank?' I shout.

'Not yet, but they cannot be far,' he shouts back.

The trees in the forest rustle in a light breeze; it is close enough to run to, but alas, only the young boys possess the energy for that now. The vigour of the blood moon is gone; adults must be content with just a brisk walk.

'Come,' I shout, seeing the side road is clear. It connects our escape route with the street parallel, but being only short, there will be little warning if a group appears. I hear talking and shouting close to Frank's position.

As the first pair reach me, Frank shouts, 'Go!' I usher the next pair across, but the group panics, loses formation, and they all pass the side road at once. That is except Robert, a balding older man, and Mildred, his young wife with dark curly hair, who hesitate.

'My goodness! You were right,' a woman shouts.

I turn to see a group of townsfolk enter the side road from the parallel street. 'Get them!' one of them cries, seeing the flurry of floating skulls. About eight men rush towards us. The women shout encouragement.

'Go! Now. All of you,' I shout. Robert and Mildred hurry behind everyone else. They don't have far to go, but they cannot move as fast as the mortals who are gaining quickly. There is another roar as a group of men run past Frank.

The boys reach the forest. The men pass me and give chase. The older boys make it safely too, and all four children run out of sight. The first of the adults mounts the wall.

'Come here!' one of the men barks. The man is running too fast.

Mildred rushes as fast as she can in her white nightgown, but her brisk walk is ungainly, and she struggles at the back of the pack. Mildred simply cannot move fast enough. She looks behind and screams. The aggressor is nearly upon her. Most of the adults vault the wall, and Robert is only yards behind them when he stops. He rushes back. 'Go!' he shouts to his wife. 'I'll distract them.'

'Robert, no!' She attempts to slow down, but Robert pushes her to continue.

He waves his skull at the approaching man, then hops to the side. The man swings but misses. Robert moves to the side again, bringing them further away from his wife who reaches the wall. 'Mildred, go! I love you. I want you to live,' he shouts. Everyone else has crossed into the forest.

Robert is busy distracting the man when another man snatches his skull. With venom, he hurls the skull against the drystone wall. It shatters. Bone shards scatter on the ground like confetti. Robert vanishes with a wail.

'ROBERT!' Mildred cries.

'Come,' one of the ladies in the forest encourages. Mildred hesitates.

'I can't live without him,' she cries.

'You have to come now,' the woman shouts.

'No.' There is a terrible air of defiance in Mildred's voice. The woman in the forest darts off through the trees and out of sight. The men approach Mildred. 'I love you, Robert. We shall be together in the next life.' She screams and violently throws her skull to the ground. It bursts with brightness. She joins Robert in oblivion.

Desolate, I slump to the ground. The men cheer having scalped two victories.

CHAPTER TWENTY

THE LITTLE CLAN OF COLOUR

T hick cloud cover prevents me from recommencing my own journey, but heavy rain subdues the towns-folk who retreat inside.

I return with Frank to his gravestone, which is distinctly lop-sided. It reads:

> *HERE LIES*
> *FRANK GRANT*
> *WHO DEPARTED THIS LIFE, AUG 20 1848, AGED 52*
> *ALSO*
> *GABRIELLE GRANT*

WIFE OF THE ABOVE
WHO DEPARTED THIS LIFE, JAN 7 1851, AGED 50
AND THEIR SON
JOSHUA GRANT
WHO DEPARTED THIS LIFE, JUL 19 1855, AGED 33

BORN INTO SLAVERY
ASCENDED WITH BRAVERY

'Where's your wife and son?' I ask.

'They were curious to meet the new arrivals,' Frank replies.

'You were a slave once, I see.'

'This bloody lot,' Frank does a sweeping gesture to indicate the whole cemetery, 'would love to see a return to such days, I believe. Too bad,' he chuckles.

'Why?'

'This place is tribal. They cluster together with those who share their surnames. Few will talk to those outside of their troupe, and even fewer will talk to the three of us. Of the thousands 'ere, we're the only coloured faces. You wouldn't think it could be lonely amongst thousands of people, but if we didn't 'ave each other, it surely would be.'

'Will no one talk to you?'

'Some do, some are very nice, like yourself, but they are not always easy to find, and then you 'ave to bloody find 'em all over again during the next full moon. Thankfully, I 'ave a great family; we're adept at entertaining ourselves. Before the red moon rose, the three of us went for a wander around the cemetery to marvel in the outrage which we caused simply with our presence. They believe they are subtle, but you can 'ear 'em murmur about 'ow such an

esteemed cemetery could 'ave permitted access to such beings.' Frank laughs with a face of absurdity. 'The worst they
can do to us is to shout abuse, and some are really easy
to irritate. Who wouldn't want to irritate such prejudiced
rapscallions?' Frank chuckles. 'We are grateful for 'em; they
are good sport.' I laugh.

Frank's enthusiasm allows the hours to tumble almost
unnoticed. I try to lament the loss of Robert and Mildred and complain about the cloud cover, but Frank will
not stand for it. Instead, he praises the inner strength that
saw me lead dozens to salvation, and he explains how this
strength will guide me to my resting place no matter how
far away it may be. Frank has performed a miracle to be able
to boost my morale after such a desolate evening.

Frank also manages to muse on topics of personal tragedy
while keeping the conversation light-hearted. It is his opinion that no one else will join their little clan because of
how their untended grave slumps so prodigiously. He also
remarks that he doesn't know the origin of his accent. It is
not the local dialect, but he claims quite a few families speak
in a similar manner. His accent is recognisable to me, but I
cannot place its origin either.

'Ah, 'ere they are,' Frank says as two people approach.
Gabrielle has long, black, curly hair, big brown eyes and
wears a bright red gown embellished with yellow flowers.
She is radiant, and this is mirrored in her smile. Joshua is
slightly shorter than Gabrielle and shows little emotion. He
has short dark hair and wears a brown suit with a lime-green
shirt. 'We do stand out,' Frank says with a giggle. 'We are
the little clan of colour; dark faces and vibrant clothing in a
sea of black suits, pink faces and white wedding dresses.' I

smile before Frank announces to the arriving pair, 'Let me introduce you to my good friend, Mr. Edward Webster.'

'It is a pleasure to meet you, Edward, I am Gabrielle.'

'Good to meet you. My name is Frank,' Joshua says.

Frank bursts into laughter, 'I said *my* name was Frank!' Gabrielle laughs loudly with Frank while Joshua maintains a stoic demeanour with just a wan smile.

'Hopeless we are, or rather, they are,' Gabrielle starts, 'it's quite embarrassing really, you see, we don't know who is who.'

'I don't understand,' I say.

'Edward, none of us remembers our names,' the man I think of as Joshua answers. 'The headstone tells us, but there is no way to distinguish which of us is Frank and which of us is Joshua. But please, call me Joshua.'

'Oh no,' I react, 'I still remember my name. Do you mean to tell me that I still have further to fall into lunacy—that one day, I will not even know my own name?'

'Yes, I believe so,' Joshua says.

'That could be a long time coming yet,' Frank adds buoyantly. 'We've been in the ground over fifteen years; plenty of the folks 'ere still know their names.'

'Perhaps they are guessing too,' I reply.

'Eddie, at the start of tonight you were lost, now you are found. You know which way to go; you need to learn 'ow to celebrate.'

At that moment, Gabrielle breaks into spontaneous song, 'Once you were lost, now you are found. The Lord has shown you the way. Praise the Lord.'

'Praise the Lord,' both Frank and Joshua instinctively echo. Evidently, this is a family that likes to sing.

The evening passes with improvised gospel song and dance and celebration. I join in. Others look on, but none of us cares. I enjoy dancing with ghouls and singing praise to God. He will guide me, and with their songs, my new friends cleanse my spirit of worry and fear. It is only when twilight seeps through the shroud above that we quell our rejoicing.

I offer my heartfelt farewell to my immemorial friends who will return to their rest, and Frank concludes, 'Eddie! It's been great to 'ave this evening with you. I 'ope you get a good start tomorrow. You'll make it back, I know it. You're a good man. God has given you the strength you need. Keep believing, and 'e will admit you into blissful euphoria.'

'Thank you,' I say as I turn away. I stroll towards the church flooded with bittersweet emotions. I am happy for the evening we have spent together, but I know that I will likely never see the Grants again. I enter the chapel in search of a dark hideout.

'GET OUT! GET OUT NOW!' The piercing shriek is from Miss Jeanette and the whole wretched episode of many hours previous floods back to me. 'Just go!' I hear no other voices besides hers. 'Go away!'

Large and impressive stained-glass windows allow just enough of the dawn light into the church to expose two figures. I stop at the back of the church pews, and at that moment, I realise my mistake. I should not have come inside. Standing in the aisle on the left-hand side of the nave is Miss Jeanette, and several yards in front is her murderer, Mr. Lawrence. Lady Priscilla is nowhere to be found; she must have returned to the roadside thicket to take her rest. I had long enough to realise that this was a likely eventuality because both predator and prey would seek shelter, but caught up in the events, I forgot all about it.

'You are not staying here!' Miss Jeanette shouts.

Mr. Lawrence's response is calm. 'Then where do you suggest, ma'am?'

'I DON'T CARE!' Her reaction is so shrill it could wake those who have just returned to their deep rest. Mr. Lawrence leans backwards and takes a single step, as though she directed a column of air to push him away in her rage.

I remember another place to hide, the tomb room. It is about fifteen minutes away, so I should make it if I go now. I turn to leave, but with my sudden movement, I am spotted.

'Sir, please sir, if you know of another place, please show this vile outlaw,' Miss Jeanette pleads. 'It would be the most inhumane torture for me to face this reprobate any longer. No woman should suffer the company of their defiler. Sir, please show me that some men have the ability for mercy. He is a callous rogue, but you, I pray, are not.' While I am deeply aggrieved with this outcome, my decision is not in doubt. Without speaking, I gesture for Mr. Lawrence to follow. As I step through the door, she says, 'Thank you, sir, you have afforded me a shred of dignity.'

I trudge out of the town and up the hillside. Just once I glance behind to see the daunting silhouette of the man tailing me. I intend to keep as much distance as I possibly can from this brute. The kind gesture to the girl is little consolation as I dread the many hours I have ahead lurking in darkness with this grotesque scoundrel.

The walk through the once-magical forest has lost all its fascination. It had been mesmerising and quite hilarious watching the animated struggles of Mrs. Walthew. The enchantment has been thoroughly dispelled. It takes merely a few minutes to pass through the barren wood with my thoughts dwelling on the murderer that pursues me.

Entering the manor, all is quiet. I dart straight to the secret room in the hope that I might shake my stalker. The stairwell is pitch black, and I tumble down, falling through the door at the bottom. I am greeted by shimmering gold and vivid colour. The sconces still light the room though the fire has died; Mr. Walthew must have forgotten to extinguish them.

'Heavens above!' Mr. Lawrence exclaims as he enters with much more grace than myself.

Why must I spend the day with this despicable fiend?

CHAPTER TWENTY-ONE

VINCENT
BARTHOLOMEW
LAWRENCE

V incent Bartholomew Lawrence prowls the vault marvelling at the curios and their historical value. I keep
to myself, squatting in the corner against the tall, colourless
statue that gazes towards the door opposite. I am not willing to engage in conversation no matter how enlightening
his knowledge of the ancient gods may be. The inept humanity possessed by this foul brute afflicts my sensibilities
to the point it quells all intrigue to the dastardly nature of
his daring schemes. This day's redemption will be found

in silence once he understands that I have no desire to be conversant.

Having examined the relics at length, he finally turns to me and says in a gruff voice, 'Whose house is this?' I stare at my feet and do not answer. 'I doubt it's yours. Why do they have such extraordinary artefacts?' I do not react. 'Not ready to talk, Mr. Blue Eyes? That's no trouble.' His calm and confident disposition unnerves me. 'These are stolen, absolutely.' At once, he laughs. 'I could not wish for a better demonstration; this entirely encapsulates the greed and arrogance of aristocracy. To plunder such treasures is testament to treason against mankind. It is SACRILEGE,' he barks, 'to conceal the birth of our history. Were these your friends?' His question is an accusation.

He pauses a short while. I feel his angry stare upon me. I thought he was bad when he was calm. 'No,' he finally decides. 'Aristocrats would not associate with someone so drab.' After a pause, he asks, 'Did you bear witness to their behaviour last night? Strip civilised peers of their lavish status and material goods and they shall unleash their primal nature. While I scorn the fact that they defeated me on the night, all of this proves that my mission had merit. They are vile folk; merely ogres protecting their opulent castles using the disguise of sophistication to persuade the meek masses of their unwarranted worth. They craft the false impression of nobility throughout their lineage to affirm their superiority across generations.' He chuckles. 'A trait which I believe they share with the pharaohs of yore. Unlike many, I saw them for what they were, and I made my mark. They betrayed their own deceitful portrayal last night and exposed their fall from grace. It was a pleasure to witness.

'That dandy, Myles, and his friends were vindictive in how they disclosed my demise and the nature of this afterlife, but I do find solace that my resolute assertions in life are unmasked in death. There is no heaven or hell, only fables reflecting the polarity of man. The fables are merely recast with time. The tales of Ancient Egypt are not so dissimilar from the myths of Christianity. Only—'

'They are not myths!' I snap.

'They are not myths?' he replies with a snigger. 'Please tell me which is true: the man whose virtue is judged by a feather in a ceremony presided over by a god; or the man whose virtue is judged directly by a god?'

I bite my tongue. I am seething. This is blasphemy.

'Ah, of course. The feather is the unbelievable part of the conundrum. Please! When will man cease to dupe itself and heed the design written in nature? It has been twenty years since Charles Darwin unearthed the truth for all to see, so why are we still cast in the shadow of our blindness? It infuriates me as much as those pompous peers.'

His aggressive atheism and assuredness is nauseating. I shall not allow him to impinge it upon me, so that at journey's end, I may bathe in God's heavenly aura.

Mr. Lawrence paces. It seems to relieve his pent-up frustration. I get the silence which I crave.

When he finally stops pacing and sighing, he sits against the stone altar beneath the sarcophagus. He speaks to me calmly. 'You are right to hate me. I went beyond the pale tonight. I am normally a very principled gentleman.'

I still do not wish to engage the man.

'You may judge me to be a villain, but that is not who I am.'

'How?' I yell. 'You defiled then murdered that poor girl!'

'No,' he responds defiantly. 'I strangled her first.' He pauses. 'It is—'

'What difference does it make what the order was?' I shout, aghast.

'She did not have to suffer the latter act.'

'Excuse me?' I have never been so angry! I add sarcastically, 'So committing necrophilia makes you a good person?'

'I cannot defend that. I was intoxicated by power. I concede such behaviour is abhorrent.'

Hostile silence reigns.

Perhaps an hour passes as fury simmers within me, but the quiet helps me restore my calm.

Mr. Lawrence is the one to vanquish the silence. 'I am led to believe that I must return from whence I came.' I utter no response. 'Law enforcement will find out who I am, and my family in Massachusetts will arrange for my body to be returned so that I may be buried with my father. It is the story that the authorities tell my dear mother and brother that troubles me now. What story can they rationally discern after last night's event? I can only hope my devious deeds remain unknown; it will disgrace my family if my name is besmirched. That is my only wish, as well as to return to rest with my father.' He pauses. 'What about yourself? Where are you going? Where is your family?'

I do not answer; partly because I do not wish to, but also because I cannot. Who am I? Besides my name, gender and the direction of my burial, I know nothing. Why I find Mr. Lawrence's accent and voice familiar, I cannot say, but he doesn't know me. So, who was I? Was I a kind man? Did I heal the sick? Did I feed the poor? Did my wife love me? How many children mourn my passing? When will we be reunited?

'Don't know? Or don't want to tell?' Mr. Lawrence asks. 'I was told that time is short for retaining mental coherence to achieve my new mission. I must therefore hurry to Lyemouth Harbour to board a steamer travelling to Boston.'

'Lyemouth?' I respond in sudden excitement. The vibrations from the utterance of that name fells one of the sentinels guarding my memory. I know it! 'How far away is it?'

'I would estimate thirty miles,' his response holds an inquisitive tone.

'Are you quite sure?'

'Yes, why?'

A surge of hope envelops me. 'I might triumph after all!'

'That is your home?'

'Yes!' I boldly proclaim. The sense of relief appeases so much angst. I could be home within a few days.

There is more. The clouds that shroud my memory break and an image rises to the surface. On still waters, a three-masted steamer rests like a sleeping mammoth. I am held high in the air above a large crowd at a dockyard. I have the impression of it being a momentous occasion, and I am filled with pride. Happiness floods and I cling to it. I have a memory of home. It is wonderful.

With joy comes horror. Horror in the form of a decision which I must make. I must return home, but I have only vague knowledge of where home is. If my bearing is out by a couple of degrees, I shall be lost after thirty miles. If only someone was travelling in the same direction and knew the route...

'I can show you the way. We can help each other.' With his offer, my options are made manifest. Either I travel with this reprehensible man or I venture forth alone.

'Why should I assist you?'

'To help yourself.' We both know it is a good answer. And we both know that I offer little to help him. I quietly ponder it.

To travel with this man is to walk with the devil. How could I be calm and civil in his presence? It would seem like an act of forgiveness. I cannot do that. We could walk in silence, but the boredom will only bring the nightmare delusions back. Talking should help keep the delirium at bay, but on what topics could we possibly converse?

'Why should I trust you, Mr. Lawrence? You are a wicked man.'

'Call me Vincent, please.'

'I am not your friend.'

'Nevertheless, call me Vincent. I understand your apprehension, but what could I possibly do to someone who is already dead?' I just stare at the man. He could condemn someone to this purgatory for eternity by simply sending them in the wrong direction, away from their home and their soul. I have no intention of giving him such an idea. 'Besides, you are safe from me. Would you like to know why?' I hold my gaze. 'Because I know you are a good man. You have said so little to me, yet this I know. You called me a *man* just now—a man with a human quality. Therefore, you are not someone to dehumanise or demean. And when Miss Jeanette asked for your help, you gave it without a word of complaint. This tells me that you are not someone who exploits others. You see—I may be a wicked man, but I am a wicked man who kills only the wicked.'

'Miss Jeanette?' I accuse.

'Alas, I am not infallible.'

'You ask me to trust you? She trusted you. You said you would help a damsel in distress.'

'You were there?' he smiles nervously.

'Yes, several of us ghosts were in the vicinity.'

'Did you hear her say she was to wed the Duke?'

'Yes.'

'That was her misfortune. The Duke is an appalling man, and,' he sighs, 'he is also my cousin.'

CHAPTER TWENTY-TWO

THE HAUNTING OF CUTHBERT WALTHEW

An antique clock on the far wall chimes for half-past four when Cuthbert Walthew dodders into the room. His heavy breathing breaks another long silence. The wizened old man surveys the room tentatively before lighting the fire.

'I should say that I know this man, but from where I am not sure,' Vincent says. 'Why does he look worried?'

'I believe that he saw the ghost of his wife a few nights ago. He seemed quite at ease last night, but with all his books on ancient curses, he must harbour some belief in supernatural forces.' These are the first words that I have spoken to Vincent since he tried to justify the murder of Miss Jeanette Davies on account of her being betrothed to his dislikeable cousin. If I am to journey with this heinous man, I cannot continue my vow of silence. That is not to say, however, that I wish to befriend him.

'Mortals can see spirits?'

'Yes, but it was only when Mrs. Walthew distorted the dim glow of the sconces that he noticed her; he saw neither of us last night.'

'Can mortals hear us too?'

'I believe it is much the same. If a spirit were to shout, a mortal may hear it as a mere whisper.'

'And you say his wife was Mrs. Walthew, do you mean the Honourable Elizabeth Walthew?' he says with a laugh.

'Yes, I understand that she was most unfortunate to have met you.'

'Certainly. She was a vile woman who spoke ever so con-temptuously.'

'So you strangled her?'

'Yes. Are you not glad?'

'Glad?'

'Society will be better without her. And, as I'm just dis-covering, she was a thief too,' he says gesturing around the room. 'I did not know of this collection, but it does not surprise me to learn that she is the treasonous matriarch responsible for purloining these artefacts. This discovery makes me prouder of my actions.' I scoff at his twisted morals. 'All these people do is oppress and steal. Speaking of which, do you know whose tomb this is?'

'Mrs. Walthew believes it is the tomb of the pharaoh depicted by that statue,' I point to the tall and colourful stone effigy in the adjacent corner to me. 'Amenhotep I is his name, but I doubt there is a mummy inside; she told the reis who acquired it that she would never open it.'

Vincent laughs. 'Such people and their infinite wisdom.' Vincent turns quiet and ponderous before his face relights. 'Now that she is dead—I wonder...' his mouth curls upwards and his smile becomes wry and cunning; I do not like this side of Vincent.

After adding larger logs to the fire, Mr. Walthew hobbles out to allow the room to heat up.

Vincent's eyes are wild as he excitedly challenges me, 'When he returns—will you aid me in scaring Mr. Walthew?'

'Scare him? Why on earth would I want to do that?'

'These ancient relics should rightly be in a museum, so mankind may learn its history. Shame on you if you wish for these artefacts to remain in private ownership?'

'You will scare the man to death!' I say. 'And, given your deeds, you cannot take the moral high ground.'

Vincent's eyes flare. 'What is the purpose of being a ghost if not to haunt? We'll frighten him into giving up these treasures. He will not die. If he believes the artefacts to be haunted or cursed, he will relinquish them to the authorities. He has so many books on curses, he surely perceives there may be some truth to it, and no decent father would bequeath tainted treasure to his son. This is for the history of mankind. Don't let this treason prevail.'

'You will not twist me to your sick dogma. Leave him be.'

'You are damned mistaken if you think I have not the courage to act.'

Our conversation falls silent; I do not doubt his resolve. I question what I can do. How do you persuade someone who has become at ease with the prospect of causing death to not act in such a way? I can think of nothing.

Mr. Walthew struggles back in with his cane for support in one hand and a clean tumbler and a newspaper in the other. He sets them on the table and proceeds to pour himself a healthy measure of whisky from the bottle he left on the table the night before. Vincent stands up and walks around the room.

'Leave him,' I whisper, so Mr. Walthew will not hear, 'he is a vulnerable old man. He will have a heart attack.' Vincent ignores me, and I watch in expectant horror. His eyes twinkle as they threaten to indulge in mischief.

'Return me!' Vincent shouts in the old man's ear. 'I am Amenhotep I, and I demand that you return me!' Mr. Walthew's finger had been tracing its way over an article but has presently stopped dead and is visibly shaking. 'Return me!'

'No! This cannot be.' Mr. Walthew's words are spoken softly to himself, but the tone of dread is clear.

'RETURN ME!' Vincent cries with thunder.

Mr. Walthew stands up slowly, grabbing his cane. Vincent moves behind him as the old man surveys the room; seeing a Victorian ghost and not a pharaoh will still scare him, but he may not believe the Egyptian curios to be cursed. In a hoarse voice, he yells, 'Show yourself!' Mr. Walthew takes a step towards the middle of the room. 'You are not real! You cannot be!' Vincent looks a little uncertain as the old man approaches the tall stone edifice of Amenhotep I. 'I knew it, it is just my imagination. I've read too many stories.'

Vincent strides towards Mr. Walthew, who is inspecting the statue. Vincent leans his head inside Mr. Walthew's and bellows, 'RETURN ME!' Mr. Walthew spasms in shock, and Vincent suppresses a laugh. It makes little sense that a pharaoh would speak English, but it appears to have fooled Mr. Walthew. 'The curse of Egypt will decimate your family! The curse took Elizabeth, tomorrow it will take you!'

'Where is she?' Mr. Walthew bawls at the statue.

'Her body will only reappear if you return me. If you fail, you will join her tomorrow. I hope Nicholas will prove wiser!'

Shuddering violently, he whimpers, 'Please. No! No!' He cowers away from the effigy.

'RETURN ME!'

The petrified old man shrieks. His cane shakes so much that it gives way. Mr. Walthew collapses to the floor. Looking up at the statue, he sobs and pleads, 'Yes, yes, I will, I will. Please spare Nicholas and return her body to me.'

I look on, terrified for the helpless man. I worry that he may be injured from the fall. Vincent lacks compassion and cannot resist one more. 'RETURN ME!'

'Yes, yes, yes, I will!' Vincent smiles as he backs away and looks at the clock.

He removes the smile and addresses me in a calm but definite tone. 'He'll be fine, but we should be on our way.' Mr. Walthew descends into a hyperactive seizure of wails and unintelligible screams befitting a madman. He flails the cane around, causing many artefacts to crash to the ground.

'He'll be fine?' I ask sarcastically with a firm stare.

'He's shaken now, but they're bound to find her body soon, and he'll recover once he knows the curse is lifted and no one is haunting him. Shall we?' We exit the room leaving Mr. Walthew slumped on the floor aggressively and uncontrollably raving.

There is loud knocking at the front door. 'Mr. Cuthbert Walthew,' comes a shout. 'It's the police. We need to speak to you!' Passing through the door at the top of the stairwell, deafening chimes suddenly ring above the heavy thumps from a standing clock nearby. It is five o'clock. The sun has set, and it is safe to vacate the manor.

'They must have found her. Great timing,' Vincent says.

Frustrated with the noise and events, I sigh and say, 'We need to leave.' I lead the way striding through the door and the policemen outside. Both shiver as though there was an arctic gust.

Thick cloud covers the sky and the spotlight from the police carriage illuminates the ground. The manor's lawn which once held a fresh, unbroken seal of snow is now dimpled with patches of green. Last night, the carpet was laid for our arrival to a mystical but monstrous realm. Tonight, it is grubby, bleak and without charm. We walk the same route through the once enchanting forest towards Ghyll. The brown scrub dominates over the clumps of snow that cling on.

I wish there were a way for me to travel alone tonight, but the cloud prevents me navigating by the moon and stars. Until I see a sign for Lyemouth, I must rely upon my murderous companion for guidance.

At the top of the crest on the opposite side of the wood, I pause, stunned by the panorama.

'Hellfire!' Vincent exclaims.

We gawp at Ghyll. The icy town is ablaze.

CHAPTER TWENTY-THREE

THE PURGE AT
ST.PAUL'S

Giant bonfires burn on the south side of Ghyll, and St. Paul's hides in their smoke. Shadows breed in the streets, dancing between pockets of flame. These fires flare sporadically as if The Beast is belching up the Earth's molten core, while unintelligible screams and shouts travel up to us on the wind.

'We have created hell on earth,' I lament. 'May God forgive us.'

'They brought it on themselves; they have a vengeful nature,' Vincent scorns. 'They should have let me be.'

'So you could kill more people?' I spit back. Vincent laughs. He is clever enough not to respond. 'I pray the Grants are safe,' I say quietly to myself. 'They do not deserve this.' A jet of white billows into the heavens closely followed by another. 'Please God, let this end!'

Descending the hillside, more souls ascend. Vincent grins.

The first sign of violence as we enter the town is at a street close to the town square. 'Get out of my house!' a man yells. He is standing beside a small bonfire outside of a house with a broken window. Various items fly out of the window and into the fire. The man pulls a few of the items out and runs into his house.

There are groans before a man is thrown out through the front door and forced to the ground. 'Get off me, you Bastard! Felix, let me go,' he growls.

'Why should I?'

'I'm not the one burning our ancestors. My parents, my wife, my two children are all in there, and you're desecrating them!'

'The graveyard is possessed. Even the vicar says so,' says Felix.

'He's just pleasing the Duke and the Earl.' They tussle as the man wrestles to escape. He breaks free and charges, then Felix is thrown into the bonfire. The fire collapses around him. His shriek is as shrill as a banished spirit, and he writhes frantically.

'Burn you bastard! How do you like it?' The onlookers rush to pull Felix out. I breathe a sigh of relief as they fan out the flames. The offender walks away calmly.

'Barbaric!' Vincent barks.

'Oh, the murderer has a conscience,' I chastise.

'Yes.'

'Abandon the pretence, I saw you smiling before.'

'Retribution is worth savouring.'

'There is no justice for you.' Vincent does not reply. I pace towards St. Paul's, Vincent follows. I need to know if Frank and his family are safe.

Large crowds surround several bonfires that dot the road leading to the cemetery. There is no one to spare these houses, they are being ransacked; furniture, paintings, and clothing are all being burned. A few families watch on with agony and scream for the police to act whilst the perpetrators shout about revenge for their actions at St. Paul's.

The police presence is concentrated on the gateway to the cemetery at the end of the road. They protect two men; one is Reverend Matthew Thornton, and the other is a smartly dressed old man with grey hair and a thick beard. Vincent informs me that this man is the Earl of Ghyll. Many in the angry crowd cover their nose and some retch; the smell must be awful, and, at this moment, I am glad that it is a sense that I no longer possess.

Towers of flame fill the cemetery behind. People scurry amongst them. Coffins have been piled in tall stacks and set alight. The newly lit pyres retain their shape, while scorched limbs reach out from collapsed piles. St. Paul's stands resolute, but its interred congregation is being decimated.

The townsfolk in the cemetery dig furiously and throw newly unearthed coffins onto the collapsed piles, while Lunatics' pleas for it all to stop fall on ears that don't hear. As one of the neatly stacked pyres caves in, a cluster of souls escape the inferno's surge, and a flurry of these spirits evanesce with their last cries.

I stare despondent, desolate. Fear does not exist when it is finally realised, and I do not possess the strength for rage. The scale of the massacre goes beyond anger; it is hopelessness, resignation. There can be no chance of Frank and his family surviving this purge. The unruly townsfolk exhibit no method of selection; every unearthed casket, limb or crumble of bones is flung on a pyre. Still they build more stacks.

I catch words glinting in the cemetery railings. Someone has chiselled a phrase into the metal. The engraving glimmers in the firelight. It reads: *The Dead Don't Rest Here.* 'Good grief,' I say. As one of the restless dead, I can attest that they're not wrong. This community has encountered frightful charnel activity, and it's exposed that not all dead rest in peace. The desecration is abhorrent, but how else are the townsfolk supposed to react? If you want to be sure to kill a weed, you must pull out all its roots. But it is no surprise that eviscerating the sacred remains of the town's ancient ancestors and the newly deceased alike has led to further unrest. 'Why is the reverend allowing the desecration of his own churchyard? He quelled some of the wrath last night, what's changed?'

'I don't know, but this is appalling,' Vincent says.

'Please don't pretend that you care.'

'I do not want them to dig up and destroy every corpse; I wish only for them to vanquish those whose skulls lay in the streets—those who hunted me.'

'Why does that make any difference to you?'

'The others do not deserve it; I was selective.'

'Did you enjoy playing God?'

'There is no such thing.' I do not entertain his heathen morals any further. I approach the crowd seeking answers.

The Reverend is talking to the group at the front. 'Madam, this is not a decision I took lightly. I leave it for God to judge my actions.'

'This is sacred ground, you said it yourself. How can you sanction it?' the woman argues.

'Madam, I saw it myself. St. Paul's has become possessed by evil. Tonight, we are taking righteous action to purge this sacred ground of all the demons that occupy it. I will not allow Ghyll to become a coven for cabbalists. There will be no evil or actors of evil in Ghyll after this is done. It is God's will to purge the afflicted puppets of necromancy to protect the virtuous heart of this town. We stand against the devil; we do not acquiesce.'

'How can you say such a thing? My ancestors were good, honest and devout in their stand against evil.'

'Madam, every soul in this cemetery was good and God-fearing, yet I witnessed their possession. The intentions of those behind this were to kill. They targeted those closest to our hearts, and they succeeded.'

'Who have they killed?' the woman asks.

'One's very own daughter, madam,' the Earl interrupts in a deep voice which exudes affluence. 'Reverend Thornton should be praised for his forthright stance against evildoers. The perpetrators of this necromancy intended to seize our most magnificent town for their purposes. The Duke of Deaconshire shares in my mourning tonight after discovering that both his fiancé and cousin, both residents of Ghyll, were found murdered last night. His fiancé suffered a demise too unspeakable to utter, and his cousin is believed to have been bludgeoned to death while aiding her defence. Indeed, a cracked skull was found at the scene and is thought to have been the grisly implement that delivered his execution.'

'My goodness!' Vincent exclaims. I gaze bewildered, though I cannot imagine how I would reconcile such events differently.

The Earl continues, 'This, my dear, is merely days after my darling daughter's disappearance, which itself was a few days after a businessman vanished who had plans to start a new venture here. I was crestfallen this morning, madam, as I was told that their bodies had finally been found. But this was not all. They also discovered the bodies of the Honourable Elizabeth Walthew of Birchwood Manor and Lord Harold Mason of Thanham Manor, both had significant interest and influence here. You see, madam, this was a direct attack on the establishment of this town. Six of our finest denizens have been slain, and the Reverend and I would likely be next. By purging St. Paul's, our response cannot be more assured. We will not harbour those of wicked will in this town.'

'I am reprieved!' Vincent cries, before laughing detestably. 'Thank Goodness, my family will retain their pride in me.' Despite being infuriated by Vincent's joy, I feel blessed relief that his family will never learn of the monster he truly was.

I do not wish to dwell on their dreadful misapprehension or encourage Vincent's euphoria any longer. I need to know if the Grants are still *alive*. This purge will surely end soon; they simply cannot burn the entire cemetery. There will be thousands of bodies to destroy; it is too many to burn in one night. The town has made its protest, and by daybreak, they will believe their message of defiance will have been heard by the evildoers. Then, if not before, they may restore what remains. If they do not, no one will want to be buried in a cemetery that is not regarded as sacred. The Grants may just need to survive tonight.

Their family plot was close to the wall where the hunt started and is also where first contact with the mortal world occurred. I explain my intent to Vincent, and we begin walking to the spot. There are a lot of mortals and spirits but no purple waistcoats, no red gowns with yellow flowers and no lime-green shirts—none of the Grants. At the junction, I turn right onto the street where the skull hunt began. My remaining hope disintegrates to ash.

'God in heaven!' I whimper. 'What have we done? Lord, please resurrect this town.'

There is only one voice here: the collective roar of rioters who mire in madness. There are no spirits or advocates for composure. Pyres burn in the streets. Coffins are hurled from beyond the cemetery wall towards the erupting mounds. Many break open, and the street is strewn with a deep layer of decaying carcasses and scattered skeletons. The townsfolk howl through makeshift bandanas, which is their attempt at suppressing the almightily foul and rotten stench. Those on the side and in doorways recoil. Their expressions are pained, and they use their hands to cover their noses and mouths. The rioters wade through the sludge of corpses while crunching bones. Some excite in using their shovels to crush what remains into mulch, while others, typically the older men who cannot muster such zeal, use their canes to push the bodies towards the pyres. The cluster of scorched limbs and the squelching of the secreted fluids is enough to bring me to my knees in distress.

When a coffin topples off a tall stack and sprays its contents onto the ground in front of me, I wail. I wail with such vigour that Vincent pulls me away and consoles me in an emphatic embrace.

I cannot remove the image of what fell from the coffin and gazed up at me from the rancid floor. It was the broken stare of dark and empty eye sockets beside a collection of bones held within a loose, tattered blue shirt and purple waistcoat.

Chapter Twenty-Four

THE MISDEEDS OF MY PAST

Traumatised, I do not speak as we leave Ghyll. I trudge behind Vincent on the dark and narrow country lanes. It begins to rain. There is solemn satisfaction as it grows heavy because it will extinguish the fires in Ghyll should the storm reach the town. It is too late for my friend and his family, but it will come in time for another. Snow becomes slush. Slush becomes water.

Sodden hooves clip and clop as they herald the arrival of the occasional cart. As the horses pull them, the carts creak softly and mechanically. Their guiding beacons signal for us to move to one side lest their metal structure knock us to the ground. The snippets of conversation enlighten us to their curious but happier lives. Distant noises are dampened by splashing and trickling all around. This soothing and peaceful lullaby has turned our stroll along these gloomy lanes into a silent trance. Oh, how I wish I could curl up and sleep. *Tiredness* is not the word; I believe no word exists to describe this lethargy and disorientation to which I have become accustomed. However gentle this ambience may be, it cannot pacify such torment.

I am walking blind with my faith in Vincent, who is quietly confident of the route. His only comment about our path being that Linketh shall be approximately halfway to Lyemouth, stressing keenly his desire to make good time. Tall bushes and dishevelled trees line the lanes. The open moorland recedes to barely tangible silhouettes.

My mind wanders, first recognising how Vincent respects my wish for silence and then to who I am. There is something terribly sad about not knowing if anybody loved you, but perhaps it is just as sad to not know if you should love yourself. After all, how can you know who you are without knowing your previous actions? We only know ourselves because of our memories. How will I react if threatened, if teased, if challenged, if applauded? I feel like an imposter behind someone else's eyes. A burden of guilt weighs heavy upon me, and it resurges each time I glance at my pocket watch. I believe I am undeserving of happiness or respite, yet I do not know why. I think most people believe themselves to be good people, but my doubt causes me to worry. My outrage at Vincent makes me believe that I am good and righteous, but then, his presence does not irk me as much as I think it should. Am I, in truth, no better than him? Like Vincent's obedient lapdog, I plod along behind him, savouring the thrum and the rhythm of the torrent.

A baby cries in the distance. That sense of guilt comes flooding back and I panic, as if someone is trying to unravel my deepest-held secrets. I shall hide this guilt from Vincent lest he think of me as his counterpart in delinquency. 'Do you hear that?' I ask, finally breaking the long silence.

'I'm not sure I hear anything but the rain,' Vincent replies.

'Sounds like a baby crying.'

With a slice of disdain, Vincent answers, 'A baby crying? No.'

It grows louder, but Vincent does not react. One moment it is on the right—a short pause—and then it is on the left. It is as if the misdeeds of my past are haunting me. Now it is straight ahead, and the cries steadily amplify. I know this to be the conjuring of my tired mind, recalling my fright at the vestigial memory of Maria Chester during the tempest on the mountain.

I distinguish a figure through the darkness and the heavy rain. The figure has long hair and stands at a corner in the road. It must be Maria, but I cannot see her face or what she cradles. The cries, however, are piercing and cut deep into my being. Vincent continues to walk, and I do not want to delay, but as I approach the figure, my apprehension builds with each step. From behind the corner, another dark figure emerges and puts his arm around her. The form has short, fuzzy hair. Could it be her husband?

I hold my breath in anticipation when two lamps beam their light upon me. They are from a carriage streaming around the corner. I startle and stand motionless in their glare. Two neighing horses charge. The cart knocks me to the ground and then rolls through me. As the coach passes, I hear footsteps.

'Might we assist you, kind Sir?' The soft and slowly spoken words are familiar. It is Maria's voice, but I fix my eyes on the ground. I know it is not truly Maria, but instead, a spectre borne of my imagination.

'That was a nasty knock. 'Ere, give me your 'and. I'll 'elp you up.' Something grips my arm.

'Frank?' I say looking up. The figure wears a tattered blue shirt and purple waistcoat but... I scream and hurry backwards, away from his frightful form lit by the vanishing carriage. I jump to my feet and rush towards Vincent. He stares, bemused at my shouts. 'Keep walking,' I say.

'Are you all right?' he asks.

'Just keep walking, hopefully, they... will go away.'

'Who will go away?' Vincent joins me as I pace up the lane.

'If you think I'm crazy—you'd be right!' I announce aghast. 'I know those phantoms were not real, but no matter how much I tell myself this, the visions, the sounds, the feelings, they seem so real.'

'What did you see?'

'The same woman that I've seen at least once before as a spectre—a figment of my imagination. I believe my mind conjures apparitions of those I've met on my journey but in a fiendish guise evoking the tragedy of their tragic demise. First, it was a woman named Maria, but now she's been joined by Frank.'

'Frank?'

'Yes, but not Frank—his spectre. Obviously. In the light of the passing cart, I saw them. It was horrid. She—she had no face. And—and Frank. He—he had those big bulging eyes of his. Just those eyes, a skeleton with short, curly hair and big bulging eyes.' I shudder and let out a noise of revulsion. 'But it wasn't Frank, it was that thing that fell from the coffin, reanimated. Tattered blue shirt, dirty purple waistcoat. The shirt hung loose like—like there was no one inside it. Bone stuck out the sleeves—not hands—just muddy, stumpy bone.'

'I didn't see anything.'

'I know! That's why I know I'm losing my mind. It is this wretched sleepless stupor that is my existence. It preys on my sanity and summons freakish phantasms to vanquish what little remains. When things are calm and quiet, they—those things—appear.'

'If they come back, Mr. Webster, talk to me. I will tell you what is real and what is not.' Vincent's words are sympathetic. Perhaps he fears it will soon happen to him, but either way, I am pleased he doesn't think I am fabricating.

'Call me, Eddie. It surprises me to say this, but I'm grateful for your company tonight. It steadies my nerves to have someone who can arbitrate fact from fiction. I can't hear the crying anymore, so hopefully, it has passed for the time being. There is something else strange about the episodes though.'

'How so?'

'Without the moon, I feel totally numb—yet—I felt Frank touch my arm. I can feel those things. My mind adds a sense of touch and feeling to the drowsy delusions. It makes the spectres seem more real; more real than if you were touching me.'

'Then it is a way to tell them apart.'

'Yes—I suppose so.'

The rain pours. Occasionally it eases but never stops. I finally make conversation with Vincent, but it is somewhat contrived as we are both avoiding the obvious subject. I am eager to talk, reasoning that an engaged mind is a sane mind.

Alas, I have to ask, 'So, tell me... Why did you murder so many people? Do you have no remorse?'

Vincent chuckles. 'Many believe that killing any man will corrupt the soul. To that I declare: nonsense! Death does not weigh heavy upon my soul, in fact, it has lightened it. There is nothing more gratifying than ripping life from someone utterly deplorable and maintaining impunity.'

CHAPTER TWENTY-FIVE

GLORIOUS RETRIBUTION

'You must think me a terrible person,' Vincent says.

'You say that murder lightens your soul; these are not the words of a saint,' I reply.

'Allow me to tell you about another terrible person, a man named Earnest Dodge. It was in January of 1865, and he is the first person that I can be sure that I killed.'

'The first person that you can be sure?'

'I was a sergeant in the American Civil War serving under General Sherman, or Uncle Billy, as we called him. Uncle Billy would say, "War is a terrible thing," and he was damned determined to prove it. He led us through hell holes and in frontal assaults in our endeavour to capture Atlanta from the Confederates. You load your weapon, and you shoot. You inflict a wound, but it is only one of many. No infantryman can be sure just who they killed, if anyone at all. War is indeed a terrible thing.'

'Why were you in the war?'

'Do you believe in slavery, Eddie?'

'No. The epitaph on Frank's gravestone read: *born into slavery; ascended with bravery.*'

'Would you fight to end it?'

Guilt rises in me again as though I am raising the guillotine above Frank's head myself. Could I allow someone to enslave Frank and his family? The concept of war terrifies me. I know so little about who I am to be able to answer the question, but there is one thing that I can be sure of: I am not brave.

'What do you say, Eddie? Would you fight?'

How has it come to this? A wicked man is asking me a question about my morality, and I fear that I fall hopelessly short. 'I don't know,' I say, but it feels like a lie.

'When President Lincoln announced his emancipation proclamation, I decided that I would join the Union Army. It was my chance to affect change.'

'How old were you?'

'I was seventeen then, though I waited till I was eighteen to appease my parents. I fought in the great and terrible battle of Atlanta; our victory ensured that President Lincoln was re-elected and helped put an end to slavery. I lost good friends to fighting and disease, former slaves and privileged men, much like myself, with dreams of a modern society led by the advancements of science and not the cracks of whips.

'After Atlanta, we marched to the coastal port of Savannah. In the state of Georgia, slavery was dyed-in-the-wool, and if we were to cut so deep into Confederate territory, we would have to forgo supply lines. Uncle Billy knew that an army was supported by its civilians, and if we broke their will, the army would collapse. Our orders were to forage food and resources, burn everything we couldn't use, free the slaves, and destroy property and infrastructure, both civilian and military. Many in our troop were former slaves, and together we reaped our retribution. Uncle Billy once said about war, "Its glory is all moonshine." We begged to differ. We developed an enjoyable practice whereby we would heat railroad rails and wrap them around trees; we called them, Sherman neckties.' Vincent laughs. 'Uncle Billy also said, "I intend to make Georgia howl," and that, I'm proud to say, we did.'

'So you venerate your general because he allowed you to forgo discipline and commit wanton destruction?'

'To affect change and achieve victory, you must be ruthless. Uncle Billy taught me that, but make no mistake, if there was one man that I wish I had throttled, even more than my cousin, it was Uncle Billy.'

'Why?'

'He is a masterful military tactician, but while I savoured the great emancipation, he held no interest in it. That was about to become abundantly clear. The newly liberated slaves had nowhere to go, and they feared the landowners would force them to rebuild their plantation houses, so they followed us in their thousands. This was proving a problem for Uncle Billy, so when we crossed a bridge at

Ebenezer Creek, he burnt it, stranding the slaves on the other side. What he had not realised, however, was that a troop of Confederates were following us; it became a massacre. The slaves had nowhere to run; most jumped in the river even though they could not swim. They tried to cross but many drowned—it was a tragedy. And there on the bank, smug and red-faced, was Earnest Dodge. His poor horse had a load to bear, and all the while, he taunted us and took pot-shots at those struggling in the water.

'I couldn't forget about him, and my admiration for Uncle Billy was lost too. But it wasn't until after the war that I came to regret that he never met his end on the battlefield. With the union restored, he turned his ruthless war strategy on the Natives. My father may be English, but my mother is half-Native, and her cousins became his prey.

'He had one final gift for the slaves, though it was purely to prevent them from following us further. He issued an order to take hundreds of thousands of acres of land from plantation owners and then distribute it amongst the slaves; an act akin to your fabled Robin Hood but with none of the good grace. So, as we marched north from Savannah, I helped oust the arrogant oppressors and delivered their land to those subject to tyranny—it was glorious retribution. Then one day, we arrived at a plantation house, and you can surmise who the owner was?'

'Earnest Dodge.'

'Precisely. He was incredibly humble, putting on a show. He was a great big man, and even though he was very recognisable, it was only me who remembered him. I ensured that I delivered the good news that slaves would own his land. He said, "You are a fine Yankee, sir, may I have a word in private?" I accepted, and alone, I followed him, but I knew something was amiss. As he waddled through his estate, he said, "I accept that you are only doing your duty and that my land is to be seized, but I do not wish for the money in my quarters to find its way into dirty negro hands." I did not reply; I was not prepared to profit from his whip. But when he reached into the cabinet in his quarters, he did not pull out any dollars, but instead, a preloaded percussion pistol.

'I dropped to the floor as the bullet flew over my head. I jumped to my feet in a cloud of white smoke and my lungs filled with the smell of sulphur. I trained my rifle on him. Earnest pleaded for his life; he became a blubbering buffoon. Later, I discovered that he had a revolver and a Springfield rifle preloaded in the same cupboard; it pertains to the considerable arrogance of the man that he would choose a traditional single-shot pistol over a revolver. Nevertheless, he had a hot, smoking gun, which meant I could return fire and maintain impunity. I shot him in the gut. Many good compatriots had received gunshot wounds to the stomach; it was a near-certain death sentence, and they died in agony.'

'That's barbaric!' I say.

'In his cellar, we found sex slaves as young as twelve. We learnt that if they got pregnant, he stopped feeding them till they either died or miscarried. When I heard later that Earnest Dodge died, my soul leapt with joy. And when President Johnson overturned Uncle Billy's order that gave slaves the right to own their land, there was no one to claim back Earnest's estate, so they are the few slaves that, to this day, remain landowners in Georgia. I feel thoroughly good about myself for that.'

'And why are you telling me this?' I ask.

'I want you to know that while I am, indeed, a terrible man, something good can come from a person's death.'

'The law exists to prosecute men like Earnest Dodge,' I say. 'It is not for you to decide.' Vincent does not reply. It is dark, and I imagine he is raising an eyebrow. 'What did you do after the war? What brought you to England?'

'I left the army, and I led a respectable life. I worked mostly as a hatter at my father's haberdashery in Harvard, and I took on the business after he passed away. I served many students who studied the sciences at Harvard University; that was my true yearning—to study to become a great scientist or inventor.

'A few years ago, I attended a lecture by Alexander Graham Bell at the Skiff Opera House. He demonstrated an electromagnetic telephone exchange whereby operators were able to receive and transmit audio messages whilst being miles apart. And last September, I visited the Blackpool Illuminations where they had a row of arc lamps at the seafront; I cannot express keenly enough how magnificent it was to experience artificial sunshine illuminating a dark, moonless night. And yesterday I read that a man named Thomas Alva Edison patented the invention of an incandescent lamp. These are truly modern and exciting times, and it was my dream to walk amongst these men and drive forward what I foresee to be a scientific revolution. I had attained the qualifications and, indeed, a place to study at the Harvard Graduate School of Arts and Sciences. Still, despite my father being part of the English aristocracy, we held none of our family's wealth, and with the haberdashery struggling, I was forced to refuse the place because we could not afford the expense.'

'Was there no means for you to attain a scholarship?' I ask.

'Sadly, I was not so fortunate, but they were kind enough to allow me a year to gather funds. That was when I discovered that my grandfather, the Duke of Deaconshire, had died. We were set to inherit!' The excitement in Vincent's voice conveys no sadness for the man's demise. 'At once, I embarked upon a voyage to collect our inheritance, and with it, I would also have the means to complete another keenly held desire—to visit my ancestral homeland. I wrote to inform the Duke of my intentions, and I boarded the Lyemouth steamer as a steerage passenger before my letters could be answered.'

'When did you arrive here?' I ask.

'It was the start of the summer, but it was not until I arrived that I discovered my family's deceit. My late grandfather, Old Albert, had put his affairs in order in such a way that my father's side of the family received nothing. Many years ago, there had been a dispute as a result of my father's marriage to someone with Native blood, and this was the result. Old Albert had, in fact, passed away two years prior, but the family refused to contact us altogether. My cousin, Albert, the new Duke, would not even meet me; I received a very politely worded letter informing me that he owed me nothing, that I should return home and that there would be no further correspondence.'

'So there was no money for your studies?'

'I did not even have funds to return home! I was stranded in a foreign land, seething with rage.'

'And you started killing people?'

'No. I held a bitter hatred towards the aristocracy within my own family and that itch for glorious retribution had returned. However, my motive was too manifest to strike with impunity, but soon I was to discover that it was not just the aristocracy within my own family that was rotten. A seed had been planted, but it took time to grow. It is a gruesome tale, but allow me to explain...'

CHAPTER TWENTY-SIX

THE ROTTEN MURDERS

'I found a job as a cabman,' Vincent continued, 'with the intention that as soon as I'd earnt enough, I would board the ship back to Boston. During the lonely journeys at the back of the cab, I'd fantasise about how I could wreak my revenge upon my British family. Of course, I would never do it, but as I rode unnoticed between the villages and the stations outlining this county, I was stewing in my thoughts.

'Each day, I'd meet the middle and upper classes, and I would attempt polite conversation through the small trapdoor while they sat in the cabin. The middle-class passengers were a mix of friendly and unsavoury charac-ters, and I did not think too much about it. The aristocrats and upper-class occupants, however, would very often treat me with extraordinary contempt, particularly upon hearing my accent. Their behaviour was reminiscent of Earnest Dodge and other Confederate slave owners. Very few would engage me in a mutual conversation. I can understand many were simply not interested in talking. I grew tired of the monotonous thrum of the cart, so I would try, and if conversation was not forthcoming, I did not force it.

'With the aristocrats, discussion was rare, but when they talked *at* me, they would sing like a bird. It was evident that many, not all, had lofty opinions of themselves and would lecture me on the way of things including proper order, etiquette and social standing. They were at the top, and I was at the bottom. I was no threat, but I was no equal either, a subject to be taught a lesson and put in its place, particularly if I told them that I have Native blood. They would openly muse about the barbaric Catholics and the noxious Irish. Most did not enquire as to my ancestry, but upon hearing my accent, they would joke about Americans and say, "at least you're not Irish!" Many went much further with shameless and brazen remarks about incestuous Yanks or how Americans are descendant from vermin and traitors.

'I was maddened by their warped opinions and sense of supremacy, but I would not react. When they spouted this utter horse shit, the journeys became more entertaining as I marvelled in bewilderment. I would despair and rage, but I would enjoy it, and I was interested to know how widespread these myths were. I conducted a little social experiment: when someone got in my cab, I would try and stoke them into talking *at* me. Soon the quieter ones would sing too, and there was a strong link between someone's social status and their level of delusion and sense of supremacy. Soon, I just targeted the upper classes, and like greedy trout, you'd be surprised how often they would bite. I would smirk the whole way through their ridiculous assertions, and they had no clue I was mocking them. One man who was a regular customer was Lord Harold Mason.'

'Lord Mason...' I say, enquiringly, 'Why is that name familiar to me?'

'Did you know him?' Vincent asks.

'Perhaps. You know, when I first heard your voice, I found it familiar too. And the name of your horse, Bella.'

'Is that so?'

'I cannot say why that is. It's like déjà vu. I had hoped that you might have recognised me.'

'I'm afraid not.'

'Well, it matters not. Please continue. I believe you were about to give a thoroughly good explanation for why you became a cold-blooded murderer...'

Vincent smirks, then says, 'I prefer the term, "vigilante". Nevertheless, Lord Mason's eyes would light up when he saw that I was his driver. He would leap onto his soapbox and lecture me further on the derangement of the former colonies by inbreeding. He charged my countrymen and me with a conspiracy to ruin British agriculture. He grumbled about his economic struggles as a result of a dramatic fall in the price of grain, which he blamed solely on imports from American prairies. He knew my mother was half-Native, and he would bemoan how poor leadership allowed the conditions for such "specimens" or "vermin" like me to be born. He referred to the American War of Independence as "man vs animal" and claimed victory was only achieved when the British finally realised its great empire should not

contain such bestial savages. He flagrantly reprimanded me
with all of this in his arrogant and righteous way. I had told
him that my mother was half-Native for the entertainment,
but his relentless insinuation that she was bestial incensed
me even beyond those Confederate slave owners. I wanted
to tear his face from his skull!

'Following the war, I was always honest and law-abid-
ing until very late one evening when I was transporting
Lord Mason, we were held up by a robber. It was a clear
full-moon night at the end of November, and it was bitterly
cold. Earlier in the day, I had taken Lord Mason to his
elderly mother's residence in Thanham, and he had asked if
I would provide the return journey to Ghyll that evening.

'I arrived at Thanham Manor at midnight, and soon, I
was enjoying another rant about how the British never lost
the War of Independence. It was on the road to Mosskene
that we came across the thief. He stole from me as well as
Lord Mason. The bastard rode off into the darkness, and his
despicable laugh made me mad.' A robber, a hansom cab,
the road to Mosskene—it is as though Vincent is retelling a
forgotten nightmare of mine. Nonetheless, I do not interrupt. 'As we rode back, Lord Mason had the nerve to blame
me for the robbery. I was amused no longer. He asserted
that the robber and I were in cahoots and that he would
explain all this to the police. I bit my tongue while he went
on and on.

'Then he got the reaction that he deserved! I pulled over,
letting him believe that I was stopping to reimburse him.
My blood was alight by the fires of fury and the flames
cascaded through my veins. Despite the surging wrath, I
calmly stepped down, walked forward and opened the door
of the cabin. The portly middle-aged man, with a large

square-ish head, sat looking at me with a vacant, slightly confused, expression on his face. I smirked as he had not comprehended my next move. The dawning shock on his face was tremendous. I rushed in and clasped my hands around his throat. I knelt on his lap to keep him still. I tightened my grip as hard as I could, his eyes bulged with terror and his arms flailed wildly and hopelessly. I had expected more of a fight, but his feeble, pathetic struggle involuntarily brought immense pleasure. I knew only then that I would see it through, and I beamed at him knowing my inferior grin would forever be etched onto his pupils. Our eyes were locked as his neck throbbed. I felt more alive than a horse with ginger up its ass, yet I felt no pain from what it seemed were tepid punches though I did bruise badly later. I held tight, constricting the pulses of the bulging blue veins popping out of his throat and forehead. "Murdered by a degenerate, how humiliating." I thought I had spoken it calmly, but I can't be sure if I compensated for the heightened emotions. A laugh erupted from deep within me as his eyes lost focus and turned glassy. Through the pulsing, I was making contact with a powerful, unseen force. I had roused the strength to purge these lands of such mindless aristocrats. Their toxic doctrine is a plague more devastating to societal progression than the impact of the Black Death on the population of Europe. I had the power to erase any man or woman who openly dehumanised a person or a race. I saw these aristocrats, not as lesser humans but as too human, too flawed, too willing to let their blind ignorance not just rule their lives but to impinge on the lives of the populace.

'Finally, the throbbing ceased, and the embrace of life lifted from his limp corpse. I was shaking with excitement and basked for a thrilling moment in my newly discovered vigour. The clean kill was a fantastic reward which aided disposal, but it still had to be carried out smartly. I had to calm myself down to think sensibly in case someone approached. The first thing I did was to prop up Lord Mason and close the cabin door. I entertained the idea of depositing the body in one of the many deep lakes that fill the landscape, but that would take too much effort and preparation. Where I had parked was too exposed, and I hadn't a shovel to bury the man, so I rode as fast as I could to the woodlands near my lodgings in Ghyll. There were no passing cabs to witness me transporting a corpse, but a solitary walker, who hailed my cab, gave me a terrible fright. I sped past, and thankfully, that man didn't report anything. I reached the woods without further detection, so I dumped Lord Mason's body, collected a spade, then returned to dig his grave.'

'Using my new-found strength, I shovelled up the mud ferociously fast. The hole was nearly dug when I saw the glow from a cart in the distance. I hid behind the wall, confident in my assertion that no driver would dare stop to investigate an abandoned cab at such an hour. Even if they did, I did not believe they would find me or the body. Sure enough, they sailed past. When I finished digging, I thought about whether I wanted to keep a trophy, but I realised that I had no great desire; what would I even take? The man had all his signet rings stolen by the thief, and if there were anything I could pawn, it would risk raising unwanted questions. I dumped the body in, and he landed face down. I didn't bother to turn him face up; I liked that it was one final indignity. I quickly piled the earth back in before carefully placing the top layer of grass and moss which I had cautiously extracted so that it would be difficult to distinguish any difference from the roadside during daylight.

'The next part of the plan I thought was wickedly clever. I cleaned off my muddy boots and reported the "abduction" of Lord Mason to the police. I felt it very likely that Lord Mason would have indicated to his elderly mother in Thanham that a "Yankee specimen" would chauffeur him that evening. I doubted that he would be able to quell his enthusiasm for his new lecturing hobby. The authorities would therefore quickly ascertain that the missing person was in my cab, so an excuse was needed, and this perfectly fit the bill. The uniqueness of the robber had presented a novel instrument for which to pass the blame. I felt it made more sense to claim it as abduction and not a typical robbery, after all, why else would he have a cab and not just a horse? A lie surrounded by the truth is the hardest to spot, and it worked brilliantly.

'A few days later, the police explained that two others had reported the strange thief south of Copsefield. It pained him to divulge that there were no leads or letters of ransom and that perpetrators of such crimes are seldom caught. Upon hearing the news, I feigned frustration, and the emotion would have been legitimate had I not turned to vice myself that night. In truth though, I was overjoyed. The policeman had just affirmed both their cluelessness to my participation, and that lawlessness here is rife. You limeys kid yourselves with the illusion of law because you have big, historical institutions and you cast aspersions on the American frontier, but this avowed that the level of unruliness is closer than many imagine. Sure, there are no Native Indian conflicts, but an outlaw can operate almost equally unabated in either setting if they are smart. If I were careful, no one would ever know, and my outlaw career—or rather—my vigilante venture could flourish. While this genuinely excited me, I felt I had been opportunistic that night as I had with Earnest Dodge, and once I had calmed, I became more hesitant in pursuing the deadly cause. That was until New Year's Eve when the Honourable Elizabeth Walthew came into my cab,' he fakes her accent as he speaks her name and chuckles to himself. 'She delivered her pompous title with such flamboyance.'

'I can understand you were livid by his behaviour,' I replied, 'but I can't believe you thought the rational reaction was to strangle him! The police would never have believed his accusation against you as it was surely only bluster. So what was it about Mrs. Walthew that made you strike again?'

'You've met her! Isn't she vile?'

'She's complicated,' I respond, keen to not pass judgement.

Vincent elaborates. 'I formed an instant dislike for Mrs. Walthew just from her introduction. It was close to ten o'clock and this helpless, but cranky, old woman approached the rank in Ghyll.

'After I replied to her introduction, she said, "Oh dear, an America, how revolting." As I closed the door of the cabin, I looked at the wrinkly skin at her neck. It would be too easy, I thought. Without a challenge, there would be no satisfaction. I was trying to suppress the dark thoughts.

'"Boy, what did you do to trick the company into hiring a degenerate specimen from the Yankee territories?" I did not answer. "There shall be no funny business, you hear?" The old hag was reading my mind. She spoke so much like Lord

Mason that I assumed they were likely good friends. It had taken only a few remarks to rekindle the seething embers stoked by Lord Mason. During the short ride, her taste for further curt assertions lit the fuse that let the cinders combust. I was engulfed in rage, and she was branded to become ash.

'I acted that night to quench my wrath and to strike this loathsome and oppressive syndicate of aristocrats. On only this occasion was there little gratification in the actual throttling as she was so hopelessly frail. I pulled over close to where I had buried Lord Mason, and it happened in much the same way except for one unexpected and utterly dis-gusting difference—she voided her bowels! The fetid smell was appalling, and it took a long time to clean up. I did not report anything to the police this time. No one knew she got in my cab, and no one thought to ask me any questions. I executed it flawlessly, and now my modus operandi was set. I was a vigilante. I left it a while to see if there was a reaction. There was only a little speculation in the local newspapers, and the passing comments of armchair detec-tives put it about that dementia or old age was most likely to blame. She was rarely seen and seldom liked by those I encountered, and they presumed the old bat had become food for the foxes.

'On Monday evening last week, I picked up a buoyant Mr. Carmichael from the rank in Deaconbury, and he asked to go to Faunton train station. With no railroad through the heart of this county of lakes and valleys, these long and lucrative twenty-mile journeys to the surrounding stations are frequent. He did not divulge what his business was, and this lack of disclosure made it sound shady. He'd arrived early that morning and closed out "the deal of his life". He was consumed with egotistical arrogance and voiced how he finally had gotten what he deserved. He eluded that he'd parted with a lot of his family's wealth and that his wife would forgive him very shortly; she supposedly had no idea. He insisted though that it would soon return double due to the Duke's influence.'

'The Duke?' I ask.

'Yes. He was very proud to drop mention to my cousin, not knowing that it branded him too. I also sensed that he craved to join their syndicate and garner social status. He was irritatingly confident about the venture, and just as Albert had ruined my dream, I wished to ruin Mr. Carmichael's. It was also an opportunity to hurt the Duke without suspicion. I went through the same procedure, except my route would not naturally pass my pull-in that was just south of Ghyll. At a junction after Lordale, I took the road north instead of south. It was risky, but I judged that with him being unfamiliar with this county, he wouldn't notice. Fortunately, he didn't realise, and unlike the previous time, it was a good, clean throttling. I won't lie, it was thrilling and thoroughly satiating. I continued working that night and returned much later to bury the body.' Vincent lets out a spontaneous belly laugh.

'What's so humourous?'

'Mr. Carmichael doesn't live near here, does he?'

'No.'

'By helping to rally the horde that slayed me, he faces the same shamefully destitute future as I.' He chuckles. 'He could have found his grave and been at peace. Instead, his body will be taken hundreds of miles south, so he must wander damnation like you and I. At least when my memory fades, I will be on board a homebound ship; he will be very much lost.

'I was getting a little carried away with my new hobby, and it was only a handful of days till my next victim. O Lady Priscilla! I liked her, at first, she was frisky—but—sadly, she was so condescending of the Irish.'

'Sadly? You didn't have to kill her!' I interject with great enthusiasm.

'The barometer for me was whether somebody stooped low enough to dehumanise another, so—yes, sadly I did.'

'You are not God or some holy emperor! It is not for you to adjudicate who lives and dies. If civilisation has come anywhere, it is that individuals do not decide life and death on a whim.'

'Ha! An emperor? It is these aristocrats that act like Caesar and his legion of followers. They make sure they keep all the power while the peasants have none.'

'They don't kill people!'

Calmly, Vincent responds, 'Oh, don't they? These are the righteous who hoard their wealth and ignore the malnourished on the streets. These are the nobles who cheer at the gallows when an impoverished woman is hanged for stealing food. They preach the notion of their high-bred dominance to ensure they are not dethroned. I've known slave owners and I've known aristocrats; they are one and the same. They have blood on their hands, don't doubt it.'

'There is no slavery here, Frank is testament to that.'

'They would soon have Frank work to the bone to try and get this land to produce cotton in the middle of any icy winter, should they have the chance. A leopard doesn't change its spots. Sure, they can't own slaves, but they still find other means to fleece the masses and purloin priceless relics.'

'You say their perception is warped, but so is yours.'

'I'm right.'

'You're not!' His calm assuredness is so infuriating.

After a pause listening to the rain, Vincent says, 'It doesn't matter anymore, does it? Do you want to know the rest?'

'Why not?' I reply despondently.

'I knew the young woman in my cab was the daughter of the Earl as soon as I picked her up. She was known for being sociable, and although I'd not met her before, I'd seen her picture. She disembarked the last train at Faunton. Living in Ghyll, I knew she had a reputation for not conforming to what the daughter of an earl was supposed to be, and I was keen to know what people meant by that. She had a rough sort of beauty, a stern face, a little rotund, and two friends who were laughing at her jokes. Her friends got a separate cab, and she got in mine alone. It is quite daring for a young woman to travel alone, but who would attack the Earl's daughter? She'd had a few drinks, and her tongue was very loose.'

'I remember I said to her, "I live in Ghyll too. What is the Earl like?"

'"Like a doe-eyed buffoon who thinks his precious daughter can do no wrong!" she was quick to answer. I laughed. "He's bright enough," she went on, "bright enough not to pry into the company I keep as he knows he would only worry. I keep coming home, and that's all he really cares about." It was quite refreshing to meet a somewhat rebellious and witty aristocrat—but—that's where my liking of her ended. She picked up on my accent. She said, "I don't meet too many Yanks—at least you're not Irish. No Irish heritage, I hope? I believe your nation is full of those cockroaches."

'I replied saying I had none which allowed her to elaborate further. What is it with these people referring to everyone as rats or cockroaches? It is detestable! It meant I had to act, and I kept to my tried and tested method. Once I pulled over though, she gave more of a fight than the others. It was very satisfying.'

'What about you kissing her and whispering in her ear?' I ask accusatorially.

Vincent lets out a hearty laugh. 'I thought I was telling the story! I'm glad it stuck in her mind,' he laughs. 'As I've said, I did enjoy it. I would add my own little flair to gall them in their dying moments. The best part was always when the spark in their eyes flickered momentarily as it extinguished—ahhh.'

'Goodness me! You were really gaining pleasure from it.'

'It was exhilarating! The surging thrill of the life-and-death stakes was wonderfully addictive. I was hooked—couldn't wait for the next person, and then the stars handed me a present with a cute little bow.'

'Miss Jeanette Davies,' I answer miserably.

'Yes,' Vincent replies. 'The snow scared everyone inside before it was even dark last night. You English like to portray yourselves as a hardy bunch, but at the sight of the first snowflake, you cower like a frightened foal. The snow in Cambridge and Boston is much worse, but I fancy I'm more familiar with how to handle it. There were not many looking for a cab but even fewer cabbies willing to risk having to pay for any damage on the slippery roads. The quiet lanes were perfect for me.'

'What you did to Miss Jeanette was depraved,' I say. 'It cannot just have been out of revenge against the Duke?'

'I didn't want to kill her. Truly, I didn't. Miss Jeanette was kind-natured and showed no malice, unlike the others. And she was beautiful. Her wispy red hair, soft pale skin, sleek emerald dress and those soulful green eyes. Oh, she was my seductress. I did not want to hurt her, but she'd told me she was the Duke's fiancée. I wish she hadn't told me because it created the perfect opportunity for revenge against Albert. It felt like fate handing me this glorious gift, but as I look back now, I fancy I was searching for an excuse.

'Her voice soothed me; her giggle aroused me. I lusted for her, and Albert did not deserve her. I held all the power, and there was no way I was going to allow her to become Albert's chattel. The thought of the beauty pleasing the beast was dreadful. I could see Albert smiling at me. I wanted to smile back. I savoured the thought of his reaction as if he could see what I was doing to his betrothed. I had now taken something from him and redressed the balance. I didn't think of her reaction because she was dead by then—' I scoff in dismay. 'I didn't know her ghost was watching. She was in a terrible rush to collect a letter, that was all. I never got a chance to read it; I hope it was important.'

Vincent seems to wait for my response. 'I don't believe it became that easy,' I say with resignation. 'It's depressing, frankly. Poor Jeanette, she didn't deserve it, she seemed a goodly soul. And her poor family; I don't believe even you can justify what you've done to her parents.'

'If the Duke starts a war, then someone will get hurt in the crossfire.'

'How can you be so unrepentant?'

'My sole aim was to remove those in society who oppressed and subjugated others, those who felt they had a divine right to keep peasants in the shackles of poverty. I could not engage in open warfare, so I had to get them, quietly, out of the way.'

Out of the way! Those words in his accent regurgitate a lost memory. In my mind, I see a cab hurtling towards me, a black horse named Bella, a passenger slumped in the cabin with a glassy stare, and a cabman with Vincent's voice yelling, *Out of the way!*

Vincent continues, 'With the regrettable exception of Miss Jeanette, I harmed only those with ill intent.'

'So, nobody else suffered fatal consequences as a result of your murderous actions?' I say.

'Not one soul,' Vincent says proudly.

'Well, that is where you're wrong.'

'Oh really, do enlighten me.'

'That man you passed on the roadside,' I say. 'If you didn't have Lord Mason's corpse in your cab, you could have given him a ride, taken him somewhere warm. But, instead, you left him to freeze to death out in the cold.'

'A wild accusation!'

'Oh, but it's not.'

'How can you possibly know that he froze to death?' Vincent asks. It may be dark, but I can see that he is grinning.

'Vincent, that man was me.'

Chapter Twenty-Seven

THE HORSEMAN OF MY APOCALYPSE

O nce upon a nightmare, a man wandered outside on a bitterly cold night. Not only was the man frozen, but he also felt abandoned and betrayed. It was as though the darkness and coldness of the night possessed those who refused to help him. But then he heard a chariot racing towards him, and the man found hope. A bright lantern glided through the darkness like a resplendent angel. Was this his moment of deliverance? Then, from the fog of night, a mare appeared, as black as the cloak of Death. This was no angel. The charioteer was a grim reaper escorting a fresh victim, and he shouted as he attempted to run the man down. Jumping out of the way spared him momentarily. But now, he lay in an icy puddle and knew there would be no rescue. As the water froze, it sunk its teeth in like a snake subduing its prey. The ice bit, and it was only a matter of time until its venom took effect.

The scene of the onrushing cab replays in my head like a spinning zoetrope. I want it to play out differently, but the ink on the paper strip is dry. It is a solitary dreamlike memory without the context of what came before or after, but the predicament tells its own tale. As such, I can only surmise that the cold is what brought me to this land of the dead.

The patter of heavy rain permeates a silence that hangs between Vincent and me. I understand why he would not stop with a corpse in his cab, but he was likely the last person to see me alive—the last person who could have saved me.

'You are a man of integrity, Mr. Webster, but how can you know that man was you?' Vincent asks softly. His grin is gone. 'You had no such knowledge until now. How can that be?'

'It was something you said,' I reply. '*Out of the way!* You uttered those words moments ago, and you repeatedly shouted the same thing as your cab raced towards me. Your use of the phrase rekindled that memory.'

'I did use those words,' Vincent says. He considers his thoughts a moment then adds, 'I am sorry, Edward. I never like to apologise as it is a hollow expression that changes nothing, and why should I apologise for what I intended? But, this, I did not intend. Due to my preoccupation, I was not concerned with your wellbeing, only what you might have witnessed. Your death could have been prevented, and it is deeply regrettable that I played a part in it.'

'You're right. Your words are hollow,' I say.

'I know it is difficult to understand, but I have been convinced of the morality of my vigilante venture—Miss Jeanette excluded—but now... I am not so sure.'

'I do not care to change your opinion. I would rather you focus on leading us to Lyemouth in good time, so I may one day reunite with whatever family I hold dear and find rest.'

Vincent remains oddly quiet. His shady figure jolts as he looks around hurriedly. 'Oh dear,' he says. 'Have we missed the turn? Darn it. I wasn't paying attention—GOD-DAMN! The turn for Linketh must be miles back. We should be next to a lake right now, not halfway up the foothills.'

My resignation at my past fate turns to anger at my current situation. 'You mean to tell me that you have been so caught up in the retelling of your vile acts that you have led us astray.'

Vincent grunts, all but confirming my assertion.

We stop and discuss whether to press forward or turn back. Neither of us knows the hour, but we both judge that dawn is only a few hours away. Vincent outlines the choice as either retracing our steps before turning to Linketh or continuing onto a small village called Elderigg, though he is less certain of the route afterwards.

Elderigg is about as close to Lyemouth as Linketh and is likely an hour or two away. The darkness would make the direct path to Linketh perilous, and the road route would risk the sun rising before our arrival. And while Vincent suspects there may be possible hideouts en route, he cannot be sure.

We are of differing opinions, but our debate is not argumentative. I think we should focus on securing a safe haven tonight without drama; therefore, Elderigg is my favoured choice. Vincent admits that his desire to follow the familiar track via Linketh is riskier, but he has confidence that we will find a solution if dawn arrives before we get there. His vague optimism doesn't convince me, and I press hard to continue to Elderigg.

'Elderigg it is,' Vincent concedes. 'I know a nice inn in Elderigg, perhaps we can find shelter there.'

As we continue, the lane sharply heaves, drops and twists. It takes significant concentration to navigate as there is so little light. When the path dips, there is not even a silhouette to follow. We either correct when we enter a hedgerow or find the path's treeline silhouette on the next rise and make a beeline for it. Vincent informs me that we are on what is known locally as the Serpent's Pass when we should have turned onto Hawne Pass.

'So if you can remember that night on the road,' Vincent says, 'perhaps I can help you recall other information.'

'Such as?'

'Do you know the name, Benjamin Disraeli?'

'Who's that?'

'He's your prime minister. You don't know the name?'

'No.'

'Sir Isaac Newton?'

'No. Why do you care?'

'I want to learn more about the person whom I have wronged. And we still have a long way to travel together. How about Charles Darwin? Do you know him?'

'Hmm. Yes, that is somewhat familiar.'

'I'm impressed. He's a tremendous man, a biologist and author. If you know him, you must know lots of exotic animals.'

'I suppose so.'

'You strike me as someone who is well-read, especially if you know Darwin. What about the poet, Wordsley? He is well regarded in these parts.'

'Yes. Yes, I know that name,' I say happily.

'Well, well, we are both avid readers, it seems. I enjoy—or rather, enjoyed—stories of the gunslingers out west, but also stories of science and fiction. I had a friend, Edward Page Mitchell, who wrote such stories for the *Sun* newspaper in New York City. The last time I met him, we spoke about a story he was writing called *The Clock that went Backward*. It is fascinating to speculate on the future advances of science. Could you imagine such a time when you could travel back and speak to the people of the past?'

'Are we not people of the past?'

'Excellent point, Eddie.'

Vincent seems to be charming me. I have no interest in forgiving the man but holding a grudge will not help me find rest. I am happy to entertain him so long as it aids our journey. 'So, what do you know of this town that we're heading to?' I ask.

'Elderigg is an idyllic village set on one side of a steep valley,' Vincent explains. 'There is nowhere like it in my home country. The backdrop of the valley is stunning, but what makes it unique are the charming, historic buildings and how they climb the sheer slopes. It is small and out of the way, so only a few passengers requested that I take them there. It has a wonderful inn too—the White House—and I would stop by when the opportunity arose. The ale they serve is so good there's a poem about it, but the woman who brews it is one hell of a battle-axe.

'This narrow trail winds its way around the valley, ending much further east; it won't be of use to us past Elderigg. It is a crying shame that it's so dark because the scenery here is spectacular. My hope is that if it is clear tomorrow, we should be able to cross the hills—it will be picturesque and much more direct. It's also a setting steeped in mystery and folklore. A lively fellow in the tavern had me enamoured with tales of the Great Serpent that gouged this passage along with stories of a Great Giant.'

'A giant?' I enquire.

'You are indeed a man who cannot resist a good tale, Eddie. It is said that the giant roamed the hills near Elderigg hundreds of years ago. When he was in a drunken stupor, he would uproot trees and hurl boulders. Some believe that he died back then and that his huge body rests atop the overhanging hillside, which has now grown to cover it. In fact, that's where the name Elderigg stems from; it means ridge of the old giant. Others swear that he only slumbers. Apparently, he likes a drink because they claim that he occasionally rises in the dead of night, searches for liquor and eventually finds it at the inn. As he staggers back up the valley, he leans on the houses, and his tremendous weight causes them to bulge and buckle. It's an odd story, but it's an interesting way to explain why the houses are so slanted and why the inn has such low ceilings and warped beams.'

The town of Elderigg is no more familiar to me, but it does appeal. Vincent continues to reflect on numerous past experiences, and it serves to keep my delirium at bay. And with his nasty account now told, I am keen not to dwell on it any further. Despite his hand in my death, I no longer view him as a devil devoid of humanity. In fact, he seems eager to atone, even if it is only by a small measure.

Some time later, we stand in the shadow of a moonless vale. The rain has subsided, and we listen to the sound of a rushing stream. Dozens of flickering flares snake their way up a steep hillside, and a thought occurs to me that it is the luminous residue of the Great Serpent. The verticality of the village is remarkable. Several of the angular edifices that catch the lamplight appear to hover directly above one another.

'This is it,' Vincent announces. The first glowing beacon reveals a peaceful church after which we follow a narrow, overgrown track uphill to the next lamp beside a farmhouse. We weave to and fro, and while the crooked houses and cottages become more frequent, they are still sparse, reaffirming the remoteness of this time-weathered settlement. Finally, halfway up the fell, we reach the White House inn.

The lamp outside illuminates the white façade though, even on the shaded side, the white walls appear to emit their own radiance. The inn stands behind a rock wall covered with a patchwork of moss and lichen and beneath the augur of the curved black belly of the sleeping giant.

'Shall we go in?' Vincent asks.

I agree and we enter the White House inn at once. We may not be on the best route to home, but at least we are safe from the torture of the sun.

CHAPTER TWENTY-EIGHT

THE WHITE HOUSE

The day passes in the cellar of the White House to the sounds of chinking jugs and half-heard boisterous conversations. To me, the foul language, loud shouts and chauvinistic laughter are disconcerting, while Vincent wishes he were able to partake. Occasionally, a balding old man, with a moustache and bushy sideburns to rival Vincent's, descends the stone stairs into the basement to fetch or restock the barrels and bottles.

Time seems to flow slowly as I cannot relax, but Vincent's light-hearted conversation eases the strain. He has a good sense of humour and natural charisma, and it is surprising when he reveals that he was unmarried. For someone so villainous, he can be quite considerate and even likeable. Being comfortable in the company of someone capable of such heinous acts troubles me greatly, but it is welcome to have someone to help ease the anxiety of such a wretched and important journey.

We discuss a plan of action though it all hinges on the weather. If we can see the moon's glow, we will use it for our bearing. Vincent says the land here is rolling hills and lakes, and he is not aware of any dangerous crevasses or gorges. He is cautious with the suggestion, but if conditions are right, he thinks it might be possible to reach Lyemouth by dawn. As frustrating as it may be, we both acquiesce to the fact that, if the weather is bad, we will stay here. Our pace in the near pitch-black will be too slow, and we could find ourselves without shelter when dawn arrives.

Vincent is impressed that my instinctive knowledge of the sky defeats my memory loss, expressing that I may now be more valuable to him than he is to me. The names of the stars I have forgotten, but the shapes and patterns of the constellations are familiar. I intuitively understand their positions as I know the sun and moon rise in the east. As a result of this understanding, and the image of a steamer in my remaining memory, Vincent believes that my trade in life was a sailor. That may be true, but why does my spirit project an unimpressive figure as opposed to a regal Navy uniform? Doubting that I could be something so noble or worthwhile, Vincent buoys my spirits and warns against a spiral of self-deprecation which, he claims, I actually enjoy. While I still do not believe his notion, his optimism and confidence is infectious.

Alas, night falls, revealing the decision of the heavens—we are to stay, for now at least. The inn is busy as they begin serving food. We are now free to roam and wander unnoticed. I lean against the stone wall in the corner, observing the various groups. By staying in a dark corner, I hope that the patrons will not see my ghost. Vincent, however, does not seem so concerned as he enjoys watching the patrons eating and drinking. No one reacts to his spirit moving amongst them, but there is a lot of movement throughout the tavern, and it is brighter than the tomb room.

Susie Blunkett is the landlady and innkeeper whose brew is infamous locally. She is an old, heavyset and bitter crone. The small, short-haired woman frequently traipses behind the bar or up the stairs close to where I stand. She is a restless soul and is always scowling, but to run such a business, I believe you need to be tough and stand no nonsense. The way the locals either avoid her or immediately obey any slight request proves her fearsome reputation.

The same cannot be said for Sally Ball, the young, tall and voluptuous servant who either follows Susie Blunkett or is subject to her barked orders and curt remarks. When the attractive brunette is in the bar, collecting the bottles or cleaning the tables, the regulars stare and the more brazen direct lewd suggestions to her, or make incredibly uncouth whistles. Sally is headstrong though, and she seems to savour the attention, often responding with her own short rebuttals. Despite the savage treatment Susie might give Sally, she is savvy to the fact that many of the men visit hoping to ogle and tease Sally. Susie, being a shrewd businesswoman, will surely keep Sally on, no matter how bad her skills are as a servant.

The barman, Kenneth, who we saw changing the barrels, is Susie's husband. He engages with each person who props up his bar and, if given the opportunity, will regale them with an old tale of his or one of a fellow traveller. He has been well trained by Susie and instinctively moves out of her way when she is close, as though he understands her current errand. They speak very little to each other, but it seems they both love their work.

The tavern itself fits Vincent's description as it slumps and creaks under the strain of centuries. The wooden support column in front of me is wildly contorted and scarred from a past infestation of woodworm. The wooden beams, supports and wainscot are a dark auburn while the ceiling and the upper half of the walls are whitewashed. There are two roaring fires, one in the large chimney recess on my right and another at the far end. Throughout the night, approximately thirty to forty people remain in the tavern, and the place is close to seated capacity. Above the bar stand empty opaque beer bottles lined up to display the variety on offer. Most people at the tables are drinking the local ale, while whisky is most popular with those conversing with Mr. Blunkett.

The inn has a smoky atmosphere due to the number of men with pipes. The male-dominated clientele are joined by a few women who appear to be boarding overnight with family as well as two middle-aged ladies who also seem to enjoy a tipple. The accents are a mix, with the more affluent travellers who can afford a room being well-spoken while the villagers hold a strong local tongue. There are a variety of game birds on the menu board this evening as well as freshwater bream caught in the brook at the bottom of the valley. Fishing and shooting are fashionable pastimes here with this passion being reflected in the multitude of paintings that adorn the white walls. My appetite does not exist, but I do wish I could savour the wonderful dishes as mortal men do. It is comforting to observe their behaviour, and while their earthly concerns are petty from my perspective, it is also beautiful to see how unburdened they are by the spectral clutch.

When two young men go outside leaving their pewter tankards on the bar, Vincent ushers me over, and we pretend they are our pints while we jovially mimic the two old men next to us talking cricket. When the two young men return, we stay, and Vincent comments on the subtext of their conversation about their spouses. For the first time in as long as I can remember, I relax and join in the fun.

The two of us mock the unaware revellers as if we are defacing a serious portrait with humorous additions. Vincent simulates being the weight on the back of a slumped and lonely old man, whose name we discover is Alasdair, who is struggling for consciousness. I then fondle the bushy moustache of the barman. Vincent makes lurid suggestions as Sally bends down and shudders in repulsion when attempting to do the same to Susie. Meanwhile, I search a man with tremendous nose hair for the sticky green nourishment that made it grow so vigorously. Vincent spectacularly mimics the waddling walk of a man we suspect has haemorrhoids before I pretend to be in deep conversation with Alasdair, who has regained some consciousness and is talking incoherently to himself. Then, when Sally struts into the private bathroom, we both follow, giggling like naughty schoolboys. The hours fly by, and our giddy state is heightened by our bafflement at their obliviousness.

The time passes half-past ten and the pub is less crowded, but the atmosphere is no less lively. The familiarity with which Sally jokes and jibes the men confirms that it is mostly the regulars that remain. The heavy rain persists outside, but the disappointment is limited as it allows Vincent and I to entertain ourselves some more.

Returning inside, I see Vincent has joined some unruly drunkards in the smoky, far corner who have started singing sea shanties. At the bar, a man with unkempt grey hair withdraws with a full tankard and a newspaper. The headline calls my attention: *The Purge at St. Paul's.* The man joins two younger men, in their late twenties, one ginger, the other dark-haired. He slaps the newspaper down as he sits. I move closer to their table in a quieter corner beside a fire, so I can eavesdrop and inspect the paper.

All three men look like they have come straight from a grubby workplace. Each man cradles a pewter mug, and the older chap starts smoking a cigar. The dark-haired man grabs the newspaper and looks up at his copper-headed friend, 'The Purge at St. Paul's. Heavens! You weren't deceiving us, James.'

'No,' the ginger man responds. 'I saw my friend earlier today.'

'The policeman?' the old man asks.

'Yes, he is due there again tonight to clean up and quell any riots,' James replies, and then explains the events to his friends, Fred and Arthur, Fred being the elder.

'You don't think they will continue the purge tonight?' Arthur asks.

'Ahah!' James exclaims. 'Hard to start a fire while it is raining, but—' he pauses and leans into the table, 'my friend told me the purge is set to continue—in secret.'

'In secret? Why?' Fred asks.

'To stop the riots and to quash this story. It is causing outrage. My friend said that when the rains extinguished the fires last night, the town went back inside to their warm homes, but he had to stay outside. His orders were to store any human remains he found. Not to clean up or rebury them. No, to search the rancid mess of mud, blood and entrails for coffins and corpses.' Arthur's gag is amplified by the tankard from which he's drinking. 'They plan to have a makeshift crematorium to burn the rest privately, and at dawn today, they publicly started the clean-up. They are urging calm and claim that they will restore the cemetery now that it has been purged.'

'Madness!' Arthur reacts.

'Oh—and my friend had another interesting story. His shift last night started with him and the Constable going to visit Mr. Walthew at Birchwood Manor. You see, they'd found his wife's body with the others.'

'I'd heard she'd gone batty and went wandering into the woods,' Fred adds with a chuckle.

'When my friend arrived,' James continues, 'they found Mr. Walthew having a nervous breakdown. Understandable because he was anticipating the worst possible news, but then he led my friend and the Constable into a hidden vault in his basement and asked them to return his vast collection of artefacts from Ancient Egypt and—'

'Bollocks!' Fred exclaims. 'So where's this story in the newspaper.'

'It's not in yet. I'm sure it will be soon.'

Vincent's plan has worked, and Mr. Walthew is safe. I withdraw from their table to tell him, but I hesitate. I'm not sure I wish to witness Vincent's gloating or receive another lecture about the vulgarity of aristocracy. I am glad that the artefacts have been recovered though.

Vincent is still singing with the men. They heartily belt out a sea shanty with lewd lyrics about a Miss Sally Brown, but they then change the name to Miss Sally Ball as the rhymes get ruder. Sally cracks a smile that is hidden from the vocal chorus. When their slurred shanty closes to a ripple of applause and laughter from the other customers, Sally announces with a straight face, 'Dream on boys! It's nearly time to return to your wives.' Perhaps on cue, Mr. Blunkett rings the bell for last orders.

'It wouldn't be the first time, Miss! I'll be dreaming of you again when Mrs. Theakston's on her back this evening!' one of the middle-aged men in the racket shouts, to the amusement of the inebriated choir.

'Even the thought of me won't help you satisfy her!' Sally shouts back. A raucous cheer erupts throughout the tavern, and knowing he's beaten, the man laughs incredulously as his drinking companions hurl further insults at him.

At once, the men leave, and Vincent returns. The bell rings once more to signify that the few remaining patrons must drink up. We join those who make their way to the exit. It is still raining. I knew it was unreasonable to think we would reach Lyemouth tonight, but we are set to make no progress whatsoever, and the thought of enduring another night and day of restive angst, with the threat of lucid apparitions, cripples me with worry.

CHAPTER TWENTY-NINE

THE NEST OF NIGHTMARES

Vincent and I sit on the floor of the dark and empty tavern, beside the fireplace. Warmth from the smouldering ashes comforts us as it releases our numbing shackles. For hours we reminisce about the various comical moments earlier that evening, and we speculate on the histories of the more interesting characters.

Vincent has some creative ideas; the two middle-aged women drink away the shame that their husbands are in love with each other, there are skeletons buried in the cellar from Susie's previous husbands, and Sally will cause many rich and powerful men to become heartbroken and poverty-stricken. The idea that the incoherent drunk was actually a sober Scotsman made me laugh the most.

Vincent's buoyant mood recedes when he starts to discuss his family back home. He articulates his sadness about not being able to hold them again, in life, and reiterates the urgency of our journey. He worries about what chance he has to locate his home even if he makes it to Boston Harbour. He struggles to remember where Cambridge lies in relation to Boston, which exaggerates his sombre disposition. Unable to map the streets between his house and the Old Cambridge Baptist Church, where his father is buried, he understands that memory loss is encroaching. It is my turn to boost his morale but finding the right words does not come naturally to me. I recommend that he outwardly reiterates his ultimate destination every hour or so to keep the memory from fading. He acknowledges that the technique has merit, and he utters aloud, 'Old Cambridge Baptist Church,' repeatedly. I am incapable of shaking his solemn demeanour; however, I realise that he wants time to grieve. He must have done so when he first discovered his fate, but he has mostly kept these emotions hidden from me until now. 'You know, I did nearly marry someone once.'

'You did?'

'Yes, she was a beautiful, witty blonde girl who was studying Philosophy at Harvard. It wasn't all that long before I came out here that we parted. I can still remember the paralysing anguish I felt when she began courting some pretentious dandy instead. Wringing that bony art student's neck would have been easier than Mrs. Walthew! I knew restraint back then,' he laughs, 'I still wanted too though. Here, I knew if it ever went wrong, I could high-tail it back home. What I didn't tell you before was that I did gather the money for the journey home, but I was relishing my new hobby. It's silly, I will be glad to forget the heartache, but it's as though this is the last chance I have to remember that part of my life. It's a part of who I am, and I am slipping away. As much as I try to grasp these memories, they slide through my fingers like grains of sand. There are things I want to speak, just to say them for one last time before they are gone.' I encourage him to do so and the final few hours before sunrise are spent with me listening while Vincent evokes stories of his past.

Amongst his reminiscing about his family and friends, he talks of the books that inspired him, the food he loves, and his passions for science and politics. Most of what he says means nothing to me. Taste, literature, history—each concept is a blank canvas to me. It is akin to someone mentioning a person without describing their appearance or personality or profession. You know what a person is, but you have no opinion about them. Vincent also speaks of his excitement for the future. While he still has memory, he can enjoy both the past and the present. I exist only in the present, so while Vincent may harbour excitement for what is yet to come, how can I when I don't know where we have been?'

We move down to the cellar before daybreak, and soon our sight readjusts to the dim and dusty surroundings. There is little down here apart from a large stack of barrels against the wall at the bottom of the stone stairs. We have a light-hearted discussion for several hours, but steadily we fall into slumbering lethargy. After a lapse in time, a frenetic tapping and scratching emerges from the silence. 'Vincent, do you hear that?' I ask.

'What's that?'

'The sound of scurrying.'

'No, I'm afraid not, Eddie.' The sympathetic tone in Vincent's response means that we both understand that my hallucinations are returning. Vincent attempts idle conversation but is powerless to prevent several furry rats from appearing and scuttling nonsensically across the floor, the walls and the ceiling. Their erratic behaviour is irritating, but they do not frighten me. The sound of their scratching grows louder and louder; they are in the walls. It infuriates. The inane dashing continues, becomes faster and their numbers multiply. The constant crescendo of senseless scurrying is giving me conniptions. The endless patter of phantom feet within the solid stone walls soon completely drowns out Vincent and the noise from the tavern. Maddeningly, covering my ears only amplifies it. At periodic intervals, my resistance slips, and I can bear it no more, so I scream aloud. It may be the act of a madman, but shrieking allows me to hear something other than ten thousand incessant claws scratching stone.

Vincent rushes over in an attempt to suppress my suffering. Staring at me with immense worry, he tries to restore my lucidity. Dead limbs do not feel his thumps, and bleeding ears do not hear his shouts. Inner-borne screams and *that* scratching is all that is audible, and his winces confirm that I vocalise my yells. The nature of my delirium has never been calming, so even though I am actively hallucinating, his visual presence provides a reassuring ratification of reality.

The spell finally breaks when the door to the cellar opens. Light billows in, causing the rats to dart for cover under the barrels.

'Oh, thank heavens!' I gasp, 'They've run off.'

'That was horrific, are you all right?' Vincent is showing genuine concern.

As I begin to recover, I break down, and with a whimper, I cry, 'I can't bear this, Vincent!' After a few sobs and a loud sigh, I try to regain composure. 'What time is it, do you have any idea?'

Vincent looks to Mr. Blunkett who is slowly descending the stairs with an oil lamp. 'I don't know but let me see if I can get a glimpse of the clock up there.' Vincent strides towards the steps. He climbs intending to pass through the old man who is cautiously going down with his lantern outstretched. Vincent steps into the oil lamp. The flame causes him to wail deafeningly into the face of Mr. Blunkett before tumbling backwards through the barrels and into the rats' lair.

Mr. Blunkett howls! He loses his balance and crashes down the remaining steps. The lamp smashes on the ground, and the flame instantly combusts the leaking oil. The pool of oil flows and the spreading fire licks the barrels. In the corner, trapped and engulfed, Vincent bawls for help. I stand and approach, but the flames keep me away. All I can do is watch. Mr. Blunkett is crying out too, he is hurt and is frantically patting at the fire on his shirt. The wooden barrels meanwhile are set ablaze.

After several moments watching their excruciating struggle, Mrs. Blunkett enters having heard her husband's commotion. Loudly she instructs, 'Take it off, dear! Just take your shirt off.' Bravely she approaches the rising inferno and helps him unbutton his shirt. With two buttons left, Mr. Blunkett rips off his shirt with incredible pace, and they both shuffle up the stairs. One of the lit barrels leaks its contents onto the burning oil. With a loud hiss, steam rises. The barrel collapses and gallons of liquid expel across the floor. The huge volume of liquid douses the oil slick, and the resultant plume of thick smoke causes the Blunketts to cough desperately. Help from the inn arrives, and they are both pulled up the stairs. The fire on the floor is extinguished but the wall of barrels, stacked to chest height, burn so ferociously it forces me back to the furthest corner of the cellar. 'What happened, dear?'

Mr. Blunkett answers apologetically, 'I'm sorry darling. I know it's stupid, but something screamed at me, it—' he pauses for a deep breath. 'It terrified me! I thought it was a ghost. I panicked and lost my footing.'

'You're getting old, dear,' Mrs. Blunkett replies condescendingly, 'we'll get you some help with the barrels from now on. Now, would you like a cup of tea?'

'What about the fire?'

'Nothing we can do, dear, it will put itself out any moment. The ale won't catch fire. It's a good job we don't age whisky down here.'

'All that ale!' Mr. Blunkett mourns.

'You're not to worry, dear, come now.' The door closes.

Vincent's tortuous cries continue as dozens of rodents escape with piercing screeches. The furnace has expunged their eyes, uncovered their broiled, muscular physique and exposed their gleaming gnashers. Now blind and skinless, the once mindless mischief of rats acts in unison. The spectres stand on their hind legs frantically sniffing out their prey. Their fearsome ivory fangs agitate as they seek out vengeance. At once their heads lock. They have found their target; together they charge towards me.

Their vicious bites send paralysing shockwaves cascading through me. I fall to the floor as I spasm with agonising regularity. Please! Let it stop. I need numbing anaesthesia. I lie writhing and screaming while the phantoms feast.

After an unbearable episode, the barrels collapse. A torrent of ale extinguishes the fire and expels the bloated vermin. 'O God, I pray they never return!' I plead and sob. It is only when I remember Vincent that I quell my blubbering. 'Vincent, where are you?' It is pitch-black, and I receive no response. 'Vincent?' No response. 'VINCENT!' I begin to worry.

'Yes—,' Vincent's reply is long and exhausted.

I sigh, 'How are you feeling?'

'Never better!' Somehow, he still finds comedy. His exasperated tone suddenly changes, 'Goddamn! How long have I been here?'

'In this cellar?'

'No! In England.'

'Oh!' I pause. 'You said it was last summer, so I suppose it has been six months.'

'God! I don't remember. I can't think straight. Argh! We have to get to Lyemouth. I recall that. Old Cambridge Baptist Church, Old Cambridge Baptist Church, Old Cambridge Baptist Church. Phew!' He gasps loudly and repetitively. 'That was goddamn torture!'

'Are you all right?' I dumbly repeat, unsure of how I can help.

'Honestly—no, but give me a minute.'

We both slump on the floor trying to recapture some poise. After a few minutes, I probe, 'What can you remember?'

'The important things, thank Christ! It hurts to think though, my mind is tender. I can remember my close family, but when I think of casual friends—HELLFIRE!' He groans. 'It is still singeing the edges of my faculties.' He sighs, 'And how are you?'

'I can't bear it anymore. I felt those rats eating me, of course they weren't, but I felt it all the same.'

'Christ!' Vincent reacts. I wish he would quell his intemperate language.

'They've run off for now—I pray. Oh, I hope nightfall will be upon us soon.'

Time passes as fast as a shambling old crone, and both our beings are too drained of vitality to muster meaningful dialogue. I try to keep my mind alert by listening to the noises upstairs and solving the riddle of what is happening. 'Do you see them?' Vincent says, breaking the long silence.

'See who?'

'The spiders?' his resigned tone means he knows my answer.

'I'm afraid not.'

'They're prancing on the wall!' He sounds almost awestruck. 'I hate the skittish bastards! I have experienced the horrors of war, and yet measly spiders are the things that flood my nightmares. These are almost comically disgusting but mesmerising at the same time. Their abdomens are grotesquely juicy and—luminescent.'

'Luminescent?'

'Yes, they each have a bulbous ass with a cyan glow.'

'I definitely don't see them. How many spiders are there?'

'Several. They pirouette through the air as they create one giant web which itself possesses a faint blue shimmer. It's kind of magical while also being monstrously hypnotic. They don't seem to be interested in me, so I will stay calm and keep my distance.'

'How big are they?'

'Those sacs are twice the size of their body—but they are quite small, thank heavens.'

Several minutes later, Vincent says, 'Wow, I didn't think I'd be impressed. The whole wall is glistening. It doesn't look real—it can't be real!'

'You have quite the imagination,' I joke.

'Nothing like yours, Eddie!'

I laugh.

A short while later he lets out a burst of fright. 'What on earth?' he shouts frantically.

'What is it?'

Nervously he stutters, 'That one, it—it's expanding. It's expanding out of all proportion!'

'How do you mean?'

'Goddamn! Keep quiet. Please.' The silence hangs. The suspense is filled with my friend's recoiling gasps and groans. In the pitch darkness, I barely make out his outline where he sits against the black stairs. I cannot see the likely grimace on his face, but his silhouette occasionally flinches. He slides down the wall still twitching in revulsion. He shuffles back up and holds still for a moment. 'Go away! Go away!' Suddenly he stands up. He opens his arms out wide and bellows, 'GO AWAY!' He paces towards the opposite wall, stopping just short.

He stares for a while before turning around and sitting in his original spot. He takes a deep breath. 'It's gone. They're all gone. Hellfire! That was genuinely frightening.'

'What happened?'

Vincent regales me. 'Ergh, it became a gigantic spider. Its toxin sac swelled three times the size of its head and was taller than me. It looked diseased! Its abdomen seemed gangrenous, and it had blotchy boils. The boils emitted an eerie green sheen. I almost fainted when one of them burst!' Vincent shudders and heaves. 'Some of it landed on me, and it burnt like acid. Those infected pockets of pus glowed strong enough for me to glimpse the full horror of the creature. It had huge, spindly legs with hairs that shimmered with the same putrid glow.

'It was not aggressive; it seemed to be investigating its surroundings like any curious animal, so I tried to remain calm and present no threat. When you spoke, it took notice. It loudly scuttled around to face you, and for something so big, it was distressingly fleet-footed. It was inspecting you when I told you to keep quiet, and then it shuffled back to face me.'

'How did you stay so calm?' I ask.

'In matters of life and death, you must compose yourself. I fancy the war and fear of the noose trained me well. When the creature's abdomen convulsed, I nearly retched. I knew I had to get rid of it—I was losing that composure. I behaved like it was a bear; I tried to make myself big. It did not attack, but it calmly slid backwards. The lurid web was swaying as if it was in a breeze and the whole wall quaked. The spider receded through the wall as though it did not exist, and it pulled its web with it until it detached. It was far beyond the wall when its glow faded.'

'You handled it a whole lot better than I would have.'

'It takes unnatural restraint, but I fancy that if you can keep your mind calm, then the creatures are too. I surmise that the apparitions mirror the state of the mind that conjures them.'

'That's easier said than done.'

'Next time you have to try; you've seen it done. If you believe they will retreat, they will.'

———◆———

Night comes, but neither of us has much enthusiasm to play or repeat the pranks of the night before. The weather is worse—atrocious, in fact. Continually we check, with the vain hope that it might improve, but we resign ourselves to yet another day at the inn.

———◆———

The day brings renewed terrors for Vincent. All his preaching about calmness is lost on him. Vincent cannot find restraint as he frantically pulls at his arms and his face and his clothes. His subconscious has discovered his kernel fear.

'Webs! I cannot get rid of these webs. Here's another!' He cries in outrage. He pulls and pulls until his voice breaks to a shriek, 'They're inside me!' He switches to clawing at himself. 'I can hear them. Ouch! They're biting.' He claws without relenting.

I fear my own experience with the rats is playing on his mind. When it started, a part of me encouraged his torment, believing the drama would suppress my own delirium. It is working, but presently his commentary has become frenzied, and I feel terrible guilt.

'STOP IT!' he bellows, shaking his head madly with his hands. 'QUIET!' My body jolts to his sudden screech. 'GET OUT!' He scratches intensely.

I try to focus his mind. I try to restrain him. I try everything. My friend is tortured, and I can do nothing to stop it.

I wither in the corner, trying not to watch as his hysterics endure, unabated, till night finally dawns.

We both agree that, no matter the weather, we cannot stay any longer in this wretched nest of nightmares.

CHAPTER THIRTY

OLD FRIENDS

B roken clouds glide slowly and complacently, thwarting our opportunity to navigate by the stars. The moon on this late January night will not rise till a few hours before the inn shuts its doors. We will travel tonight, we are adamant of that, but why walk blind and aimless when we know that our guiding moonlight will soon be at our side? It cripples to even entertain the notion of delaying our exit any longer, but we reason that we must. We return and loiter in the crowded tavern.

The old drunk, who did not appear last night, is back at his favourite table. Alasdair is still quite cognisant at this hour, but amusingly, he is Scottish. Tongue in cheek, Vincent professes his genius for correctly judging that he wasn't drunk at all, while I jokily point out how the Scotsman's ale flows faster than the village stream. In his current coherent state, I am able to understand Alasdair, albeit with considerable concentration. The inebriate sits close to the bar and occasionally interjects in all the various discussions that he overhears. Most ignore him, but as his stupor thickens, more patrons encourage conversation for their entertainment. He is the definitive village drunk, and as he stumbles past people, they look and snigger.

Alasdair has wild grey hair and a face full of wrinkles. His clothes are a muddy brown colour that exaggerates his unkempt appearance. His eyes are a striking and vivid blue, like my own Vincent tells me, but they hold a great sadness within.

The antique clock behind the limping Mr. Blunkett tells the time is close to nine. Vincent remains beside Alasdair as he is still the best source of entertainment. Returning from another check on the weather, I walk back to Vincent and ask, 'Anything interesting?' As I walk between Alasdair and the bar, Alasdair lifts his head up from staring into his beer. He appears to look at me rather than through me.

'I couldn't tell you if what he said was interesting or not,' Vincent answers. 'Perhaps you can translate.' Vincent hadn't noticed Alasdair look at me and now I doubt myself as he is clearly looking for the barman's attention.

Standing by the vacant seat at the table, Alasdair glances at me again. He speaks softly to himself in his thick Scottish accent, 'I'll get ye one pal.' He speaks up, 'Kenny! Can ah get another and also a wee dram o' whisky?'

'Whisky?' Mr. Blunkett responds with surprise. 'You don't drink whisky. Who's that for?'

'Ne'er ye mind.'

'Which whisky do you want?'

'Airdmore please, nae ice nor water.'

Mr. Blunkett gives a strange and knowing nod upon hearing the order, 'That's the one from Skye, right? It's been a while since you've ordered that.'

'Aye.'

'This one's on the house,' Mr. Blunkett kindly offers.

'Cheers, Kenny! Yer a good'un.'

'It's nothing. Do you ever think of returning to Skye?'

'Aye, I miss the place, but ma home is here now.' Mr. Blunkett shuffles over with the mug of ale and whisky tumbler. 'So wha' happen to ye?'

'It's silly. I fell down the stairs in the cellar.'

'He saw a ghost!' a young man at the bar adds cynically.

'Ye did?' Alasdair asks with intrigue.

'I thought I did, but I couldn't have done,' Mr. Blunkett replies with a sombre tone. 'I'm getting on now, and things play on your mind in that dark cellar.'

'Do nae doubt yerself, Kenny!'

'Thanks, Ali! You're the first tonight who doesn't think I'm crazy,' Mr. Blunkett adds cheerfully.

'Aye, I believe ye.' Mr. Blunkett smiles and limps back to the bar.

'I'd believe you too if I was plied with free drink,' the young chap at the bar implies hopefully.

Alasdair slides the glass of whisky to the empty seat where I am standing. He states quietly but boldly, 'Billy! Here ye are pal.' Staring at the seat, he continues, 'Was nae sure it was you t'other night. Ye lookin' young but ah recognised yer cap. Hope they be keepin' ye well up ther.'

'Who's Billy, Ali?' the man at the bar asks having overheard. His smile suggests his only intention is to deride

Alasdair, who ignores the question. The man looks to Mr. Blunkett for an answer.

I catch Mr. Blunkett's hushed response, 'Billy was Ali's old drinking partner. For years they'd both come in and sit there. Ali ordered the ale and Billy always drank whisky neat. Billy was a local farmer here, but ever since he died last year, Ali has been coming in by himself. He won't ever let anyone take that empty seat. It's unusual for him to order Billy's favourite whisky though. He must be having a rough few days.'

'What brought him down here?' the young man asks.

'Ali was a trader in antiques, and he would occasionally stay here. That's one of his, in fact,' he says pointing out the rustic clock. 'He met his wife here and has lived here ever since. Agnes sadly passed several years back, they never had any kids, so the poor man is a little lonely these days.'

'Oh, that's sad.' The juvenile at the bar looks over his shoulder at Alasdair with new respect.

'Take a seat would ye?' Alasdair asks.

'Vincent, I think Alasdair saw me. He—he thinks I'm his old drinking partner,' I say.

'You'd better have that drink then!'

'How?'

'Well if he can see you, he won't want to see you just looking at it.' With that, I squat down, so it looks like I'm sitting on the chair, and I reach for the whisky.

Before I can do anything else, Alasdair picks up his tankard and toasts, 'T' old times, pal!' In response, I raise my right hand, pretending to be holding the glass and return the gesture. 'Do nae worry about me Billy, but could ye do me a favour pal? Just one thing. Tell Aggie ah still love 'er. Tell 'er I have nae forgotten 'er, far from it. Am nae sad, am glad ma English dove is soarin'. Cheers, pal.' We toast again, and Alasdair finishes his brew. Vincent looks at me dumbfounded. 'Another please, Kenny!'

'Right you are.'

Looking at the untouched whisky, Alasdair adds, 'I'll help ye out, pal.' Alasdair throws the whisky to the back of his gullet and his face gurns as he swallows. 'Ergh, I'll ne'er understan' why ye liked tha' so much.'

With that, I slide out of view so as not to haunt the old boy any longer. 'Shall we go and check the weather?' I urge Vincent.

We step outside, and above the hills across the valley, we see a brilliant white aura behind streaks of thin, broken cloud. We decide to go, but there is an ill omen in those clouds; they claw at the midnight pearl with the haggard fingers of a banshee.

CHAPTER THIRTY-ONE

THE MARE AT THE MERE

Strolling away from the inn, passing its stables, the clanks and brays of restless horses supplant the clamouring of intoxicated patrons. Within moments, we move through the village centre which consists of only a post office, a general store and a farrier's shop. We ascend the steep lane that weaves through the crumbling houses. The dim ambience escaping through the curtains and the columns of black smoke billowing out of slanted chimneys publicise the inner warmth of these abodes.

The last lamp heralds the end of this small enclave of civilisation, and its meek lustre portends as the harbinger of uninviting pathways. Four routes are presented: a narrow path, clutched closely by agitated oaks, that arcs back to-

wards the village; a sheer track leading towards the summit
of the giant's belly; an eerie, exposed farm track that also
trails up the hill; and an overgrown lane which rolls adjacent
to the ridge.

We take the farm track, as it is most suitable for our
north-western heading, and we bid farewell to the antiquated settlement. The guiding lanterns fall deep into the
basin and are partially concealed by pillars of black smog
and covering vegetation. The waning celestial pendant,
scratched by the dark oracle, hangs low. It offers enough
brightness to hint at deep green and reddish-brown colours
in the foliage up ahead and along the ridge. We crest the
rise and peer over the other side. The snoozing sheep in
the farms on either side are soon lost to the hill's shadow.
Further along our bearing, the ground steadily swells, and
formidable peaks impose off in the distance. The darkness
to the south suggests a depression while the terrain is rugged
directly north. We peel off the muddy track when it turns,
and we cross the last farm. Using only the moon, we gait
through the knee-high moorland brush.

Time is lost effortlessly as conversation flows, naturally
veering down strange tangents, as it does between age-old
friends. It is the first time, however, that I appreciate how
oddly puerile Vincent's laugh is. This must be partly why
I now feel so at ease in his presence. It softens the sharp
aspects of his character, which his steely calmness and
square-jawed, moustachioed countenance inherently portrays. Our stimulating exchanges halt whenever the moon
unmasks its hazy shroud, allowing the breath-taking landscape to bask in its anaemic glory.

Vincent extols, almost starry-eyed, about the polarity between the jagged peaks and the unruffled lakes. I marvel

as I gaze upon the vast reservoirs that shimmer as they wait—but what do they wait for? I get the sense that they wait to shatter so that they can cast their chosen charm to restore and reseal their unbroken silver mirror. It is the mystique of Mother Nature that something so submissive can be so assured. The pallid, monochrome vista stirs many spiritual thoughts within us, and although we differ wildly and defiantly in our beliefs, we are unified by our sense of awe.

The hours tumble. I attempt to gauge time's passage by the height of the moon. Our slow hike through the steep, tenebrous topography assures that there will be no miracle of us reaching Lyemouth tonight. The night inevitably slips in its bid to resist the relentless surge of dawn. The sky is still black, but I perceive dawn to be only a few hours from us. The cloud layer has sunk, and we enter a delicate mist as we crest a minor peak. We continue across flat terrain through tall, spiky scrub. The fog reduces visibility to a few hundred yards, though the moon's light still reaches us. At the edge of visibility, the fuzzy vegetation subsides to a dark, smooth surface. Something is moving—twinkling. A bright white phantom dances elegantly in the moonlight. Its form is unclear, but it possesses a certain grace and majesty.

'Do you see that or is my imagination rebelling?' Vincent asks nervously.

'Yes, I see it.'

'Phew! I don't know what it is, but it's alluring,' he says. I grunt in agreement. 'It looks like it's under a lake.' There is a definite shoreline between us and the gleaming apparition. Water distorts its effulgent form. The mirage slides side to side before it holds firm in front of us. This shining beacon then swells in size. We edge forwards, with the lake's shore less than fifty yards ahead.

Without a splash, the mysterious phantasm emerges from the lake. Out of the water, it resembles a familiar creature, and bounding towards us, it lets out a lively whinny. We halt as the spirit-animal advances upon us. Unleashing another high-pitched neigh, the horse circles us twice. The phantom's sheen sparkles with strange splendour. It gallops back to the lake, and its playful nature entices us to follow.

Dumbstruck, I look to Vincent. 'That isn't an ordinary spirit,' I say. 'What could it be?'

'It didn't seem threatening, but I'd say it's luring us to the water. But even so, what can it do to harm us?' A silence separates us, and as we creep closer, he says, 'Are you sure a spirit projection cannot appear like that?'

'I've never seen a spirit quite so—shiny!'

'Hmm—,' Vincent's response lengthens as he audibly ponders. Warily, we encroach further forward. Reaching the edge of the lake, the horse stands stationary, and the perception is that it is leering at us from under the surface.

Smooth pebbles cover the miniature shoreline. There is a dark void a dozen or so feet into the mere. The water's surface ripples gently, presumably from a breeze too weak to disperse the fog. Standing at the edge, we watch the vivacious creature renew its coax by darting deeper into the lake. The surface below the shallow water is coated with a lattice structure formed by omnidirectional strings of prismatic moonlight that wave softly and mesmerisingly.

Cautious, I assess whether crossing the lake is our best option. The thin mist is only capable of obscuring a hill that rises beyond the opposite shore, not hiding it. Either side, however, the fog drapes an impregnable wispy, white blanket over the panorama. Is it cunningly concealing safer passageways, or does it help us obviate perilous pitfalls?

'It doesn't look too far; we shouldn't get lost if we cross underwater,' I say.

'I agree. Are you ready?' Vincent responds.

'I am worried, though, that I might panic purely because I am underwater. I know it is a foolish concept, but I suspect I have been pretending to breathe even though it is obsolete.'

'I believe I have too, but it is mind over matter. We will descend slowly to get used to it. If you need to rush out, do so, I will come with you. If I feel suffocated and retreat, will you join me?'

'Of course,' I respond plainly. It is dubious to consider that he will retreat first. Nonetheless, it is this non-judgemental and comforting reaction that endears me to him.

'Thank you, we must stay together. It is not far, but it could become dark down there.'

'All right, I'm ready,' I say. My words belie my worry.

We step forward slowly, and our feet enter the mere. If anything, the minor heat from the moon is amplified by the water. Reaching the dark patch, we test the bottom and determine that the descent is not too sudden. We keep a slow, steady pace, and I see the silvery white horse pirouetting as we submerge.

'—good?' Vincent tries to speak, but his voice is bass and muffled.

I try to reply '*Yes*', but in my own ears, it is just a loud, indistinguishable reverberation. It is not possible to talk down here. I look at the lake's still surface inches above my head. The pallid rays sway brightly over the black void.

We descend further, and I am relieved that I do not feel unduly anxious. I check on Vincent, he is fine too, but it is getting darker. We submerge deeper. The darkness emboldens and attempts to cloak us in its cape. I very briefly greet Dread before Fear shunts him into the black void beside me. What if Vincent and I lose sight of each other? What if the cape hides the moon and renders me lost and blind? But there is still a great brightness ahead of us; we cannot be cast adrift while we retain sight of this creature. Yet more encouraging is that the dazzling beast is ahead—no longer below us. Realising that we do not need to descend any further and with Vincent still visible at my side, the lesser evil that is Dread returns and ripostes Fear. Then the gleaming, amorphous shape prances towards us and both Fear and Dread are banished for good.

The creature's luminosity brightens both our beings but not the lakebed. It's the same way the souls within the skulls only illuminate the enigmas of this spirit realm. Up close, this soul-revenant of a mare halts her canter and lowers her head. She has a pink nose and a brilliant white mane which covers the left-hand side of her neck. Vincent and I, together, reach out to stroke this pearlescent pony. The frigid moon offers a slight sense of touch. Her milky coat has a gelatinous texture, and I brush my hand through the soft, water-like threads that comprise her mane. The water horse is receptive to our petting, and she lifts her head friskily with little echoing whinnies. Excitedly, she skips away before returning. She is just a playful pony. Vincent and I are beaming at one another as the maritime mare bounces and leaps between us as though we are her first playmates in centuries. Then Vincent boldly attempts to mount her, and though she retreats in protest, she continues to frolic.

We allow ourselves to momentarily forget our time-bound mission to cavort with this resplendent beast.

After a short while playing with the horse, Vincent points to suggest we leave. Begrudgingly, I nod, and orientating the moon to our left, we continue to the far side of the lake. The unctuous mare continues to harass us in the hope that we linger. We pet her as we walk, and she frantically bounds around, encouraging us to stay. We are close to surfacing. The mare darts out from behind us in her typical lively fashion and nudges us both backwards. She really doesn't want us to leave. We stroke her some more before continuing forwards. We break the surface.

We step on dry land. The shimmering horse pokes her head above the surface and nickers. She is sad.

'I'm sorry horse, but we must go,' I explain pointlessly. We turn our back to the lake and climb.

Through the mist, at the top of the hill, a castle towers. The intricate, gothic architecture of the daunting edifice welcomes Luna's ghoulish kiss. The castle's gloomy dereliction hangs over us like a spider hidden in the rafters waiting to drop from its silk thread to claim its morsel.

'Pleasant creature,' Vincent says, breaking my building apprehension.

'What was she?' I ask.

'What do you mean?'

'She wasn't a normal spirit. She was radiant. She lit us up like the souls *that* night.'

'I have no idea.'

'I think she's lonely.'

'Yes, and we will be lonely too if we do not continue,' Vincent warns. I am not distracted; we must continue.

We rise above the thin layer of mist. Without the haze, the castle's sharper contours are no less unnerving. Four octagonal towers, in various guises of decrepitude, line the rocky ridge with an immensely high wall linking them. Each of the two nearest towers holds, within their structure, a tall, narrow watchtower. Crenellated battlements run the entire length with worn spikes protruding at random intervals, and atop these spikes, ravens perch and peer down upon us like silent sentinels. The looming walls contain many dark fissures, both uniform and irregular. Arrow slits, window hollows and the open arches of an elevated walkway denote its use, while its crumbling edges and the numerous, large, serrated cavities narrate its history. Its current semblance of partial ruin infers a fierce battle and its subsequent abandonment.

The mist below is backlit by the moon's reflection off the mere, presenting the perception that the lake is smouldering. From where we encountered the horse, the lake arcs south, then turns west, and hides behind the hill and the castle ruins.

Cresting the ridge, we follow the base of the oppressive medieval monolith. All is not quiet! There are muffled but painful cries, moans and wails emanating from inside. My essence tingles with foreboding and forgotten goosebumps. 'This place does not sound benign,' I say, to no reply.

We both listen to the stifled sobs for clues. Reaching the end of the high wall, we continue forward and inspect the entrance. Two octagonal towers stand as a barbican protecting the narrow entry portcullis. Both faces either side of the entrance are heavily disfigured as if it has been chewed by a gigantic hound. This castle's gargoyles are its ravens; every shiny, black beak points at us, but they all remain oddly silent. Ravens do not possess the ghostly guise and their stare follows us, so they must be able to see spirits.

'It is a most unnerving place,' says Vincent, 'but the sun will surely rise soon, and we would be foolish not to search for somewhere to shelter.'

'I could not bear to listen to that wailing all day. It could serve only as a last resort.'

'Agreed.'

Vincent traipses towards the gatehouse of the forsaken castle, and timidly, I follow. We pass through the wooden portcullis.

The ravens find their voice at once.

Chapter Thirty-Two

THE CRYING CASTLE

The walls devour me with their soaring authority and impose a claustrophobic sensation. A hideous shadow lingers on the ground ahead. It is borne of the gibbous moon whose lambent rays penetrate through the gnarly cavities in the castle walls. The narrow bailey, in which we stand, extends to the third set of cylindrical turrets where a prominent edifice marks the entrance to the keep. The castle and the disquieting projection may daunt; however, it is the inauspicious sounds which attempt to banish my composure.

Silently and confidently, Vincent strides towards the keep. I waver in my pursuit. The ravens' calls are shrill, but the crying is louder and more harrowing. There is no singular source of the shrieks and woeful whimpering because it wholly surrounds us. The amorphous terror woven into the strident symphony deranges beyond anything tangible and recognisable. The essence of eldritch uncertainty causes me to furiously fight the urge to flee. I cannot stem the idea that the fortress's intimidating aspect of ruinous abandonment foretells our own fate.

As abruptly as the ravens' call started, it ceases. Vincent and I look at each other, and then behind and around. Nothing appears to have changed, except the ravens have turned their winged backs on the outside world as they all leer at us in the bailey, like silent sentinels once more. The crying persists, and the watching eyes of the carrion birds do nothing to dispel the forlorn augur.

'Vincent, I don't want to know what is causing this crying,' I say. 'We cannot stay here. We need to leave.'

'The whines appear to emanate from around us but not from above,' Vincent says. 'If we can make it up to the watchtower, it should be much quieter, and we may find it to be a suitable sanctuary. It could also prove to be a good vantage point. If we climb these steps, then we will know, and we can leave.'

'The stairs have probably crumbled.'

'Perhaps, but we will proceed carefully.'

Vincent diverts towards the octagonal tower beside the keep. Passing through the open entrance, we begin to climb the spiral staircase. The wails are so loud that I would struggle to hear Vincent if he spoke. Vincent tests the footing because the darkness is jet black. Arrow slits are the only indication of our progression until we reach an archway. Passing the arch that leads out to the covered parapet walk, we realise that we are close to the top of the tower. We ascend further, and the shrill nature of the shrieking softens. 'Stop!' Vincent shouts.

'What is it?'

'No floor here—hold on.' I wait and spy the numerous large cracks that exist in the exterior surface. 'I don't think there is a way up. We should try the bridge.' My hesitancy is notable as I lead our short descent and step through the archway.

Moonbeams illuminate the ornate architecture at the opposite end of the parapet walk, and the floor there is plain but sturdy. It hints that the entire walkway is solid, but the ground before us is made invisible due to its gothic blackness. My worrisome disposition senses a trap set to plunge us into a treacherous ravine. Vincent takes the lead once more, and I attempt the impossible task of placing my feet exactly into his concealed footsteps. Vincent's pace is quicker than my own, and I hover above the great rift as he dismounts this bridge of indeterminate width. He waits patiently as I test for myself that each new step is firm.

Success! We leave behind the underpass and ascend the tight upper staircase of the castle's corner tower. At the next opening, we exit into the night air and stand on a circular platform fenced with crenels and embrasures. This is not the top of the tower. A slim lookout turret rises higher still, and in a bid to move further from the wailing, we climb its narrower stairwell. The darkness is all-encompassing and the walls are close, but while the noise is lesser, the baneful cries still seep through. The fortification's shroud finally breaks overhead, revealing the solid final few steps. The sight of a reprieve from this suffocating stairwell ushers my mind to release its anxious clenching.

A few ravens fly away as we exit into open air and gaze over the full length of the lustrous battlements whose sharp shadows are cast in silver. The regal castle rises steadfastly from the encircling cloud that fills the valleys and cushions the lakes. The smooth peaks that protrude above the soft blanket do not threaten the fort's claim as King of the Hill. With great pride, the monarch, both visually and symbolically, sits upon his throne as this land's shimmering crown. He beams with honour, knowing that he has foiled nature's attempt to cloak its gleaming treasure yet again. And so, the weathered but enduring sovereign basks in the secreted splendour of the vibrant cosmos, while his adorning nimbus lingers, poised and ready, to deliver his life-giving dew onto the rippling bed of suckling, subordinates below.

'That's a fine sight to behold,' Vincent comments. I join him by the crenels where he peers out towards the west.

Close to the base of the castle, a thick, evergreen forest extends into the valleys. It manages to catch its breath above the low cloud before diving below and re-surfacing to part the grassy hills further north-west. Its quiet breathing is steady, but a little chaotic, and I infer that the leafy canopy and smothering mist conceals a flowing brook. A vast swathe of mist shimmers below the moon in the south-west, and it arcs around to the east by where we met the mare in the mere, hiding the entire lake. Rising through the fog to the south-west is a wonderful sight; a stalwart spire beckons us to its sanctuary. The chapel promises a calm shelter away from this screaming before, what is hopefully, our final journey. Due to the cloud, however, the structure beneath the spire and the village itself is not visible.

'I believe we have found our home for the day,' I say.

'A church in the clouds,' Vincent says. 'That sure is a heavenly sight. It is both remarkable and strange how suddenly it transitions from dense fog to clear air.'

'I doubt it's as thick as it appears.'

'I fancy you are right but do not get too aroused about it being a good omen. It will be all too easy to become lost in the misty forest. We shall take care with our approach.'

'Absolutely, but it is helpful that the moon provides our bearing. Shall we?'

'Yes,' Vincent responds, and he leads the way down the spiral staircase.

On the shadowy parapet walk, I perform the same hesitant theatrics, despite Vincent powering across it, and this time, he ridicules me as he waits. Back at ground level, with the weeping and bawling at its awful apex, Vincent pauses beside an archway leading further inside rather than out. In the darkness, he appears to raise his hand and shouts to be heard, 'I shall take a quick look. Wait here.' He shuffles slowly into the dark room, and I poke my head in. The night beckons through a large gap in the outside wall. What looks like a metal bar blocks a slim portion of the external scene. Shifting my head sideways, I spy a couple more bars. Are these gaols? Above the background racket, I distinguish the loud sobs of a man. His cries do not come from this room. They are nearby, but they originate from below.

A Scottish accent and a few identifiable words blend in with his begging moans, '...please don't... I see them... army of cockroaches... chewing their droppings... control them... eat me... like barnacles... roof of the cave... maggot eyes... thousands... please don't...' His voice becomes shrill: 'CONTROL... DON'T EAT... PLEASE!'

'What's going on?' I ask Vincent, horrified by the impli-cations of a scene truly too bizarre to be a reality.

'Come here, you'll see. But watch your footing, serious-ly.' I shuffle forwards, and from his voice, I know he is not far into the emptiness. 'Kneel and peer through the gap in the floor. It's some form of dungeon pit. There are three Scotsmen down there.' I do as he instructs.

The well must be at least thirty feet deep. There are in-deed three soldiers, all brightly lit and wearing a blue tartan uniform with a kilt and a blue beret. Two rest peaceful-ly: one slumps against the wall and the other lies face up on the floor. Their pigmentless souls glow brightly within their skull's sunken recesses, and they shine through their shuttered eyes. The brightness of their souls makes their gleaming spirits appear ghostly, and they illuminate a third spirit who cowers in the middle of the chamber.

At this proximity, all this restless spirit's words are dis-tinguishable above the surrounding cries. 'Please, don't eat me, not anymore,' the tortured man appears to address the two Scotsmen who enjoy rapturous sleep. 'The bats are waking up, there are thousands of them. Let them sleep, let their droppings become a mound so high that I can climb out. You can control them, you—No! Let them sleep, they're waking up.' The man stands up slowly, turns his gaze upwards and takes a step backwards. 'Why? How? I have been devoured countless times.' He shouts, 'Stop them!' The soldier cowers as he steps back again. He puts his arms up to shield himself. He jolts violently. He shouts in anger. He jerks again releasing a sharp cry of pain. The man collapses to the floor convulsing. His wails dramat-ically judder as their pitch rises uncontrollably. His body contorts in a wholly unnatural and perverse manner, while his woeful and wavering screech eclipses the pain threshold of any mortal ear, man or beast.

The episode eventually ceases, and the soldier regains a humanoid form. He sits up. 'I think they've gone,' he says with a sigh of relief as he glances around. 'What is that?' He grabs his arm. 'What is that? I can feel it. It's—' he yells out as he recoils. 'Poison? It—it—'

'Poor son of a bitch!' Vincent interjects. 'Even when this castle finally crumbles, he is stuck. How do you get out of such a hole? There's no hope for him to reunite with his soul; he's doomed to spend eternity wallowing in this mad pit.'

'This place is diabolical,' I say before sheepishly asking, 'Shall we leave?'

'Definitely! I'd like to help the poor bastard, but I don't see how.'

Cautiously, we exit the gaol and walk through the adjacent stone archway and out into the bailey. Saddened by the man's plight, we amble silently towards the gatehouse.

'Oh, good morning gentlemen!' The squeaky female voice derives from the feet of the shadow-creature on the ground. 'How art thou this evening?' Her tone is friendly, and as the woman approaches through flashes of lunar light and shade, she comes to a halt in a patch of broad moonlight. She casts no shadow of her own. The full extent of her naked and fiendish spirit projection is on display. Her kind smile reveals discoloured teeth beneath a short, thin nose and greasy black hair. Her body wilts somewhat, and I estimate her to be in her late thirties. As much as I try, I cannot ignore her more obvious characteristic. Her face, her large, drooping breasts and much of her upper and lower body are covered with what can only be one thing—blood.

CHAPTER THIRTY-THREE

THE WITCH OF HAVELOCK

I stand in shock without any inclination to respond to this naked and bloody woman. Surely only the most despicable person would clutch a moment of such barbarity so close that it lingers for eternity as their spirit projection, which as far as I know is a mental conjuring of how a person perceives themselves. It typically harkens back to a moment of youthful beauty or former glory or, if an image does not resonate so strongly, it is their appearance just before death. I don't believe the image can be fabricated. This means that, in a moment of naked ecstasy, this wretched woman once bathed in the blood of a most unfortunate soul.

'How do you do ma'am; don't you look rosy this fine evening?' Vincent says. I am glad to have a stout and confident friend by my side because I wish to cower.

'Oh my, American and handsome, I am a lucky lass,' the woman giggles and flirts.

'Thank you, ma'am,' Vincent replies. 'It is most pleasurable to make your acquaintance. My name is Vincent Bartholomew Lawrence, and this is my good friend, Mr. Edward Webster.'

'Good morning,' my voice almost breaks as I nervously utter those few words.

'Thou hast marvellous blue eyes,' she says, and adds in a voice of false affluence, 'Well then gentlemen, it is only courteous to offer my own introduction. I am Miss Alice Shelton. What bring'st thou to Draymere Castle?'

'Miss Shelton, we are attempting to reach Lyemouth Harbour,' Vincent says. 'We have come from Elderigg and are seeking shelter for the day. What brings you here?'

'The ravens. Their call is a warning; this is not a safe place for spirits such as thyselves, and I have come to ward thee from danger.' Alice stifles a giggle.

'And what danger might that be, Miss Shelton?' Vincent asks.

'Prithee, just Alice,' she says with a smile to Vincent. 'Dost thou not hear the cries? Those spirits endure the most dreadful fate, but thou art close to Lyemouth. Tomorrow thou wilt arrive, and I will show thee a dark place within these castle walls, so thou may pass the day.'

'We are just leaving ma'am,' I jump in, keen not to accept any offer from this wretched hag, whose crimson paint drips with infinite viscosity. 'We saw a church from the tower, and we plan to reach it before sunrise.'

'O my darling, that would be a fool's errand,' Alice replies. 'The church thou seek'st is more ruinous than this castle.'

'How so?' Vincent asks.

'It lieth beneath Draymere Lake. The village was flooded to create a colossal reservoir.'

I recall the front-page story of the newspaper that Mr. Walthew was reading about the disappearance of a man named Walter Henderson. It related that sightings of a silver horse—a mercurial beast which I believe we've met—were near the Forest of Blackmoss and the *flooded* village of Drayside. While I inherently distrust this woman due to her bloody appearance, she may be being truthful.

'Is there not somewhere in the village for us to shelter?' I ask.

'No, the whole settlement is sunken. Dost thou refuse my succour?'

'Your offer to show us to a safe place is most welcome, Alice,' Vincent says.

Damn you, Vincent! We cannot stay here. 'Is there another town or village?' I press politely.

'Dost thou not know the hour?' Alice says, agitatedly. 'The nearest town is a few miles through the dark forest and much further by way of the ridgeline. It is too treacherous, and there is no time.'

'How deep is the lake?' I ask, grasping for an alternative.

'Extremely deep, and it has become deeper since they flooded it, but that lake is the lair of the Kelpie.'

'The Kelpie?' Vincent asks.

'A kelpie is a creature known in Celtic folklore. It is a horse that appeareth by lakes at night and will encourage you to ride it. If you do though, you soon realise that you cannot dismount! The Kelpie will gallop deep into its lake, drowning her rider.'

'We met her,' Vincent replies. 'She would not let me ride her.'

'Alas, thou art dead already,' Alice's words create a sombre pause. 'She is the fabled mare of Draymere. The Legend of the Silver Horse is cast over centuries. There is a fairy-tale that portrays her as a kind soul who once saved the princess of this fair castle from drowning, but she is now rightly sullied as an evil being. She was responsible for many a disappearance in the village, and soon, no one would live there. 'Twas a ghost town before its sinking. She is a fearsome creature and her legend hath expanded her lair.'

'She seemed pleasant,' I say.

'She is not,' Alice bluntly replies.

'What is she?' Vincent asks.

'There art beings with extraordinarily powerful souls, both good and evil, and when such a being doth die, its transcendental power fuses soul, spirit and an element, which was water in her case. If a water horse hath a tainted soul, it is a Kelpie; if the steed hath a pure soul, it becometh a Dionnair.'

'This is nonsense,' Vincent says.

'Believeth what thou wish. Doth the soul not possess divine power?'

'It is not divine or transcendental. It is unexplained—that is all,' Vincent replies resolutely.

'Humanity exulteth in the masquerade of the divine, for it shalt not permiss the unexplained,' Alice says. 'Alas, is it not thy deific scripture that walloweth in the mire of ignorance, for it readeth, "*Thou shalt not suffer a witch to live*"?'

'You are a witch!' I accuse. Her eyes turn wide and wild. A grin grows. With a roar, she lunges at me. I fall to the floor. I stare up at demented eyes. She cackles detestably. It was a prank.

'Enough!' Vincent scolds like a father. 'Edward, here—' he holds out a hand and pulls me up. 'There is no such thing as magic, hexes, foresight or—witches. They are the inventions of a world blind to science.'

Alice swoons. 'Art thou my sweet prince! Such wisdom and courage. If I could, I would keep thee forever.' She giggles childishly. 'If thou had'st been in this courtyard on that fateful day, thou would'st have been our knight of saviour. My darling, our only crime was recoiling from the oppression and intolerance that choked our existence. Perhaps thy reasoning would have dispelled their indoctrination and spared the felling of eight exiles by the hangman's noose.'

'You died here?' Vincent asks. Alice clasps her hands demurely, and gazing at Vincent with doe eyes, she gives a single sheepish nod.

'Our whole coven was charged with cursing a man and the death of someone who disappeared,' she says with feigned sorrow. 'There could not be a greater falsehood. They called their society civilised, but it would not abide uncertainty or the unexplained; rumour and greed ensued and, facing hysteria, the authorities sought recourse.'

'Which was to convict the members of your covenant?' Vincent asks.

''Twas indeed,' Alice sulks. 'We had been marked one Good Friday when all citizens were ordered to church. We worship the old gods and follow the beliefs of the peoples that roamed long before the marauding invaders and zealous Christian hypocrites defiled this land. On that day, our coven rebelled from the sullying sacrament, and we engorged ourselves during a Celtic celebration in defiance.

'The rite took place atop Havelock Hill. Our group has many ancient secrets learnt from the lore of sacred groves.' She gleams at me with a wry smile. 'It is not how thou would'st describe witchcraft, but there art some truths buried within the tales of the occult. We hold such practices dear and do not inscribe them for fear of discovery or betrayal. One of our secrets resides with alchemy which one in our coven, Selma, used so effectively to treat ailments of the townsfolk. The ancients had learnt the power that flora possesses. We witnessed its power countless times. Selma was a kind-spirited soul and took pity on many of the villagers who she felt timidly succumbed to the imposing regime. By helping them, she had gained great favour. Her powers were feared though, but while Selma remained friendly and life was uneventful, they would not spout aspersions of her being a witch. The rest of the coven generally kept more of a distance which roused minor suspicion, but we did not plot against them.'

'Sounds like witchcraft to me!' I bark out of frustration. This artist of alchemy is not the victim she attempts to portray. 'If you were truly innocent, why is it that you stand before us naked and bloody?'

'It is the same reason why I stand before thee without the accursed infliction of memory loss—it is the rites we perform. They provide immortality with shrewd sanity. I bear knowledge from three centuries whereas thou can'st muster merely a week.'

'Three centuries! How?' Vincent asks. 'What is it about the rituals that preserved your memory? Might I be able to save the little memory that I still possess before it is lost?'

'Preserve—that is the correct word.' Alice smiles her ugly smile. 'It is within peat bogs that our bodies are buried—preserved. The Forest of Blackmoss begineth outside these walls, and it possesseth one of several sacred glades around Deaconshire. Burials within the peat bogs will brilliantly preserve the flesh—and thus—the memory.' She beams with pride. 'Alas, my darling, if thy corpse is not embalmed, thy mind wilt soon be lost.'

'Hellfire!' Vincent reacts. 'You finally speak something plausible. Preserve the brain and you protect memory. Ingenious! One more question if you will, ma'am.'

'Prithee.'

'If you were hanged, how was it that you came to be buried in the bog?'

'Well—I don't mind telling thee that!' Alice joyfully says. 'There were two friendly faces in the crowd that day. The Greyfernes were our spies; they did us a great service that night. Once the gathering departed, the gravedigger was instructed to bury our bodies in the forest earth.' Alice pauses.

'And?' Vincent asks expectantly.

'O darling, thou art of astute mind, no?' she cackles coldly. 'When Havelock was awoken by the Great Wolf's howl early the next morning and the gravedigger's body was discovered outside St. Martin's Church, our legend was born. Terrified, they would only whisper the name which they coined for us, the Havelock Harpies.' Alice titters childishly. 'Our lust for revenge was not satiated though,' her giggling does not relent. 'Oh, we tormented those cretinous swines! We stalked Havelock, whose residents we had never harmed. Their reaction was to swear never to visit Haunted Havelock Hill, as they christened it. They found no sign of our bodies in the Forest of Blackmoss and feared the worst. Stories arose that it was our witchcraft which twisted the spire of St. Martin's, and that evil has lingered within the village for centuries. Such was the hysteria, the general advice became that anyone suspected of witchcraft, upon death, should be buried head-down in a tall, narrow grave with a heavy boulder placed over the top to prevent resurrection and escape.'

Angrily, I reply, 'You worship blasphemous gods and frighten the good folk with the false pretence of satanic resurrection, AND you attest that your coven murdered a man and enacted sacrificial rituals, AND *YOU* have the gall to criticise the justice of civilised society for preventing such barbarism?'

Alice leers at me. 'Yes, we held sacrifices, but we would use willing volunteers though thou would'st not believe it. The suspicion thou hast shown explains why *thy good folk* charged six women and two men, who had done no wrong to the people of Havelock and sentenced them to hang in the most excruciatingly cruel way. *Thy good folk* demanded absolute adherence and those that did not were flagrantly branded heretics or witches. And so, in *thy God's* name and by the decree of *thy King, we* were sacrificial lambs for slaughter. Those convicted, even without any substantial evidence, were hanged, burnt alive, drowned and much more to *cleanse* this land. We merely took a lowly peasant for our recompense. Pray tell, who are the real worshippers of a satanic and barbaric death cult?'

'How dare you, you loathsome murderess!' I shout. 'How dare you besmirch those honest, God-fearing men and women who were rightfully defending themselves. The god's you claim to worship, *require* a wicked sacrifice and would have the devout followers of the one true God pilloried for eternity!'

'Enough! Both of you,' Vincent cries. 'Anyone can twist the events around them so that they conform to their own beliefs and make all others appear immoral. Can we put aside this futile debate?'

I acquiesce.

'I can ne'er forget the trauma of the noose,' Alice says, adopting a sombre disposition. 'It is a burden to recall the circumstances of thy death. That is one thing that I will be glad to forget. That evening, Selma was the first. She was the kind one to whom so many in the village were indebted. They kicked the stall out from under her feet, and the vicious crowd roared. To cheer the death of the person who cured thine ailment is the most detestable betrayal. One by one successive roars resounded. The rapacious rope finally bit hard. There was barely a drop. 'Twas to be tortuous strangulation. The noose sunk its teeth in further, leeching our life. I writhed, against my will, due to an involuntary seizure. As I unwittingly twitched, I caught gasps momentarily. The noose willed to savour the moment. It slowly tightened, and my gasps became more infrequent. As I wriggled, I caught glimpses of my petrified friends convulsing. Young Jane Hargraves, Selma's granddaughter, was animated beside me, but, before long, she became pendulous. Her white eyes stared as she gently swayed. The creaking of straining rope lessened and the cries from the merciless onlookers revealed that I was the last struggler. They revelled boisterously, heckling my dangling dance of death, blind to the religious hypocrisy. That was when the earth shook! From a distant source, the Eldritch Chime boomed.'

CHAPTER THIRTY-FOUR

THE FORGOTTEN PLACE

V incent, having wished just a few nights ago to be able to converse with, 'people of the past', is excitably asking the odious oracle about the events of the last few hundred years; evidently, he has no need for a clock that turns backwards. I, however, harbour little interest in entertaining any of Alice's noxious notions. I wish to be away from her and this terrible castle.

I have to attest that Alice answers Vincent's questions too quickly to be inventing it all, but I still distrust the bloody woman. I fancy, as I'm sure Vincent does too, that she was incredibly fortunate to stumble across the secret to preserving the mind in this afterlife. Somehow, a spirit must have communicated it to one of her ancestors. She may like to linger in this nightmare realm, but for me, this is just the place through which I must journey to reach the paradise that awaits. It stirs another thought; is there rest for the wicked? As a result of her crimes and beliefs, I surmise that she does not experience such bliss, which is why she is not lying in rapture tonight. If I ask, she will probably lie, so why bother?

Even though the conversation on the surface is at least more amiable, she tells stories with aggressive arrogance while her mood swings wildly. Alice is still visibly swooning over Vincent but also displays other strange and unfathomable behaviour. Her mind seems wholly erratic and unpredictable. She gabbles about details that are beside the point, and some of her stories obviously contradict themselves. Vincent, I can tell, mostly from his occasional glances at me, is wise to it. To him though, Alice is entertainingly passing half an hour. I, however, am not amused. Mercifully, the sky is showing the first signs of dawn though I regret that I did not attempt the route via the ridgeline when I had more time. Vincent was quick to accept staying in the castle, and I still do not have an alternative suggestion.

If Alice's account can be believed, the castle was built in the late 1200s though she does not know much about its history before her demise. The dank cesspits beneath the gaols are called oubliettes. She says this is a French word meaning, the Forgotten Place. I also agree with her opinion that these dungeons were far worse than the gaols. She explains how the pit is a bell-shaped prison, and an enemy would be lowered or thrown in from a trap door in the ceiling; they were supposed to simply die and rot.

'We saw three Scottish soldiers in one of the pits, who are they?' Vincent asks.

'Ah,' Alice smiles, 'There art four men in that pit, but only three Scotsmen. Captain Campbell and Lieutenant Robertson art the two men at rest. Captain MacCulloch and a nameless wanderer, who fell in whilst seeking refuge, art the unfortunate spirits who gaineth no rest.

'There were only three, ma'am. No nameless wanderer,' Vincent responds.

'It is not possible to escape,' Alice states. 'Perhaps he was experiencing a brief reprieve from the terrible nightmares. He is a very recent addition to the pit, and I do not yet know what vexes his visions. Captain MacCulloch, however, has been a squealing inhabitant for over a hundred years. He hath a recurring nightmare that he is being eaten; it is either at the hand of his compatriots, or if they art not hungry, they summon creatures—who act upon their behest—to devour him.'

'Over a century—goddamn!' Vincent responds. 'Why are they down there?'

''Twas during the Jacobite rebellion,' Alice continues, 'but I've no pity for Captain MacCulloch, for he, and the other captain, capitulated when the battle was nigh won. I despise the English; I do not consider myself such. They arrogantly seek empire and it hath spread across the world. I applaud thy countrymen for their victory.' Vincent nods graciously, not wanting to disclose his English heritage.

'These Scotsmen cowardly surrendered, expecting mercy. I was pleasantly surprised that the English did no such thing. Their captor, Winston Reynolds, taught me a few new tricks,' she sniggers. 'He threw Captain MacCulloch, naked, into the oubliette. He broke his leg in the fall, and his howls kept the men awake. I sat in the cells and watched; they were unaware of my presence.

'The English were after revenge and information, but realising they had been duped, information was not forthcoming. The poor coward died,' Alice giggles. 'Then they threw in Captain Campbell, but still they did not talk. After a few days, they raised Captain MacCulloch's decaying body, upon a butcher's hook, for all to see,' Alice chuckles some more. 'The coward's body was yellow and bloated, full of blood blisters and was strewn with bite marks.' Alice howls with laughter. She is perverted to get such satisfaction out of desperate cannibalism. 'Maggots reanimated his eyes, regurgitated from his mouth and burst from every orifice. The men vomited, except one man—Lieutenant Robertson. He was a strong, courageous man—a true warrior. He was boastful about how he had maimed the English soldiers. Oh, he could have had me.' Alice makes a sultry smile. Her perversion is staggering.

It occurs to me that the length of time that the captain's corpse had been on display in Alice's tale would be similar to the length of time since Vincent's death. Presently, his body must be in a similar state of decomposition. The thought bothers me, and I cannot shake the idea of Vincent being the actor on stage in her story.

Alice continues, 'The butcher-hooked coward's eyes went black, and his mouth was grinning wide. His cadaver squelched and spasmed and oozed liquid into the rancid pit below. Winston Reynolds lit candles, so his putrefaction was always on display. Captain MacCulloch's spirit was going mad in the darkness below.

'The other coward soon died too. The Lieutenant remained dauntless, and the gallant warrior was flung in next. The others finally crumbled and gave up their information. The English buried the captain's body, dooming his spirit to replay his compatriot's cannibalism over and over for a century and more,' her words bounce with the laughter in her throat. 'The remaining Scotsmen were hanged. It was a longer drop than my own, and death arrived with swift dignity. Soon after, the English left. Lieutenant Robertson was forgotten, and Draymere Castle lay abandoned.'

'That is a haunting tale,' Vincent says. 'In such a dark environment, devoid of distraction and stimulation, I do not believe it is possible to stem the lucid horrors that the withered consciousness, sneakily and consistently, conjures. Captain MacCulloch's spirit must endure for aeons. He has no hope of escape, he can only pray that his body was badly buried so his skull can finally crumble.'

'Yes indeed, so heed my warning: stay out of the pits,' Alice says with a happy smile. It is a smile that signifies that we have understood the deeper moral of the story.

I remain quiet; I understand. As grotesque as their deaths were, it pales to insignificance when you consider Captain MacCulloch's relentless suffering as a spirit. But the captain is just one of the dozens of spirits who share this tragic fate. They are the forlorn who serenade this castle with a harmony borne of their cries as they painfully endure purgatory. If Vincent and I do not return to our graves, we too shall spend eternity shrieking at shadows.

Alice breaks the silence. 'Thou can'st witness an inciteful side to mankind by gazing into the pits. Strong and mighty men are fearful of such silly things—one man is scared of brambles; another keeps choking on a button!' Alice giggles. Vincent laughs too. I do not find any comedy in this person's misfortune. 'Each person tends to have a horror that reoccurs. The most common fear is from little furry animals, cats and rats mostly. I await to see what traumatises the new nameless guest with the Scotsmen.'

'There is no one with the Scotsmen,' Vincent responds irritated.

'I do not deceive thee.'

'Then I shall prove to you that he has escaped.'

'By all means. And then, I will show thee the dark corner in which thou can'st pass the day,' Alice offers.

'Very well,' Vincent says as he leads the way back to the pit. I do agree with Vincent that there were only three in the oubliette, but my glance was short, and I have little interest in proving a point.

I wait at the entrance to the gaols. The wailing is sickening. The Scotsman's screams reach a new octave. The phantom bats are biting. You need to shout to be heard.

Through the gaps in the walls, the twinkling stars fade into the twilight. The cavities allow the gaols to be dimly lit. There are rows and rows of metal bars, rusted and warped. A series of square holes are noticeable along the corridor between the gaols. These were once the trapdoors to the pits.

Alice peers down, and shouts, 'One, two, three,' she pauses, then adds with a delightful tone, 'four! He ain't got away. Look here.'

'Nonsense!' Vincent barks. Alice takes a step back, and Vincent squats in front of her. He gazes below. He shouts the count, 'One, two, three—there is no f—' Alice jolts. Vincent's cry rises to an unsettling pitch.

'FOUR!' Alice unleashes a piercing howl of laughter. 'Oops!' she giggles revoltingly. She's kicked Vincent into the oubliette. 'Thou should'st believe little old Alice.' Her childish chuckle cascades into ludicrous laughter.

'Vincent!' I cry. Vincent is doomed. He has no hope for escape. I leer furiously at Alice. 'You witch! You deceived him!'

She opens out her arms and shrugs. 'Witches play tricks!' she cackles. The wanton gaoler of ghouls then leans over the pit. 'I will keep thee forever,' she says to Vincent. 'How dost thou like being my new pet?' She pauses. 'No answer? Oh well, thou wilt find thy voice very soon. Thou art the newest chorister for my fine opera.' She sniggers, then cries, 'Let the madness begin!'

CHAPTER THIRTY-FIVE

HELL OR HIGH WATER

I stare, startled. Vincent shall cry in purgatory forever-more, and Alice is making quite sure he knows it. This may seem quite a fitting fate for his dastardly deeds, but I am sick with sadness. He is a wretchedly flawed man, whose actions I cannot excuse, but to me, he has been sympathet-ic and encouraging. We have suffered together, journeyed together and found hope together. Now, only I hold the mantel of hope. But my hope burns brighter than ever be-cause I am so determined to succeed and, when I do, his loss shall not be in vain. Upon their deaths, Vincent's family will mourn a name on a gravestone, for they will not remember to whom it belongs. They will correctly presume only one thing: that the fate of Vincent Bartholomew Lawrence is hell.

'Come now, Edward,' Alice calls, 'I see now that there art FIVE in this pit.' She pauses. I stand facing evil. 'Prithee, come. I promise to be a good girl,' she smiles with false sincerity.

I take a step back. 'Stay away from me, witch!' She cocks her head. Her smile grows. Her eyes inflame.

'Eddie! Get out of here!' Vincent shouts from the oubliette. 'Don't let this hag lure you into one of her traps. Get out of here!'

'Vincent!' I shout. 'I'm sorry I could not—'

'Go now, goddammit!'

'Yes, I shall.'

'Goodbye Eddie. You will find your home.'

'Farewell.'

'Where art thou going to go, Eddie?' Alice squeaks with excitement. She is perversely savouring this moment. She steps over the pit and walks towards me. 'The sun is rising. There is nowhere but this castle, wilt thou stay here with me in my house of tricks?' She giggles.

'Goddamn! Spiders!' Vincent roars.

Alice turns. 'Spiders? So utterly predictable,' she groans. 'Why could'st thou not be more like the button man?'

Vincent roars again. His cry is deep and throaty. Alice leans over the pit. 'O songbird!' she swoons. 'Thy double bass shalt handsomely complement the high falsetto of my symphony. Thou art a fine addition.'

Her back is turned as she peers down. Now is my chance. I am a coward no more.

I rush towards her. She stands up. I lunge to push her in. She hops out of the way. I stumble towards the pit.

Gleaming soul-light beckons. I catch my fall, jump over the hole and land in a heap. Alice stands beaming. She moves to block my escape.

'Thou art a fool, Eddie. Where art thou going now?' she titters.

I rise to my feet, turn and stride away from Alice. I pace down the long corridor. I shall not wrestle this witch; wasting any time on her will only condemn me to this castle. There is an exit on the far side of this gaol. I walk on the left to avoid the traps down the middle.

'Which pit awaiteth thee?' The witch's voice is close behind me. She is trying to scare me so that I will fight her. She does not scare me. She cannot run. She cannot catch me.

The traps pass by. Each has a different pitch as though they are the holes of a flute, each playing a different note. The gaols are kissed with the dim dawn light. I am going to the church. It may be sunken, but it is standing, so it should be dark.

I exit the gaol to the base of a crumpled spiral stairway and enter the open bailey. I stride towards the portcullis.

'O darling, won't thee stay? The sun shalt claim thee.' I glance behind. Alice emerges into the bright bailey. Her pace has slowed. This is her last attempt to tempt me—to trick me.

Closing in on the portcullis, I distinguish a sonorous soloist in the sonata of chirruping choristers. Vincent's eternal terror has begun. There is no way that I am staying here. The question now is whether I can reach the church in the lake before sunrise.

'Edward,' Alice tempts again.

I step through the portcullis.

Out in the open, I turn towards the forest. I hasten towards the spire though I cannot see it because of the verdant wood. The evergreen forest meets the plateau and drops down into the mist. I gaze behind. Alice has not emerged through the gateway. She knows how close daylight is; she will shelter in the castle. I must hurry.

I walk beneath the gloomy canopy and start my descent. Unfathomably, light seeps through the dense awning to penetrate the haze. Sprawling branches, dripping in moss, grope the misty air. They extend ungainly from the skinny bodies of wart-ridden warlocks whose faces are hidden by their dark hoods. A brook gouges a path but trickles innocently. The creatures of the forest floor hide in tall and tangled vegetation. The flora that straddles the stream is dank and diverse with big, brown ferns, fallen trees painted white with fungi, spikey bushes, and rocks buried within a mossy carpet. I search for vegetation that may be thick enough to hide in, but nothing is suitable. I peer through the dense jungle and spy the mere. The lake is aglow!

Specks of light, distinct from the mist, swirl and sway in a slow dance between the trees. It is as though the mist is infested with glow-worms or fireflies. I would not describe the things as such, however, because the bugs emit a glow that is lightning-white. As I descend through the obscuring mist, the lightning-bugs multiply. Some appear to glide in a patch of barren forest while others cluster together further out into the mere. The lake dances with shifting constellations of light. What are they? The bugs share the same hue as soul-light. Is this a lake of souls?

Slender pine trees contain the gloom within the forest. Beyond, brightness mesmerises. The descent steepens. The black canopy from the evergreens recedes. The pines below stand tall but bare. Have the bugs leeched the life from these trees? The summoning glow of the lake approaches. As I pass the last of the evergreens, I pause and gawp. The lake and the forest are one.

I step into submerged, knotted roots. Dead tree trunks—that have lost their branches—stand tall within the still lake, like pillars of a temple ruin. Ahead, amongst the graceful beacons, only their stubby tips break the surface. The lake devours the forest like a snake eating a crocodile.

The dead forest captures the radiance of the brightening sky. I am fortunate that the sun has not yet risen; it feels overdue. The shadow of the spire looms through the fog. It stands steadfast in the quiet lake.

I tread deeper into the lightning-bug-infested swamp. The water rises—to my waist—to my chest. The orbs shift as lazily as the lake ripples. A listless lightning-bug approaches under the surface. It glares with the eyes of a predator. The water reaches my neck. The predator is within reach. I submerge.

Chapter Thirty-Six

LIGHTNING-BUGS

B lack velvet drapes my legs. Scarlet strands wisp over the pale face of a sleeping beauty. A young redhead floats by. Her flowing dress gleams in the dawn light. Her peaceful, closed eyes appear ghostly as her skull beams behind her face. A soft current in the lake causes the skull to bob slowly along the sunken forest floor. Her spirit follows her soul like a kite on a string. I watch as her skull becomes wedged in a tree root. She lies still. Her body appears to be cut in half by the thick tree trunk that her spirit passes through.

I push deeper into the underwater forest. The pines rise floor to surface. Spirits are strewn across the floor. They glide past like drowned bodies while their skulls leer with a sickening gloat, intent on reminding you of your own demise. Up close, the soul is a shimmering globule that illuminates its spirit, but in the distance, through murky water, they appear as a colony of lightning-bugs dancing. Their bolero mystifies as I walk amongst submerged trees that break the aether.

I leave the forest and enter a ghost town. The sunken street has a dozen houses on each side with a tavern and a church at the far end. This ghost town may be bereft of life, but it is not devoid of the dead. Immemorial beings drift through the street and cluster in cramped corners. They all slumber having released their last breath in a time long forgotten.

The street is so crowded that I am forced to push my way through. The ghouls do not disturb. The sunken village stands eerie as it bathes in the cloudy light from a liquid sky. The fluid firmament hangs low over the roofs. The church's pointed spire exalts to the heavens above. A stone plaque reads 'Drayside' and another informs that Alnustone lies one mile away, and Lyeminster is two and a half miles in the same direction. The doors and windows to the houses are all missing. The houses themselves are mostly intact, but some have gaping holes, and their contents are scattered across the lakebed.

If the village was purposefully sunk, these beings did not die in a flood, but why are they here? Have they rested like this for centuries, or did they pluck their skulls from the sunken cemetery during the Night of the Souls? Why are there so many bodies? There are too many for a hamlet so small.

I cannot speculate. I must find a dark place to shelter. I peer into the nearest house. There is only rubble. I go upstairs. Again rubble, except for two spirits who commandeer one of the rooms. Their skulls rest neatly in a corner in a slot made by masonry debris. The skulls rest on their side, and a young businessman cradles a lady in a pink dress. Their position is too quaint such that I fancy it unlikely that they arrived here as a result of shifting currents.

This room will be too bright for me, but is it not for them also? Do the spirits rest peacefully by night but endure pain by day? Or does the soul subvert the spell cast by the sun? It matters not; I must find somewhere darker.

I leap through the window and hasten my trudge through restful spirits to reach the tavern. No signage exists to tell the tavern's name. The bar has collapsed. Bottles are encased within the debris, and the inn is full. A multitude of fiendish skulls glare as I attempt to find the basement, but with such wreckage, I am unable to.

Please, God! I need shelter. Your church is my only option now.

I hold dreadfully little hope because the chapel's entrance has caved in. The windows are without stained glass, but they are too high to clamber up to, and a ghost can't swim. I climb the rubble that was once the entrance.

I find a way to reach the roofline, where I gaze down through a collapsed section. Several Lunatics float amongst a deluge of masonry. If the spirits did choose their resting place, the tavern was the favoured option. Should I drop in? If I do, will I ever be able to get out? I can't see how I would. Should I try the clocktower?

A tingle. A singe. I look up. The surface of the lake dazzles with the sun's morning rays. I need to find somewhere now.

A thunderous cry! I jolt away from the lofty ledge for fear of further collapse. Another shrill cry. Its high pitch reverberates in the water and judders through the debris beneath me. I turn. The Kelpie stands in the street. She spins, then runs deeper into the murk. Is she ushering me to follow?

Kelpie or not, I need a saviour. I jump from the wreckage, land at the base and follow its flare. The lake scalds like dipping your toe into a hot bath. I scamper across as if treading on hot coals. The horse re-emerges into focus. It stands beside a blackness. Nearby, a spirit and its skull float towards the precipice between light and dark. It crosses the black hole and sinks into the abyss.

I scream as the sunlight scorches. I reach the horse, but she dives down. I leap after her. I fall into a twilight trench and land beside a luminous heap of spirits and skeletons. The lake here is so deep the sun barely penetrates, and mercifully, its inferno quickly subsides. The trough in which I have landed appears to nonchalantly collect cadavers. It seems that once they drift in, they are unlikely to drift out. The skeleton horde is bright with souls and an eclectic cast of illuminated spirits.

In the gloom, fish excite over one freshly rotting carcass. They nibble at their delight throughout the day. There is light above, but besides the soul-light, my surroundings are dim. One side is too steep to climb, but on the opposite side, I am able to explore away from the sunken mass of soul-streams. I do not venture far, however, because I climb blindly into darkness. I do not allow the giant orb of souls to stay out of sight because it would be too easy to get lost in the dark depths of the lake. When the surface loses its brightness, I will find an escape—I hope there is one.

As I wait for nightfall, a few skulls and spirits drift by, yet to be ensnared by the deep trench. The currents do not naturally direct the Lunatics to this underwater ossuary.

I spend much of the day petting the pearlescent creature. She has the energy of a young foal and her insistence to play grows tiresome, but I am indebted to her for sparing me a day of infernal torture, and the entertainment she creates keeps the drowsy delusions at bay. My morale is further boosted by the thought that if the horse is not trapped down here, then neither am I.

The brightness above disappears. The terrain hides. I walk blindly up the shallow climb. Tonight, I hope to reach my home and finally rest.

The mare follows me; she wants me to stay. She spins around, dashes in front of me and nudges me with her head. I rub her pink nose and continue past. This will be the second time that I've upset her by leaving. She just wants a playmate, but it cannot be me.

A lightning-bug helps me maintain a course before I make a beeline for another high on my left. I rise and reach a restful child. Another lightning-bug glows further up—then another. I ascend from the depths. The horse still follows me.

One by one, more lightning-bugs appear in the darkness. The bugs glide sporadically all around. Their stare is like starlight, and it is as though I am flying through the cosmos. Amongst the stars is a dense nebula. I turn towards it, and soon I find the submerged forest and the sunken houses. The lightning-bugs do appear to emanate from the cemetery, so I surmise that they rose during the blood moon but were locked out when it faded.

At the church tower, the horse bounds in front of me. I stroke her as I walk past. She spins around to get back in front and rears up on her hind legs. She neighs loudly—deafeningly. Her hooves flail high above my head. They crash down and pin me to the floor. Her pearly-white snarl divulges that her new hostile temperament is intentional.

The charger nickers and steps back, releasing me. I stand. Her head lowers in a fighting stance. I back-step to keep my distance from the unpredictable and insistent nag. How do I get past her?

I reason that I must approach her and then slip by. I pet her pink nose; she still bares her teeth. She holds her ground. I make my move.

I slip to her side and rush past. She bolts. I approach the surface as she races towards me. She rears up to pin me, but I dodge underneath. She darts back to face me, then she spins. Her hind legs fly. Her hooves thrust into my chest, tossing me away. As I rise to my feet, she kicks me again—and again—and finally, I plunge to the shimmering depths where fish sharpen their teeth on bone.

CHAPTER THIRTY-SEVEN

ETERNAL PLAYMATES

T he mare corners me in the trench and encourages me to play. I do not. She nudges, nibbles and nickers, hoping that I do not remember her snarling assault. I understand what she is now; she is indeed a kelpie, but she is lonely too. She yearns for an eternal playmate. There may be hundreds of spirits in her den, but their souls are here too so they find rest, and she remains lonely. I, however, cannot rest, so either I sulk or I play.

I shun her attention, but her play becomes rough and heavy-handed. She kicks me away, and as I get to my feet, she kicks me back again and again. She runs the relay. When I stay on the floor, she picks me up by my neck, like a dog carrying its pup, and deposits me where I am supposed to be. I am her rag doll to be played with, discarded and left to rot in a hidden corner. I acquiesce to my role as her toy but refuse to play in the hope that she will become bored. If she leaves, I can reattempt escape. For what feels like hours, the malevolent mare persists.

Eventually, she leaves her den and disappears into the dark lake, so I attempt to sneak away from this ghoulish trench before she realises. I begin to ascend the bank using lightning-bugs as waypoints. I emit no light of my own, but I must keep my distance from the waypoints because soul-light will illuminate me like a candle in the night. I continue to ascend hidden in the mere's cloak of darkness, and my hope rises too. Then, from the murk, the shimmering kelpie re-emerges and gallops back to her nest of skeletons. She unleashes a distressed neigh that booms in the water. Her doll is gone.

A lightning-bug drifts closer. I rush to keep a good distance to remain invisible. The nag speeds along the trench as I ascend. The glow of the hamlet beckons me. I wish to avoid passing through because the mare will see me, but its bearing will ensure I emerge on the correct side of the mere. The kelpie is racing up the bank, she knows I will try to leave via the village. The hamlet comes close, and I divert for the forest where there are fewer lightning-bugs. Will she see me before I reach the woodland?

She races past, behind me. She is far enough away that my spirit does not glow in her luminosity. I hide in the ghostly forest. She searches the old street, trampling on the many sleeping Lunatics. I turn to leave by climbing through the woodland. She reads my mind. She dashes into the forest. In response, I pace towards the hamlet.

The souls of the slumbering spirits brighten me with their lustre. I look back. A white haze flashes amongst the murky columns of trees. I pass a couple of houses. She neighs then charges towards me. I've been spotted.

I dart into a house and hide upstairs. It is the house with the cuddling couple. I peer out the window. The kelpie stalks the street. She cuts between houses. I wait. Her search does not relent. It is as if she can smell me. I wait some more. The nag's pace slows, but she refuses to withdraw. I cannot wait till daylight. I must escape now.

I judge that I can jump from the window, land and dive through the ground floor window of the next house. I don't believe she can enter the houses, but she will definitely not catch me if I go upstairs. It is the grimy alleys when I will be vulnerable. I wait for an opportune moment.

When she enters an alley a few houses away, I enact my plan. As I rush through the ground-floor window, a soul hidden in the corner of the room places its spotlight upon me. She sees me and races over from the next house. I approach the stairs. She tries to bite me through the doorway. I dodge and climb up. Glancing out from the top floor, I see her head peering through the window. I jump down again and into the next house. Debris blocks the stairs, so I hide below a window that faces the street.

The kelpie prowls the avenue, nickering through frustration. She is looking through each window inspecting each house. Her gleaming head appears above my own. My spirit catches her light, and I hold my breath. She does not look down; she has not yet seen me. The kelpie lingers. Her trembling neigh nearly frightens a yelp out of my bosom, but I keep quiet. She continues her search.

There are a couple of houses before the tavern and the church. The church is nearest the forest shore. It will be hard to hide by the church as it has crumbled and the souls in the street will irradiate me, but what if—I pause the thought. It is a terrifying prospect. What if I lie in the road? What if I crawl beneath the Lunatics? She will think I am just another slumbering spirit who only wake through their own volition. It will be like slithering through corpses, but I am prepared to do anything to escape. The bodies strewn in the street lead past the church. They grow sparse by the forest, but I must try.

When the kelpie is out of sight, I vault the window and crawl under the Lunatics. They are not aware of me shifting them. I creep. Gaping skulls terrify. I crawl into an open space and lie still. The nag continues her prowl. Her distressed whinnies grow in frequency and volume. She is worried. I halt and remain still. Before my frozen gaze appear two fetlocks flowing in the stream. I hold my breath. They stutter an inch forward. Her cry startles as it deafens. She bounds away. I continue my crawl. At the edge of the forest, I sneak without cover. She cries and charges towards me.

I dart into the trees and climb the embankment. The mare invades the woodland, but I break the surface. I hide amongst thick ferns as she emerges. Only her radiance will brighten me. If I keep my distance, she will not see me, and I will be free.

'My Goodness!' The voice is a man's. 'Do my eyes deceive me? Good heavens! Walter was right. There are silver horses that roam the sunken pines.' The sound of snapping twigs perpetuates a pause. 'You are a most beautiful creature,' he says.

The kelpie whinnies excitedly in response. I dare not give away my position, so I do not look.

'What are you?'

The nag nickers playfully. The man laughs. 'My goodness,' he repeats, 'you are magnificent—majestic. Your hair is like—like water. What in heaven's name are you? Do you know where Walter is?' The man laughs and then stutters, 'You want—surely not—' The horse neighs. 'Ride you? To where? Do you know where my friend is? I need to find him. The police believe I killed him. Are you going to take me to him? Is he injured? Is he safe?'

It dawns on me that I have met Walter Henderson. It is his carcass on which the fish feast. Alice claimed that if you ride a kelpie, you will not be able to dismount, and she will drag you into her lake and drown you. I know now why so many skeletons fill the deep lake. How can I stop the kelpie claiming another? I want to scream at the man to tell him not to ride her. I want to—but—if I do, she will see me, and he will not. After so many victims, does she not comprehend that her victims will simply slumber after their initial shock? They will not play with her for eternity—that is why I am her real prize—I will not slumber.

The man marvels. 'You are a magnificent beast. I cannot wait to tell my little boys what I saw—what I rode!' His excitement is palpable. That is about to rapidly change, and I cannot bear the thought. I am powerless. His fate is imminent and preordained.

The man releases a cry of distress—then another—and another. With a flash of white through the ferns, the kelpie bolts. I gaze out. The man has sunk to his chest into the horse's watery bulk. With his hands, he tries to push to release himself, but his hands are swallowed too, and he cannot remove them. The man screams. Branches and pine needles scrape his face. The kelpie turns around. I see the man's bloodied face demented with fear. The mare rides him back and forth through the grotto of spines. She does not wish to drown him yet; she is sadistically savouring the moment.

Up and down she rides. 'Help me!' the man bawls. 'WALTER! HELP ME!' The petrified man shrieks so terribly that those crying in the castle would pity him. What can I do to help? He is condemned.

The horse neighs with wicked excitement and diverts towards her lake. Soon, the man's screams are muffled by the mere. The night turns calm as water fills his lungs. Silence hangs like a noose. I stand and gaze into the lake. Bubbles rise. The wind's whispering ballad sings in step with the equine ballet. Draymere Lake feigns its innocence by disguising the bubbles as soft ripples. I watch and wait in trepidation...

BONG!

From the lake's erupting spire, the Eldritch Chime thunders.

CHAPTER THIRTY-EIGHT

A PHANTOM FOR THE OPERA

I stroll through the Forest of Blackmoss in mournful silence. That man had little boys, he said. They don't know it yet, but they've lost their papa. They will never hear from him. Hopefully, they do not go searching for him because they may share his foul fate. As for the nameless man himself, he is, at this very moment, in a world of despair. He has no one to welcome him to this spirit realm but the illusory creature that castrated his life's ambition. He will gaze upon the nest of skeletons, witness fish slowly devour his body, and be pestered to play by his captor. I pray that he perceives it all as a mere bad dream. He will rest in death, however, so he may yet be more fortunate than I.

I exit the forest and climb a steep hill. From the ridge, I should be able to plot my route. The night is clear, but the moon has not yet risen. The sign in Drayside made mention of a town called Lyeminster. Judging by the name, surely it is upstream from Lyemouth, so if I find Lyeminster, then I can follow the river home. As I climb, I spy ruinous Draymere Castle in the distance against the horizon. I see it now for what it truly is: an ugly king whose deviancy endures far beyond his reign.

I reach the summit where three ridges connect; one goes towards the castle, one follows the Forest of Blackmoss in the other direction, and the other leads to city lights. Is this Lyeminster? Down on my left are the gas lamps of a small village—Alnustone? A small chapel is alive with the light of the living and the song of hopeful hymns. It is encouraging. I am returning to civilisation.

Draymere Castle catches my eye again. The unsightly wart repulses me. It is all that is uncivilised, and like a guilty conscience, I cannot ignore it. There are forces in this nightmare realm that go unchallenged. The witch continues to claim spirits; the kelpie continues to claim souls. I have fled from both the nag and the hag. What happens when another unfortunate spirit comes upon the castle? What happens when another poor soul encounters the kelpie?

It angers me to think of them lying in wait, and it enrages me that I have done nothing. I have told myself that I am helpless, but am I? I failed to push the witch into her own trap, but tonight, I could catch her off-guard. As for the kelpie, I do not know how to tame her, and I will not sacrifice myself. Walter's disappearance stoked rumour of the Legend of the Silver Horse. Will this new disappearance enhance it to the point that they fear it, or will they believe a guilty man fled?

Clangs and whispers from Lyeminster whistle on the wind. All the churches are alight with Sunday evening service. It invites me with the promise of exultation, but duty shackles my ankle like an iron ball on a chain. How can I expect to exult knowing that I did nothing—knowing that others shall suffer purgatory in that witch's pit?

I walk the ridge. I walk the ridge towards Draymere Castle.

The ruin remains a distant eyesore when, at once, discordant and shrill quorks pierce the night air. The ravens call for the witch. It cannot be for me that they call; another spirit must have entered the castle. Their grating alarm quickly subsides, but its echo of crying spirits persists.

The ravens all gaze into the castle as though they are entranced, and my approach goes unnoticed. Is there some foul covenant between witches and ravens? Alice may not be the only witch to claim spirits, and I have witnessed ravens devour souls. Perhaps ravens offer witches spirits, and witches offer ravens souls?

'Dear child, what is thy name?' I overhear as I creep up to the portcullis.

'My name is William Wells, Miss Alice.' Why do I recognise his name?

'What bring'st thou to Draymere Castle?'

'There was a monster.'

'A monster?'

'It was chasing me, Miss. I came here to hide. I hope you don't mind?' he says in a hurry.

'Mind? Dear child, I do not mind. Thou art most welcome to stay here. There art no monsters here. If thou wish, thou could'st make this thy home.' Alice disguises a snigger with a cough.

'Why do you speak so strangely, Miss?'

'Dear child, I am a very old woman—a very old and very wise woman—and I speak an old tongue. Dost thou wish for me to show thee a place of sanctuary from thy monster?'

This unspeakable witch; she is luring him to the pits.

A cold breath kisses me. The rising moon delivers a frosty embrace. I peer through the portcullis, careful not to be seen by Alice or the ravens. The moon's light shines through the castle's cracks. A young blond-haired cherub gleams in its aura; his spirit projects a choirboy. 'What is that awful screaming, Miss?' the boy asks.

'Thou shalt soon see that that is not awful screaming but cries of ecstasy. Hast thou ever heard an adult cry in pleasure?'

'No, Miss.'

'Did'st thy mother ever tell thee how thee was born?'

'I don't remember, Miss.'

His mother... That's how I know his name. I met his mother, Joan Wells. She yearns for his return. This witch will not claim her boy. I won't allow it.

Alice continues her ruse. 'Dear child, when two adults wish for an infant—they cry in ecstasy and joy—and God listeneth to their cry and granteth their wish. This is a place where spirits lie in euphoria. Come, I will show thee.'

William follows.

Alice leads the choirboy to the same entrance to which she led Vincent and me. 'Thou must possess the voice of an angel,' she says. I am quite sure that she will attempt to drop him into the same pit as Vincent because, in her twisted mind, their contrasting voices will complement each other's very nicely, as part of her ghastly opera.

As they enter, the ravens on the high walls all turn in unison, like a clockwork contraption. Now they all face outwards, and I am able to sneak in without alerting Alice. I gain admittance to the gaols through the closer archway, whence I exited at dawn. I peer inside and keep to the shadows. Alice is on the far side of the corridor of gaols, but the boy waits at the entrance. Alice turns her back to me and squats to look down at Vincent and the Scotsmen in their pit. 'Come,' she calls.

'I'm scared, Miss.'

'Do not be. There is nothing to fear.'

William hesitates, taking only one step closer.

I approach, keeping to the side and away from the trap doors. The howls and screams surround me once more; they remind me of the peril that awaits should I fail. I had safety in sight, yet here I am. I sneak beside the bars of the cells on the internal wall; William will see my silhouette if I walk in front of the moonlit vista. If he startles, he will alert Alice.

'O darling, prithee come,' Alice coaxes William another step. 'Good boy!' she encourages, but William stands still. A finger on his lips holds his uncertainty.

I have become accustomed to feeling numb, but now that I need to sneak, my legs no longer feel attached to me. They progress forwards with some impulse that I pray is my own will. If they decide to deceive me, they could cast me into an oubliette. I must also remain silent. As I am a spirit, Alice does not hear my footsteps, but in moments of jeopardy, our instinct is to breathe deep breaths. So, I fight to hold my breath as I approach on dead legs.

'William, come,' Alice says, with a little frustration.

'What is down there?'

'Thou shalt not know if thou lookest not.'

William edges towards the pit. I creep behind Alice.

'That's it,' Alice cajoles. She reaches out her hand to William. William's restraint falls with his finger as he rushes to her.

I hurry in. William yelps and recoils as he sees a dark man in the shadows. Alice turns. I kick her. My legs are numb, but it feels fantastic.

Below, Vincent is whimpering and cowering from spectres of his nightmares when Alice collapses on top of him. Her shrieks and shouts would strip a layer of skin from mortal ears. She joins Vincent in hell, becoming the final phantom in her macabre opera.

CHAPTER THIRTY-NINE

THE LEGEND

The devious man, who hid in the shadows, carries a screaming child away; William thinks I am kidnapping him. The ravens start when they witness William and I emerge through the portcullis. Alice's screams hold their own shrill note in the choir, and the ravens, hearing her cries, flee the castle in a flurry of glossy-black feathers.

I lower William to the ground but hold him firm, so he cannot escape. 'William!' I shout to arrest his bawling. 'Your mother is waiting for you.' The boy's countenance balances hope with suspicion. 'She loves you, William. Her name is Joan Wells. Do you remember her?'

'Joan—' he ponders.

'I met her in Lordale. She stays awake, night and day, waiting for your return.'

'Lordale?' William's face starts to open. I release my grip.

'Yes, that is your home. Joan is your mother. Do you remember?'

William's face is bright with optimism. 'Yes—I do. Yes. Thank you, sir.'

'That's quite all right.'

'That woman, Miss Alice. She w—'

'Don't think of her. She is not as nice as she let you believe.' I then point towards the east, and say, 'Do you see the moon?'

'Yes.'

'Run at the moon, William.'

'Run at the moon, sir?'

'Yes. Run towards it. Your mother waits for you in Lordale. The town is south-east from here. The moon is in the east, but it will move to the south during the night. If you run towards it, you will be a long way south-east from here by the end of the night, and hopefully, you and your mother will be reunited.'

'You really think so?'

'I know so!' I say emphatically.

'Oh, thank you, sir. Thank you ever so much.'

'Come. I wish to see you past the lake.'

I hold William's hand as we walk to the ridgeline. If he follows the ridge, he will not need to pass beneath Lake Draymere. I do not want me or him to get too close to the kelpie.

'Sir,' William says as we reach the rim, 'what about the monster? I wish it was cloudy.'

'Cloudy?' I ask.

'The monster does not come out when it's cloudy.'

'How so?'

'It lives in the cosmos, where the moon dares not cross,' he says, pointing north. 'Those stars are its eyes—they cover its mane—they descend whenever I approach—it chases me, but it has not got me yet,' he adds with pride. 'I keep running away from it.'

'William, I have experienced similar visions, but that is all they are—visions. It is our tired minds that give life to such spectres, and the more we fear them, the more they seem real, but trust that they are not real. Do you understand?'

'Yes, sir.'

'There is one more thing: as the spectres are borne of the psyche, you can control them.'

'You can?'

'Yes, my friend showed me how. If you can keep calm and really concentrate on how much you want to reunite with your mother, then you can tame the monster. Do you believe me?'

'Yes, sir.'

'Good, you have to believe it else it will not work.' I squat down and face the angelic child. 'Your mother misses you, William. Run at the moon, run as fast as you can, and look for signs for Lordale. I am afraid I cannot come with you, but you can run faster than me.'

'Thank you so much, sir.'

I embrace the boy with a hug, then he sets off running. I watch as he dashes across the ridge and say quietly to myself, 'Good luck, son.'

I turn to face the mere. It mirrors the stars in the night sky, but it is not a reflection. With no mist tonight, I can see the lightning-bugs scattered under the surface. From my vantage point, the souls from the kelpie's trench glow as bright as a second moon.

There are more lightning-bugs, however. A dozen or so upon the hillside across the lake, like fish out of water. They move slowly as one. What could they be? Are they Lunatics returning to the mere? Why did they leave the lake with their skulls?

The Lunatics of the mere could leave at any time to scare villagers. It would be a smart way to get retribution on a miscreant, and it need not be the Night of the Souls. I ponder—the Night of the Souls. Could it be? Could it be the dozen or so Lunatics who Frank and I helped escape?

Two lightning-bugs rush ahead towards the lake's shore-line. It is them—it must be. Those running are the two children. The new family has found a home. They will share it with the kelpie if they stay, but she won't bother them while they rest. It is a blessed relief to see them all still together.

I think to my good friend, Frank. His actions have ensured he has a positive legacy in this nightmare realm. And with this, the fall of Alice, and William's rescue, so have I.

I return along the ridge as civilised bells argue the midnight hour. There is just one last thing to do before I follow the River Lye home.

In Alnustone, I find the Pickle and Pike Inn, and I haunt it. The *Deaconshire Chronicle* named this establishment as being the place where Walter Henderson recounted the Legend of the Silver Horse before his disappearance. Now, in the ears of the Innkeeper and the late-night arrivals, I bellow, 'Fear the silver horse, for she hath taken another!' I think the old English impresses the message more keenly. And having got their attention, I stand within them, so they tremble in the icy chill of my being. It is my mission to haunt all those awake at this late hour, and after frightening several people in the quiet streets of Alnustone, I progress to Lyeminster.

Thick smoke billows from the chimneys, and I stride through a maze of dingy alleys and across clumsy cobbles in search of mortals. When I hear uncouth cries, I sniff out the source like a hungry, slavering hound. I find homeless drunkards crowded around a fire in a makeshift shack. I shout in their ears, 'Fear the silver horse, for she hath taken another!'

I spy two policemen, and again I yell, 'Fear the silver horse, for she hath taken another!'

I accost reprobates, travellers and carters who bustle at such an hour and spread my warning. Many attest to witnessing my ghost, but this is good. For my warning to be heeded, many must hear it, and seeing my ethereal being will enhance their belief. When the poor and affluent from these two towns tell the same tale then learn that my prophesied disappearance has come true, they shall all believe, and they shall fear the kelpie.

Upon finding the river and various moored vessels, I turn around and smile. The town is muttering, and their mutterings seed the creation of a new legend, and this new legend will become my legacy. I do not know what I did in life, but in death, I have saved many souls.

CHAPTER FORTY

THE GHOSTS THAT HAUNT ME

Hope touches me like a faery; the shape carved into stone unveils that the myth of home is real. The etching reads, 'Lyemouth'.

The sign marks the start of a riverside path and informs that my hometown is seven and a half miles away. I should be there before dawn.

The waterside path is dark and overgrown. Soon, the smoke from the chimneys clears and the stars are no longer choked. The river has tamed the surrounding lands to be flat and open, and I follow its arduous winding route with ease and safety.

The farmland yields to a forest glade alive with hooting owls. The nocturnal calls and the swishing river are calming. I can almost smell home.

I push through the woodland and return to open countryside. The river calms as it widens, and soon, my feet sink deep into the marsh. New streams steadily join the slow torrent towards Lyemouth. The laborious winding walk protracts. The persistently bare horizon frustrates. The scene must crack soon.

A baby cries...

'Good evening, Maria,' I call out. 'Where are you?' I say it slowly, to help keep my composure. Vincent has shown me that these hallucinations can be controlled. If I remain calm, then they will too. And I have not come this far to crumble so meekly.

From the peaceful waters up ahead, three figures emerge. As their forms rise in the water and step onto the marshland, I remain poised.

These are the ghosts that haunt me—the allies that I have encountered during my gruelling journey whose disastrous fate my mind cannot shake.

These three apparitions epitomise the hopelessness which permeates this nightmare realm. The fated trio stand ready to greet me. As the moon catches them, I shudder, but that is all. Their frightful form no longer petrifies; I am in control. 'Please stop crying,' I say politely. The crying fades away.

Before me stands Maria Chester, the angel-voiced spirit who lies restful but lonely, wondering whether anyone will ever join her; Frank Grant, the man who helped me rescue over a dozen souls from the Purge at St. Paul's, only to be cast into oblivion; and Vincent Bartholomew Lawrence, the American murderer who endures eternal damnation.

My mind insists on portraying their spectres fiendishly. Maria stands cradling her invisible baby with rats rustling through her hair and skull sockets. Frank is a sorry sack of bones in a baggy blue shirt and purple waistcoat with bulging eyes inset in his skull. And Vincent imitates Captain MacCulloch's tragic end as a butcher's hook pierces Vincent's naked body that's bloated with decomposition, while maggots froth out of his mouth.

I step to the side of them, and as I pass, I say, 'Walk with me.'

For once, I lead, and they follow. 'It's been a hell of a journey,' I say. 'I'm sorry I couldn't spare you.'

'It's all right, Eddie,' Frank replies, 'ain't nothing you could 'ave done about it.'

'It is I who should apologise to you,' Vincent says. 'If I hadn't entertained the stories of that wicked woman, I might be walking with you as spirit and not a figment.'

'Do you know if anybody will be awaiting your arrival?' Maria asks with slow, clear enunciation. 'Will you have someone to dance with at the full moon festivals?'

My heart sinks. Maria's fate feels very close to how I perceive my own. Who cared about me in life? 'No,' I respond. 'I have no idea.'

'What do you 'ope for?' Frank adds.

'Is it appalling for me to request a welcome party?' I joke. 'No, I don't want that because then I would know that everyone who greets me is no longer enjoying the pleasures of the flesh. The thing I yearn for is, simply, rest. The week in my memory feels like a year because you suffer every sleepless moment. This realm is dark and numb; I wish for somewhere bright and warm.'

'But you cannot desire to be lonely,' Maria adds softly.

'I want my name to be the only name on the plaque—but—I would like there to be a memorial wreath to know that I meant something to someone,' I reply. 'Then at full moon festivals, I would like to greet and dance with ancestors much older than I.'

'What do you fear?' Vincent asks.

'Vincent, you would be the devil on my shoulder. I worry I will discover why I feel a terrible sense of guilt each time I glimpse my pocket watch—I don't want to learn that I was a bad person. But, mostly, I fear I will find a fourth horrific destiny that renders our little group—the Fated Four.'

'It 'as a good little ring to it,' Frank says.

'That's what I'm worried about.'

'What do you fear?' Vincent repeats. Evidently, my subconscious has more to unveil.

'You are persistent,' I answer. 'I fear Lyemouth is not my home, and I will be lost. I fear the death of someone I love and that that person is lost, and like Joan Wells, I will forgo euphoria to ensure that person returns safely. I fear I will not be admitted through the pearly gates of heaven, and I will remain in purgatory. I fear my body will not be in my grave—that perhaps my body is missing, and I will have to search aimlessly like Mrs. Walthew. I fear the unknown. I fear so much.'

'You need not fear,' Maria says. 'You are a kindly gentleman. You will be happy and adored.'

'Maria, I believe you are the angel of my subconscious telling me what I wish to hear.'

'A frightful angel if I may say so,' Frank jokes.

'Have you looked at yourself in the mirror lately?' I re-buff. Frank and I laugh.

'Eddie, if Maria is the angel on your shoulder and Vincent is the devil, what am I?'

'You're the bothersome persona that doesn't know when to leave.' We laugh.

'We are here,' Vincent announces. A serrated bulk rises in the distance like a slumbering wyvern.

We walk in silence; they sense my nervous apprehension. What *will* I find?

What was one spire is now several. Hulking brutes invade the unruffled river, hiding its snaking path. Chimney stacks line up like reptilian scales but only the boldest vent soot during the dead of night. Firelight breathes out of shady pits and twinkles as it wrestles with the smog. This ashen haze swells around the thorny spine of the civilised dragon. Even while sleeping, this dragon is more domineering than its younger sibling, Lyeminster.

Reaching the quiet but cluttered harbour, I halt, almost paralysed. Its contours line up with the image that I have retained in my mind. It is a poor match, but just as two signatures are never alike, they still hark from the same source. The mundane detail paints in the blurred edges of my mind's sketch while the steamer and two large sailboats tessellate differently. The picture that my eyes resolve with subtle motion is akin to the negative image of an ambrotype photograph without the black background—the picture that I recall was during daylight. While the light sources may differ, I know this is the place I have sought. As I look around, the artist in my head paints furiously, slowly reveal-ing shapes of increasing familiarity. Yes, this is my home.

I feel the hands of my friend's spectres on my shoulders. I have calmed the daemons that have plagued my journey, and now they wish me well.

'Good luck,' Frank says buoyantly.

'Rest in peace, Eddie,' Vincent says.

'Sleep soundly,' Maria says.

'Farewell,' I reply.

The fated trio stroll towards the steamer. They enter the water. Slowly they sink deeper until they disappear below the surface. I stand alone. What awaits me? Will I finally rest in peace?

CHAPTER FORTY-ONE

THE DAWNING OF THE DAY

I am being reacquainted with my hometown as I walk. The sense of *déjà vu* is marvellous. I seem to know where I am going.

The eerie desertion welcomes me with its solemn stillness. I see no one, yet a distant clip-clop tells that someone stirs amongst these gloomy alleys. My unguided wandering twists and turns and leads me steadily towards a steeple. That is where I will look first. Hopefully, it will be easy to find the warming presence of my soul. While I feel anticipation, there is also trepidation that I may fail to find it. I turn a corner to see hallowed ground and that fear eases. It is the warm reception from an old friend whose name you are mortified to have forgotten. As I approach, the artist paints rapidly and skilfully with both hands. The wind swirls, momentarily catching a sound like childish laughter; even this feels familiar.

The lunar bonfire prickles with stray embers, and as they land, they singe with excitement. Two conifers guard the lych-gate entrance. I venture into sacred ground as the looming black edifice crackles with an unexpected welcome. Four steel rasps echo like a whetstone sharpening a sword. The towering black knight stands attentive over the quiet graveyard adorned with monuments that dwarf me. Does one of these hoary relics shield my fireplace?

The moon shines from behind the church, through the spindly branches of a large, old ash tree. Small clumps of white snowdrop flowers are scattered throughout the cemetery with their heads bowed in respect. I weave through weathered headstones. I feel no warmth at my feet, and I struggle to read any names. I meander methodically over to the far side as I search with increasing desperation.

My eye catches a figure praying at a gravestone. The headstone's shade partly obscures her, but a flowing white wedding dress catches the lunar rays. To be so bold and unblemished on muddy ground, she must be a Lunatic; it would certainly be odd behaviour if she were not. The tell-tale sign that she is a spirit, however, is that she does not possess the ghostly guise. Perhaps she has seen my name on one of the tablets. I approach cautiously, not wanting to startle her or intrude on her respectful mourning.

I stand close by, but she does not notice me. Shadows hide the names on these gravestones, but their edges are not so weathered or so sharp. She caresses an array of flowers that poke out of the shadow.

'Excuse me, ma'am,' I say. 'I'm sorry to disturb you, but you may be able to help me.' By her movement, I deduce that she turns her head to face me, though the tall headstone still conceals her face from the moonlight.

'Dearie?' My whole being tingles as a nervous flood tries to sweep away my shaking legs. Those sweet Irish syllables greet me with immense affection and warmth.

My voice breaks to that of a trembling child. 'Mama?'

She stands. Her fiery red hair shines through the ghostly veil of her bridal dress. She lifts the veil back over her head to uncover her youthful complexion, brown eyes and radiant glower. Her cheekbones rest beautifully and contently, and they wrinkle to frame a smile of pure happiness. I know it well! That smile has greeted me so many times. Each time it cast an enchantment that was sweet and encouraging. The periphery of those memories is a blur, but that smile of optimism and joy bursts open the door of memory, and exhilaration pours out. I rush to my guardian lioness, my protective Cat.

'Eddie, dearie. I was so worried.'

I remember her embrace so keenly. The moon's embers above and my soul's vigour below reward us with full feeling. My head nestles in that familiar shoulder divot, and her arms squeeze me in an all-encompassing hug. I savour the moment. I am home.

Without breaking the embrace, Mama softly says, 'O darling, my fleeting hour of life has come. I am sorry; I was too weak to bear it.'

'Mama, I am sorry too. I forgot who you were. I tried so hard, but memory escaped me. I thought I'd never see you again.' We both squeeze harder.

'Hush now, my cub, there will be no more apologies. You found your way back to me. That's all that matters. God knows how much I have prayed that he guide you. I've been so terribly anxious since I saw you were not here; I didn't know what to do. It is wonderful to have you back in my arms, dearie.' Pressing hard, she kisses me on the side of my head.

'The night was so long and frightening. But the night-mares seem so far away now—now that I know I am safe. But—I am sad for my friends, Mama. They—they are not as fortunate as I.'

'I'm sorry to hear that, Eddie.'

'Mama, I was hopelessly lost, afraid and running scared. They helped me—calmed me. They showed me the way and taught me courage.' She comforts me by rubbing my back as she did when I was young.

A faint snigger dances amongst the gravestones. I look at Mama with excitement, and say, 'Charlie!'

Mama grins.

'He is up too?'

'We've both waited for you.'

'Charlie,' I shout. 'Where are you?' A distant tombstone giggles.

I remember Charlie, my younger brother. I remember all the times I visited this headstone, asking forgiveness for my terrible sin. I remember too what it was that I did—or rather, what I didn't do.

'Charlie,' I shout again. A different gravestone chuckles. I smile. 'Coming, ready or not...'

My walk turns to a prowl. Me, George and Charlie used to love playing, *Ghost in the Graveyard*. How apt that name is now. As he was the youngest, we always made Charlie the ghost. We gave him a minute to hide in the house with only a single candle to light each room, then it was the first to find him. If we called his name, he had to make a noise. Charlie was never very good, but I often pretended not to know where he was. Typically, I let George find him; he didn't like losing. But all our training has led to this showdown. It is me versus Charlie in an actual graveyard and we are real ghosts.

'Charlie, where are you?' His giggle is near the entrance. My prey hides in the shadows. I scour the gravestones; they all tilt so much that I worry one will fall. In the shadows, I see nothing. 'O Charlie.'

His laugh is behind me. I turn and search. 'Where are you, Charlie?' His laugh is behind me, again. 'You've been practising, haven't you, Charlie?'

Charlie sends me in circles, in and out of the shadows. He is as swift as Vincent's shovelling. I try to corner him, but he keeps slipping passed me. My hunt goes on. Occasionally, I see flashes of blond amongst the grey, but the memorials are so tall and so densely packed that it is like being trapped in a maze. He chuckles on my left, then behind me, then on my right, then in front. It is disorientating, but Mama acts as a beacon. In her beautiful white wedding dress, she stands as the nacre pearl of this oyster-grey cemetery. I follow his flash of blond, but every time I look behind where he hides, he has gone.

'Come here, Charlie...'

I see him rush. Moonlight illuminates him like a hare in a fox's glare. Fate's reminder is cruel. He finds cover behind a tablet, then he shifts across slowly. He is close to Mama and I see him crouching. I've got him now.

I stalk the gravestone which he hides behind, but it hits me that I am about to get my wish. I can finally say how sorry I am. No matter how practised my speech may be, he should not accept it. I don't want him to accept it.

Approaching the tombstone, I smile like a wolf approaching an injured bird. I squat low and prepare to pounce. He is facing away, so I know that I can grab him from behind. With a roar, I strike.

'GHOST IN THE GRAVEYARD!' I cry. Charlie wriggles and giggles. I've caught him. Mama watches happily.

'You cheated!' Charlie shouts as he gets to his feet. 'Mama, did you tell him where I was?' He stands in the moonlight, sulking. His long blond hair and big brown eyes remind me how he was always the angelic one.

I hug the boy. It is weird. It is an adult hugging a child, but it was never like that.

I was fourteen and he was nine. George had left home, and I was in charge as the two of us walked to the train station, en route to our aunts and uncles. I was always jealous of Charlie. He used to cry so much, and he stole all of Mama's attention. His crying as a baby kept me up every night, and I hated him for it. Seeing his face, I remember the distinct pattern of his cries. His bawling still haunts me. It is his crying that accompanies my apparitions of Maria. The guilt never left me.

That day, Mama told me to hold Charlie's hand. I didn't. We were waiting at the station, but the next train wasn't stopping. It was quiet and Charlie was bored; he wandered off. I only noticed when the train belched to announce its approach. Charlie was on the tracks. He had climbed down from the platform and was playing. There was time to save him, but I did nothing.

I simply said, 'Train's coming.' He didn't react.

At first, I thought it was a test, he was trying to make me panic. But I quickly saw that he was distracted and not listening. Then I did panic. I was utterly petrified. I startled as if a pistol had been pointed at me. I have come to my grave knowing that there was still time to save him. But I froze. I foresaw all the possibilities: me tripping on the tracks; me saving Charlie but slipping as I tried to climb to safety; me holding Charlie as the train hit us both. I stood there and I watched. I watched as Charlie ran. I watched as Charlie cried. I watched as the train rolled past. I watched as they picked up the pieces. There wasn't much of him that remained intact, but his pocket watch survived. I have carried it—and that moment—with me ever since.

From that day, I lived further inside my shell. My sin was deadly; my sin was sloth. I am not guilty of laziness but inaction. They say for bad things to occur, it needs nothing more than for *good* men to look on and do nothing. I did nothing.

A thought lifts my spirits. There may well be another boy reuniting with his mother tonight. A boy who I did help. A boy who I spared a terrible fate. By acting to help William Wells, I finally did something that was not nothing.

<hr />

I hold my little brother so tight. 'Charlie, I am sorry,' I say.

'Eddie, please. I've heard it enough.'

I look at the boy, confused. He looks bored.

'He has heard you,' Mama says.

'Heard me?'

'We spirits can hear those who talk at our grave.'

'You can hear the living while you rest?'

'Yes, dearie. Their kind words float effortlessly through the peaceful aura.' This is excellent! Mama smiles as my face brightens. 'Yes, you will hear them soon. You will hear your papa, George and your sister-in-law very soon.' I recall them all, including Lucy, George's wife.

'How are they?' I blurt out, desperately.

'They are all very sad because we are not with them, but they are doing well. Our family may be split, but we are strong, and now that you have found your way back to us, everyone has someone to embrace.'

I beam at Mama and then Charlie. 'You really heard all my apologies?' I ask him.

'Yes, you wouldn't stop crying. I was trying to rest.'

'I got my revenge then...' I choke, half laughing, half crying.

'We heard them when they came to visit after church yesterday,' Mama says.

'Will I hear them soon?'

'Yes, and soon, you'll hear another voice.'

'Whose?'

'Your niece or nephew,' Mama smiles. 'Lucy is pregnant. They spoke with such pride today; Lucy is doing very well. Isn't it wonderful?'

'Mama, it's fantastic!' I say, overwhelmed with joy. Knowing that new life is due, consumes me with hope as our family lives on, and it is a relief to learn that we are not so abruptly cut off from their lives.

I think back to all those times when Papa spoke to his parents here. The first thing Papa would do when he returned from a long voyage was to visit this cemetery. I remember it partly because it was the day after I saw a ghost. I was so proud of my papa when he arrived back on the new steamer. So proud, in fact, that my memory still clings to that image. I quarrelled petulantly because I wanted us to play in the park. Papa insisted we came here. I thought it was silly; we were talking to an inanimate slab. But they could hear us. My Grandma, who I have never met, has heard me and must know me well. Diana, that's her name. She is the doting soul who would have spoilt us boys given half a chance.

'Mama, will I get to meet Grandma soon?'

'Yes dearie, we saw Peter and Diana at that peculiar full moon festival soon after I arrived. They will be thrilled to welcome you.'

'Tonight?'

'Let them rest tonight, but they will be up when the moon is full again.'

'Why are you not resting?'

'I had to be here for you, dearie. I couldn't have you come by and miss us. Though, I was lost in worry when you finally did arrive.'

'And Charlie?'

'I woke him up. I knew how much you would want to make your peace with him.'

I beam down at Charlie as he clings to Mama's leg. I rustle his hair, and he shies behind her, complaining.

'Would you like your rest now, Charlie?' Mama asks. He sheepishly nods. 'All right, dearie.'

Mama ushers him to our gravestone, but Charlie rushes towards me. I squat down to my little brother as he embraces me. 'I missed you, Eddie,' he says.

'I missed you too, Charlie.'

'Can we play again soon?'

'We certainly can.'

Mama's face is a picture of serenity. All she ever wanted was for her boys to play nicely.

After we bid Charlie goodnight, I ask Mama, 'What is it like? When you rest, I mean. Is it heaven? Have you and Charlie met God?'

'Dearie, you will find out soon enough. But it is wonderful, and it will be much better now you are with us.'

As we talk, Mama repeatedly gazes into my eyes—it pleases her. When I ask why, she explains, 'I'm sorry, dearie. It is great to see your piercingly blue eyes again. I always loved how you looked at me. You were the only one to take your papa's eyes. When I identified your body, I witnessed your empty stare. It haunted me—every day. Ravens had got to your body before anyone could stop them. They targeted your beautiful sapphires. It fell to me to place a coin over the vacant voids that they left.' Her voice breaks. 'They took your blue eyes, Eddie!' I hug her and squeeze tightly. 'I never recovered,' she weeps. 'The trains—they brought all three of us here.'

My heart breaks because of what she implies, but in an attempt to ease her sadness, I joke, 'Those bloody trains!'

Mama gives a snort as she laughs through her sobs.

We converse till dawn. It seems the only memories that return to me are the strongest ones etched in my soul, and even then, I believe it is only the sight and sound of Mama and Charlie that unlocks them. Given that the Grants forgot who was Frank and who was Joshua, I understand that, in time, even these memories will fade. But they are not gone yet!

Then, in a soft, slow and very peaceful way, Mama begins to sing. It revives a few more memories from a time when all five of us—Mama, Papa, me and my brothers—visited Mama's birthplace. She awoke us and sang this Irish melody as the sun was rising on a beautiful morning. I recall the name of the song to be *Fáinne Geal an Lae* which translates to *The Dawning of The Day*. She sings it again now, and though I do not know the Gaelic words, it brings joy to my heart.

That morning she sang several ballads. Many were in English, and their lyrical and poignant message ignited a love of poetry. So, as Mama sings sweetly, I think of my journey and rekindle, in thought, that pastime of old:

I hid in a cave, lost and astray,
Fearing a creature to which I was prey.
How long I had been there, I cannot be sure,
Then I fled from a phantom of a time before.
New companions kept my hope aflicker,
And with their aid, my courage grew thicker.
My tearless weep accompanies Mama's song,
For I have returned to where I belong.

From darkness, despair and disarray,
I behold the dawning of the day.

I stare up at the towering steeple. It has rung for every hour that has passed and each toll shakes the ground. The sky is bright, and the hands on the dial below the tall spire are approaching eight o'clock. Mama's song comes to an end, and I know it is time.

I turn towards the tall gravestone with its straight sides and pointed apex. I can now resolve the words due to the light of dawn. The stone carving reads:

IN LOVING MEMORY OF
CHARLES WEBSTER
BORN 12th AUGUST 1852
DIED 2nd JUNE 1862
ALSO
EDWARD WEBSTER
BORN 26th JANUARY 1848
DIED 29th NOVEMBER 1879
ALSO
CATRIONA WEBSTER
BORN 17th MAY 1819
DIED 26th JANUARY 1880

At the base, it adds:

BELOVED

Even though I have long accepted my fate, it is dreary to see our names engraved into Charlie's tombstone. I don't think I ever thought about our names being added to it.

Mama indicates that I am to go first and that I should not dawdle. I kneel at the flowers at the base of the headstone. The ground is warm, soft and spongy. My knees sink in. I continue to descend naturally and slowly. I turn onto my back and look upwards. Mama is beaming, and the gothic spire, rising behind her, points to my destination—heaven. The scene fades to a soothing, brightening white. A warmth immerses me.

The soft church bell echoes eight times—at first. Soon, the mellow, metallic sound reverberates again, and again, and again, and again. The ringing metronome is my only indication of time. In resplendent and peaceful slumber, its passage becomes imperceptible and irrelevant. And so, I am finally at rest, beneath the chimes.

Author Note

I wish to thank you for reading my debut novel. Writing this tale began six years ago with a desire to journey through a realm of romanticised horror, steeped in eerie mystery.

I drew inspiration from the classics in literature and from gothic fiction across modern media. I imagined someone unearthing a lost book from the era of the classics, rediscovering it in some dusty, forgotten archive, mixed in amongst penny dreadfuls and tales by Stoker, Shelley, and Poe. I wanted to create that book, to make it truly original, and for it to serve as an ode to gothic fiction, new and old.

Although I envisioned this book on the shelves of a Victorian bookshop, it won't be found in any bookstore today, as of its release. When my attempts to publish this tale via traditional means ultimately failed, I decided I couldn't let this book die in digital obscurity on an old laptop. I vowed to self-publish and to employ a series of creative geniuses to make this as good as any traditionally published book.

Connecting with a reader audience is my most valued goal; however, many avenues to this are closed to self-published authors. The best way to break down these barriers and to help others find this tale is... Reviews. So, if you feel this novel deserves to be discovered in a bookshop or online, please consider leaving a review. N. P.

Acknowledgements

First, I must thank my mom, Joy. You are the self-sacrificing soul who would forego all things for me. You are endlessly encouraging and would be impossible to forget. And, to my dad, Nigel, thank you for always being supportive, even when I write strange horror stories that delve into areas that may make you uncomfortable.

Special mentions must also go to my brother, Simon, and some of my best friends, Adam Pritchett, Stephen Hegarty and Ryan Broomfield. Your feedback shaped this tale and spurred me on. Having friends who are excited to read my stories is so heartening.

To consider a former bookshop manager and a retired Head of English as close friends is equivalent to having an "ace in the hole". This is certainly not your speciality of Children's books but, David and Elaine Chant, you've really helped me refine my prose.

I must also thank Dr Stephen Carver for his manuscript critique and subsequent edit. To find an editor who loves gothic fiction and "gets" what I'm striving for has been invaluable.

All of you at the Brighter Writers group in Lytham have truly helped me make the step from fledgling writer to published author—you've been excellent. You've read and proofread my book, critiqued tricky passages, passed on your wisdom and much more. I can't name you all, but I am so grateful.

I harbour a special appreciation for everyone who read my novel whilst it was just a printout as each person has helped me build my foundations as a debut author. So, in addition, I extend huge thanks to Richard Lord and David Knowles.

Finally, I would like to share my gratitude to the fantastic artists who've contributed towards this publication: my cover artist, Fay Lane; my map designer, Dewi Hargreaves; my chapter heading illustrator, Keegan Eichelman; the audio and visual artists behind my promotional material, Adam Pritchett (again) and Iulian Gutu; and my logo designers, Wendy and Rachael at ZPQ Designs. Your artwork and skill are the flourishes that I could not give.

About the author

N. P. Arrowsmith is an author of adult horror fiction and a Chartered Engineer with the Royal Aeronautical Society. He lives in Lancashire, England and can be frequently found hiking in The Lake District, the inspiration behind his fictional county of Deaconshire. His other passion is to explore weird and wonderful places all around the world.

Upcoming Releases by Author N. P. Arrowsmith

Edward's journey is the first of many *Deaconshire Tales*. If you wish to explore deeper into the dark and mysterious corners of this gothic county, keep an eye out for the following stories, coming soon:

THE DREAM HOUSE

A novella featuring a haunted guest house that is stuck in the past.

HAVELOCK HILL

A novel featuring witches and beasts that brings the origins of All Hallows Eve to the modern world.

Release dates for these titles will be announced on the author's website: **nparrowsmith.com**

Made in the USA
Middletown, DE
10 December 2024

66584591R00210